The verdict is in on Melinda M. Snodgrass's

CIRCUIT

"Something different! A well-presented tale . . . set against a backdrop of action and political intrigue."

—Roger Zelazny

"Provocative . . . she keeps it moving along at a rocket pace!"

—Albuquerque Tribune

"Brisk pacing and intelligent speculation . . . Snodgrass, a former attorney, has the background and skills to make *Circuit* a landmark in science fiction."

—Chicago Sun-Times

"Diverting, fast-paced . . . the courtroom theatrics and the spacegoing shootouts keep the action boiling."

—Publishers Weekly

And now . . .

CIRCUIT BREAKER

Berkley books by Melinda M. Snodgrass

CIRCUIT
CIRCUIT BREAKER

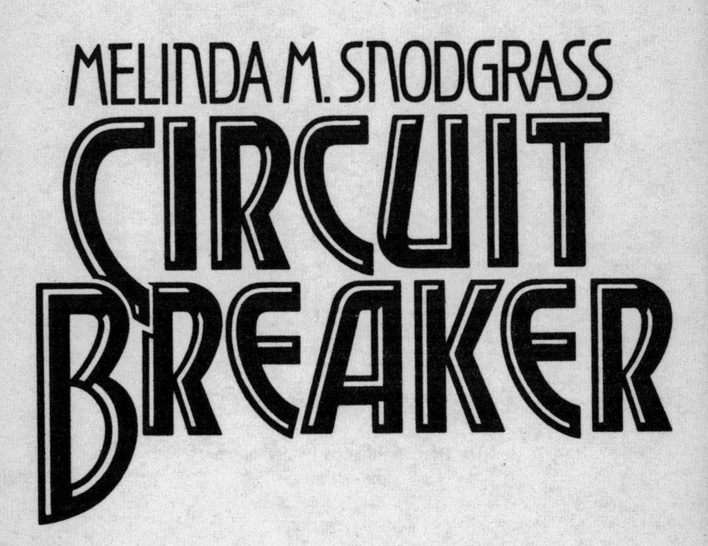

BERKLEY BOOKS, NEW YORK

CIRCUIT BREAKER

A Berkley Book/published by arrangement with
the author

PRINTING HISTORY
Berkley edition/May 1987

Illustrated by Don Dixon.

ISBN: 0-425-09776-5

A BERKLEY BOOK® TM 757,375
Berkley Books are published by The Berkley Publishing Group,
200 Madison Avenue, New York, New York 10016.
The name "BERKLEY" and the stylized "B" with design are
trademarks belonging to Berkley Publishing Corporation.
PRINTED IN THE UNITED STATES OF AMERICA

Acknowledgments

A number of people helped me create this book. I'd like to single out for special thanks Alan Hildebrand, Department of Planetary Sciences, University of Arizona, for invaluable technical advice and for pulling me out of a terrible crack into which ignorance had plunged me. Thanks are also due to the good people of American Aircraft Inc., manufacturers of ultralight aircraft, who patiently led me through their factory and didn't even turn a hair when I proposed ultralights on Mars, just suggested technical innovations to accomplish my purpose. For service above and beyond the call of duty—Ruth Kovnat—my former environmental law professor. She thought she'd seen the last of me in 1977; she certainly didn't expect to have me back in 1985, looking for advice on how to create a ticklish off-world environmental problem. Thank you, Ruth, the case law was impeccable. Finally I would like to mention two books that greatly influenced my work on this novel: *Progress and Privilege* by William Tucker; and *Private Ownership vs. Public Waste* by Robert J. Smith.

This book is again for Vic Milán, whose faith and support gave me the courage to stay on my little soapbox.

MARS/EDEN PROJECT

Environmental Impact Statement

Final

No environment, no impact.

Preparer: Jasper Mendel, Ph. D.

Chapter One

There was a vigorous rustling of paper that set an odd counterpoint with the spatter of rain on the skylights and against the bay windows of the breakfast room.

"Well, I'll be damned."

Jennifer McBride, a plate of toast in one hand and a butter knife in the other, stuck her head inquiringly out of the kitchen and peered at her lover. Cabot Huntington's face was hidden behind the sheets of the *Washington Post,* which he still stubbornly insisted on printing out rather than reading straight from the screen. Visible only was the top of his head, the black hair still damp from his early-morning walk. Mere weather alone was not to interfere with this ritual. Each morning at six he would vanish from bed, head down the cliff trail, and walk for thirty or forty minutes down the beach. Jenny thought it was a way for him to survey his kingdom—the great stone house sprawling on the top of the cliff, the narrow strip of sand at the rocky base, and the seal rocks beyond—but Cab vehemently denied that interpretation. He claimed it was mental and emotional therapy. At the moment Cab was canted back in his chair, booted feet propped easily on the hand-hewn breakfast table. This unusual show of informality brought a smile to Jenny's lips. She stepped into the room.

Juggling the plate in one hand, she caught the paper between middle and forefinger and pulled it down to reveal the thin, intense, patrician face that had become so familiar over five years of legal partnership and now, during the past weeks, familiar in a far more intimate way.

"No doubt," she replied.

He ignored her raillery. "I've been returned to the corridors of power, the councils of the wise, and presumably to public respect as well." His tone was flat, expressionless, as if he were holding in emotions that he feared to release. Jenny raised one coppery eyebrow inquiringly. "Look."

His long forefinger with its perfectly manicured nail marked the headline.

HUNTINGTON TO RETURN TO BENCH.

"Well, so much for your impeachment."

The toast was deposited before him, and she stared out the window, seeing not the scudding gray clouds racing north before a brisk wind but instead a great wheel spinning against a backdrop of stars, a white space-suited figure ringed by a halo of frozen blood, a courtroom jammed with people. For a long minute she thought back on the tumultuous events of the past four months, and the part she and Cabot had played in shaping those events. First had come the creation of the Fifteenth Circuit, the newest federal court designed to bring a coherent system of justice to the Earth-Orbit stations and the outlying colonies. Or so she had thought initially. In fact, the Circuit had been created to exert a measure of control over the increasingly independent System colonists. In an effort to serve a cause he had believed just, Cabot had handed down a decision barring the sale of Soviet Moon ore to independent companies. That had been bad enough, but there had been worse to follow. The Soviets, eager to teach a lesson to their errant colonists, had dropped a tactical nuclear missile on the mining collective, with the tacit approval of the government of the United States. Fortunately or unfortunately, depending on one's point of view, three people survived the bombing and brought word of the atrocity to the world. Then President Tomas C. deBaca had looked to his old friend for a bail-out, but Cabot, disgusted by what he had unleashed, refused. After a series of moves and countermoves that included the occupation of a civilian space station by troops of both the United States and the Soviet Union, murder and attempted murder, Cabot had handed down a decision censuring both superpowers.

His action had brought about the fall of one government, for deBaca had been swept from office in the largest defeat in American history, but there was still enough time between November and January for him to fire one final, bitter salvo at his former friend. He had initiated impeachment proceedings against Cabot. Now it seemed that President-elect Richard Malcolm Long had canceled that proceeding and was going to return Cabot to his former position. It was irritating, however, that he had not bothered to tell them and had let them discover their return to favor from a newsfax article. Her hand tightened on the hilt of the butter knife.

"Nice of Long to tell us."

"Perhaps he was busy," Cabot replied soothingly. "The inauguration is only a few weeks away."

"He couldn't assign some junior clerk to make a call?" Cabot shrugged. "Why do you always make excuses for these people?"

"Because I understand the reality of their situation. Things can get lost in the—"

"You weren't so understanding of Tomas's situation."

His face hardened, and he shook the pages of the *Post*. "That was a different matter entirely. Tomas abused his office, and he deserved everything that happened to him. Long is a different kind of man: scholar, outdoorsman, artist. He didn't come up through the smoky wardrooms the way Tomas did, and I think he's cleaner for it." He looked challengingly up into her set face and pushed on as if determined to convince her. "He's already attracted some of the best minds out of the universities and colleges, and his wife has connections with the East Coast aristocracy and top European society. Long's going to make a difference."

"Your family is going to shit when they hear you speaking in such glowing terms of a member of the loyal opposition." Her tone was a little sharper than she had intended, for Cabot had yet to introduce her to any of his blue-blooded relations, and the oversight rankled. Mainly because she wasn't certain if it was an oversight or if he was somehow embarrassed by their liaison.

Cab's face had closed down into an expression of frozen disapproval. He hated crudity or vulgarity in women. "Jenny, please, you know how I—"

He was interrupted by the chiming of the comnet.

"Shall I get it?"

He lunged out of the chair and headed out a side door. "No, finish with breakfast."

"Yes, sir!" She gave his retreating back an ironic salute with the butter knife and wondered again why she had ever permitted their relationship to develop from friends and colleagues to lovers.

That's a stupid notion, she thought as she returned to the kitchen, replaced butter knife with bread knife, and began hacking at a loaf of white bread. It was not something people could weigh and consider—it just happened. She realized that she was attacking the bread as if it were some kind of enemy, and she glanced in dismay from the sloping angle she had left on the end of the loaf to the uneven slice that lay waiting to be toasted. She could already hear Cab's comments on her inexpert surgery. He was one of those irritating people who could slice a loaf of bread on a perfectly straight line, never got greasy carving a turkey, and squeezed a lemon without showering everyone else in the room with juice.

And she was maundering. Worse, she was doing it in her own head. She tossed the piece of bread into the toaster and, turning to the stove, began preparing Cab's egg and sausage. As for herself, she had lost her appetite and she didn't know why. They were returning to space and to their work; something they had vowed they would do when the impeachment had pulled them from the EnerSun station. They would see their friends, Lydia, Andy Throckmorton, Lighting—or perhaps not, she amended as the sausage began to sizzle and spit on the griddle. They had finished the first leg of the circuit and presumably would have to move on to their next stop—Mars.

She shuddered and tried to contemplate living on—hell, even *visiting*—that bleak, windswept, red world. She had felt comfortable with their assignment to the space station. She had done a lot of research before their arrival, and it was relatively close to home. Mars was another matter. It was a frozen red cipher some two hundred and seventy million miles from Earth.

There, she thought, comforting herself. *You do know something about Mars. You know how far away it is from home.*

She shuddered again, an involuntary reaction, born of a fear she couldn't identify. Cab came bounding into the kitchen and, lifting one of the links from the griddle, took a quick bite. He then just as quickly dropped the sausage back to the sizzling surface and puffed vigorously around the mouthful of hot meat. Jenny eyed him, noting that despite his momentary discomfort, he looked well pleased about something.

"So who called?"

"Richard Long." His tone was thick with satisfaction.

"Calling to tell you that the article in the paper was a misprint?"

He gave her a sharp look, not missing the sarcasm and bitterness in her voice. He rubbed his fingers together, and his eyes flicked about the kitchen searching for something on which to wipe the grease. He headed to the sink and rinsed his fingers.

"No, he called to apologize because I had to learn of his decision from a newsfax article. An overeager staffer sent out the release before he had a chance to call me, and he wanted to assure me that I was not being overlooked."

"Um."

Cabot pivoted slowly and leaned back against the edge of the counter. "And . . ." He drew out the word while his cat-and-canary smile deepened. "He's invited us to Washington for the inauguration, and to his and Jennifer's private ball at the Kennedy Center." He gazed at her as if daring her to continue her unenthusiastic response.

She swept up the sausages with a spatula and deposited them on a paper towel to drain. "Another Jennifer. This could get confusing."

"Is that all you have to say?"

"What do you want me to say?"

"This is pretty damn exciting."

"I don't know why. You've been to a lot of inaugural balls."

"I thought you would be pleased."

She kept her eyes on the stove, concentrating on cracking an egg perfectly. "Cab, I've never much liked politicians. After what happened on EnerSun, I really despise them, and I don't trust them. I was worrying a few minutes ago about going on to Mars. Now I wish we could leave tomorrow and avoid all this—" She gestured helplessly in the air before her.

"Long is a different kind of man," he said, repeating his earlier statement. "While Tomas . . ." He hesitated for a moment, then rushed on as if realizing that vilification of Tomas deBaca could only reflect back on him; they had, after all, been friends for over twenty years. He coughed and awkwardly switched the subject. "And you have to admit that the system worked. The abuses were uncovered, and the people gave judgment on Tomas. He's out of office."

"But if you and Evgeni had been killed, or Lydia proved less stubborn, or Joe less determined, then the abuses wouldn't have been uncovered, and *the people* would have marched in and obligingly voted Tomas back into office."

"So you don't want the people to have any say in who is chosen to govern over them?"

"That is not what I'm saying. It's just that—" She stopped and tried again. "Living with the colonists and doing some thinking over the past few months has made me realize that terms like *society* and *the people* don't mean much. *Individuals* make up societies and peoples, and they're being ignored and manipulated by the system. So is it really working, or does it only appear to work?" she mused.

"And terms like *the system* don't mean much to me." She inclined her head to acknowledge the hit. Cab peered beneath the fringe of her lashes, forcing her to look at him. "So what is it you want? To chuck everything and start over again? I don't know about you, but I don't have the wisdom to redo it all."

"And I'm not saying I do. I suppose I want to preserve those parts of the Constitution and the law which protect the rights of the —" She stopped abruptly, blushing to the roots of her dark red hair.

"The people?"

Chuckling, she slipped the paper from beneath the sausages and deposited a very hard and very overcooked fried egg on the plate. Leaning in close, she handed him the plate.

"Individuals."

They were so close that she could feel the warmth of his breath across her face. He tilted his head and bestowed a soft kiss on her mouth, then glanced down at the plate that pressed against his belly just above his belt.

"You are a brilliant, talented, and beautiful woman, but you can't cook," he whispered.

"True, and I also don't do windows."

"Do you dance?"

"Yes."

"Will you set aside your objections long enough to dance one waltz with me next month?"

"Yes."

"And will you go to Mars with me?"

"Oh, yes." He took his plate and headed into the dining room. "Rather go there than to Washington," Jenny murmured to the stove, and she knew from the way his brisk footsteps on the polished brick floor faltered, then resumed their even rhythm, that he had heard.

He remembered that remark now as he stood staring at the Comnet. The image of Fred Downs, Long's urbane and smiling press secretary, had just faded from the screen, leaving Cab feeling frustrated, confused, and filled with a vague sense that he was in the midst of affairs over which he had no control. Downs was the highest official Cab had been able to reach, the rest being busy with "preparations" or "affairs"; though what business could be pressing at seven P.M. on inaugural day when not a cloud marred the political horizon, he didn't know. Further, one presumed that preparations had been completed long since.

He snapped his gold plastic embossed bank card beneath his thumbnail and tried to make sense of a politician—hell, even a politician's lackey—turning down an offer of money. Still fiddling with the card, he returned to the front room of the suite he had rented at the old Jefferson Hotel. Jenny was seated in an armchair with her left leg extended toward the ceiling, her hands smoothing the deep blue stocking with its network of shivering and sparkling silver lights. This latest fashion craze had been sparked by the development of tiny light-emitting diodes that were powered by body heat. Once enough energy had been built up, they would discharge, creating a shimmering and random pattern across the wearer's legs. A gown of twilight blue, decorated at the hem and bodice with the same twinkling lights that adorned the stockings, lay across another chair. A long slit ran up the left side of the gown, and Cab contemplated the effect she would make with her flame-red hair; slender, graceful body; and the twinkle of magic lights glittering enticingly through the gap in her gown. The stereo set into the wet bar was filling the room with some piece of classical fluff, on the level of eighteenth-century Musak, and Cab frowned at it before flopping down into a chair.

"Want to go to Mars?" He propped his chin in one hand and gazed at her.

Jenny lowered her leg. "What? Now?"

"Uh-huh. I'm beginning to think you were right about not wanting to come to Washington."

She rose, picked up the gown, and stepped into it with a rustle of silk. "My, my, we're grumpy."

"Not grumpy, confused."

"Zip, please." He obliged, running his thumb up the strip of self-sealing material on the back. "Confused about what?"

"Nobody will take my money." He waggled the card at her, then slid it into the inner pocket of his jacket.

"Now, Cab, surely that's an exaggeration. Somewhere in this great bureaucratic Mecca"—she flung her arms wide—"there must be someone who will take your money. I'm sure if we called the IRS, they would be happy to oblige you in your desire to give it away." She moved away with a whisper of silk. "Let's talk in the bathroom. I have to do my face."

"Don't be flip," he said as he followed her into the brilliantly lit and mirrored bathroom and seated himself on the toilet.

"Then don't be cryptic."

"Jen, we're going to this ball for free."

"So? Long invited us."

"You don't understand. Only a handful of the President's closest friends ever get to go to an inaugural ball for free. I even paid to attend Tomas's."

"How much?" Jenny asked, a foundation-covered finger poised over her nose.

"Five thousand dollars was the going rate last time around."

"Dear God!" She turned back to the mirror. "Well, I should think you would be relieved to avoid that kind of expense."

"That's not the point."

"So what is?" Her hands were busy among the various jars

and bottles, and he could tell that she wasn't really paying attention. He rose and leaned in on the counter at her side.

"I'm not a close friend of Richard Long's."

She glanced over at him. "Maybe he's just trying to be nice. You said he seemed to be trying to make up for the way you were treated by Tomas."

"Well, maybe." He gripped the edge of the counter with both hands and frowned down at the white carpeting between his stockinged feet. "It's just that I have this sense that I'm being . . . used."

She swung around to face him and fluttered a sable makeup brush beneath his nose. "Now hold it. *I'm* the one who's supposed to be suspicious and skeptical, but in this case anything that saves us five thousand dollars is okay in my book. A federal judgeship doesn't carry a princely salary, and mine, as your clerk, frankly sucks."

"Don't be lewd," he muttered automatically.

"Cab, stop worrying. It's probably nothing. Besides, I thought the essence of politics was people using each other."

"It is, but I like to know what I'm being used for. I don't want to think that they're trying to set me up again." He fell silent and shook his head. "Tackling another president would be all I need." He pushed off the counter, only to be stopped by her hand on his arm.

"Don't. Let's assume they're smart enough to learn from past mistakes."

"Yeah, a mistake that swept them, against all expectation, into the White House."

"A mistake that they couldn't have capitalized upon if it hadn't been for *you*."

"So it must be a payoff for services rendered." He forced a lightness into his voice that he didn't feel.

"Don't be bitter or feel guilty. You didn't ruin Tomas; he managed to do that all by himself."

"But I was supposed to have been part of it. Part of the team designated to reassert control over the colonies."

"That's over now, Cab. Now you're just their judge, you can concentrate on dispensing justice, and to hell with all the rest. Let Lydia and Joe hammer out the System's relationship with Earth. It's not our problem anymore."

"You're right, and thanks, you comfort me." He lifted her hand from his arm, bestowed a quick kiss on the slender fingertips, and moved to the door. "I still wish I were on Mars," he called back to her.

"I've been wishing that for weeks," she said, then made a shooing motion. He left her to finish her preparations.

The foyer at the Kennedy Center was a riot of flowers. Looped in garlands between the chandeliers, overflowing from massive tubs by the doors, blossoming from centerpieces on the tables. The perfume of hundreds of roses, orchids, hyacinths, and lilies mingled in the smoke-filled air. If the decor had been designed as a means to reduce the effluvium from cigarettes, pipes, and five hundred bodies, it had failed. The end result was a chokingly sweet yet acrid miasma that filled the room and sent people periodically bolting out onto the long balcony overlooking the Potomac in search of some relief. Doors opened and closed, sending gusts of icy late-January air swirling into the room.

The final chord of Strauss' *Artist's Life* hung pure and clear in the thick, overheated air, and the conductor, his violin bow poised over his head, stood beaming at the dance floor. He seemed not the least bit disturbed that it was occupied by only three couples, and Cab, with Jenny clasped gently in the circle of his arm, shared the conductor's pleasure. Dancing as an act of social and sexual converse was a dying art, and people who could still practice the arcane skill were viewed with varying degrees of awe, jealousy, and displeasure. Since it allowed Cab to have the dance floor to himself, he endured the glares with equanimity.

He also knew he had had an advantage; his mother, for all her political acumen and the various ambassadorial posts she had held, was a bit of a crank. She had always wanted to live in the nineteenth century, so she had filled her various homes with fine antiques, learned to ride sidesaddle, and insisted that her only child learn to dance.

Jenny's ability was come by more honestly. She had been destined for the ballet and had studied and performed for fifteen years before being sidetracked into the law. But whatever their reasons, they made a striking couple, a fact of which Cab was well aware and which filled him with pride. He bowed formally over Jenny's gloved hand, and she swept him a curtsy. Her face was flushed with exertion and pleasure, and she laughed up at him.

"This makes it all worthwhile."

"Yes, but they're starting to play something ugly so that people can jerk and gyrate, so let's retreat."

Tucking Jen's arm beneath his, he guided her through the crush of people. Another glass door was shoved open, and fingers of cold air shot up the slit in Jenny's dress, dampening the fire of the heat-sensitive diodes. She sucked in a quick breath and clung tighter to Cab's arm.

"Just as a point of trivia, did you know they still don't have this building paid off?" he remarked.

"Well, that's certainly significant, but I'm not sure why."

"Would you like a drink?"

"Yes, hot coffee."

"Sorry, I don't think they have that."

"Bad planning."

Their table was almost in sight when they were brought up short by a tall, stoop-shouldered man whose long, sad face was overlaid with a flash of momentary happiness at the sight of the couple.

"Cabot!"

"Mr. Secre—Oh, sorry, Taylor. How are you?"

"Fine, thanks. I was admiring your dancing." His eyes crinkled with a deepening smile. "Although I must say that you looked like the figures on the top of a wedding cake."

Cab stiffened at the joking comment, correctly assuming that it was a reference to his size while Jenny, who had never been particularly disturbed by her diminutive frame and assumed that since she managed to make Cab look tall, he wouldn't mind, either, sighed and looked heavenward.

Taylor, realizing that he had managed to tread on a sore spot, coughed, his eyes darting nervously around the room. "No sign of the President yet. I admit I'm a little surprised to be here."

"No more than I am. Jenny thinks Long is paying off those of us who put him in the White House." He paused and glanced from Moffit to Jenny. "Do you two know each other?"

"Only by reputation," Jenny answered, and extended her hand to the former Secretary of State. "You're the man who got the goods, so to speak, on Tomas."

"Uh, yes . . . well." Taylor knotted his fingers and once more gave that dry, nervous little cough.

"Still, if this is a payoff, Joe Reichart and Evgeni Renko ought to be here," Cab added.

"It's a long way to come for a dance," Jenny replied, pointing toward the ceiling and the distant asteroids.

"True, but you'd think Joe would come back home now that things have been settled."

"I don't think Joe trusts any government now, no matter who's at the helm, and speaking of . . ." She went up on tiptoes and gazed toward a flurry of excitement and activity near the main doors.

"The man himself," muttered Moffit.

"Are you likely to be offered a position in the new administration?" Cab asked in the sudden silence that fell when the orchestra stopped playing.

"Uh, no."

"Too bad. Any administration needs people of integrity no matter what their party alignment."

Taylor turned away, his voice muted. "That's not me. Better you or Joe. I had to be forced to do my duty."

"I think we all did."

Cabot lightly touched his left shoulder, which ached suddenly in memory of the wound he had taken saving Evgeni Renko from an assassin's bullet. He closed his eyes, his brow furrowing at a pain that was not entirely physical.

So many deaths, and all because of one man's need to prove his power and to hang on to that power.

He opened his eyes and studied the handsome, boyish face of Richard Long as he moved joyfully through his guests. In the group that surrounded him he spotted the honey-blond elegance of Jennifer Long, three professors of economics and political science from top Ivy League colleges, a world-renowned pianist, and a scion of royalty from some small European country.

Please God, let him be a good man, he added mentally, almost like a little prayer.

And as if the President had sensed the thought, Long paused in his earnest handshaking and moved swiftly to Cabot. Looking up into the tanned, square face, Cab for the first time felt the great personal charisma of the man, a charisma that was being favorably compared to that of the legendary Jack Kennedy or Gary Hart.

"Here's the man I wanted to see." Long gave Jenny and

Moffit a friendly but dismissing nod and dropped an arm around Cab's shoulders. "Come up here where they can see us."

A double row of camera lenses gazed blankly and, to his mind, malevolently, at Cab, and he felt his smile freezing on his face. This was one of the reasons he had chosen law over politics and broken with six generations of family tradition. He hated to be in the public eye. He also had a momentary surge of panic at what the rest of the family would say when they saw him cuddled up with the leader of the opposition party. He rejected the thought as being really stupid. The Huntingtons had always admired leadership, and Long had already demonstrated that he had that special, ephemeral, and God-given ability to draw all sides together. Now that his initial nervousness had faded, Cab found that he rather enjoyed being within the aura of Long's eminence. He pulled about himself the dignity he felt animated him when he was on the bench and tried to match Long's stride. An equal among equals.

Jenny, finding herself abandoned, decided not to fade unobtrusively back into the woodwork. She fell into step with the President's party and found herself next to Jennifer Long, the President's perfectly groomed, perfectly beautiful, perfectly poised, and perfectly supportive wife. They exchanged brittle smiles and returned their attention to their men. There was something between the two men that made Jenny think that Cab was in the inferior and vulnerable position, and it wasn't just because Long was President or that he physically towered over the small judge. Seven years in various courtrooms had taught her to read the signals, and the signals were clear: Something was going on here just below the surface, and whatever it was, she didn't like it.

Long mounted the dais that held the orchestra, drawing Cab up to stand beside him. Thrusting one arm up into the air, he shouted, "Well, here we are!" A roar of approval from the crowd met the statement. "And we're here because it was through *our* efforts that the American people learned that an evil and power-hungry man occupied the White House!" He paused and surveyed the room, his voice dropping dramatically, "And they didn't fail us. They responded with the honest indignation and integrity that we have come to expect from the people of this great nation. They swept our opponent from office and placed the reins of power into our hands. God grant us the wisdom to use it well."

He bowed his head, a humble little gesture that gave the crowd and the reporters an excellent view of his now famous tousled cinnamon-colored hair. *"We"*—Long's hand tightened convulsively on Cab's left shoulder, and Jenny saw the judge wince at the pressure on the imperfectly healed bullet wound —"had the courage to tell the world what evil was being planned and executed in the corridors of power."

"Funny, I thought *we* had a little bit to do with it," she muttered in an undertone, unable to hold back the words. Several journalists shot her interested glances, Taylor looked nervous, and Jennifer Long sent her a venomous look. Jenny stared back defiantly and added in a somewhat louder tone, "And we paid for it . . . with our blood."

She stared down at her right hand, feeling again the kick and pressure of the rocket pistol with which she had blown away the assassin who had killed Peter and wounded Cab. The memories dampened her bravado and indignation, and she subsided, feeling resentment claw at her throat. She forced her attention back to Long's speech.

"But we're not going to rest on past laurels. From this moment foward I am pledging to use the mandate given to me by the American people to lead all of us—earthman and colonist alike—into a new era of friendship and prosperity." He turned to face Cab and held him at arm's length like a man admiring a new acquisition. "So it is to that end that I have instructed the Senate to drop all impeachment proceedings against Justice Huntington, and I have instructed him to resume his circuit. He will be acting on my behalf to carry this message of goodwill to the colonies and to right any injustices that may remain because of the actions of my predecessor."

Pride, embarrassment, confusion, and frustration warred within Cab. There was another stab of pain radiating out from his shoulder as Long once more tightened his grip, and for one wild instant he considered saying, "I didn't notice you up there taking this bullet for me." Good sense, and an intimate knowledge of how politics worked, intervened. The words died in his throat.

Besides, he thought. *Why should I expect to take credit for stopping Tomas? My actions started the whole mess and doomed those people at the collective, and it took me a bloody long time to recognize what I had done and break with Tomas.*

No, better to lend his support to Long, the man who was faced with the touchy and delicate task of reforging the links between Earth and the System, and forget his own pride. He pulled himself up to his full height, took his place firmly at the President's side, and gave Long a warm, supportive smile.

"Say something, Cab," Jenny hissed. "He's being used like a damn *prop!*" she raged to Taylor Moffit.

"What do you suggest he do?" Taylor asked under the cover of the applause. "Dash Long's hand from his arm and bellow out that it was the two of you, plus Lydia Kim Nu and Joe Reichart who had the courage to break the story of deBaca's treachery to the world? Long's got him over a barrel, and Cab's smart enough to know it." Taylor's pale eyes flickered for an instant with grudging respect. "Long's a consummate politician."

"I would take that as an insult."

"You're not a politician."

"Thank God! And I don't think Cab is seeing anything except how he's once more buddies with a president." Her tone was bitter, and the President's party drew unobtrusively away from her.

Long descended from the dais like a pope stepping forward to bless the multitudes; indeed, as soon as he reached the floor of the ballroom, he was engulfed in a throng of well-wishers, office-seekers, and hangers-on. Cab, looking small and somehow bereft, pushed unnoticed through the crowd. Unnoticed, that is, by the other guests. Several journalists rushed to intercept him. He brushed them aside with sharp gestures.

"Why don't you talk to them?" Jenny demanded without preamble when Cab reached her.

"And say what?"

"How about setting the record straight and giving credit where credit is due?"

"It would look like sour grapes if I now start moaning to the press about how it was really *my* doing and how Long ought to be grateful to me for putting him in the White House. Let's not make the man's job more difficult for him. He has to lead this country and her colonies."

"Okay, then if not for yourself, how about for Joe or

Lydia? Don't they deserve some of the credit? After all, they've been fighting this fight for years."

"They're both ardent System rights people, and they don't carry a very good odor right now. Especially if they're going to set themselves against Long simply because he exists and not even give him a chance."

"So you're just going to stand by and do nothing?" Her green eyes were glittering, and a gust of air from an open window lifted her hair like a red flame.

"What do you want me to do? Make a scene? Pillory the man in public? Denounce his goals and aims? They seem like pretty damn good goals to me. Let's give him a chance. A lot of intelligent people whom I respect seem to think that he deserves one." Jenny opened her mouth to argue, and Cab cut her off. "Would you like to dance?"

"No! I want to leave. I've lost my taste for this affair."

"All right, fine," he said soothingly.

"And maybe the colonists who might be watching will notice your absence. We can hope," Jenny threw bitterly at him.

Taylor fell into step with them as they headed for the door. Behind them, the orchestra had renewed playing. The spritely fox-trot set an odd counterpoint to Cab's and Jenny's grim expressions.

"Excuse me for being obtuse, but what are you two battling about? Sure, Long took credit for everything, but that's just typical political jockeying."

Cab accepted his overcoat from the coat-check machine and said nothing. It was Jenny who leapt to answer, biting off the words as if they pained her.

"Because Long has just told the colonists that Cab is his man, and now they'll have no reason to trust us. Everything we went through to prove ourselves to them has been swept away by a sentence."

"You're *wrong*, Jenny." The words were forced past clenched teeth.

She rounded on Cab. "Oh, really? Well, let's wait and see who's right."

Chapter Two

Dawn was reaching across the rocky, dusty red plain of Elysium, striking radiance from the thin mists of carbon dioxide and water vapor that cowered in the low-lying channels and craters. As the sun climbed higher the sky lost its brilliant white-gold fire and settled into its standard pink-tinged beauty, and with a sigh of wind the mists gave up their unequal battle and vanished, absorbed by the thin, dry air.

High on a crater's rim, President Darnell Hudson, Prophet to the Jared Colony, yawned and stretched, the seals and joints of his pressure suit creaking with the motion. Reaching out a gloved hand, he stroked the red rock wall of the temple and assured himself yet again that he had done right to build it here.

"It'll never withstand the winds." "It'll cost too much to insure that it will." "It shouldn't be this far from the colony."

The arguments had swarmed about him, but he had remained adamant, and eventually his own faith had convinced the Seventy and, with them, the quorum of the people. Here on the rim of the crater, he had reasoned, the temple could be a beacon and an inspiration to all who approached. From the main dome of Jared City and her attendant domed farms, nestled in the bowl of the crater, the people could pause in their work, gaze up, and be refreshed; and outsiders approaching the colony would know that it had not been money and technical ability alone that had built Jared but faith and service to God.

He craned his head back and gazed up the side of the incredible structure. The low Martian gravity had allowed him to indulge in his dream-born fantasies, so thin spires like wentletrap seashells twisted into the sky, the clerestory extended several hundred feet and contained fifty lancet arch windows. In place of stained glass Darnell had had the panes cast and rolled from volcanic dust brought from Olympus Mons. They swirled with fantastic colors; deep purples shot through with traceries of yellow, green, iridescent blues. In short it was a dream structure, a fairy palace, clearly too fragile to survive, but survive it did, for Darnell had believed and had backed that belief with action. The finest engineers and architects had been brought in to supervise the planning and building, and now, seven years after the foundation stone had been laid, it was complete. All that remained was to bolt in the pews and fit the pipes into the massive organ, and those pipes would arrive on the next transport from Earth.

Hudson shaded his faceplate and peered down into the artificially deepened crater. A line of sand crawlers was heading up the slope toward the chapel, bringing the day's contingent of workmen. For an instant he resented them for interrupting his private moment, then with a chuckle he released the emotion and started for his own vehicle. He had done enough dreaming and self-congratulating; the day's work awaited him.

He had just climbed onto the seat of the oversize dune buggy when he spotted a Piper Light coming in low from the southwest. With its extremely elongated wings, designed to catch the thin Martian atmosphere, and its oddly shaped pod, which tapered from a narrow nose, adorned with a canard wing like a mustache, to the bulbous aft section, the plane had the look of a pregnant dragonfly. This insectoid illusion was heightened by the luminescent dragon that adorned the flyer. Darnell, recognizing that distinctive design, gave a whoop of delight. Jumping up, he balanced precariously on the seat of the crawler and waved his arms over his head. The Light responded with a wobble of its fragile wings, and a few moments later it had settled with a whisper onto the sand about five hundred meters from him.

Dropping down onto the seat, Darnell kicked the engine to life and went rolling toward the Light. As he approached, the cockpit door opened, and a tiny, suited figure leapt out.

"You crash into my temple and I really will have your ass."

"Meaning what?" Even distorted by the suit radio, the voice was music; soft, lilting, and chiming.

"I'll make you marry me."

"First, Jeanne wouldn't like that. Second, I thought you had me all picked out for Seth—"

"I'm that transparent?"

"Yes. And finally, I fly too well ever to hit anything."

"You fly like a maniac."

Darnell climbed off the crawler and folded the visitor in his arms. Through the faceplate he looked down into the delicate, doll-like face of Amadea Kim Nu. A few tendrils of jet-black hair had escaped from her tight bun and trembled on her cheeks. Darnell contemplated what it would be like to push them back, to stroke that petal-soft skin, but it was an unworthy thought from a married man of his age, and he pushed it aside. Amadea seemed to sense the storm she had raised within him, for she peeked impishly out from beneath her long bangs, her eyes a startling green in that ivory and carnelian face, and gave him a wink.

"I'm surprised to see you. I thought Dave would place us officially off limits to any station personnel."

"He tried, but I never listen to anything that jackass says."

He gave her a small shake. "Or anybody else."

"Not true. I *always* listen to *you,*" she said in an exaggeratedly innocent tone while opening her almond-shaped eyes to their maximum width.

He snorted. "Got time for a cup of tea?"

"Of course. I came to gossip, and I don't intend to go home empty-handed." He dropped an arm over her shoulders and they walked toward the crawler. "I was wondering what response you'd gotten to the impact statement?"

"Nothing yet, which sort of surprises me, but maybe after that blowup on EnerSun, the feds have decided they shouldn't mess with us."

"I wouldn't bet on it," Amadea drawled as she hopped up

behind him on the crawler and wrapped her arms around his waist.

"Why are you always such a pessimist?" he asked as they went bouncing and grinding their way down the hill toward the city.

"My experience with, and observation of, people."

"Oh, it's just Dave who's soured your outlook. By the way, how are you coming on the setup out there?"

"Slowly." She hunched one shoulder as if rejecting something particularly unpleasant and changed the subject. "And how's your mining base doing?"

"All right. The deposits just get better and better, but it takes an awful toll to get the diamonds out, since we don't have proper equipment. We lost another person last week."

She patted his shoulder. "I heard. I'm sorry. How many does that make now?"

"Forty." The response was terse, and his mouth twisted with concern and frustration as he considered his foster son, now living and working at the mine. The moment passed, and he shrugged philosophically and added, "Still, it's a risk you run when you leave the nice comfortable womb of Earth. And there are no guarantees. Nobody promised us life would be safe or easy."

"True, but does it have to be quite so grim?" Her tone was low and overlaid with a tinge of bitterness. Darnell craned his head around to stare at her, and she quickly smiled. "Don't mind me, I'm just crabby."

They rolled up to one of the dome's five locks and cycled through into the city. Since domes were expensive and vulnerable, the bulk of the colony's population lived in quarters that had been bored deep into the crater's side. The main dome was reserved for public buildings, parks and playgrounds, militia headquarters, and the newly completed thirty-room hotel. One of the major attractions of Mars, aside from scientific inquiry, was her awesome natural formations: Valles Marineris, the five-thousand-kilometer canyon that cut from five to seven kilometers into the crust of the planet; Olympus Mons, the Solar System's mightiest volcano; and other equally spectacular vistas. The colony had pulled in a nice supplementary income from a steady, if somewhat tiny and erratic, trickle of tourists who each year made a trek to the red planet; in an effort to boost that income they had committed to build the hotel. As several people had said during the congregation meeting that okayed the project, it beat having to put the strangers up in their homes.

They drove down the main, tree-lined boulevard and into the mouth of a large tunnel. Just off to the left was the crawler park, an enormous, dimly lit cavern filled with various types of vehicles. A short walk through various pedestrian tunnels and they arrived at Darnell's home. He pushed open the front door and stepped aside so Amadea could enter first. She found such old-fashioned courtesy amusing, and she told him so, only to be interrupted by a quick call from the kitchen.

"Don't you dare tell him that. Not all of us are energetic young women who want to shoulder equally the burdens of modern life. I *like* a little respect now and then." The tone was sharp, but the smile that crinkled Jeanne Hudson's already very wrinkled face took all the sting from the words. "I'm making doughnuts. Shuck those suits and come in and have some."

They shucked, hung the suits, set the tanks to recharging, and hurried into the kitchen, but at the sight of the long, lanky figure sprawled at the table, Amadea froze and almost retreated. Dr. Jasper Mendel raised his head and gave her a toothy, sardonic grin. Lifting a dripping doughnut from his coffee mug, he sucked noisily on the pastry, chewed, swallowed and said, "Come on in, I don't bite."

"Yes, but Dave would if he knew I was in the same room with you," she replied smoothly, recovering her poise.

"Dave's an asshole."

"Undeniably."

She slid into a chair, Jeanne set a cup of herb tea in front of her, and Amadea helped herself to a doughnut from the loaded plate.

"I don't suppose I could get a cup of real coffee?" Amadea asked, greedily eyeing Jasper's steaming cup.

"Not from my private stock you don't, and if you come among the godly, you'll just have to accept the consequences."

"So why aren't you?"

"Because I'm a permanently unrepentant sinner, and I've blackmailed Jeanne into making coffee for me." He grinned up at the older woman, who gave him an affectionate slap on the shoulder.

"We don't force our beliefs on outsiders . . . but we never stop praying for you to come around." She drifted back to the counter to continue with her cooking. Darnell joined her, and they stood talking in an undertone while she dropped gobs of dough into the sizzling oil. Amadea sipped at the grassy-tasting brew and warily eyed her former colleague.

"So how do you like working for the Mormons, the lack of caffeine aside?"

"Sure beats working for those lamebrains in SPACECOM." He gulped down some coffee. "How's the station coming?"

"Fine."

"Don't lie. It's not becoming in a person of your age and sex."

"Don't be patronizing or sexist."

"Then try being up-front with me."

"All right, I will. Things are lousy. Dave is pissed because you schemed and maneuvered until the Command ordered us to take a look at the pyramids and then you left."

"A well-developed instinct for self-preservation and a natural desire to be where the action is."

"A possible alien artifact not being interesting enough for the great Dr. Jasper Mendel."

"A little too broad, my dear. To be really successful a sneer needs to be subtle. A mere flick of the eyelid, an infinitesimal curve of the lip, and a tightening of the nostril."

"You must remind me to take lessons from you sometime."

"You were speaking of an alien artifact?"

"I thought that would interest you. We haven't done any real investigating yet since Dave decreed that we should set up five kilometers from the pyramids, but I did take a fly past the big four. They really are incredible, particularly that one big monster. A mile and a half high, Jesus Christ, and yes, you were right, there does seem to be something on the top." She shook her head in wonder and disgust. "I just don't understand why Dave is being so obstructive. I sometimes think he's deliberately trying to arrange matters so we don't discover a thing."

"Of course he is."

She looked up, startled. "But why?"

"Would you have made that remark about an alien artifact if you weren't with that nut Mendel but rather in the company of 'serious' scientists?" She bit at her lower lip and said nothing. He laughed, a loud, braying sound, and thrust a forefinger at her. "Aha! Another classic example of the scientific community's desperate need to be safe and conservative at all costs, lest they lose their fucking federal grants."

Amadea frowned and began to break her doughnut into tiny pieces.

"But back to Dave," Mendel went on. "He published a very pompous paper several years back attacking my contention that the top of the pyramid was too regular to be natural." He raised his voice to include the Hudsons in the remark, and satisfied that he now had their attention and a larger audience, he continued. "Anyway, he stated quite emphatically that SPACECOM shouldn't waste money on investigating the pyramids, and they listened."

"And then you got into the act and pulled every string available, called in old favors, and God only knows what else, to get that decision overturned."

He smirked and settled back in his chair. "Did it too."

"And promptly cut out leaving the rest of us to face Dave's foul moods."

"Facing Dave in any mood is foul."

"Don't give me that ingratiating smile. You left us in the lurch." She smacked her palm on the table.

"I found Darnell's project to be a good deal more interesting and with greater potential benefits then peering at pyramids, be they ever so fascinating. We're going to change the face of Mars." Mendel's dark brown eyes glowed with an inner fire, and he waved his long arms in the air over his head. Jeanne moved quietly to his side and refilled the coffee cup. Her solid, down-to-earth manner brought him back to himself, and when he continued, it was in more moderate tones. "Besides, we're only a few miles from the plain. I can pop over during my free time and see how you're coming."

"That ought to be a wonderful meeting, you and Dave. Remind me to be in Eagle Port or, even better, on Earth."

"Coward."

"You're damn right. But enough of this scientific rivalry. Tell me about the project. I've only managed to pick up bits and pieces through the gossip mill."

Now that they were talking about *his* project, a topic that interested and excited him, Darnell joined them at the table.

Jeanne drained the last of the doughnuts and also pulled up a chair.

Mendel hunched forward in his chair and clasped his hands between his knees as if trying to keep them still. His long, homely face had taken on a kind of beauty as his animation cast a glow over his features.

"Okay, here's the drill—"

"You know our goal has been to turn Mars into a real home and not just another barren outpost," Darnell interrupted, unable to contain his enthusiasm. "We were willing to commit six or seven generations necessary to transform the planet, but we had figured it would be another forty years before we were able to start."

"Then you found the diamonds."

"Right. We've been digging those suckers out with our fingernails and stockpiling every gem. We now have enough to pay for the extracting and processing equipment we need, so orders have been placed, and when the machinery arrives—" He stopped and rubbed his hands together gleefully.

"You'll be able to remove diamonds at an amazing rate," said Amadea.

"Correct. And if the deposits are only half what we estimate, it will still be enough to finance our terraforming effort."

"We're also getting a lot of support from the church back on Earth," added Jeanne.

"Suffice it to say we've got the money to start," Jasper growled, a little piqued at losing his position at center stage. He pushed back his chair and stood with feet planted firmly apart, one hand behind his back and the other upraised in a professorial attitude. "Two things have to happen rather simultaneously if we're going to succeed: we've got to change the albedo of the planet, and we've got to free up some water to start an atmosphere.

"To accomplish that we're going to seed the north pole with this new super-algae that's been developed by Meadow's team at Berkeley. The stuff has been genetically engineered to survive and thrive under Martian conditions. It's dark, almost blue-black in color, and here's the real kicker." He grinned like an oversize gremlin. "The crap will slowly alter its metabolism to match the increasing levels of oxygen, water, and pressure." He gave her a wink and an A-okay sign. "Slick, huh?"

"Amazing, but are you going to wait for this super-algae to heat the poles enough to start melting the caps?"

"Nope. We're going to hurry things along a bit, at least at the north pole, by slamming several big comets—iceteroids—into the cap. I've been negotiating with some independents out in the Belt, and they've located the first likely ice ball for us. Once the charges are in place, they can start nudging it toward Mars. It should be here in about two years, and then *wham!*"

"Little tough on the algae."

He frowned at her. "The algae will be seeded in a circle around the impact area, and after the comet hits, we'll cover the area with big mats of the gunk to keep the freed water from evaporating. As the atmospheric pressure increases, water won't evaporate as quickly, and it will become a self-perpetuating engine."

"So how long until we don't have to work in pressure suits?"

"Few hundred years and we'll be down to just supplementary oxygen."

Amadea eyed the Hudsons. "You people do think in the long term, don't you? I can't picture any government getting behind a project for that length of time."

"Which is precisely why we didn't ask a government to do it for us," Jeanne answered in her soft voice. "We can think in terms of our children, and our children's children, and so forth."

Amadea stretched and pushed back her chair. "You're sure going to ruin our scientific playground."

"I know. I've been hearing nothing but screams from the various scientific missions on the planet," Darnell conceded. "But it seems insane to keep an entire world as a playground for a few rich tourists and a handful of scientists."

"You'll get no argument from me, but a lot of people will argue that turning it into a playground for a handful of Mormons is equally insane."

Jeanne frowned. "That's not our intention. Once the project is complete, we'll naturally open the planet to colonization from Earth."

"With no limits based on race, creed, or color?"

"No limits," replied Darnell.

"Okay, that reassures me, but"—she waved a hand in a vaguely ceilingward direction—"I don't think they're going to take this quietly."

"What can they do?"

"I have no idea, but they'll probably think of something."

The room sang with power. The accompaniment consisted of the chink of tableware against fine china and the ring of ice cubes in crystal goblets, but the main theme was made up of voices, several hundred of them, all rising and falling in quiet conversations that would sell a company, get a bill through committee, buy a senator. Smoke-filled back rooms were all well and good, but it was more fun to conduct business, shape events, and in short, be a mover and a shaker out where your peers could see you doing it, and wonder.

In one corner of the restaurant exactly such a conversation was beginning to take place.

"Now look, Devert—"

"How's your beef?" The man named Devert leaned inquiringly in, fork extended as if to poke at the other man's plate and perhaps steal a bite.

"Uh, fine."

"And the soup?"

"It's fine too. Look, I didn't some here to talk about the food!"

Devert sank back in his chair and speared a piece of sautéed carrot. "Relax, Honkay. We'll get to business, and you may not find it's as urgent as you thought." The smooth, handsome black face radiated satisfaction and a smug sense of power that fit well with the expensive tailored suit, gold ChronCom watch, and discreet pearl tie tack. He popped the carrot into his mouth, chewed, and swallowed.

Honkay stared down at his plate. "I'm risking a lot helping you people. If what I'm doing is so unimportant . . ." He started to push back his chair.

"Sit down, Lewis, and finish your lunch. I'm not trying to diminish your contributions, it's just that Gemetics has other sources of information."

"Well, they can't know about this." He reached into his inner breast pocket, removed a long brown envelope, and shook it emphatically in the air between them. "It came in yesterday, and as soon as I received it, I knew it was something that would interest you." He laid it on the table and attempted to slide it across to Devert. It was not a very successful attempt; the envelope snagged on the white tablecloth and one corner crumpled.

With deft fingers Devert smoothed out the wrinkle, extracted the folded sheet, and quickly scanned the page. "Interesting, yes, but unexpected, no. We already knew about this undertaking and have a good deal more detail concerning their plans than has been provided by this statement."

Honkay goggled. "But how? I mean . . ."

Devert took a sip of white wine, rolling the crisp, dry liquid over his tongue. He finally swallowed and gave Honkay a knowing smile. "We have an agent already in place on Mars."

The door to the Oval Office came open even as she reached for the knob. Disconcerted, Lis Varllis drew back and gazed into the equally disconcerted eyes of her boss, President Richard Long, and the cool, steady gray eyes of Justice Cabot Huntington. She had never met the man whose escapades aboard the EnerSun station had handed them the election, so she spent a few moments weighing and evaluating the slender, compact, jurist as she said, "Sorry, sir, I didn't know you had anyone with you. Shelley indicated that you were free."

"I swear, that woman would lose her head if it weren't screwed on. Sure wish Dani would get well and get back. He's my regular secretary," Long explained to Cab. "This one is his replacement—"

"And I think it's time to replace the replacement," broke in Lis. "We can't have this sort of mix-up. It wastes too much of your time."

"Ah, my ever-efficient chief of staff." He paused and glanced from the blond woman to Cab. "Do you two know each other?"

"Only by reputation," Cab replied.

"Lis, Cabot Huntington. Cab, Lis Varllis." They exchanged handshakes and how-do-you-dos. "Okay, Cab, bon voyage, good luck, and all the rest, and I'm sorry I didn't get a chance to talk to you sooner, but you know how it is, picking up the reins of power and such." He gave his boisterous, youthful laugh and slapped the smaller man on the shoulder.

"I understand sir. I'm surprised you called me in at all."

"Well, I wanted to let you know that I was behind you and quiet any doubts you might have had. After your last experience dealing with the White House—"

"Yes, Mr. President, I understand that, too."

The words were a shade too cold, and the tone, together with the interruption, indicated that this was not a topic the jurist wished to pursue. Lis's estimation of the man rose with the show of spirit, but she also felt some concern. He looked like he could be a pigheaded son of a bitch in the right circumstances.

Looks like, hell! Can be, she amended to herself. This man brought down Tomas deBaca because he got a cramp in his soul. He'll bear watching. She made a mental note to do so. She didn't want Huntington doing unto Rick what he had done unto his great, good friend deBaca.

The two men made their final farewells, and Cabot strode away with his back ramrod-stiff, as if trying to add another inch or two to his height. Long stepped back so Lis could precede him into the office.

"Stiff-necked Brahman. They're a breed that give me a pain where I sit." He flung himself into a chair and sprawled in loose-limbed ease.

"So why see him?"

Lis deposited the file she had been carrying onto the desk and looked back at the man she had followed and help propel from an Oregon governorship to the senate to the presidency. She had his trust and reliance, but she had never had the man. That right belonged to Jennifer, and Lis's soul writhed every time she contemplated that fact. Still, maybe it was better to be the king-maker rather than the king's concubine. She forced her attention off this painful subject and back to Rick, who had begun speaking again.

"I don't know. Guess I just wanted to feel him out and hope he would leave here my friend."

"And did the old Richard Long magic do the trick?"

"Who can tell with a tight-assed, closemouthed customer like that? So what do you need?"

"Your permission to handle a situation."

"You don't need my permission for that."

"All right, I don't, then, but I would like to brief you on the circumstances so you won't be caught flat-footed if there should be any questions."

"Are there likely to be?"

"I doubt it, but one should never underestimate the ability of the press to ferret out pointless minutiae."

Long folded his arms behind his head and propped his feet on a nearby coffee table. "Okay, shoot."

"Gemetics."

"Name is familiar."

"It should be. They contributed a million dollars to your campaign." Long straightened and brought his hands down. "They're in the business of making synthetic diamonds for industry and growing zero-gee crystals for the computer business. Both are very lucrative activities—the diamonds more so than the crystals. Recently Gemetics has been facing some competition from Mars."

"Mars?"

"Apparently the . . ." She paused and referred to her notes. "Tharsis region . . . there are a bunch of volcanoes there," she explained "and they're just packed with diamond deposits. Right now a group of Mormons, who settled on Mars some twenty-five years ago, are mining the sands. It's only been a trickle so far because of the unique and hostile conditions faced on Mars."

"Worse than the Moon?"

"Much worse." She seated herself on a corner of the massive desk. "According to some experts I consulted, Mars has no atmosphere to speak of, so a man has to wear a pressure suit to survive. On the other hand, there is just enough to kick up monumental dust storms. Some have even been known to envelop the entire planet. A big storm can kill a man if he's out in it long enough. In short, it's a bitch to mine under these conditions."

"So what's Gemetics' beef? Doesn't sound like they're going to get much competition out of these colonists."

"The colonists are planning to change that. They've been stockpiling diamonds and have ordered a load of heavy mining equipment. Once that arrives, they might be able to control the market."

"What in the hell are these people going to do with that kind of money?"

"Terraform the planet."

"Quite an undertaking."

"It seems they're capable of doing it, and meanwhile they'll hurt Gemetics . . . badly."

"So what do you want to do?"

"I'll get to that. First, let me lay out a bit more of the background."

Long subsided, rebuked.

"All right," Lis continued, "the colonists have filed an environmental impact statement with the EPA per the 1993 additions to the act, but the statement itself is rather a slap in the face to the department." She reached back and removed a sheet from the file.

"Great, more damn colonists," Long groused as he stumped over and took it. His jaw tightened as he surveyed the single line. "This kind of challenge to a federal agency infuriates me. Have the EPA deny the request," he ordered. "That will solve Gemetics' problem and give a clear message to the colonists that I'm not going to brook this kind of challenge."

"I don't think that's a very good idea. It would be a red flag to the colonists and might bring back too many memories of that confrontation with deBaca. It was, after all, only four months ago."

"So what do you advise, Ms. Cunning? I can see the devious wheels turning." He grinned, not the least offended by her curt disagreement. He was used to following her lead, and as he gazed down into her delicate, oval face, framed by a cap of dark honey-gold hair, he was again struck by her brilliance and loyalty. Lis's lips parted in an answering smile, and her lashes slowly lowered to veil her elongated violet eyes.

"I think we should ring in a third player."

"Such as?"

"The Protectors of Worlds, a.k.a. POW. They're big supporters of yours, and they would love to sink their teeth into this one. When they find out that the colonists are planning to slam comets into the poplar ice caps, they'll come unglued."

"Jesus, *I* may come unglued. What makes them think they have the right to undertake those kind of destructive activities without consulting anyone else?" he asked rhetorically as the old emotions and reactions of a longtime Green Peace activist came to the fore. He took a quick turn around the room and stood drumming his fingers on the back of a tall leather chair.

"Okay, you have my permission. This makes us look good to two of our supports, eh?"

"Absolutely." She pushed off the desk, gathered her files, and headed for the door. "I'll get things started. Oh, I'd also like to involve some of the other agencies; SPACECOM, OSHA, maybe the Commerce Department."

"Fine," he agreed. She was relieved when he didn't ask for any details. Sometimes Rick could be a trifle naive, and she didn't like to tarnish his innocence.

"Thank's, Lis, you're invaluable," he said rather absently, his mind already on other matters.

"I aim to please."

And to stay invaluable, she added silently as the door closed behind her.

The act of exercising power had her blood singing, and she stretched out until her strides matched that internal singing. Several young aides gave her surreptitious and admiring glances, and she smiled that secret little smile that had led several newsfaxes to dub her the "Mona Lisa of National Politics." It pleased her that at thirty-eight she still had the power to fire a man's blood. It also amused her that virtually everyone in the campaign, and now at the White House, thought she and Rick were having an affair. It did neither of their reputations any harm, and poor, dear Jennifer sat in unconscious innocence. But then Jennifer hadn't noticed much of anything beyond her poets, writers, and musicians for a good many years now.

So maybe the time was right to take that final step into Rick's bed, she mused.

Still, she didn't want to do anything that would diminish her effectiveness. She was the first female ever to hold the position of chief of staff, and she wasn't going to blow it. Through the years several other poor dupes had been shunted into the vice-presidency, but it had been a sop and everyone knew it. If only one of those male presidents had had the courtesy to die, something might have been accomplished, but they hadn't, and women had been frozen in the number-two spot. Rick hadn't even given a nod to that tired old tradition. He had picked a male running mate, a sad-eyed man who had delivered the South as promised and now kept politely out of sight.

She swung into her outer office, and Susan Donetti looked

nervously up from her computer. She was an incredibly beautiful twenty-three-year-old whose dark Italianate looks made a perfect foil to Lis's golden radiance. That was part of the reason she had been hired. The other reason was that Lis Varllis liked to have women working under her.

"Get Lucius Renfrew on the com," she ordered as she swept past and into the elegance of her private office. The door slammed behind her.

"Yes, ma'am," Susan replied politely to the blank panel.

While Lis waited for the call to go through she lounged in her chair and admired her latest acquisition, a delicate and icy abstract by a young Chinese-American painter. It went well with the rest of the room which had been decorated in shades of white. There were only discrete touches of color in the room, provided by an elaborately blown twelve-inch vase of swirling and iridescent shades of purple and lilac that sat on a pedestal near the window, an enormous Chinese rug whose pattern was expressed in the same pale lilac, and the pale peach desk set.

Her predecessor in this office had been a man, and the room had reflected it. Heavy dark paneling, massive walnut furniture, and a thick plush carpet in dull beige. Others no doubt would have described it as powerful, but she saw only typical male insecurity.

Hanging on to his balls with one hand, and waving his hose with the other, so people would know he was tough stuff.

She chuckled aloud and gave the blotter an infinitesimal shift to the left. She preferred to work more subtly.

The com chimed and she switched on the screen. The narrow, intense features of Lucius Renfrew stared challengingly out at her. With his shaggy blond hair falling limply to touch his collar, his pinched mouth, and the affectation of his wire-rimmed spectacles, he looked like an out-of-work Russian revolutionary. Lis suspected that was why he dressed as he did. He wanted to appear dangerous—and he was. He and his group had cut off more than a few research projects of which they had disapproved. Under Lucius's direction they had combined loud and sometimes violent protest with a judicious use of money and the courts. He was a good weapon to have at hand, as long as one was always careful to keep it pointed in the right direction.

"Hi, Lucius, how are things going?"

"Busy." Being laconic seemed to be his latest mannerism. She could remember a time when any question, no matter how banal, was a trigger for a long, impassioned speech on Christ alone knew what.

"Look, I've got a little something here that I think will interest POW. As you know, President Long has always been a strong defender of the environment, and he's appreciative of the support you people gave him during the campaign, so he wanted me to pass this along to you." He remained silent, and she decided this latest affectation was far more irritating than its predecessor. She sighed and pulled the impact statement from the folder. "I'll send it through to you."

"Fine."

She fed the sheet into the Comnet where it was scanned and pulsed across the country. For a few moments Renfrew's face disappeared from the screen as the information reached his office, then he was back, mouth pursing into an even tighter pink bud.

"This is outrageous! Does the EPA mean to approve this?"

"Yes, of course. We have no real grounds on which to deny the permit."

"Well, you can be sure that *we'll* act." His mouth twisted. "Hope Long won't get his little feelings hurt by our suing the EPA."

"The President understands the realities, and I trust you do too."

"Yeah, better us looking like bad asses to the colonists than the sainted Richard Long." His tone was putting Lis in a slow burn, but she held back the anger. "I'll get this matter before our legal department today, and we can have a complaint out in a week. Give that asshole Huntington something to do." He smiled bleakly, and Lis felt the room momentarily tilt around her.

"Huntington?" she repeated faintly.

"Fifteenth Circuit, remember? I'd say this is definitely in his bailiwick."

"Oh, right." They exchanged a few more remarks, then Renfrew cut off, leaving Lis to stare blankly at the darkened screen.

Huntington, the man who had at the final and most critical moment sided with the System colonists and broken a President. Was it likely to happen again? No, surely not.

She shook her head, and the golden chin-length cap tickled at her jawbone. She had failed to take that into account, but she wouldn't accept that it had been a miscalculation. At least not yet. And if it turned out she had erred . . . well, nothing was irrevocable. Even judges could be handled if it was done properly. Subtlety, that was the key.

Chapter Three

Jenny fingered the hammered silver of the concho belt and rubbed a forefinger on the inset turquoise stones.

"It's a beautiful piece," offered the young Navajo man behind the counter. "Part of an estate sale. You don't see turquoise like that anymore—real sky blue." He rested his elbows on the glass case and leaned in. "My grandmother's got trunks of the stuff. Still pulls it out at every opportunity. But she's real old-fashioned."

"Wearing the family wealth?" suggested Harry as he also slouched against the counter, and Jenny hid a smile. The old McBride magic was definitely at work again.

It had always amazed her the way people would strike up a conversation with her father. In restaurants, on street corners, on trains, and in planes. Even in other countries. Once in Vienna they had found a socialist workingman's restaurant, and while they had stuffed on wiener schnitzel and noodles, the burly men had maintained a running conversation with Harry. It didn't seem to matter that he couldn't speak a word of German; his smile was enough to encourage them. She mistily regarded the small, rotund form of her father and realized she was in danger of becoming maudlin.

"Yeah. We used to measure our wealth in sheep, horses, and turquoise. Now it's tougher. It's hard to get a feel for electronic money."

Jenny removed the belt and with a clash of silver returned it to the counter. Harry lifted the belt, running it through his hands. "Feel is important." He grinned at Jenny, his gray eyes soft and a little unfocused behind the lenses of his glasses. "We'll take it."

"Dad, no, it's—"

"Wear it on Mars. I think it's creator—whoever he might have been—would be pleased."

"Mars?"

"Yep. My daughter's leaving in a few days for Mars."

"To settle?" He turned his black eyes to her, and there was a glitter over the obsidian.

"No. My work's taking me there, and I'll only be staying a couple of months."

"I've thought about heading out, but I don't know. I'd miss the mountains and the sunsets."

"Other mountains, other sunsets," said Harry softly.

"True." He took McBride's card and the belt and went to ring it up. "But there's family too. Be hard to leave them."

Jenny suddenly found a shelf filled with brightly painted and feathered kachinas to be irresistibly interesting. Cradling a comical little mudhead in her hands, she stared down into the open *o* of its mouth and concentrated on being sad. Six months ago she had said good-bye to her father, thinking it would be a year, at least, before they saw each other again. Now she was back doing it again, and it was harder the second time. Thoughts of Cab came slipping in, winding tendrils of resentment about her sadness, creating an uncomfortable melange of emotions. A nudge in the ribs brought her back to her surroundings.

"Want to wear it?"

"Please. And thank you."

"My pleasure."

She took his arm, and they stepped out into Santa Fe's central plaza. Tatters of dark gray clouds were racing north toward the mountains, driven by a brisk, clean wind. Each cumulus mass was a distinct creation, fascinating in its individuality, capable of being viewed with joyous imaginings. The pale February sun seemed to dart between the clouds, and an alternating pattern of dark and light flickered across the adobe buildings and the small patches of snow that clung in shadowed crannies. The sun also seemed to draw sparks from Harry McBride's silver-white hair and deepened the lines in his round face.

The smell of roasting chili and wood smoke added a pungent bite to the winter air. Jenny sucked in a deep breath, shivered, and tightened her grip on her father's arm.

"Have you seen your mother?"

"I called her a few days ago and said good-bye."

"You should go."

"I don't want to." McBride looked distressed. "Dad, you couldn't live with her. Why do you expect me to get along with her?"

"Just wishful thinking, I guess. Let's walk, shall we?"

They did. Across the plaza and down East Palace Road past tiny shops selling hand-woven goods, Indian pots, rugs, and jewelry; art galleries—five of them within a half-block radius—and all displaying what Jenny had contemptuously dubbed "Indian Gothic" after her first visit to her father's retirement home. It wasn't that she had anything against pueblos or adobe houses nestled among aspen trees, but after viewing sixteen paintings offering different angles of the Taos Pueblo and innumerable adobe houses—most of which were badly executed—it devalued the good work that was being done.

She realized that she was indulging in head games to avoid thinking about her mother. That line of thought drew her inexorably to thoughts of Cab because Vivian was currently living in Paris, and that was right across the channel from England where Cab was visiting his family. . . . She gave herself a shake like a filly irritated by gnats, and her father raised an eyebrow.

"Not still mad at your mother, are you?"

"Yes and no. Remind me when I have children not to play control games with them, okay?"

"Meaning that we did?"

"Yes."

"Are you angry about it?"

"Less toward you than toward her, which supports the premise that daughters are sweet on their daddies."

"I just hated to see you wasting your intellect."

"And Mom hated to see me turning into a carbon copy of you."

Harry looked at her, startled. "She said that?"

"Oh, yeah. She never forgave me for giving up ballet and realizing your dream instead of hers."

"I did always want to be a lawyer." His voice was low.

"I know."

"Do you really hate it? Did I drive you into something that's made you unhappy?"

"No. There are aspects of it I despise, but overall I'm happy and glad I didn't waste my brains. Dancers wear out too soon. I'm looking forward to being ninety, on the bench, and an obnoxious old beldam who eats young attorneys for breakfast."

"That's a long way away."

"Sixty years. God, I wonder where I'll be in sixty years. Things change so fast."

"I have a hard enough time coming to grips with where you'll be next month."

"Are you going to miss me?"

They were strolling past the Scottish Rite Church, a soaring monstrosity of bright pink stucco. Harry sighed, pulled his arm from Jenny's, and seated himself on the low stone fence that ringed the church and its grounds.

"Bunches and bunches."

She joined him, leaned her head on his shoulder. "Me too."

"Why didn't he invite you?"

She didn't pretend not to understand. "Damned if I know."

"I've known senators. Been a real pillar in the New Mexico business community."

The dull resentment that had been gnawing at the pit of her stomach ever since Cab had decreed that they would visit their families, but hadn't offered to take her along to Oxfordshire, flared when she heard the mournful tone in her father's voice. He had always been very sensitive about his standing in society, and he was assuming that no invitation had been issued because he hadn't been rich enough or famous enough to insure her acceptance in the circles frequented by the Huntingtons. She remembered how devastated he had been when, at sixteen, she hadn't been selected as a Donita. She had been secretly relieved to avoid all that debutante rigmarole but had suffered for him and somehow felt she had let him down. Just as he now felt he was letting her down. For an instant she reflected on how strange and convoluted human emotions could be. She wanted to bring it all up and reassure him, but there was so much and it would take so long, and they had so little time left together.

"Dad, it doesn't matter. I live with him, not with his mother, and I don't think the Martian colonists are going to be all that impressed with how much money the Huntingtons have or how many presidents they've served."

"Is he going to marry you?"

"This is not the nineteenth century. Is he going to marry me!" She made a face. "How about asking if *I'm* going to marry *him?"*

His laugh was boisterous and very much at odds with his seventy-four years. He cuddled her close and kissed her, his mustache tickling and bristly against her cheek, the scent of his after-shave strong in her nostrils. Tears sprang into her eyes, but she didn't try to force them back. That was one of Harry McBride's virtues—he was not a man to hide his own emotions, and he respected and acknowledged emotions in others.

Moisture fogged his glasses, and blinking rapidly, he pulled them off and polished the thick lenses. "You'll wear the belt and think of me?"

"All the time. Dad, it's not like it's forever." Her voice was husky with unshed tears.

"I know, I know, but I didn't expect all that trouble last time, and this is even farther out—"

"Dad don't . . . don't give voice to my inchoate worries. I've got an irrational fear about this circuit, so don't make it okay for me to be scared."

In one of his blinding mood shifts he shook off his depression, dried his eyes, and gave her a stern look. "You're going to be just fine. You're tough and strong and smart, and you can handle anything life throws at you."

"In other words I'm a lot like you."

He looked pleased, then frowned and harrumphed. "Come on, let's get home. There's homemade vegetable soup and my justifiably famous French bread."

"Maybe I'd better not introduce you to Cab," she said as he lifted her down from the wall. "He'll want to know why with a gourmet cook for a father I can't poach an egg."

• • •

Dust motes spun in lazy, golden patterns, driven by the final rays of the sun slanting in through the door of the barn. Cab leaned his forehead against the flank of a big, dappled gray hunter, who was named Rufus, listening to the muted rumblings from the horse's gut and drinking in the warm, musty horse smell. Periodically the animal's hide would wiggle, trying to dislodge this irritating pressure, but he was a polite beast and never made a really big issue over Cab's presence. Also, his hay net had just been filled, and all down the line of wooden box stalls came sounds of contented munchings and stampings.

Less contented was the commanding voice of Cecilia Huntington, who was busily lecturing the unfortunate farrier who had come to shoe her favorite hunter.

"I wanted calkins on the shoes and you didn't do it."

"If you'll forgive me, ma'am, but calkins don't make a bloody bit of difference. The weight is on the toe when a horse lands after a jump." The man's deep basso and elongated West Country vowels set an odd counterpoint to Cecilia's clipped Boston tones.

"Then I'm an ignorant old woman, but humor me! Cabot, quit skulking in that stall and come out here and give me some support."

Cab sighed and gave the horse a slap on the rump. Rufus reponded with only a flick of one ear, which proved that one should not look to horses for comfort or encouragement. Reaching over, Cab pulled the latch and let himself out of the box stall. Hawkins, the blacksmith, was hunched over a hind foot fitting a shoe to the black mare while Cecilia leaned against the wall, arms folded tightly across her chest, riding crop beating lightly against the wall behind her.

At sixty-one she was still a striking woman. Diminutive, probably no more than five feet tall, but animated by a power and presence far greater than her size. When it was down, her hair hung to her waist and was a dull ebony. Cab knew the color came from a bottle but would never dare to say it to her. She was whip-lean, and her face tapered to a sharp, foxy chin. He had inherited that chin and felt it looked better on his mother than it did on him. A few discreet crow's-feet etched her eyes, left over from her face-lift. She had wisely decided not to have all the wrinkles removed; after all, they gave character to a face. She had looped the skirt of her riding habit over one arm, and in her polished black boots and white cravat she looked like a tiny nineteenth-century doll. A somewhat imperious doll, however, for unfolding her arms, she began beating out an irritated tattoo on the top of her boot with the braided whip.

"So what do you say?" she challenged, blue eyes flashing from behind the fragile netting that adorned her riding hat.

"Nothing. I haven't been on a horse in ten years until today, and I never was an expert on shoes. I left that to you."

"How aggravating you can be. I do hope you show more forcefulness of spirit on the bench. Please see these shoes reset, Mr. Hawkins, and in the future save yourself an extra trip by doing what I say the first time." She beckoned, and Cab followed her obediently out of the barn.

The sun vanished with that gray suddenness that characterizes an English winter, and tendrils of fog were beginning to rise from the turf. They wrapped themselves about the great, white bulk of the house, creating the illusion that it was floating somewhere out of time and space, and the golden light that spilled from the mullioned windows added to the fairy like quality.

"You should be more forbearing with your farrier. There aren't that many of them left."

"And there aren't many people who own fifteen horses left, either. He should be grateful for the work."

"You can be a most aggravating woman."

She chuckled, a light, silvery sound, and Cab could easily see why she had been the joy and despair of a generation of young men some forty years before.

"Why didn't you bring your lady?"

"I knew you wouldn't approve of her, and I saw no reason to make all of us uncomfortable."

"Cabot! I am never arbitrary. I would have judged the girl on her own merits."

"Mother, you have never liked *any* woman I've brought home. You can't blame me for paying more attention to what you do rather than what you say."

Her delicate, upswept brows drew together in a sharp frown, and Cab clamped his teeth. He didn't want to totally prejudice his mother against Jenny in case there should come a time when he did introduce her. Cecilia swept in a side door, down several heavily paneled hallways, and into a fire-lit library. A silver tea set rested on a low table, wisps of steam rising from the spout of the pot. A plate of cakes, and one of sandwiches, lay next to the cups. Cecilia, flinging herself onto the Queen Anne love seat, swept up a cucumber sandwich and took a large bite. Her blue eyes roved about the room until they came to rest on a briar pipe still smoking in an ashtray. A frown again creased the white expanse of her brow.

"Damn the man, now where has he gotten to?"

"Probably fleeing for cover in his bedroom. Why did you insist on invading his private sanctum?" There was that inward cringe again as he realized he had once more baited his mother. he wondered what was wrong with him. Why, after all these years of adoration, was he finding Cecilia so irritating?

"He ought to spend some time with us."

"We took a long walk this morning."

"Hello, dear, did I leave my pipe?"

Gerard Huntington hesitated in the doorway, hands thrust deep into the pockets of his gray wool pants, gray hair drooping into his eyes. There was a nervous, apologetic air about him that aroused feelings of anger and pity in his only child. His brothers all had brilliant public careers, while Gerard had, without warning and for apparently no reason, refused to run for a second term in the House of Representatives. He had retired to his books and airplanes—he was one of the foremost designers of prototype planes and ultra-lights in the world—and left the public stage to his more energetic wife. Most members of the Huntington clan referred to him as "poor old Gerard," and most people tended to forget he existed. Cab remembered John Malcomb on the EnerSun station saying he would marry Cecilia if there weren't such an age difference, and anger shook him again.

He's not dead yet, he thought, and something must have showed on his face, for Gerard gave him an inquiring glance.

"Right here, Papa," he said, to cover his feelings and to prevent any outburst from Cecilia. He moved swiftly to the table and held out the pipe.

"Well, I won't disturb you any—"

"You're not disturbing us. Please"—he laid a hand on Gerard's arm—"stay and have some tea."

"Perhaps I will." He and Cab arranged themselves on the

sofa across from Cecilia. "Wish you had brought your young lady," Gerard remarked as he absently stirred four spoonfuls of the sticky, dark brown English sugar into his cup.

"According to Cabot, he was scared to because of the way I'm prejudiced against all his ladies." The tone was pure acid.

"But you are, my dear." He turned to Cab, either unmoved or unaware of his wife's furious look. "Did you know they're flying my design on Mars?"

"What?"

"Ultra-lights. They're using my design."

"I should have thought they'd use rocket-powered craft."

"Oh, they do, for long trips and when the winds kick up, but for the day-to-day, ultra-lights will do. With that new ceramic engine that weighs only three pounds, LegerSteel for the struts and frame, and a tedlar covering, the weight is negligible. All it requires is enough wingspan for lift."

"Jesus, they must have the wingspan of a 747."

"No, you can compensate for wing length by upping the horsepower. They're long, but not as long as you'd expect."

"What's the range on those?"

"About fifteen hundred miles. Speed's way up, too, around three hundred miles per hour, and—" He shut his mouth and rolled a nervous eye toward his wife. The clearing of his throat erupted in the room like a backfiring engine. Cab's fingers tightened on the handle of the Wedgewood teacup, driving the blood from his nails. Gerard breathlessly added, "But you will be careful out there, won't you, Cabot? You got into such trouble last time."

Cab shot a glance at Cecilia. They had never directly referred to the events on the EnerSun station. Cabot hadn't mentioned anything because he still had ambivalent feelings about the whole affair and because he feared that at base his mother did not approve of his siding with the colonists.

"I really didn't have a lot of choice."

"Oh, I know, and I'm pleased by the way you handled things."

"Glad someone is—I'm certainly not. I should have stood up to Tomas a good deal earlier."

"Tomas was clumsy—stupid, even—but his position was sound. The authority has to originate *here*." Cecilia slapped the table for emphasis.

"There are a lot of people living out *there* who wouldn't

agree." Cecilia sat up and leaned in, hungrily anxious and ready to debate. Cab could sense his father preparing to flee at this show of intensity from his wife and hurried to add, "But I really don't want to get into it all over again. It's done, and I'll be starting out fresh."

"President Long seems to like you," murmured Gerard, helping to spread oil on the troubled waters.

"Yes, and I like him. He seems to have a real program."

"I wish he were a little less chummy with this Lucius Renfrew, however; the man, and his little gang of galloping Luddites, are quite worrisome."

"Your father fancies himself a real scientist now that someone actually bought and built that ultra-light design."

"I'm glad I'm not a real scientist. It's a nervous time for technocrats. People welcome the technological advances for the comforts they bring, but they're also frightened by the speed with which the world is changing. Fundamentalism continues to advance—"

"But about Renfrew," Cab interrupted hurriedly before Gerard could start riding his favorite hobbyhorse.

"There was an article in the *Times* today. It seems that POW has convinced the federal government to close down Dr. Meadow's research laboratory at Berkeley, pending further investigation of the super-algae they've been testing there. People are afraid the stuff will creep out a ventilator shaft and eat the planet." His mouth twisted with derision.

"There have been problems."

"Grossly exaggerated. Of course there are risks, but scientists are responsible people. They have to live on this planet too. And I still can't forgive the fact that earlier groups blocked the development of an artificial insulin for thirty years because of the same irrational fear. Lunatics!"

"I'm a member of Green Peace."

His father shot him a crooked smile. "And you're not a lunatic."

"Thank you," he replied dryly.

"Cab, I agree that watchdogs are useful, but if we decreed that nothing could be attempted until it's certain that it's absolutely safe, we'd still be living in caves." He snorted. "No, it's these fringe groups like POW that I object to. It's interesting how their philosophy parallels Nazi rhetoric in the last century."

"Papa!"

"I'm serious. There was the same distrust of urbanization and technology. The attitude that the greatest value was to be found in nature. That was part of the propaganda against the Jews—that they were responsible for the rise of cities, and leading the good peasant stock astray. No, old Reichshinnie Himmler would have felt right at home with POW. And frankly if Lucius Renfrew can refer to human beings as "cancers" I think he's the moral equal of Heinrich."

This conversation was not to Cecilia's liking, violating, as it did, her desire that her home be a haven of nineteenth-century fantasy. She frowned down at her husband and asked her son, "Do you want to go to the opera with me tomorrow night?"

"No, I'm going to head home tomorrow. I want at least two days in my own place before leaving again."

"How long will you be gone?" asked Gerard.

"At least a year. Probably not too much longer."

"That's a very long time," Gerard murmured, and dropped another spoonful of sugar into his already oversweetened tea.

"I'm going to check on dinner," announced Cecilia, and left.

Father and son sat for a few minutes in uncomfortable silence. For some reason the departure of Cecilia had left them tongue-tied and awkward. Cab wished he could put his arms around his father's stooped shoulders and tell him he loved him and would miss him, too, but the words stuck in his throat. Gerard gulped down his tea and, muttering something about a book that he was reading, wandered from the room.

Cab stretched out on the sofa, his cheek pillowed on one hand, and stared into the flames. He hoped Jenny would cut her visit to Santa Fe short and be back in California when he arrived. While he wanted to be in his own place, he didn't necessarily want to be there alone.

Jasper Mendel came in low over Elysium's highest pyramid and peered down at the object that sat in splendid and mysterious isolation at the exact center of the summit. Yes, Amadea had been quite correct—it was not natural. Still, what did lie beneath the crust of Martian dust was unclear, and Dave was dragging his heels about actually laying hands on the alien object. Perhaps he's scared alien boogey monsters will erupt out of the object and eat his head, thought Jasper sourly, then smiled a little at the picture presented.

There was an explosion of sound from the Light's radio, and an all-too-familiar voice came yammering out of the speaker.

"Mendel, you clear off! This area is off-limits to—"

Jasper sadly allowed his imaginary alien to release Dave's head, then, jabbing at the send button, he snapped, "Fuck off, Dave, you don't own Mars."

"And neither do you and your gang of religious lunatics, and now you never—" The director cut himself off, as if aware that he was saying too much.

"My, my, word travels fast in the sticks."

"You can't land here!"

"What, you going to come out and stand in front of me? King Canute might have admired you, but the nose of my Light is going to hurt a hell of a lot worse than waves." There was an inarticulate splutter from the radio. Jasper laughed, cut the connection, and arrowed in on the expanse of rippled red sand at the base of the pyramids.

The base was obviously makeshift; five quonset huts ringed the buried living quarters, giving the impression of circled wagons from an old Western film. Jasper wondered if he fell into the category of Indian, probably hostile. The living quarters themselves consisted of old landing modules salvaged from earlier bases and buried beneath a yard of soil to shield the scientists from cosmic radiation.

The Light rolled to a halt; Jasper popped the hatch and jumped to the ground. Three suited figures approached, and he easily recognized Amadea from her size and the ease with which she handled herself in the low Martian gravity. Having been born and raised in the orbiting stations, she was at home in low-grav, null-grav, and Earth-norm.

We really are breeding a new kind of human, thought Jasper, and it was both sobering and exciting. A little jealous-making too. He wished he could be one of these new adventurers instead of lanky old Mendel, the crank of Cal-Tech, who felt like the clay of the home world had wrapped itself firmly about his feet and would forever hold him back from his dreams.

The little knot of scientists had reached him by now, and

Jillian Green, Dave's downtrodden assistant, gazed at him nervously through her faceplate and licked at her lips.

"Dave says this base is off-limits to you, and you won't be permitted inside." Her plump, good-natured face was mournful, and her eyes kept darting away, refusing to meet Mendel's amused gaze.

"Jilly, dear, I won't bite. I know that left to yourself, you'd never have delivered such a half-witted message, and I'll assure Dave you made every effort." He gave the glowing blue figure of Berto Bunny, Mexico's most popular cartoon character and which adorned the nose of his Light, a fond pat and started toward the lock.

"You're going in?" came a squeak.

"Of course. I came to visit my old buddies, and I'm not going to do it standing by the back door. And if Dave persists, I'm going to accuse him of anti-Semitism."

Amadea chuckled and, linking her arm through his, escorted him to the lock.

Dr. David Lucas was waiting, his lips so tightly compressed that his mouth was a thin slash in his pale face. Two bright spots of color were burning on his cheeks and—the real acid test by Jasper's way of thinking—his bald dome was also flushed a faint pink. Long brown hair formed a circlet about his head and hung in a heavy pageboy to his shoulders. It made him look rather like a mad monk.

Jasper pulled off his helmet. "Hi, Dave. How's it going?"

"Out! Get out! This is my project now, and I'm not going to have you coming around upsetting my people—"

"Am I upsetting you folks? There, see? No problem," he added when none of the other scientists said a word. "By the way, I'm the one who got the project off the ground, and these were *my* people before they were yours. Remember? You're going to benefit from *my* brilliant training of your team." There was a rude sound from Amadea, and Jasper slapped her on the rump. "They're going to make you look like a genius."

Jasper made no effort to disguise the obvious contempt in his voice. For a moment Lucas stood frozen, breathing heavily through his nose, then he reared back, planted a hand in the middle of Jasper's chest, and gave him a hard shove. Jasper stumbled back into the lock and emerged with a hot light burning in his deep brown eyes. It consisted of equal parts of anger and pleasure; the offer of a good fight was always a source of joy to Mendel. But his former colleagues knew him too well. Before he could land his punch, he had Amadea hanging off one shoulder, Jillian swinging from his arm, and Conrad, another of the team, gripping his fist. The last he saw of Dave was the man's back disappearing through a doorway.

"Asses and elbows," he said disgustedly.

"One of these days you're going to land in jail," said Conrad.

"Won't be the first time," he smirked. "And it's bound to be better than the one I ended up in in Ecuador. Did I ever tell you about that?"

"Yes," the three announced as one. Jasper looked hurt, then grinned, and launched into the story, anyway. A chorus of groans punctuated the oft-repeated tale as they shed their suits and went to the mess hall.

An hour later, Conrad and Jillian had departed. Jillian to see if her boss was going to kill her and bury her out beyond the huts, and Conrad to check the results of his spectographic analysis of the object on the summit of the pyramid. Amadea, canted back in her chair with her booted feet propped on the table, regarded Jasper over her mug of chocolate.

"Okay, so what's up?"

"You haven't been by recently."

"Been busy."

"If you'd been busy, you'd be on the top of that pyramid by now."

"Dave's a sissy. He's scared aliens are going to eat him."

Mendel crowed. "I knew it, I knew it."

But his momentary flash of pleasure faded, and he frowned off into space while his fingers drummed out the first movement of Rachmaninoff's Piano Concerto #3 on the edge of the table. It was one of his more irritating habits, and Amadea laid her slender hand over his big-knuckled one and squeezed.

He stared at her from beneath knotted brows. "We've got trouble."

"What? Darnell have a vision and discover that God's not a Mormon?"

"That was nasty."

Her green eyes flicked away, and she bit at her lower lip. "Sorry, that was a bitchy thing to say. Please don't repeat it to Darnell." She looked back, her beautiful doll face contrite.

"My only excuse is Dave, and that's not a very good one for laying into your friends."

His momentary sense of shock faded, and he patted her on the shoulder. "Hey, that asshole would try the patience of a saint. It's okay."

She clasped her knee with both hands and gave him her full attention. "So what is up?"

"We're getting squeezed, and I'm not sure why or by whom. Well, I guess I do know by whom. It's that fanny with ears, Lucius Renfrew, and his POW gang. They're suing the EPA to stop the terraforming project."

"What?"

Jasper smiled grimly at her goggling response. "They say it's not for the benefit all mankind. Although how keeping Mars a frozen ice ball for the private use of a handful of scientists and tourists is going to better benefit mankind is beyond me. Anyway, they're yapping in the courts, and it will have to be heard when that judge arrives. But the bigger problem," he went on before she could speak, "are the agencies. We're being nibbled to death by ducks.

"You know that SPACECOM has full authority over what goes into space. It grew out of that damn mission-review policy that was passed back in the early ninties, and it allows agencies within the federal government to control or suppress private launch activities. It's got all these wonderfully vague phrases like 'international obligations,' 'national security,' and 'foreign policy implications,' et cetera, and they've used it to embargo our mining equipment until the POW suit is resolved."

"But what does POW's suit against the EPA have to do with the Jared Colony's legitimate right to mine its own stake?"

He raised his shoulders. "Your guess is as good as mine. And that brings me to the final problem. SPACECOM has set a quota on what can leave Mars, and guess what's the *only* item that's been limited?" She shook her head. "Go on, guess."

"Not the—"

"Yep, the diamonds." He threw his arms over his head. "So even if we could find a ship to carry the equipment, we can't get payment to our suppliers. Sweet, huh?"

"But how can they get away with this?"

"Damned if I know. Oh, did I say that was the final problem? I lied." His hands dropped heavily into his lap. "Darnell's off at the mine right now trying to convince OSHA that the conditions aren't unduly hazardous, but I'll bet you dimes to doughnuts he doesn't succeed and they shut us down there too." His arms were windmilling about his head again. "*And* there's Meadow's team at Berkeley. Renfrew, that fascist, convinced whatever nervous old lady is overseeing genetic engineering projects right now that our super-algae is a dangerous Martian substance, and God knows what could happen to dear old Mother Earth if any of the stuff got loose. Hell, as the stuff exists right now, it would wither and die in the high-oxygen content of Earth."

"I thought you said it could adjust to higher concentrations of oxygen?"

"Yes, but over time. It will mutate slowly, at the same rate the carbon dioxide in the Martian atmosphere is being slowly reduced and replaced with oxygen."

She laid an arm across his shoulders. "Jasper, I know it's a pain, but you'll just have to wait and have the mess resolved in court."

"If it were only waiting for Huntington, I wouldn't mind so much. I talked with your mother a few days ago, and she said she was pretty confident that Huntington would see things our way."

"Oh, really?"

"Yeah. But even if he is on our side, they could tie us up in court for years what with appeals and such. So we're damn well not going to wait. Your mom, who is a veritable font of wisdom—"

"Oh, undoubtedly."

"Suggested that we get in touch with Joe Reichart out in the Belt."

"What can he do?"

"I have no idea, but Lydia seemed to think he could help, and we're willing to grasp at any straw right now."

"I'd be a little careful about that if I were you."

"Why?"

She drew lines through the circle of moisture left on the tabletop by her mug. "Joe's a good man, but he tends to use people in his own games, and sometimes those people have found their interests being shoved aside in favor of Joe's grand schemes."

Mendel rubbed at his chin. "Hmm, well I'll mention this to Darnell. And thanks for the word of caution. Maybe we'll go a little slow on this thing."

"That would probably be best. God knows I want to see you all get your dream of paradise, but I'd really hate to see you get sucked into a bigger fight than you bargained for."

He smacked a kiss onto her cheek. "You're a sweetie. Can I tell Darnell and Jeanne that you'll be by soon? They've missed you."

"And I them. Yes, tell them I'll come soon, just as soon as I tie up a few more loose ends."

Chapter Four

"Joe, call for you."

Reichart looked up from his lap screen where the month's figures for the Reichart station were crawling across the palm-size screen. Stinson White swung through the door of the observation dome and gazed out across the dark, cratered surface of Ceres. The sun was a brilliant globe of light against the black-velvet backdrop of space. Away from its golden corona stars began to appear, but the constellations were confused because of the presence of other starlike objects, some of which crawled perceptibly across the background.

"You shouldn't be reading out here, it's too dark." He leaned in over Joe's shoulder, the twisted white scars and black eye patch making him look like some ancient demon in the shadowed light of the dome. With a touch he saved the data, and snapped off the tiny computer.

Joe shook his curly, grizzled head. "The numbers glow, and stop acting like my father. I'm older than you are."

"Sometimes I feel a thousand." Stinson grinned, twisting the ravaged left side of his face into an even more hideous shape. Ironically a smile utterly transformed the other side, making him look like an ebony god. He dropped a hand onto

Joe's shoulder. "Sorry, I don't know why I'm so gloomy lately."

"Musenda again?" Joe asked as he rose, bounced, and caught at the back of the chair.

The surface dome was at Ceres' normal gravity, which meant almost nonexistent, but personally Joe preferred that to the experimental artificial gravity inside the hollowed asteroid. Joe had no idea how the gravity generator worked. He just knew that it had grown out of the now almost perfected unified field theory. Unfortunately the key word was "almost." It had a disconcerting habit of cutting out at the most inopportune moments and leaving people floating.

"I think children should be locked in a closet from the time they're fifteen until their eighteen," Stinson said as they moved to the door. "It would be so much easier that way."

"It will pass, believe me," he said, then added as his thoughts went to the woman who had borne one of his children, "Who's calling? Lydia?"

"Nope, some guy on Mars."

"Mars?" He frowned. "I wonder if it could be Cabot?"

"Come and find out."

Darnell huddled in a chair in front of the communications board with his two counselors, Levi Coltrin and Rich Young, gathered close about him. Mendel paced up and down, chomping hard on a piece of rock candy.

"Jasper, do stop *chonk*ing. It is driving me quite crazy," said Jeanne Hudson in an aggrieved undertone.

He removed the offending object from his mouth and tossed it into a waste can. It landed with a loud bang, and several of the elders gave him varying glances of disapprobation. "You ought to let me talk to him."

"This has nothing to do with the terraforming project," replied Darnell curtly.

"It sure as hell does."

"Jasper, stop being childish. Darnell can talk to Mr. Reichart just as well you can." He was pouting, but Jeanne chose to give him the benefit of the doubt and call it a frown.

"Uh . . . hello, hello, Mr. Reichart?"

"Yes, how do you do?"

"Fine, sir." Darnell regarded the weathered, smiling face on the screen before him and decided this was what was meant by the word *charisma*. Occasionally the image would waver as lines of static broke up the feed, but the voice always came through clearly. "I'm Darnell Hudson, leader of the Jared Colony here on Mars."

"Ah, yes, I've heard of it."

"We've got a problem, and I think . . . well, you seem to be rather experienced in this area."

"Making money or pulling the nose of the feds?"

There was a nervous titter from Levi Coltrin. "The latter, sir."

"Mr. Hudson, please stop calling me sir."

"Oh, okay."

"So, let's hear the problem."

Drawing in a deep breath, Hudson launched into an explanation. It all seemed rather convoluted to him, but Reichart kept nodding, obviously following every twist; POW's injunction to prevent the terraforming project, SPACECOM's embargoes, the closure of the lab in Berkeley, and OSHA's closure of the mine. Darnell actually felt a bit aggrieved at the ease with which Reichart grasped the ramifications. It had taken him weeks to begin putting it all together, and he had been involved.

"So now OSHA's got us shut down because of unduly dangerous conditions in the mine, which—"

"Which you can't correct without heavy equipment, which you can't have shipped until the POW suit is settled, and which can't pay for even if you could get them lifted because you can't ship the diamonds."

"That about sums it up. We knew you had mining interests in the asteriods, and you have a reputation—" He broke off, uncomfortable with what he had been about to say.

"For being a troublemaker, a gadfly, a hair up the ass of the government. Yes, I know, and it's well earned." He paused and pulled thoughtfully at his lower lip. "We'll find someone to sell you the equipment you need, Mr. Hudson, but a sackful of diamonds isn't going to be much use to the miners out here. They need a somewhat more negotiable currency."

"And for that we need to get the stones to Earth and get them sold, which we can't do." Darnell's voice was heavy with hopelessness. "Nobody here will carry those diamonds. The American missions are tied to universities or to SPACECOM and are vulnerable because they're also tied to Congress' purse strings, and the other missions—Soviet and Japanese, mostly—don't like our terraforming plans and wouldn't be sorry to see the whole project go down the tubes."

"So the ship that carries the equipment will simply have to go on to Earth carrying the diamonds."

"But we'll have the same problem. The SPACECOM quota still stands."

Reichart smoothed his sideburns and tugged at the lobes of his ears, then the sunny smile was back. "We've got a little time to puzzle on that one. In the meantime you send us a list of what you need. We'll find the equipment, get a contract signed, and start it on its way to you. Meanwhile I'll try to come up with some appropriately sneaky and underhanded way to deal with the quota. You're looking uncomfortable. Why?"

"I don't like the idea of us doing anything illegal."

Joe spread his hands. "Who said anything about illegal?"

"All right—disloyal, then."

"Mr. Hudson, I admire your desire to return good for evil, but I submit that you're being royally screwed by your own government. Why, I'm not sure. I don't know what possible interest it is to those lamebrains in Washington if you sell diamonds or not, but apparently it is. In the meantime you have a God-given right to continue to pursue liberty and happiness, and your right to make a living definitely falls within those categories. Outwitting the agencies on this one issue is not going to undermine your country. Besides, you're a System man now."

"Does that mean I abandon the planet of my birth?"

"I don't know. Does it? But I do think the time is coming when each of us is going to have to answer that question." Joe clapped his hands together and rubbed them briskly. "But those discussions are for another day and another hour. Get that list out to us and we'll get rolling."

He broke the connection, and Darnell fell back in his chair, not knowing whether to feel elated or uneasy. He finally decided that he felt both and that it was all right. He suddenly snapped his fingers and ran a hand through his gray hair.

"Damn, I forgot to ask him about this Huntington man. He'll be the one hearing the POW suit."

"He's a government goon," Jasper exploded. "He was right

there cuddling up to Long, and it's Long's administration that's doing this to us."

Young cleared his throat. "Like Darnell, I'm not very comfortable with this kind of talk. I consider myself a Mormon first, an American second, and an Earthman third."

"And how about Martian?"

"What?"

"A Martian, a Martian—you know, the place you live." The scientist's chin jutted forward challengingly, and Jeanne laid a soothing and warning hand on his arm.

"Prophet, are we perhaps into something that we can't control?" asked Coltrin, ever the peacemaker.

Hudson shook his head helplessly.

"More to the point," broke in Jasper, "do we have any choice?"

The three Mormon men looked distressed and thoughtful while Jasper glared pugnaciously about the room. It was Jeanne who answered for them all.

"We'll do as we must and leave it to God to sort it out."

"Hello, beautiful. Looking for this apartment?" William Devert's teeth were very white against his black skin as he grinned down the length of the hall.

Lis Varllis advanced toward him with that swaying, hip-leading walk that had always made him think of a tigress. They embraced briefly, more for old-times' sake than any other reason, but the rather melancholy thought that they were no longer lovers couldn't dampen his enjoyment of the taste and feel of her lips beneath his.

Lis slipped free and stepped past him into the apartment. "I'm breaking one of my unwritten rules by being here, Bill, so this had better be good."

"The lure of my lasagna has been known to make strong men weep. So why not a powerful woman compromise her ethics?" He slipped the silver-fox coat from her shoulders and admired the winter-white wool pantsuit and high blue leather boots. She always dressed like a human iceberg—back at Standford all those long years ago he had even called her the Snow Queen—but he had to admit it was effective. Every person in any room was instantly aware of Lis from the moment she entered.

"Sweetheart," she said as she flung herself down on the

couch, crossing her legs neatly at the ankle and lounging back against the pillows. "Not to denigrate the fact that you'd make some woman a wonderful wife, I didn't come for food or sex."

"But having come, you will eat?" A subtle emphasis on the final word turned the sentence into a vibrating double entendre.

Lis dropped her lashes to cover her lilac eyes and smiled her Mona Lisa smile. "I think I could be convinced."

"Have some wine," Devert said, indicating the bottle and glass on the coffee table, "while I check the mushrooms."

He disappeared from the front room, and a moment later the redolent smell of stuffed mushrooms filled the room. Lis sniffed, sighed, poured a glass of wine, and laid back against the pillows. The bite of the dry red wine was like a restorative, and she felt the muscles in the back of her neck beginning to relax. She sensed more than heard his return. She knew he was leaning on the back of the sofa gazing down at her, and she allowed her lashes to tremble on her high cheekbones and her lips to soften into a beckoning cupid's bow.

"You said on the phone this was a Gemetics problem of which I was aware—"

"And since you didn't want to discuss it on the phone, I suggested dinner."

"And I accepted because from your remark I gleaned that you were referring to our little Martian problem."

He rolled gracefully over the back of the couch and stretched out on top of her. The ripple of muscles beneath his shirt and the ease of execution reminded her poignantly of the glamorous gymnast who had been the joy and despair of every woman at the university. She alone had broken through his reserve, and they had become lovers. She had been there when he had won a silver medal at the Paris Olympics. . . . She gave herself a mental shake. Memory was a dangerous thing.

"Hello? Earth to Lis. Are you with me again?"

"Yes."

"I hope you weren't thinking about work. The blow to my male ego really would be too much."

"Tell me your news and then maybe I'll tell you. If I told you now, you might get distracted." Her fingers palyed softly through his wiry hair.

"Yesterday we got word from our employee on Mars that the Jared colonists have contacted Joe Reichart." Lis came upright. If Devert hadn't moved fast, he would have been bounced unceremoniously onto the floor. He poured out a glass for himself and drank before continuing. "It will come as no surprise—knowing, as you do, his reputation—that he's agreed to help. The Jared people will be purchasing equipment from miners in the Belt, and *that* delivery no power on Earth can prevent."

"Payment?"

"Ever the quick one, my lady. Yes, that is the one sticking point for the colonists. The miners quite rightly want payment for the extraction and processing machinery. The only thing the colonists have to offer are the diamonds already stockpiled. At this point the Belters don't have too much use for raw stones. They want cash, so—"

"The diamonds have to get to Earth."

"Yes, and naturally we'd prefer not to see this happen. If the colonists find a pipeline, they're going to hurt us—badly."

"They won't find a pipeline. SPACECOM has full control over what enters or leaves a planet or station, and the diamonds are embargoed."

"Yes, I agree it looks like they're locked up tight, but this is Joseph Reichart we're talking about. If anyone can find a loophole, it's him, so I'd prefer that we find it first and plug it. I've got Legal taking a look at the situation, and if they should find any of these loopholes—"

"Tell me. I'll see them plugged."

"Ah, it's good to have friends in high places." He set his glass on the table and moved in on her.

"Is there anything that would spoil from waiting an hour or so?"

"The mushrooms."

"Butter and crumbs in the bed. It sounds delightful." She held out her hands, and he pulled her to her feet.

"Meet you in there," he called at her retreating back.

Jenny pressed her nose against the port and watched the moon receding majestically behind them. For a moment she had an odd sense of déjà vu; eight months before, she had pressed her nose to a port and had her first glimpse of the spinning wheel of the EnerSun station. It had been unfamiliar territory, terrifying and exciting all at the same time, but now it had all the welcome contours of home and, like any good home, held friends and loved ones. She had even waved at the distant point of light as the deep stage shuttled had swept past the station, bound for its rendezvous with the jump-point accelerator. Immediately after she had felt embarrassed, but fortunately no one had noticed. Cab was sunk in his own thoughts, and the Mendelssohn Trio he was listening to on his tiny clip player. The other passengers—mostly military personnel—were visiting with friends, nursing hangovers, or listening yet again to taped farewells from friends and lovers back on Earth.

"I certainly hope this thing is safe," muttered Cab.

Correctly interpreting that the remark did not refer to Mendelssohn but did refer to the deep-space ship they were taking to Mars, she said brightly, "Safe as houses." The oldfashioned phrase had come to mind perhaps because of her thoughts about EnerSun.

"What?" Exasperated, she pulled the clip from his lobe, pulling the almost invisible leads from his ears at the same time. "Ow."

"Then don't ask me questions when all you can hear is music."

"I hope you told me the ship was safe."

"I did."

He twined his fingers through hers. "But do you have any knowledge to support the claim?"

"No," she replied with a chuckle. Cab shuddered and closed his eyes. Smiling gently, she leaned in and pressed a kiss onto the corner of his mouth.

"S-speaking from experience, I can tell you that after s-seven years aboard one of the antimatter s-ships, we've never had a major propulsion problem" came a new voice from behind them.

Both Cab and Jenny slewed around and looked into a deeply tanned, lean face. The man's eyes were like two slivers of blue Arctic ice in his dark face, and his hair was a unique platinum blond. The darkness of his skin and the hint of a wiry curl to his hair bespoke an African forebear, and Jenny —with a twinge of guilt toward Cab and a mental apology—thought he was quite the handsomest man she had ever seen.

"What constitutes major?" Cab's eyes flicked to the rank

designation on the shoulders of the man's pressure suit. "General . . . ?"

"S-Saber, Ingvar S-Saber." He thrust a hand over the back of Cab's chair and they shook.

"Justice Cabot Huntington. My clerk, Jennifer McBride."

"That name can't be real," said Jenny as his slim hand enfolded hers in a warm clasp.

"Honest to God, my mother's of S-Swedish descent, and s-she thought it would be just great to honor the old grandfather. It could have been worse. Dad was a real wag, and he wanted to call me Hilt."

"Now *that* you are making up." Jenny suddenly became aware that her hand was still resting lightly in the general's, and she withdrew it with what she hoped was not undue haste.

The Air Force officer slid his eyes back to Cab. "Major means life-threatening."

"How about life-*ending?* Ever had one of those?"

"Yes, but in the thirty years s-since the first antimatter drive s-ship became operational we've only had one catastrophic malfunction."

"And what does that mean in people language?"

"The s-ship blew up."

"Oh, great!"

Saber winked at Jenny and sent her a warm smile. She responded, then shot a quick glance to Cab. The judge seemed oblivious, but Jenny knew from long experience that his sleepy, lazy-eyed look could be deceptive. Sometime tonight, after he had folded her into his arms, she might be hearing about General Saber and her response to him.

"It only happened once."

"Once is enough if you're unlucky enough to be on board. And that argument doesn't comfort me. There aren't very many antimatter ships in operation."

"The deep s-space fleet now consists entirely of them, and Congress has just authorized the building of five more."

Jenny pulled a face. "And just what are these supposed to be protecting us from?"

Saber spread his hands. "Who can tell?"

"I think it's a damn waste of taxpayers' money. There are only three commercial antimatter liners in operation, but SPACECOM gets seven, with five more on the way." Cab's expression caught her attention. "Oh, am I being rude again?"

"Yes, very."

"No, please, people s-should s-say what they think."

"Well, she did and I did. Now it's your turn."

"Oh, I think it's great we're building more, but that's because I get to command one of these beauties."

"Isn't that somewhat modest, General? Don't you in fact command the entire deep-space squadron?" Jenny looked surprised.

Saber grinned shyly. "Yes. But back to the original point. You're going to love these s-ships, too, especially when you consider the alternative: s-six months to Mars with nothing to do but play cribbage."

"Is that mandatory? Couldn't we play bridge or chess or tiddlywinks?" teased Jenny.

"Absolutely mandatory. It has to be cribbage. If you'll take a look, we're getting within range to s-see the antiproton factory."

Jenny scrunched against the window with Cab pressed against her shoulder. The antiproton factory was in fact a giant acceleration chamber one thousand miles in circumference, powered by solar satellites. The long oval caught the light of the sun and shone like polished bronze, creating the feel of a Jules Verne novel. A small station spun lazily in the center of the oval with two deep-space ships nuzzled up to it like nursing baby whales.

"It's quite incredible," said Cab.

"Yes, but not incredible enough. With enough distance we can push right up to the s-speed of light but without crossing it." Saber shook his head. "I'm greedy, I want faster-than-light s-speed drive."

"There was talk, when this technology really got rolling, of building big colony ships and heading for some of the closer star systems."

"Right now it's s-still too expensive for private industry to finance, and none of the governments will touch it." He frowned and tugged at his upper lip. "I'm not sure why."

"Loss of taxpayers?" suggested Jenny.

"But they'd have a whole new planet to tax."

"And what's to stop the crew from never phoning home?" Cab's gray eyes were alight with amusement. "If I had just discovered a new Eden, I'd pretend the ship had been lost with all hands and let Earth wonder."

"Cab! I'm shocked. There is a revolutionary streak in you." He smiled a secret little smile. "When the first ships fly, will you be on board, General?" asked Jenny.

"No. I have this image of plowing along at just below the s-speed of light while the years pass back home, and then the big s-scientific jump takes place, and suddenly they have light s-speed and I'm s-still out there s-slogging. There was an old s-science-fiction s-story about just that—three guys on their way to Alpha Centauri being met by their descendants, who had arrived there years ago."

"But we're not talking hundreds of years to get to another system."

"True, but what if none of the planets are habitable? Or if the sun has no planets. It could take a while to find an appropriate s-system."

"But what if that great s-scientific leap forward never comes?" Cab frowned, irritated and embarrassed at his inadvertent imitation of Saber's stammer. The officer merely smiled, and Jenny, who found the delicate little hesitation rather endearing, coughed behind one hand.

"It will, it will. I've learned to distrust pompous s-statements of 'it can't be done' from eminent s-scientists. They're almost always proved to be wrong."

Jenny clasped Cab's arm beneath hers and gave it a hard squeeze. "Oooh, want to be hearty pioneers on Alpha Centauri?"

"No. My children are going to be raised on Earth."

She bridled at his flat tone and pulled back. "Who said anything about children? And first you have to find someone to bear them for you."

Saber glanced from Jenny, pink-cheeked and rigid, to Cabot, lips pressed tight and pale face made even paler by his anger and embarrassment, and gave a nervous cough.

"Ah, the docking klaxon."

He fell back in his seat and watched as the pilot maneuvered them in for docking. Cab returned to his music, and Jenny sat staring bleakly down at her hands. She tried to analyze how she felt about Cabot's arrogant pronouncement about *his* children, her feelings about children, and more to the point, children by this man, but all that kept running through her head was: Dumb fight. Dumb fight.

• • •

They were still feuding when seven days later their shuttle settled onto the scorched sands of Eagle Port. During the voyage from the jump point to Mars, Cab had become icily correct and had refused to lay a hand on her. She wasn't sure what he was punishing her for; her interest in Saber, the tiff over children, or perhaps he was just nervous about the coming session and was taking it out on her. She decided that he was being unfair and unreasonable, and nursing her anger, she withdrew to the far side of the lock.

She stared at the door of the shuttle, listening to the whistle of the air being cycled out of the lock, and wondered about the people who waited beyond that door. Would they like her and Cab? Would they like them? Suddenly she decided that making a good first impression was more important than her pride, and she walked to Cab's side. She had resisted apologizing to the judge, hoping that he would do so first, but it hadn't happened, and now other matters needed to take priority.

She stepped directly in front of him. "Cab?"

"What?"

She smiled and raising a hand to her helmet, kissed at her gloved fingers, then pressed them against the front of his faceplate. "I'm sorry. I'm not really sure what we're bickering about, but let's start fresh."

"I'm sorry too," he said gruffly. "It was a stupid argument—"

"It wasn't even an argument. That, at least, would have generated some passion.

"I guess I'm tense about this session."

"I am too." She leaned against him, his arms, going instinctively about her suited body. "Let's release some tension real soon, okay?"

"Okay."

Sighs whispered through their helmet radios in unison, and they stepped reluctantly apart as the door swung open. Jenny placed a foot on the top stair and suddenly realized that in a few moments she would step down onto the surface of another world. And instead of savoring this moment, anticipating it, she had been wrapped up in an emotional turmoil with her lover over a really very minor matter. How typically human, she thought disgustedly, and followed Cab down the stairs.

Just before she reached the surface, she paused and

scanned the horizon. Cab was already down on the seared soil of the shuttle landing field and surrounded by a crowd of welcoming, suited figures. For a moment she regarded him enviously. *He may not be at ease, but he'll bloody well be in control of any situation. Of course, I don't understand how he can stand talking to people when there's* this *to look at. Is it lack of imagination or are people simply intrinsically more interesting to him*?

For herself she found her first sight of Mars too fascinating to be drawn into immediate conversation with her hosts. Shading the glare off her faceplate with a hand, she scanned the panorama. To her left three other shuttles lay berthed and waiting for passengers or cargo to ferry back up to the inter-planetry transport. The great freight doors of her shuttle were open, and men were handing out large crates with an ease that would have been impossible on Earth. As she watched, one of the welcoming committee broke away and hurried over to stroke and pat the long boxes like a nervous hen asessing her brood.

Straight ahead was the town of Eagle Port. All that was visible were the conical cooling towers of the buried nuclear power plants, a row of sturdily constructed greenhouses and warehouses, and cylindrical bumps beneath the red soil indicating the actual living quarters, bars, brothels, and God knew what else that made up the city. It wasn't really a city, though, not the way Jared-City was. It was an embarkation point and the oldest scientific colony on Mars, but it was not and never had been intended as a permanent settlement. People rotated in and out of Eagle Port on three- or five-year cycles.

Overhead a few wispy clouds painted a stark white picture against the pink-tinged sky, and off to her right was Mars without the evidence of human habitation. Dust-eroded rocks protruded from the wind-rippled red sand. In the far distance a tiny dust devil went dancing along the foot of a towering, flat-topped butte.

She bounced experimentally on the steps, testing a gravity that was one third of Earth's. It felt wonderful, and when Cab beckoned to her, she felt no hesitation in launching herself from the stairs to the ground. It almost turned into a disaster, for her sense of equilibrium was off, but she managed to catch herself with only a hopping little step and remained upright.

Near the crates, a suited figure leapt forward, and a powerful hand closed about her arm. She looked up, irritated, into a craggy face. The glint off the faceplate created odd lines and crevasses in his face, but the effect was still one of warmth and humor. This first impression, a favorable one, was ruined when he said with paternal condescension, "Whoa, little lady, you're lucky you didn't land on your snout. Better not try anything fancy until you've become accustomed to the gravity." Jenny stiffened.

"But I didn't fall, did I?" she replied as she lifted his hand from her arm.

"Jenny is a former dancer, and she still works out every morning. I'm quite certain she can handle the environment," added Cab, almost in tandem with her remark. The defense and praise felt good, and she flashed him a quick wink and a small smile. "Jenny, this is President Darnell Hudson," continued Cabot while the older man harrumphed and tried to find something to do with his hands.

Watching him, Cab realized how limiting pressure suits could be. The pull on the earlobe, the hand through the hair, the scratch at the nose, all were denied to the System colonist whenever they ventured outside their sealed environments. He wondered what the long-term effects would be. Three or four generations down the line, would they be left with a breed of people who no longer talked with their hands? People who would express a variety of disparate emotions with only the flick of an eyelash or the jerk of a shoulder? It was an odd thing to consider.

"Pleased to meet you. I'm Jennifer McBride, Justice Huntington's clerk. And please forgive me, I didn't mean to bite, but I tend to be rather prickly when people try to protect me."

Hudson was staring bemusedly down into Jenny's heart-shaped face, and Cab enjoyed the effect she was having on the President. Like most liberal males, he disapproved of the Mormon attitude toward women, and he liked to see Jenny rocking the Prophet and his counselors off-base.

"Ah, yes. Mr. Young, Mr. Coltrin, Dr. Jasper Mendel, and my wife, Jeanne." There were murmured greetings all around, then Darnell gathered them like a farmer shooing chickens. "Well, we'd best get on our way. There was a dust storm predicted, which is rather unseasonable, but after you've been on Mars awhile you learn she's as unpredictable as a woman."

"Interesting, since the planet is named for the god of war.

So maybe it's the male military mind that the planet is emulating rather than women," suggested Jenny sweetly.

Jeanne laughed softly and linked her arm through her husband's. "Better look out, she's going to be as spirited as Amadea."

"About the dust storm . . ." prodded Cab.

"Oh, yes. We brought the jump ship rather than ultra-lights because of the prediction, but just the same, I'd rather not be flying in a big blow. The sooner we're back to Jared, the better I'll like it." He glanced at Cab. "You probably feel the same. I expect you'll want to see your courthouse, and—" he gave an uncomfortable little cough—"and there's already a bit of work for you to handle."

"Local matters?"

Glances were exchanged among the Martian residents. "Some. But it's more this thing from Earth that's got us concerned."

The five colonists stared intently at Cab, and there was a prickling at the back of his neck.

"From Earth," he repeated.

"Yes, from Earth," said Darnell, laying a subtle emphasis on the final word.

The exchange was becoming both comic and exasperating, and Cab wanted to snap, "I have no idea what *you're* talking about, so why don't you just tell me why this is so significant?" He restrained the impulse and settled for a mild murmur of interest. In fact, he was very interested.

Who from Earth would have filed a suit on Mars, and why? And why wait until he was in transit? Was it done to keep him in the dark? He cautioned himself not to read too much into the matter, but it was hard; the events on EnerSun had made him touchy. As they walked across to the ship, the russet sand gritty beneath their boots, he continued to worry and gnaw at the question. Probably just some supplier suing the Mormons —a simple breach-of-contract suit—he would welcome that. What he didn't need was an earth-shattering, or at least government-shattering, case, like the ones he had heard on the first leg of his circuit.

Behind him, Jenny was chatting with Jeanne Hudson, already getting a feeling for Jared and the people who inhabited the city. He again envied her her ease in dealing with people. He had to force himself to talk with new people, but it was always a strain and he was always nervous they would . . . His mind shied away from the source of his fear.

I probably would have done better as a legal scholar or law professor, he thought.

"You'll be staying with the Keys. They're a lovely young couple who've just had their first child. Sasha is the sweetest baby. I keep telling Darnell I'm going to steal her and bring her home, but he seems to resist that idea."

"How nice. I can't wait to see Cab dealing with a small person. He's never been of the doting school, since he doesn't have any little nieces and nephews to coo over."

Cab looked over his shoulder to glare at Jenny and noticed that Jeanne missed a step.

"But Justice Huntington will be staying with us," she said, and then her hand flew to her faceplate as if she realized she had blurted it out.

The party faltered to a stop, the Mormons all looking embarrassed and distressed, the silent scientist, Mendel, looking amused, and Cab and Jenny trying to remain natural.

"Er . . . well, ah . . . " stammered the Prophet.

"Ah, come on, Darnell." Jasper slapped him firmly on the shoulder in good-humored raillery. "Not everybody shares your outmoded views of morality."

"It's not a question of morality," Cab said stiffly. "It's a matter of convenience. Ms. McBride and I have to work very closely, and it facilitates matters if we're together."

"Right," drawled Mendel. "Facilitates other things too."

Cab felt the blood burning in his cheeks, and he cursed Mendel for being a churlish buffoon. His explanation had provided everyone with a face-saving way out of the situation, and now the scientist had ruined it. His gray eyes met Jenny's green ones, and there was a plea in them. He knew he should acquiesce to the Hudsons' arrangements for the sake of peace, but the thought of four to six months without Jenny's familiar presence next to him in bed was insupportable. Granted, they could probably slip away to Eagle Base for a fast fuck, but when he winced over his own designation of the situation, he realized that wouldn't work, either.

He looked desperately to Jenny, but it was obvious that she was going to give him no help on this one. He coughed and carefully gathered his words.

"Ms. McBride and I are more than associates. We are accustomed to living together and would find it . . . difficult to be separated." Mendel snorted and Cab glared, deciding that he didn't like the man. "And while we respect your beliefs, we do not feel that we should be constrained by them."

Coltrin muttered something about setting a bad example for the young people, but Jeanne stepped forward with that brisk way she had and took Cab by the arm.

"Well put, Judge. You must be quite eloquent on the bench. We'll see to it that you and Ms. McBride have a place of your own."

"But . . ." Hudson began, but Jeanne frowned at him.

"Actually, before we all hustle off the ship, I might mention the lack of stimulants at the colony." Mendel dug an elbow into Cab's side. "No caffeine and no alcohol, so if you want something, you'd better speak now so we can buy it while we're still among the iniquitous."

"Thank you, that's probably a good suggestion." Cab turned to Darnell. "May we take fifteen minutes for Jenny and I to shop?"

"Sure. Jasper's perceptions of us notwithstanding, we do not try to force people to accept our customs. It would be better for them if they did—" But Mendel, sensing a sermon, had already shifted direction and was leading them toward the Eagle Base colony proper.

The party fell in behind him with Cab and Jenny dropping back so they could talk.

Cab chinned his radio to a private channel. "Well, we're getting off to a great start—offending our hosts within the first fifteen minutes. And there's something else going on too."

"Oh, caught that, did you?" replied Jenny. Her gloved hand slipped into his. "Cab, why have I got such a bad feeling about this?"

"Probably because trouble seems to follow me around like a black crow," he said gloomily.

Chapter Five

"This is so stupid," announced Jenny. "Suing the EPA because they authorized the terraforming project. It's stupid."

Cab continued brushing his hair, noting as he did that the silver over his temples was getting larger. He then focused on Jenny's image in the mirror and made a noncommittal noise.

She was an alluring sight as she sat in the bed with her long red hair spilling over her bare breasts and her anger giving a glow to her white skin. Off to his right a teakettle was singing on the tiny stove, and since the bed had not been folded back into the wall, the room felt like a storage closet at a furniture dealership. Still, he wasn't going to complain over the one-room cubbyhole they were occupying. The alternative might have been more comfortable, but it would have meant he couldn't stand and admire Jenny while she bristled.

Also, the courthouse offered real compensations for the inconveniences of their private quarters. Though small, it was a real federal building with offices for the tiny Jared-City police force, three cells (rarely used in this peaceful community), administrative offices for the various departments, and a tiny jewellike courtroom. It was a strange feeling to come down the tree-lined boulevard toward the two-story red-stone building, see the American flag hanging limply from the flagpole out front, and then raise your eyes to the dome glinting high overhead and the red sky glowing beyond. There had been no System flag to hang next to the American one, which had been rather disappointing to Cab. He thought it showed how far he had come and how much he had modified his views since that first disastrous session on the EnerSun station. He had walked into his courtroom, seen the two flags hanging behind his bench, and ordered the System flag removed. It had been an inauspicious start. He wondered if he ought to suggest to Darnell that the colony obtain one of the midnight-blue flags with its mock-up of the Solar System set against a glittering starfield.

"Are you listening to me? Are you paying any attention to me? Or do you think this is absolutely wonderful and don't want to make me mad by saying anything?"

"Yes, yes, and no."

"Then can we discuss this?"

"Yes."

"Cab," she shrieked, slamming the papers down onto her sheet-covered knees. As always, he had instantly printed out the complaints that awaited him so he could have that sense of permanence only paper could give.

"What?" He sprawled across the bed and massaged her foot through the sheet.

"Stop staring up at me like a sex-starved bull."

"Jenny!"

She chuckled. "Well, that's what you look like."

Disgruntled, he sat up and arranged his coat. "Now, seriously, is this a silly complaint or is it a silly complaint?"

"I would agree that it seems to lack certain substantive content, but I want to hear some evidence before I consider . . . well, whatever it is I consider. Besides, it's up to EPA to move for summary judgment." Raising a cautionary finger, he added, "And these environmental cases are always a little nebulous."

Jenny worried her upper lips between thumb and forefinger. "Cab, do you think this ties in with the other things that have been happening?"

"You mean the embargoes?"

"And the OSHA thing. I mean, really, why should SPACE

COM care if the colonists sell diamonds or buy mining equipment?"

"I don't know, but frankly I can't see any connection between an environmental problem, or a perceived environmental problem, and the colonists' mining activities."

"Oh, I can—mining . . . environmentalists. It's always gone hand in hand."

"Then why not sue the colonists directly over the mining and not ring in the EPA at all? The feds have a lot more money than the colonists, which makes it a tougher fight."

Jenny sighed and ran a hand through her hair, the strands lifting and rippling like a cascading red wave. "I suppose you're right. Do you think our experiences on EnerSun have made me paranoid?"

He stretched out next to her and began playing with several long strands of hair. "Yes, and me, too, but I really don't think Long's that kind of man."

"There are a lot of other people in the government other than Long."

"Yes, I know," he said testily, and slid off the bed. "But we've got to stop seeing conspiracies under every bush. There must be some cogent reason for the embargoes."

"Jasper says not."

Cab frowned. "Jasper says a great deal, most of it hogwash."

"I like him."

"I think he's a buffoon."

"Brilliant lunatic is probably closer to the mark." She waved her hands about her face as if shooing away insects. "But that's neither here not there . . . can we at least reassure Darnell and the others that we're on their side? I attended one of the Mutual Improvement Association—"

"What in the hell is that?"

"It's the youth organization, although apparently adults are involved. According to Jeanne, they provide not only wholesome instruction but wholesome recreation and activities for the members as well. And stop staring at me like I've lost my mind. I went because I thought it might be a good idea to get a feel for the life of this community. It would behoove you to do the same."

"Maybe I could have them research my genealogy," he

suggested thoughtfully but with just a hint of a gleam in his gray eyes.

"Stop being a pig," she ordered, but there was a catch of laughter in her voice.

"I'm sorry, and yes, you're right. I do need to get out and about more, but I've been busy reading over the complaints and trying to get a feel for exactly what we're going to be dealing with over the next few months."

"Well, I hope you will . . . get out, I mean. For one thing I miss you and would like to be doing things with you. But we're off thc subject. The point is that there's a lot of rumbling from that youth group, and I think we should defuse some of the fear and suspicion. They see this action of POW's"—she scrabbled about on the white sheet, gathering the scattered pages—"as being a direct assault on their goals and dreams for terraforming the planet."

"And how do you suggest we do this?"

"Oh, I don't know. Just get across that we're sympathetic to the System's goal of autonomy, and freedom from Earth interference." She stared up into his set face, and her brows drew together. "We are sympathetic, aren't we?"

"Yes, in principle, yes. And I think another whole planet for humans to spread out on is a good idea. . . ."

"But?"

He sat again and took her hands in his. "We're the representatives of justice out here. For better or worse, the local arbitration boards have been dismantled, leaving . . . us. The colonists are willing to accept us now, but we cannot appear to be biased in any direction. If we show favoritism in this case —however much it may please the Jared people right now—it will plant a seed of doubt about our overall impartiality, and they'll wonder when it comes to a dispute between a colonist on Mars and one in the asteroids, or one on the Moon and a station dweller, whether we can be trusted to deal fairly.

"If I say to anyone other than you that I don't think much of the POW case, I'll be leaving myself open for removal because of bias or reversal by a higher court. You think too much with your heart, Jenny," he added softly. "And now you'd better get that teakettle before it boils dry."

"What are you, crippled?"

"No, I have another more pressing need," he said, standing

and moving toward the bathroom with its coffin-size shower and postage-stamp-size washbasin.

"Well, I guess I'll let you."

She rose, slipped on Cab's dressing gown, rolled back the sleeves to her elbows, and filled a teacup with boiling water. She was just adding a tea bag when there was a knock on the door.

"Who is it?"

She had no desire to open the door to one of the Mormon hierarchy. She had a feeling that none of those middle-aged males would be comfortable if they found her dishabille. At least not on the surface. What wickedness might lurk within the hearts of even Mormon men, she couldn't say.

"Amadea Kim Nu."

For an instant she had a sense of total dislocation, then realized that the first name was different. It was not the powerful, autocratic manager of the EnerSun station come to visit. There was a rush of water, and Cab came hurriedly out of the bathroom, sealing his fly. He gave her a questioning look and she shook her head and shrugged.

There were certain facial similarities between the woman who stepped through the door and her mother, Lydia. The same elongated eyes and high cheekbones, but Lydia was tall for a woman of Oriental descent, while her child looked like an animated doll. She was no taller than Jenny, but she made the other woman feel heavy and awkward with her slender, graceful limbs and gliding walk. Her hair was a river of ebony down her back, reaching to a point just below her buttocks, and her eyes were a pure jade green.

Cab stood staring like he'd been poleaxed, and Jenny suppressed a strong desire to kick him. She prided herself on being intelligent and well adjusted and able to accept the fact that men could find women other than their wives and lovers to be attractive, but until this moment she had never felt threatened by his interest. But the look in Cabot's eyes brought an agitated flutter to her gut.

Amadea stepped in toward Cab and extended her hand. "How do you do? Mother insisted that I stop by, make you welcome, and offer my services as tour guide, resident Martian expert, and general factotum."

"Thank you, and how thoughtful of your mother," Cab said, still holding her hand in a light clasp. "I hope this didn't work a hardship on you. Taking you from your work . . . ?" His voice trailed away.

"Oh, Mother's never backward about offering my services, whether it's convenient or not, but this time it was a pleasure," she hastened to add. "I've heard so much about you." She flashed a quick smile to Jenny, adding, "Both of you." But to Jenny's mind it sounded decidedly like an afterthought. "And, yes, I do work on Mars. I'm a geologist, although right now I'm busy uncovering something that may be an alien artifact."

"Really, how fascinating." Cab led her to the table and pulled out a chair. "I'd very much like to hear about it. Would you like some tea?"

Jenny, staring at his back, thought he wouldn't have cared if Kim Nu had said they were digging up *actual* aliens. He probably hadn't even heard what she had said, he was so busy undressing the Eurasian with his eyes.

"Please."

Cab signaled Jenny, and swallowing her resentment, she obligingly poured out another cup. She's probably just one of those women who can bewitch any man within a hundred-foot radius. It's not anything they can control. This is Lydia's daughter. The thought mollified and reassured her, and with a genuine smile she handed around the cups.

"So you're the lady who kept us informed about Joe's whereabouts during the EnerSun crisis."

"Yes, he and Irina made a brief stopover here before catching the next ship for the Belt."

"Do you hear much from him?"

"No. Now that the emergency is over, he once more communicates directly with Mother. As is always the case with great movers and shakers, they move and shake and the rest of us wait on their pleasure—"

"That sounds rather bitter," Jenny broke in, deciding she had been a passive participant for too long.

"If it did, I didn't mean it. My mother and Joe Reichart are great people. It isn't often one is born into a time with truly great people, much less get to rub elbows with them."

"Are your other siblings—four, I believe,"—Cab said, looking to Jenny for guidance; she nodded—"also involved with System politics?"

She laughed, the silvery sound darting about the room.

"Ah, no, of the five lovely Kim Nu girls, Rohanna is married and raising a family on the Moon, Tasya is a lieutenant in the Air Force, serving on a drive ship, Perdita is a teacher, in the asteroids, and Jamila is a researcher for Botts-Hammerfeld on the Reichart station."

"Your mother never mentioned your father, and she's not someone you question about her private life." Jenny clasped her hands under her chin. "Still, I'm curious, so I'll ask you."

"Kim Nu is my mother's maiden name." She smiled at Cab's expression. "Mother was far too independent to ever settle on one man, but she wanted children, so she revived an early colonial tradition of bearing children by several men. In the early days it made sense because there was usually a limited gene pool among the colonists, so they played mix-and-match. We all have different fathers. Mine got croaked in a construction accident when I was three, so I don't remember him, but the other four are around and love to play indulgent uncle. And yes, Joe did sire one of my mother's children. Perdita is his daughter."

"And you're the youngest."

She inclined her head in a graceful, geishalike motion. "I'm the youngest." There was a thoughtful silence while everyone took a swallow of tea, then Amadea said softly, "I thought Mother and Joe would finally marry, but perhaps their causes are just too alluring. Mom isn't about to leave her station, and Joe seems to be permanently fixed in the asteroids now."

"Does that bother you?" Jenny asked.

"Not bother, no. *Depress* is perhaps a better word." She gave herself a little shake and drained her cup. "Well, I've taken up enough of your time. Thank you for the tea and hospitality."

Cab's chair clattered back as he came swiftly to his feet. "May I escort you somewhere? I was about to leave for my office."

Amadea's hand delicately touched her breast, then fluttered gracefully back to her side like a small white bird. It was a beautiful expression of shyness and pleasure. "If I'm not rushing you . . ."

"No, no." His eyes followed Amadea's as they slid to Jenny, standing quietly at the sink. "Jenny still has to shower and dress, and I have things to do at the office. She'll follow along in . . . thirty minutes or so?" he said, turning the statement into a question.

"Yes, thirty minutes or so."

He hurried forward to hold the door, and he and Amadea stepped into the hall. They walked silently along, side by side for several minutes, then she slipped her arm through his, and he felt the blood rushing into his face. Amadea seemed mercifully unaware of the effect she was having on him. Good God, a forty-three-year-old man salivating over her—he was old enough to be her father. The thought was unbearably depressing to him, and his free hand slipped up to brush lightly at his graying temples.

She then raised her eyes to his face and smiled, and he realized he was fooling no one. She knew! But she didn't seem to mind. In fact, there was a unmistakable invitation in those green eyes that left him breathless.

"This really is a thrill for me," she said, her soft, lilting voice making a caress of the words. "When I saw you on the newscasts during the hearings, I thought you were quite the sexiest man I'd ever seen." She laid her fingers softly over his mouth. "Don't say anything. I know you're involved with Ms. McBride, and I'm not a home wrecker. I just think that when you feel something, you should say it, and if it has the added benefit of making the person feel good about themselves, all the better."

He obeyed her dictate and didn't speak. He wasn't certain he could find anything to say that wouldn't sound foolish or as if he were fishing for more compliments. Instead he tightened his grip on her arm, squeezing it against his side. They emerged from the tunnel into the central dome, and he instantly looked up. Dust was peppering against the dome and then sighing off its curved sides.

"Sandstorm?" he asked.

"This? Good heavens, no. You'll know a sandstorm when it hits. It's like an avalanche of yellow dust hundreds of meters high bearing down on you."

"Sounds dangerous."

"It is and it isn't."

He laughed. "How can it be both?"

"The winds aren't as fierce near the ground as they are in the upper atmosphere, but it is impossible to fly a Light in a storm, and a man in a suit would be in tough shape if he had to be out in one for more than a few hours." She added with a sideways look from her exotic eyes, "I'd like to be alive three hundred years from now to see Mars resurrected."

"You're giving me a significant glance. May I ask why?"

"I'm wondering about that POW complaint. It has the colonists in a real dither, and since I'm very close to these people, I'd like to know if they have something to worry about or not."

"You and Jenny. You want me to rent a soapbox, take up a position in the center of the dome, and reassure everyone—"

"I didn't say that. I just wanted you to tell me and *I'll* tell the colonists." She gave him a look like a mischievous elf.

He stopped and took her hands in his. "I'm sorry, but I can't discuss this, or any other case, with you."

"You discuss them with Jennifer?"

"Of course. She's my clerk, and she also has strict orders not to reveal the substance of our discussions. Also, I don't make up my mind about a case until I've heard the evidence."

"But you must have some opinion, some sense about the case from the beginning," she protested.

"I'd be more than human if I didn't, but that doesn't mean I have to abide by my first impressions, and I'd be out of line if I did, and even more out of line if I discussed those initial feelings with anyone. I'm the impartial trier of law. That's my function."

"A man of integrity in addition to being almost fatally attractive." She laughed and patted his cheeks. "You look ten years old when you blush. All right, I won't pester you. I'll just pass on to my friends that you are fair, and godlike, in your impartiality."

"Please . . . don't," he muttered, his eyes flicking about, trying to find anything other than her face to focus upon.

She stepped away, and almost without volition, his hand reached out and caught hers. "Don't work too hard. I hope I see you next time I come to visit."

She moved slowly away, pulling her hand languidly through his. The friction of her skin against his made his breath catch in his throat, heat licked through his groin, and he knew he was in danger—terrible danger—and it didn't seem to matter at all.

• • •

Seth Hudson was holding the floor when Amadea arrived at Jeanne and Darnell's apartment. This was nothing new, for command seemed to come easy to the gangling teenager, and he never missed an opportunity to exercise it. He was standing with one hand locked in the small of his back and the other alternately gesturing or thrusting like a swagger stick at the twenty young people gathered about him. With his straight, fine brown hair, black eyes, and pale skin, he looked nothing like the people he fondly, but somewhat facetiously, called Mammer and Pater, but that was natural, since he had been adopted by the couple following the freak accident that had claimed both his parents.

His father, Barnaby Mayburn, had been a less than perfect Mormon, and his mother too ill and colorless to exert any real control over the boy. Levi Coltrin, after one of Seth's particularly trying and expensive pranks, had been heard to prophesy that the boy would be hung before he was fifteen, but under the firm but loving tutelage of the Hudsons he had mitigated his behavior enough to reach seventeen. He had been an indifferent scholar and craved excitement and adventure the way a plant craves water, so Jeanne had cajoled, and Darnell had finally allowed him to leave school and join the crew working at the diamond mine. Now that the mine had been shut, pending an upgrade in the safety measures, he was home, and Amadea knew that his parents were already worrying over what mischief he could find or concoct.

"I think we should open the talent show with a salute to the ranking figures present. Gustav says that's what they do in Vienna when the president attends a performance."

"Ranking figures?" asked Sarah, a plump fifteen-year-old who was overwhelmed at being in the same room with her god, and eager to attract his attention even if by a stupid question.

"That's my folks, the counselors, and probably bishops too."

Sarah giggled. "Sounds like we'll be saluting everybody."

"What about those of us in the orchestra?" piped up a new voice before Seth could respond to Sarah. "We should get to play a few solos so we'll be heard."

"You'll be playing all night so I expect people will hear you," Seth snapped, and Ben looked mulish.

Amadea stepped in before Seth's notable lack of tact could lead to another blowup. She was a little surprised that Jeanne had not moved to smooth ruffled feathers, but she then noticed the older woman huddled with Darnell, Jasper, and Coltrin in the kitchen.

"It sounds like you're talking about some sort of talent show. And since instrumentalists are talented, too, I think you ought to give them their moment in the sun, so to speak."

"See, she understands."

Seth ignored Ben's parting shot. "Hey! Amadea!" He caught her hand and rubbed his cheek against the back of it. She noticed with gentle amusement that there was still no beard. "Since those fuckers"—his voice dropped on the last word and he shot a quick glance to his parents—"on Earth have shut down the mine, I've got nothing to do, so I'm back to kid stuff." He gestured at the other teenagers.

"Always the soul of tact," Amadea murmured, and pulled him down with her onto the floor. "But what's this all about?"

"The annual talent show. But we're trying to give it a little tone this year. Gustav—"

"Gustav?"

"The Austrian guy who came with the pipes to install them."

"Pipes?"

"You know, pipes. Honk, honk, hoot."

"Oh, the *organ*."

"Yes, stoopid. The organ. Anyway, he was being homesick and talking about the great concerts in Vienna, so I thought, *hey,* let's do it the European way."

She patted his knee. "Sounds like fun. Maybe you and I should do a duet."

"I don't think that would be such a good idea. First of all, you sing like a bullfrog, and second and worst of all, Dad would get notions about you and me again."

"That wasn't very gallant. You mean you're not interested?" She looked out of the corner of her eye at Sarah, who was almost holding her breath waiting for Seth's answer.

"Forgive me, but no. You're too old."

There was a spate of protests and laughter from the other young people, and Amadea covered her eyes with a hand and said in faltering accents, "Twenty-three. Yes, I can see that I'm quite, quite over the hill. So I'd best go join the graybeards in the kitchen. Keep up the good work." She dropped a light kiss on the top of Seth's straight brown hair. "And do try to be polite."

She half expected Darnell to be staring at her like a hopeful basset pup, and she was looking forward to shattering his romantic illusions where she and Seth were concerned by repeating the boy's remark about her age, but the Prophet was not even aware of her approach. His brick-red cheeks were redder than usual, and a blunt forefinger was tapping out a nervous tattoo on his belt buckle as he listened to Jasper.

"May I join this council of war? That is what it is, isn't it?"

Jeanne gripped the younger woman's upper arm like a person grasping for support in a powerful windstorm. "Yes." She switched her attention to the scientist and glared. The expression set oddly on her pleasant face. "Jasper, what you are suggesting is monstrous. I can't believe it."

"There is no other explanation! This ship starts out from the asteroids, it's name known only to us and our suppliers, and suddenly it's known on Earth, and the FAA and SPACECOM are moving to rescind Captain Gupta's license. Somebody has to be feeding information to Earth."

"You think someone's deliberately spying?" whispered Amadea.

"Yes."

"I'm with Jeanne. I simply can't accept that. No one in this colony would do that." She tugged thoughtfully at a strand of hair. "We're familiar with everyone—"

"Except you." Mendel leaned back, hard-eyed and cold, against the counter.

"Jasper!" gasped Jeanne, and wrapped a protective arm about Amadea's shoulders.

He ignored her. "You've never said much about the project, just listened and listened. And what's this *we,* white man? You're not a member of this colony."

"Neither are you." Both tone and eyes were level. "God knows you're erratic; joining one project, leaving after sometimes only a few months." The man's hands were clenching and unclenching at his sides, and his nostrils were white and pinched. "You hit me, Jasper, and I'll find someone to wipe the landscape with you. I said what I did to you show you how stupid and paranoid you're being. There are a lot of people in the asteroids, and like in any colony, they gossip. The word could just as easily have been sent to Earth from the Belt as from here."

Darnell grunted, shifted, and the tension washed out of his shoulders and back. "She's right. Damn you, Jasper, for upsetting everyone and almost turning us against one another. We're a family. We stay together, we believe in each other, and we defend each other. We'll hear no more of this."

"At least until next time," the scientist muttered sotto voce.

Amadea pinned him, her green eyes cool, and after a moment his gazed dropped and he shuffled nervously. A hand thrust out. "You're right, I was being an asshole. Friends?"

She accepted the overture, saying as they shook, "Friends, but if you ever unjustly accuse me like that again, I'll cut off your nuts and feed them to you one by one."

"Good Lord."

"One of my mother's more colorful threats. I rather like it."

"You don't have nuts."

"I'm glad. After long observation it appears to me that semen tends to back up through the body and affect the brain."

"Uugh," Jeanne said succinctly while she loaded cookies on a plate, filled a pitcher with water, and added instant milk. "Did you find Justice Huntington and deliver your message?"

"Yes." Amadea picked up the plate and followed Jeanne into the living room. "I went first to his office but he wasn't there, so I tracked him to his apartment. Apparently he and his lady had just gotten up. She was still in a bathrobe, and I felt a little awkward."

"Real hardworking," drawled Jasper, and crammed a cookie in his mouth.

"Well, maybe they were working at home." She set down the plate. There was a surge of movement from the teenagers, the plate vanished, and seconds later reappeared empty.

"Did you like him?" Jeanne asked, carefully filling glasses.

"Yes." She paused and glanced sideways at the older woman. "Probably more than I should, given the fact he has a—how shall I say it?—significant other?"

Jeanne slid back on the couch and clasped the pitcher, an expression of almost comic dismay on her wrinkled face. "Oh, dear."

Seth's dark eyes flicked from Amadea to Jeanne and back again. "I think I'm going to get jealous."

"Why? I'm too old, remember? You can't have it both ways." She joined Jeanne on the sofa. "There is one thing that disturbs me. He's so cautious, never revealing what he's thinking. It's hard to tell if he's maintaining his impartiality or if at base he really doesn't favor our position."

A shudder ran through Seth, and he whirled, milk sloshing out of the glass and onto his hand. "Fucker!"

"Seth!"

He sucked at his hand, catching the running liquid with his tongue. "Sorry, Mammer, but if that guy is going to screw us over the way he did that mining colony. . ."

"He acknowledged he was wrong and tried to rectify matters."

"And what's to say he won't revert and *really* screw us?"

"People *do* change, Seth. And we do not continue to crucify people over errors in their past. If we did, *you* would find things rather uncomfortable." There was steel in her voice, and the boy flushed and bit at his lower lip.

"Hey, hey. I didn't mean to start a battle. I only said that that's how *I* viewed him, and I don't even know for certain. It could have just been me having a bad day."

Jeanne gave Amadea's hand a nervous pat where it lay between them on the sofa. "That's fine, dear, but please don't repeat that to other people. We don't want to create anxiety or make Justice Huntington's job any harder."

"I don't like being at the mercy of a stranger," said Seth, frowning down into his glass. "Wish there were some way to find out. Maybe I ought to ask—"

"I'll tell you what. I'll spend some time with him—God knows I want to, anyway—and see what I learn. I won't pry, I promise," she said in answer to Jeanne's uncomfortable grimace. "I'll simply listen. I'm good at that."

"You probably shouldn't even be seeing him, given the situation. . . ."

"I like him, but that doesn't mean I'm going to try to take him away from his lady. I have some ethics. If, however, they should drift apart, and *if* I continue to find him this attractive, I'd be in position to catch him on the rebound." Jeanne was looking decidedly agitated, and Amadea, with a silvery laugh, leaned in, kissed her, and gave her a squeeze. "I'm only teasing. I should be getting back. I'm abusing flextime as it is."

Jeanne glanced at a clock set in the wall. "Time for you kids to get back to school. Lunch is well past."

"If we get a tardy mark, will you cover for us, Mrs. Hudson?" asked Sarah as she gathered up her belongings and headed reluctantly for the door.

"Yes, I suppose so."

Seth, seated on the floor with his back propped against the couch, gave a languid wave to the departing youth group. "Have fun, children. We'll have another meeting tomorrow."

"Seth, you must stop rubbing it in to the other boys that you're out of school. We allowed you to drop out early because it clearly didn't suit you, but—"

The closing of the door cut off the rest of Jeanne's lecture. Amadea, following slowly in the wake of the chattering children, decided to delay long enough to invite Cabot out to the site. He had said he was interested.

Chapter Six

"There aren't as many craters as I had expected."

Cab shifted a bit in the cramped backseat of the Light and gazed out the front of the clear canopy, watching the red-rock-strewn ground flow away beneath them. If he squinted up and to the side, he could distinguish the LegerSteel wing ribs through the clear tedlar covering, but he tried to keep his eyes away from the long, fragile wings. It was nerve-racking to think that plastic only one mil thick was serving as the lift surface. *Wish she'd painted all of the wing surface to resemble a dragon's wing,* he thought. These disconcerting flashes of the interior parts of the Light made him nervous.

But on an artistic level perhaps she was right. The clear plastic sections in the dragon's wing heightened the sense of butterflylike delicacy. He had been around Jared long enough to notice that everyone had their Lights painted with fantastic designs and had asked Amadea why. "A way to pass the time?" she had suggested with a shrug. Or perhaps a way to create a sense of community, because literally everyone on the planet did it whether they had any talent or not. They even had an annual Light show (small giggle when he groaned) where prizes were awarded for the various designs. Last year, Amadea had added with pride, she had won best of show.

He glanced quickly up, thinking he had seen a warping or shivering of the tedlar covering, but apparently it had been only his imagination. *I wonder if this really will hold. I just can't believe—*

"I just don't see why a group of people living on Earth ought to be able to dictate to those of us living on Mars," commented Amadea pointedly.

"I wonder why that is?" Cab mused, returning to his opening remark about the craters in a determined effort to remain obtuse.

"It doesn't seem fair."

"I wonder why the southern hemisphere is more heavily cratered?"

The Eurasian slewed around in her seat, and Cab suppressed a desire to catch her by the shoulders and put her attention back on her flying.

"Is this deliberate or are we talking at cross-purposes for no particularly good reason?"

"I don't mean to be rude, but as I've told you before, I won't discuss cases that are pending before my court."

"I'm not asking you to discuss the case. I'm asking you to explain to me—*legally*—why POW can sue and why you'll hear it."

"That's hairsplitting."

"You ought to be used to it."

"Touché. Okay, quick lesson on the limitations on the exercise of judicial power. There are several grounds upon which the Supreme Court and the federal courts can refuse to hear a case. There's the concrete controversy, which basically asks how eyeball-to-eyeball the disputants' confrontation must be. There's the prohibition against advisory opinions, and the case-or-controversy requirement. There's ripeness. And finally, there's standing. Still with me?"

"Barely . . . no, not really, but go ahead."

"The criterion for standing is whether the litigant has a sufficient personal interest in getting the relief he seeks—"

"That does not apply to POW."

"*Or* . . . is a sufficiently appropriate representative of other interested persons. During the last century the courts, sensitive to growing environmental problems, began to expand the concept of standing. In *Sierra Club* v. *Morton,* heard in the 1960s, Justice Douglas wrote a famous dissent, arguing that trees should have standing. But since the trees couldn't come toddling into court to speak for themselves, it was appropriate to have interested persons speak in their behalf, i.e., the Sierra Club. Well, in 2003, in *Sierra Club* v. *Bustemonte,* the Douglas dissent became the majority opinion of the Supreme Court. I feel that Mars offers a similar circumstance."

"Also, the POW complaint is predicated on the idea that the members are asserting the rights of people worldwide. This is, I grant you, a rather large group, but there is precedent growing out of the Pierce and NAACP exceptions, which state that a group's nexus with its members is sufficient to permit it to act as their representative before the court. This was profoundly extended in the Hung Li case in 2035, which removed the requirement of membership and allowed sufficiently active organizations to speak for the rather amorphous concept of the worldwide public interest. The Supreme Court was waxing very spiritual and metaphysical in that decision, and so I always think of it as the Weltgeist case.

"Now"—he scooted forward and rested his arms on the back of her seat, his helmeted cheek next to hers—"this all dovetails with the long line of environmental cases growing out of the Scenic Hudson case in 1965, which established the public's right to environmental protection."

Amadea began to laugh. Cab stiffened, then shrugged sheepishly. "I'm sorry. Am I boring you?"

"Not at all. I am just amused by your enthusiasm. You're such an internal person that I didn't expect this kind of energy and involvement—certainly not about something as dry as the law."

"But it's not dry. The passion of ages is contained in those cases."

"Boiled-down . . . very boiled-down."

"True, but the pedantic delivery of the justices doesn't detract from the very real feelings that were roused over these issues."

"Would you rather have been a professor?"

He sighed and slid back in his seat. "Yes. I sure as hell don't want to die a judge. If this first circuit is any indication, I wouldn't live very long—worry and agitation would burn me out before I'm fifty."

"Joe said there was an old law-school adage about the *A* students . . ."

"Ah, I know the one. The *A* students become professors, the *B* students judges, the *C* students practicing attorneys, and the *D* students go into politics."

"And what were you?"

"An *A* student, but I seem to be working my way backward through the catechism. With luck I'll never devolve all the way back to running for public office."

There was silence for a few moments, then Amadea asked, "Is this leg of your circuit really that bad?"

"No, not bad, but nerve-racking. I was hoping for nice, dull, routine cases while I was here, and instead I get hit with this major environmental problem."

"'No environment, no impact,'" she quoted. "So where's the problem?"

"The issue isn't the environment. Not in the traditional sense of something destructive being done to it. It's the UN treaty preserving the planets for all mankind, and POW's argument is that the best and highest use for this world is as a national . . . international," he amended, "park."

"This leaves me very confused and rather ambivalent," said Amadea. "Maybe we should leave some things alone and not try to play God with the cosmos. Maybe we should have some places that are left pristine, with people simply coming to visit and observe, and not change them."

"Won't Jupiter do? It's rather unlikely we'll ever set up colonies in the clouds." There was a touch of sarcasm in the words. "And I'm a little uncomfortable with what you're advocating. It seems to me that having a new world on which to expand would certainly be in the interests of all mankind."

"Then you *are* sympathetic to the Jared colonists."

Cab frowned, irritated with himself for revealing so much. "It's a factor I'm considering. One must also ask if a private religious group should have the control of such an awesome undertaking. Perhaps it might be better in the hand of an international tribunal. Of course, it's not for me to make a decision like that—"

"Would that be an advisory opinion?"

"Exactly! You catch on fast. Have you considered a career in law?"

"No thank you. Geology's enough for me. Especially when a person gets to work on a project of this magnitude."

"You're certain you won't get in trouble for bringing me out here?"

"I would . . . if Dave was around, but I'm cautious in addition to being a coward, so I picked a day when he was in Eagle Port. He does seem to be making an awful lot of trips there," she mused.

"Is that significant?"

"I don't know. He's a strange man and actually far more comfortable being alone in the field than among people. Which is why I'm puzzled by his trips to the port."

"Perhaps there's something he needs there. Or perhaps there's a woman—"

"What there is, is privacy and a really *big* transmitter."

"I beg your pardon? Excuse me, but I'm lost."

"And I'm probably seeing spooks that aren't there, but someone's been feeding information about the colonists' plans to Earth, and I just wondered." She shook her head. "No, Dave's too wimpy to be cast in the role of agent-provocateur."

Leaning forward, Cab massaged her shoulders through the thin material of her suit. "I don't think that's the phrase you want. An agent-provocateur is a person who incites others into actions for which they will be liable."

"Hey, I'm a scientist, not a literary scholar. So what is the word I want?"

"*Judas* leaps to mind."

"Oh," she said a little hollowly, and he tightened his grip on her shoulders.

"I'm sorry. I didn't mean to upset you. I'm sure this man you work for isn't selling out the colonists."

"What makes you so sure?"

"There are a lot of people on this planet. Information, gossip, and rumor must bleed off here like . . . like . . ." He groped for an appropriate phrase.

"Like air out of a suit puncture?" suggested Amadea, glancing back over her shoulder. Her smile and the mischief in her eyes made his breath go short.

"Something like that, yes," he forced past a suddenly dry throat. "Is that the base?" he asked inanely, pointing out the front window. Of course, it had to be. They hadn't seen any sign of habitation for a hundred miles, but he made the remark simply to gain time and to distract her before she could notice the devastating effect she was having upon him.

"Yes, that's the base."

"Do you land this thing like you fly it?" he asked as he settled back in his seat and rehooked his seat belt.

"Not you too! Everyone criticizes my flying, and I'm a very good pilot."

"You're a very . . . dashing . . . pilot."

She flashed that grin again, her small teeth a pearly white against the rose of her lips. "I think people should live on the brink."

"Living is the operative word in that sentence," muttered Cab to himself, gripping the edges of his seat as they came screaming in for a landing.

Jillian and Conrad met them as they climbed from the Light, and the first thing Cab noticed was that the man was packing a shotgun. It was obvious from the awkward way he was holding the weapon that he hadn't the least idea what he was doing, and Cab kept a wary eye on him, not wanting to be on the receiving end of an accidental load of shot.

Apparently the presence of arms at the camp was something new to Amadea. Hands on hips, she surveyed her fellows. "Are we under attack?"

"It's Dave!" grunted Conrad, disgust laying heavy on the words. "He's gotten it into his head that Jasper and the Jared colonists are going to come stealing over in the night and take his precious discovery."

"Oh, Christ! He's flipped. In the first place, there wouldn't have been any discovery without Jasper—"

"But he left the project, so Dave will get the credit," interrupted Jillian.

"And furthermore, he's got more important things on his mind."

"More important!"

"Yes, Conrad. It's clear that the creatures who left the marker came through some five million years ago. I don't think anybody's going to work up a real big sweat over that."

"I disagree. I think that what we have discovered is of profound importance. It settles the decades-long argument about life on other worlds. It means we are not alone."

"It's been five million years. They haven't come back.

They're probably dead. And since nobody's been calling to say hello, I can't work up a lot of enthusiasm."

"Amadea, you have no soul."

"I have other things that I think are more important."

From their stance and the rising decibels he could tell the two scientists were winding up for a fight. Cab cleared his throat, bringing the attention to him. "I think your project leader is off-base about the Jared colonists, but it probably wouldn't be a bad idea to post a guard here. Especially once you uncover the object and make an announcement. The fundamentalists aren't going to like having their ethnocentric view of the universe upset. Also, you might want to have the media and other dignitaries out for the final days of work. That will preclude any accusations of fraud."

"A modern-day Piltdown man scandal," Jillian said.

"Something like that, yes."

Amadea clasped his arm and gave it a squeeze. "You're so clever and devious."

"No, I'm not. I've just learned to anticipate deviousness in others. Actually what I've begun to realize is that I'm really very transparent and gullible. It's quite depressing."

"Excuse me," said Conrad. "But who the hell are you?"

"I'm sorry, I'm forgetting my manners. Conrad Weisman, Jillian Green, this is Justice Cabot Huntington." There were polite murmurs all around. "I'm going to take Cab up on the pyramid and show him the object."

"Won't be much to see. We still aren't down to the object itself, but you are now able to get a sense of its shape and size."

"And what is its shape?"

"A six- by ten-foot dodecahedron."

They were walking toward the looming bulk of the great pyramid of Elysium. Cab gave a self-deprecating little cough. "This is going to sound really stupid, but you don't learn if you don't ask, so I'll go ahead and risk sounding stupid." Three faceplates swiveled to regard him. "You keep talking about aliens 'passing through.' I wondered if there was any chance that they were homegrown aliens? From this Solar System."

"You mean, like Martians?" asked Conrad.

Cab blushed at the veiled amusement in the other man's voice. "Yes. I'm not a scientist," he added defensively.

"No, Cab. If there had been some sort of semi-industrial civilization on Mars, there would have been indications of it elsewhere on the planet," Amadea explained. "There aren't, and since I don't buy the existence of Atlantis, I can't even make an argument for early humans creating a space-capable civilization and then falling back to total barbarism. We're hoping there will be some sort of writing or symbols on the object to prove our thesis, but for now it's the simplest and most reasonable explanation."

"Occam's razor."

"There, you do know some science."

"I know buzzwords."

Amadea looked to Conrad and Jillian. "Are you people going to come along?"

"No, I'll stay here and guard against the phantom hoards."

"And I have work to do. See you in a bit."

They circled the quonset huts that stored the team's lights, recovered a crawler from vehicle storage, and crossed the five-mile expanse between the base and the pyramid. It was an awesome sight with the sunlight striking off one of its three sides, and shadows lying deep in the grooves and crevasses of the other two. There was something brooding and ominous about the great mass of stone rising 3,300 feet off the plain of Elysium, and Cab felt the hairs at the back of his neck prickling. Perhaps the secret this monolith guarded was not something men should disturb or explore.

But that's what men do; they disturb and explore, question and probe. And I'm being silly and finding significance where it doesn't exist. If we didn't know there was an alien artifact on the top of this monster, I'd view it as just another awesome natural formation.

They reached the side of the pyramid, and Cab reached out to touch it. The red sandstone was gritty beneath his glove. Each face had appeared smooth from a distance, but such was not the case. As he studied the side of the pyramid he realized it consisted of a series of giant slabs shoved and rotated to form the pyramid shape.

"I read one book on Mars that dismissed all the theories on how these things formed and suggested that they were constructed."

"No, they're quite natural." Her arm arced out, including the other smaller pyramids that dotted the plain. "As a geologist, I can say it was a pretty weird sequence of events that formed them, but it was natural. As to why the aliens selected this site for their marker?" She shrugged. "This pyramid is a pretty major feature on the face of the planet. It's visible from orbit, and they might have wanted to draw attention to the marker for future travelers. Who knows? After all, they were alien, with all that word implies."

A freestanding lift had been erected next to the pyramid, and as they slowly creaked up toward the summit Cab gazed out across the Martian landscape. Three tiny dust storms were whirling between the lesser pyramids, like mad pink dervishes involved in a joyful game of hide-and-seek.

He nodded toward the distant dust devils. "They act like they're almost alive."

"Yes, In lieu of pets we tend to adopt dust devils. Some of them can last for several hours, and on slow days we've been known to name them, place bets on their speed and direction, play tag with them, and in general indulge in other kinds of strange and bizarre behavior that would get us committed back on Earth."

"No pets," mused Cab as the elevator jerked to a halt. "There's something very sad about that."

"Life out here is one long series of sads."

"You sound bitter."

"Do I? I don't mean to, and I shouldn't be bitching. I had life easy being raised on a station, and I did have pets—a fat and venerable old cat named Humongous. But I think of the children of the asteroids."

"That sounds like the title of a novel."

"It does, doesn't it?" She jerked at the waist-high gate, and it clashed back. "Perhaps I'll write it someday, but first I'll have to do some research."

"You've never been in the Belt?" They walked side by side, Cab with his hands firmly clasped behind his back.

"No. Civilization has too strong a hold on me."

Cab gestured at the empty red landscape. "Like this, you mean?"

"Don't be snide. You haven't experienced a big night out on the town in Eagle Port."

"Sounds heady. It might be more than I could handle."

"I'd be happy to go along and make sure you get home safely."

They had stopped walking and stood regarding each other, their faceplates only inches apart.

"I may just take you up on that."

"Please do." She gave herself a little shake. "Well, here's our little mystery."

Cab picked his way over the mounds of sand that had been removed from around the artifact. It was rather like moving through a colony of particularly busy ants who had constructed an ant metropolis and then moved on. The object itself was still shrouded in a layer of sand, but the twelve-sided shape of it could be discerned through its russet veil. The judge slowly circled the dodecahedron, his hand reaching up to touch the top of the six-foot-tall object. He then froze and looked inquiringly back over his shoulder.

"May I?"

"Of course. There's still seven or eight inches of sand between you and it, and we've been chipping away at it for days without it biting back."

"I'm not afraid. But I don't want to trespass."

"Oh, sorry. Please." She gestured, and he continued his walk, gently trailing his hand along the edge. A fine rain of sand followed behind, creating a whispering counterpoint to his crunching footfalls.

"It's quite, quite awesome." He turned back to face her, folding his arms across his chest as if hugging himself. "How on Earth did anyone ever notice it?"

"Jasper has a keen eye. He was looking at orbital photos and realized it didn't look quite natural. Still took him five years of agitating before SPACECOM would authorize the project."

"Mendel!" he said incredulously. "I didn't realize he was involved."

"*Instrumental* is a better word."

"Oh," he said lamely. He took two quick steps toward her. "Doesn't it make you crazy having to work so slowly? Don't you just want to grab a shovel and see what's under there?"

"Yes, but Dave is afraid it's fragile, and Sharon, our resident archaeologist, concurs, so we work at a snail's pace. Personally I think it's stupid. We know the thing's been here at least five million years without eroding, which doesn't suggest fragility to me."

"So when will you break through?"

"Probably another week. And I think your suggestion of calling in the press, and various bigwigs, is well merited." She was moving back toward the lift, and Cab hurried to fall in step with her.

He slipped an arm through hers. "Do I qualify as a *big-wig?*"

She pulled her arm free but only so she could slide it around his waist. "Do I take it that you want to be present?"

"Please, ma'am."

"What's it worth to you?"

"Are you asking to be suborned?"

"Um-hmm."

"Madam, I'm shocked!" His gray eyes were alight with amusement.

"Isn't that how things get done in the legal profession? It is in the scientific community."

"In the legal profession we call that unethical behavior, and you've shattered one of my treasured illusions." He paused. "So, what do you want?"

She leaned back against the side of the lift. "Dinner in Eagle Port?"

He jerked shut the gate. "That's all? I thought I might have to sacrifice my manhood, or my integrity at the very least."

"Who knows what that night might bring." She threw the elevator abruptly into motion, and he grabbed at the wire-mesh cage for balance.

Jenny listened to the air cycling and thought again how strange it was to enter a church through an airlock. Every day, in every way, things become weirder and weirder, she thought as she slithered out of her suit and set it in the recharge room. Her heels rang out on the great red flags that paved the nave as she walked toward the chancel. The great windows of the clerestory with their predominately blue and purple colors created a sense of being underwater; very restful, but also somewhat suffocating. Jenny analyzed the feeling and then decided that her sense of breathlessness came more from her own disordered emotions than from the church.

Suddenly a barrage of sound erupted from the choir as all seven thousand of the pipes on the German organ let loose. For a moment the wall and the vaulted ceiling flung back a cacophony of runs, scales, and chords that slowly resolved into the opening chords of Bach's awesome Toccata and Fugue in D minor, then the mood shifted as the unseen organist began the final movement of Mozart's *Exsultate*. Jenny fought the temptation, then surrendered to it, and began to sing the Alleluia. She was startled when her sweet, light soprano came echoing back to her, and she realized that the acoustics were as perfect as everything else about this improbable church. She stopped, embarrassed, and a moment later the organ died too.

"Don't stop," called a familiar voice, and Jeanne Hudson's gray head came popping inquisitively over the rail of the choir.

"I'm embarrassed."

"Don't be. You have a beautiful voice. Come on up," she added, and returned to her playing, not waiting to see if Jenny would accept the invitation. This time it was Handel.

She stopped as soon as Jenny's red head appeared through the top of the stairwell and folded her gnarled hands in her lap. "Are you a triple threat or only a double one?"

"I beg your pardon?"

"In my day we called someone who could sing, dance, and act a triple threat. I know you dance and now I know you sing, so I wondered if you could act too."

"I liked to imagine I could, back in high school and college, but it was all purely amateur stuff."

Her fingers resumed their quiet play across the keyboards. "And so is my playing. I took a music minor with my major in child development." Her hands dropped back into her lap. "And then discovered I couldn't have any children. Ironic, isn't it?"

"But Seth . . . ?"

"Adopted."

Jenny leaned against the side of the console. "It isn't the sole definition of a woman."

"It is in the Mormon church."

"But with the modern techniques couldn't you have—"

"There's something wrong with my eggs. The genetic code somehow isn't there. We could have had Darnell's sperm fertilize some other woman's egg, then implant it in me, but he viewed it as a kind of betrayal of me."

"And you? How did you view it?"

Jeanne dropped her head and regarded her nails. "I would

like to have had a child. But that's ancient history and not very relevant to the present. What brought you up here?"

"It seemed a good place to think. Actually it's probably my Catholic upbringing rising up to slap me in the face. In times of trouble, run to the bosom of Holy Mother Church."

Jeanne shifted on the bench so she could face the younger woman straight on. "Is this a time of trouble?"

"No, I just used that as an—"

"Jennifer!"

"I'd rather not say anything. Cab would hate it. He's a much more private person than I am. I like to talk about my feelings. I think he sometimes wishes he could remove his."

"We're not talking about Cab."

"It involves him."

"Bless you, child, I'm not a lack-wit. I know that." She patted the bench next to her invitingly. "Why not pretend I'm your mother."

Jenny sat, but she was perched warily on the edge of the padded cushion that covered the bench. "That would be guaranteed to silence me. My mother's . . ." She paused and shrugged. "Let's just say I've always been more comfortable talking with my dad."

"Okay, then how about pretending I'm the kind of mother you would like to have had. There are some things that boy people can't comment on as easily as girl people can," she added softly.

Jenny pressed an experimental finger down on one key. A forlorn honk filled the church. "I'm wrestling with one of my demons."

"I don't suppose its name would be jealousy?"

"Yes." She sighed. "I guess I'm very transparent."

"Well, you do wear your heart in your face. It's not very hard to read how you're feeling."

"Cab went off to the Elysium base with Amadea." The words came pouring out of her. "Nobody even thought to ask if I wanted to go along, and I really wanted to. I'd love to see that alien thing. But when I said something, Amadea said that there wasn't enough room in her Light, but we could have taken another one. I'm sure Darnell wouldn't have minded, and I've flown. I wouldn't have upset her little tête-á-tête, if that's what she was worried about."

"That's very noble of you. If I had a woman making eyes

at my Darnell the way Amadea does at your boss, I'd cut her off at the knees and feed her feet to the garbage disposal."

The remark, coming as it did from the normally sweet-faced and placid Jeanne, pulled a surprised burble of laughter from Jenny. "I keep telling myself that I don't own Cab and that I should be understanding and liberal, but I want to hit him. I want to kill her, and I'm embarrassed about it because I count her mother as one of my dear friends, and I shouldn't feel this way about her daughter."

"Just as the sins of the parents shouldn't be visited upon the children, neither should their virtues."

"I thought you liked Amadea?"

"I do, but not when she behaves this way."

There was again a sigh. "I know things are different in the System. Lydia had five children by five different fathers."

"Not that different," Jeanne replied acidly. "People may be more open about sharing their spouses and lovers, but they usually have the courtesy to all sit down together and discuss it."

Jenny threw her head back and scraped her hands through her hair. "Oh, God, that really would kill me if Cab and Amadea came in and said they were going to have an affair. And I don't think it's going to happen. Cab's blown away by her beauty, but I don't think he'd hurt me by sleeping with her."

If Jeanne had any doubts, she hid them well. Reaching out, she gave Jenny's hand a motherly pat where it lay between them on the bench. "I'm sure he wouldn't. Come, let's do the Mozart, and then you can sing next time we have a musical evening."

"If you want someone to sing, Cab is your man," Jenny said, climbing to her feet. "He has a beautiful baritone voice."

"All right, then you can dance, Cab can sing, and Amadea can feel quite left out because to my knowledge the girl has all the musicality of a stump."

"That's mean, and I shouldn't be laughing."

"What's the good in being female if you can't indulge in a bit of cattiness now and then?"

She whirled her hands in a theatrical motion and began the energetic introduction of the *Exsultate*. Gazing into that seamed, pink-cheeked face, Jenny was suddenly seized by a strong sense of love and gratitude for this woman, and before she could think and hesitate, she leaned down and gave her a brief but fervent hug.

Chapter Seven

Cab peeled back the top slice of bread and peered suspiciously at his sandwich. "Mayonnaise. I hate mayonnaise. I told you I wanted butter."

Jenny chewed and swallowed. "So next time make it yourself."

"My word, you're prickly."

"Did you have a nice time in Eagle Port last night?" The words were edged with acid.

"Yes," he said in a tone that did not invite further questions.

The couple was seated on a blanket beneath one of the young trees in the park. Across the street the government building sat, smug and serene-looking, like a set piece out of a 1908 historical movie but a movie with jarring incongruities: like the new System flag that had been added at Cab's suggestion and now hung limply directly below the American flag; the delicate pink sky; and the shimmer of the dome overhead.

Cab frowned out across the park, chewing and trying to avoid Jenny's green eyes. Suddenly Hudson, Young, and Coltrin erupted out of the front door of City Hall and went hurrying toward the small hotel. Several other elders of the community were also converging on the squat, whitewashed building with its red, Spanish-tiled roof. Peter Yeates, manager of the hotel, appeared in the door, gesturing passionately, his mouth moving in a wild counterpoint to his swinging arms.

"I wonder what's going on?" mused Cab as the group of men vanished into the hotel.

"What?"

"Every bigwig in the colony just went into the hotel."

"Probably church business. Are we going to talk about this or not?" she asked abruptly.

He didn't pretend not to understand. "No. There's nothing to talk about. Amadea is fulfilling her promise to her mother by showing us around."

"You. Showing *you* around!"

"You went off alone with Peter the entire time we were on the EnerSun station."

"That was different."

He crammed the remains of his lunch back in a sack and rose to his feet. "Yes, it was. *I'm* not involved with Amadea."

"Could have fooled me," Jenny muttered after his retreating back as she dusted the crumbs from her skirt and folded up the blanket.

An hour later, as they sat in Cab's office reading cases for an upcoming trial, the com chimed. Cab answered, listened for a moment, then switched on the intercom.

"—want to set up our people at the hotel there in Jared—as you know there are no facilities in Eagle Port—but the leaders of the colony have refused."

"Padget MacKinley," Cab mouthed to Jenny, and her brows flew up to meet the fringe of her bangs. The last person she expected to hear from was the slick, young attorney for POW.

"Now," the lawyer continued, "I can file a formal complaint, but that will take time, and meanwhile we're all camped out in the passenger lounge at Eagle Port. So I thought of you. If you could intercede on our behalf, we'd really appreciate it. We don't want to make the colonists look any worse than they already do, and if the world finds out they're denying us service—"

"Why are you issuing these threats to me, Mr. MacKinley?"

"No threat intended, Your Honor."

"Forgive me if I misunderstood you, but that last remark did sound very much like a threat to me."

"Whatever you say, Judge." Cab glowered at the com. MacKinley went on. "Now, about this business of the hotel . . ."

"I'll talk with the colonists and be back to you."

"Don't take too long. We're a little uncomfortable—"

"My time is my own," snapped Cab, looking a little white around the mouth.

"You know precedent is with us."

The smug certainty, and the implied suggestion that MacKinley had to refresh Cab's memory on the law, shattered his control, and the judge furiously broke the connection.

"No wonder he's been found in contempt of court three times!"

"I'm following most of this, but could you please fill me in on the part I missed?"

"Lucius Renfrew is here with Padget MacKinley and twenty POW supporters."

"Rather a large cheering section, isn't it? I would have thought Renfrew and MacKinley would have been enough."

"Subtlety had never been POW's style. They like to try every case in the press, and several judges have bent under the pressure, ruling in POW's favor to avoid crucifixion in the media." She raised her eyebrows inquiringly. "Nobody wants to be known as a murderer of baby bunnies." He sighed and ran a hand through his thick black hair. "Thank God there's no natural fauna on Mars."

"You don't sound like you like them."

"I don't. I have nothing against environmentalists—God knows there've been abuses—but this gang is on the outside edge of crank." He held up a warning finger. "And don't you dare repeat me."

"You and your damn impartiality."

"It does rather go with the territory."

"I'm too passionate. I'd clearly make a poor judge. So, do we go to Darnell or call him here?"

"I don't want to seem unduly antagonistic or arrogant. Let's go to them."

"The mountain to Mohammed."

"Jenny . . ." he warned.

Five minutes later they entered the front doors of the hotel. Seven men were there and the faces were grim. Yeates was behind the desk with the other men clustered about, and Darnell perched on the counter. It was a jarring image, the big-bellied, red-faced man swinging one leg like a coquettish girl. A second later Cab realized why the leg was moving. It enabled Hudson to beat out an angry tattoo against the side of the desk with his boot heel.

"War party?"

"Church business," grunted Darnell, and looked pointedly back at the door.

"My business now." There were murmurs, and Cab held up a hand. "I just got a call from Padget MacKinley, the POW attorney. What are you thinking about, trying to deny them accommodations?"

"They're our enemies—"

Cab turned on Coltrin. "No, sir, that is not correct. Their lawsuit was filed against the EPA."

"Legal hairsplitting," snorted Darnell. "Fact is, it'll cause bad feeling in the community."

Cab eyed Hudson. "Undoubtedly, but that's not sufficient legal ground to bar them. A good deal of bad feeling was generated in Skokie, Illinois, when a neo-Nazi group decided to march in their town, but the courts unheld the Nazis' right to do so. I think the Jewish citizens in that city had more cause to complain then you."

Jenny leaned in and whispered into Cab's left ear. "Climb off the high horse, please." He drew in a quick breath and nodded to acknowledge her.

"Damn it! This is not a public street. This is our home!"

"No, this is a public hotel." Cab spread his hands in a placating gesture. "Look, Mr. Hudson, I came over here to mediate between you and the environmentalists. MacKinley is prepared to bring suit against you to force you to house them, and they're dedicated enough to endure sleeping on the floor of the shuttle lounge until this thing is settled. They'll also make political and journalistic hay while they wait, and ultimately they'll win. I'm a judge, and as such, I've sworn to uphold the law—all the laws—even the ones I may not like or agree with."

"You mean to tell me that I can be forced to associate with people I don't like?"

"No, Darnell, that's not what I'm saying." He squeezed the bridge of his nose. "This is a little complex, but bear with me. In 1964, there was a case—*Heart of Atlanta Motel* v. *the United States*—that challenged the constitutionality of Title II of the Civil Rights Act of 1964. The motel had been refusing to rent rooms to blacks, and they wished to continue this practice. Congress had based the act on the Equal Protection Clause of the Fourteenth Amendment, as well as its power to regulate interstate commerce. The Supreme Court upheld Congress' right to eliminate the evil of segregation by both means, saying that discrimination against persons moving in the flow of interstate commerce worked a hardship on that commerce.

"Through the years that case has been significantly expanded. In 1997, the Court held in *Martinez* v. *the United States* that the concept of interstate commerce extended to system colonies that held the status of American territories—which you do."

John Guisetti, a skinny young man with thinning hair and a prominent Adam's apple, who was also the resident attorney for the Jared Colony, spoke up. "Couldn't we argue that we fall under the private-club exclusion?"

"Your suggestion is a good try, but it won't wash. This hotel cannot be construed as a private club."

"But wait, wait, these guys aren't Negroes," objected Yeates, obviously missing the point.

"Race is not the only grounds on which you can deny someone equal protection. You're discriminating against them on the basis of association—their creed, if you prefer. Also, you've placed yourselves squarely within the parameters of *Heart of Atlanta*. You've solicited patronage outside of the colony using various national magazines. I've seen the ads in *Leisure* and *Time* and *World Traveler*, and believe me, up until six months ago I never dreamed I'd be coming to Mars. If you made an impression on a casual reader like me, you've definitely been getting the word out."

"So we'll have to accept them?"

"I'd strongly advise you to do so. Otherwise there's going to be a big fight in the press, and you'll come out looking the worse for it."

"Fuckin' crazy Mormons acting like money-grubbing elitists again," muttered Young, and though Darnell frowned at him for the obscenity, he didn't disagree.

Hudson sighed, a huge, gusting sound that seemed to originate in his toes and erupted from his nose like a windstorm. He shook his head. "Okay, Your Honor. We'll take your advice, but I'm damned if I can make heads or tails out of all this commerce and interstate traffic stuff. Seems like a lot of mental gymnastics to me."

"To a lot of other people too," replied Jenny. "Just think of it as a sort of legal Dadaism."

"That's a little strong," objected Cab.

"Cabot, even you think the modern interpretation of the commerce clause gives the feds far too much power."

"I may think it . . . a lot, but I don't say it, or least not often. It's not a popular position."

"Especially not with your big bosses. Sort of like biting the hand that feeds you" came a muttered remark from someone in the knot of men, but it was said too quickly for Cab to identify the speaker.

He debated about challenging the remark but, for better or worse, decided against it. It was frustration and high-tempered talk, and he didn't want to embarrass the man—whichever one it had been.

"Shall I inform Mr. MacKinley of your decision?"

"I'm a big enough man to eat my own serving of crow," said Darnell, and then wiped the back of his hairy hand across his mouth as if already removing the taste. "I'll call 'em. Besides, it wouldn't look too good for you to be chatting up the other side. We wouldn't want people to say you were biased."

"The POW people probably feel the same way about you. After all, I've lived among you for several weeks. They probably think you've talked up your side of the argument and completely swayed me to your side."

"And have we?" asked Coltrin.

Cab just smiled and started for the door. Jenny hesitated and dithered, torn between a desire to stay and reassure the Mormon leadership and the implicit command in Cab's ramrod-straight back. Her lack of anything concrete to say to the frowning men and her habit of obedience to her irritating, fascinating, and exasperating boss sent her after him.

Cab waited outside for her, staring moodily off through the

top of the dome at the fantastic spires of the church on the crater's edge. The strange, pink-tinged sky; the fairylike building; and Cab's thin, pale features combined to make Jenny think of some bygone tale.

She laid a hand on his shoulder. "You look rather like Prince Charming when he's first sighted the forest of thorns around Sleeping Beauty's castle."

"I don't feel very charming. *Thorny* is actually a very good word."

"Toward . . . whom?"

"Padget MacKinley."

"Oh."

He smiled at her surprise. "Were you afraid I was going to say 'your beloved colonists'?"

"They're not *my* colonists."

"But they are dear to you."

"I think there's a lot to admire in them."

"Don't be defensive. I'm not disputing that."

"I don't know, Cab. I sometimes get the feeling that you still have a certain superiority where the System dwellers are concerned."

"That's not fair." His hand went reflexively to his shoulder. "I think I pretty well proved where my loyalties lay during the EnerSun crisies, and I think you're using this as a way to take a slam at me. Not because of the colonists but because of—" He bit off the words, flushed, and pressed his lips together, but Jenny could finish the sentence.

Amadea.

She was angry and feeling as if she'd been unjustly accused, but upon reflection she realized that he was right. Her motives weren't that clear. Maybe she was looking for a way to dig at Cab.

He's right. If I'm going to be a bitch, I ought to at least be a bitch about the right item. But I'm too much of a coward. How can I accuse him of stepping out on me when he keeps insisting there's nothing between them? Maybe we should have established this as an open relationship from the beginning. But he would never have accepted that. So it's okay for him to step but not for me?

That rankled. Still, she had no proof that he *was* stepping, and God knows, most men lusted in their hearts. Though perhaps a different part of their anatomy ought to be invoked for that phrase, she thought with a momentary flicker of amusement.

Her thoughts continued to tumble like flotsam in a whirlpool, and she realized that she neither wanted to deny his allegation, acknowledge it, nor comment upon it. In short, she didn't have any idea what to say, so she simply walked away. It was a very unsatisfying conclusion.

President Carmella Alvalena Rodriguez rested her elbows on the wrought-iron balustrade of the Presidential Palace in Managua, Nicaragua, and surveyed the stream of gaily dressed people passing through the street below. The deep-throated boom of the cathedral bells rang out over the city, and the bobbing porcelain head of the saint being carried on a flower-decorated litter at the head of the procession seemed to be keeping time. She wondered if that were blasphemous and added a mental apology to Saint . . . Her thick, black brows pulled together as she struggled to remember his name and the reason for the celebration. Finally she shook her head and admitted defeat. She couldn't for the life of her recall it.

And you, a novice nun for a few years, back in your foolish youth, she chastised herself.

A slow smile creased her plump face as she remembered the fiery young Anglo who had been visiting during one of her brief visits home, whose drive and passion had fired her imagination, and whose body had convinced her that chastity was not a concept she wished to embrace. A man was much more satisfying. When Joe had left at the end of that idyllic two weeks, headed south for Ecuador, she had revealed her decision; a decision that delighted her father and prostrated her mother with strong hysterics for three days.

They had sent word to the convent in Granada that she would not be returning, and she had entered Mexico University. She did her graduate work in economics at Harvard, returned to Nicaragua, and entered politics. Forty years since that magic summer and so much had happened. Joe had married her sister Amparo; a marriage that ended tragically four years later in an air-car crash. She believed that grief had helped push him to build his empire of the stars.

And her? She had convinced the various governments under which she had served to adopt the free-market theories of her professor, mentor, and guru, Dr. David Morgenstern, and to do business with the newly formed Reichart Industries. The results had been spectacular for Nicaragua and had kept the country out of the American net, woven from the subtle economic dependence and outright military aggression that had trapped so many of the South and Central American nations.

Her secretary, Carlos Salazar, came cat-footed out onto the balcony. "Señora, there is a call."

"Business?"

"Personal."

She sighed, released her reminiscence, and, squaring her shoulders, prepared to deal with yet another crisis generated by her youngest son. She loved Guillermo, but when he continued to plunge from scandal to scandal, she could find herself wishing there was still a draft. Shagging ass through the swamps and mountains of Nicaragua with a drill sergeant chewing said ass all the way might be exactly what he needed.

She thumbed the accept switch, expecting to see the faded features of her mother or her husband. She saw instead curly gray-brown hair, dancing brown eyes, a strange, almost mocking smile.

"Joe!" she gasped, and fell back in her chair, laughing.

"That's one hell of an effect I'm having on you. Am I becoming so ludicrous in my old age?"

"I'm not laughing at you. I'm really startled. I was literally *just* thinking about you, and I'm not just saying that."

"I believe you."

"You don't often call."

"I don't often need a favor."

"Whatever it is . . . yes."

He held up a hand. "Wait, hear me out before you so rashly commit yourself." She settled back more comfortably in the big leather chair and nodded. "I need you to grant registry to a ship out of the asteroids and to sign an entrance-and-importation agreement with the Jared Colony so the ship can offload cargo at your port. It's an anitmatter drive ship and not designed for Earth's deep gravity well, so you'll have to use shuttles to transfer the cargo."

"That's no problem. We have an agreement with the Saudis. But tell me, where is this ship currently registered?"

"In the United States."

"Are they involved in something illegal?"

"No, they're simply trying to ply their trade. It's the U.S. government that's doing something illegal." And in a few quick sentences he filled her in on the situation with the Martian colonists and the diamonds.

"So you want me to pull the great bird's tail feathers for you?"

"You know I'd be more than happy to do it myself, but this is one I can't handle. I'm not a nation state."

"Is Long involved?"

"Doesn't seem to be. My spies"—his mouth twisted in a grimacing little smile—"indicate that the orders are coming from the White House Chief of Staff."

"Lis Varllis," and Carmella made a face like a person who has bitten into a rotten piece of fruit.

"Oh, goody, have I found a hair-pulling situation?"

"Yes. That . . . lady was extremely rude and condescending to me at the last International Women's Conference."

"Well, of course she was. You had the audacity to apply Morgenstern's theories, bring your country up to a level of prosperity unheard-of in Central America, and avoid baby brotherhood with your white fathers to the north."

Carmella slapped her hand down on the polished surface of the desk. "Yes, Joe, I'll do it. And love every minute of it. Do you want this announced with a fanfare?"

He worried his lower lip between thumb and forefinger, then shook his head. "No, let's keep it low-key. I don't want you in a real confrontational position with the White House. Your country's too small, and Long might suddenly decide he's got six-gun fever, like some of his revered predecessors, and decide to prove how macho he is by invading Nicaragua. And there's the matter of . . ." He paused.

"Yes?"

"There appears to be a very large leak in the Jared Colony, and I know they'd like to see it plugged. Maybe if we give our shadowy spy another tidbit to pass on to Earth, he'll tip himself."

"This is sounding all very cloak-and-dagger."

"But what fun, my dear! Now here are the particulars."

A few moments later and she had the information, and they had turned to more personal matters.

"How's Guillermo?"

"Awful. Don't ask."

"Send him to me. I'll keep him too busy to get in trouble."

"I wish I could, but he'd never go. His pomaded locks would stand straight up at the thought of a bit of hardship. He's addicted to the soft life here on Earth. Skiing in San Moritz, sunning on the Riviera, dancing the night away in Budapest." She shook her head. "No, he'd never go."

"Don't be too hard on him. It's not only soft Earth kids who want to hang on to the nipple. We lose quite a few of the younger generation once they're old enough to leave. The lure of Earth is a big one."

"At least they come here and do something."

"So cut off his allowance."

"I should, but I'm still a doting, fuzzy mama where he's concerned. Don't worry. It's only going to take one or two more scandals before I blow and get tough."

He winked and mimed a gunshot at her with his forefinger. "Get tough? You are tough. And think of the frustrations you can take out on Lis Varllis!"

She smiled a dreamy, contemplative smile. "I am, I am. And won't I love being an uppity Spic. Which is how she'll view it, of course."

"She sounds like an unpleasant person."

"Worse than that. I think she's a dangerous one."

Peter Yeates huddled behind the desk and watched with growing apprehension as the level of Scotch in Jasper Mendel's bottle continued to drop. The lanky scientist lounged in an armchair in the tiny lobby, and periodically his brown eyes would flick toward the stairs and the elevator. Though his body looked like an unhung scarecrow, there was nothing in his expression to echo that boneless slump. His eyes were glittering, and two dull spots of color were burning on each cheek.

The clatter of feet on the stairs brought Pete's head up like a startled gazelle, and Jasper sank even deeper in the chair, an anticipatory smile pulling at his lips.

"What we have here is a classic example of more being not enough. It's greed, pure and simple, that's motivating these people, and anyone who sets the accumulation of wealth as the sole object of their life is of necessity an uneducated class, inferior in intellect, and more or less cowardly. It is physically impossible for a well-educated intellectual or a brave man to make money the chief object of his thoughts."

Renfrew's voice had taken on that strident, forced quality it held whenever he was lecturing or haranguing, and he descended the steps like Napoleon going forth to inspect the troops. A step behind him was Padget MacKinley, his freckled, boyish face set in an expression of cool arrogance, and three paces behind him were the faithful followers. Twenty strong, they were all young and intense, and they gazed at the back of their leader's blond head with reverent awe. In the case of the women, this adoration was tinged with lust.

It brought to mind cult movements—the girls worshipful and horny, the men stalwart and strong-jawed, and the messiah busy dispensing wisdom to the flock. Jasper stretched, long and slow, like a cat moving out of a sunny corner, and took a long pull on his Scotch. Peter Yeates glanced from the scientist to the activists and back again, then surreptitiously switched on the com and picked up the tiny headset to insure privacy.

Jasper was on his feet and moving now, and when Renfrew reached the foot of the stairs, he found his way blocked. He looked up and up, then retreated back three steps so his eyes would be on a level with this tall, lanky, curly-haired man. Jasper gave his toothy grin and leaned nonchalantly on the banister. Every inch of his six-foot-four frame exuded contempt for the smaller man.

"If you're going to quote, you at least ought to give credit to the man who wrote it. John Ruskin was just as fuzzy-headed as you, but he deserves the credit—or the blame—for his stand."

"Who the hell are you?" gritted Renfrew.

"Hello, Jeanne, this is Pete Yeates over at the hotel."

"Peter, I can hardly hear you. Why are you whispering?"

"I have to. Is the Prophet there?"

Jeanne frowned and pushed back a strand of hair, remembering too late that she was still holding a dust cloth. No one in the colony referred to Darnell as Prophet unless it was in a formal meeting or there was trouble. So there had to be trouble.

"No, Pete, he's gone to the mine and won't be back for two days."

"Oh, sh . . . shoot." The innkeeper moaned, amending the curse word at the last moment.

"What's wrong?"

"Jasper's here and he's looking for blood."

"Those environmentalists?"

"They're all right here making a really awful tableau at the foot of my stairs."

"I'm on my way."

The silence of the apartment lay like a dusty curtain over her thoughts, and she realized that she didn't feel capable of handling this situation. She ran through possible allies: Darnell and Seth gone to the mine; Amadea at the site; Young and Coltrin were too emotional . . . *Huntington*. She dropped her cloth and went.

"Dr. Jasper Mendel."

Renfrew rocked back on his heels. "Ah, the man who wants to play God on a planetary scale."

"That's right. I figure God gave us an intellect so we could solve problems and better the human condition."

Renfrew's forefinger jutted out, jabbing Mendel in the chest. Yeates closed his eyes and muttered a quick prayer, but the scientist wasn't ready to blow quite yet. He, too, wanted a chance to lecture.

"But you're not helping mankind. You're destroying an entire planet for the benefit of a small group of users. This world should remain the property of the people of Earth. To endanger its magnificent vistas—" Renfrew voice was spiraling ever higher.

"Destroying? Destroying?" Jasper bellowed, cutting through the man's oration like a power saw through plywood. "Would you care to explain to me how terraforming a surface area of 144,202,000 kilometers and opening up vast new areas for colonization can possibly be viewed as destruction? You look surprised. Well, there was never any intention to keep the entire planet for the sole use of this colony. You should do your homework before you open your yap."

"And how would all these new colonists obtain land? Buy it?" Renfrew sneered.

"Damn straight. The Jared people deserve to make some money back, since they were willing to take the risk and make the initial investment of time, money, and work."

"That would limit it to the wealthy. The poor would never be able—"

"Oh, fuck me to tears! You don't give a damn about the poor. Yours is the most privileged minority in the history of the world. You're the fucking aristocratic status quo. You want nature preserved so you can go forth, 'leave no footprints,' get in tune with the spiritual animas of nature, and to hell with those struggling millions behind you on the economic scale for whom technological progress is the only hope. Your no-growth philosophy doesn't cut a lot of ice in Africa or South America, does it? Because those people know that their chance to rise above subsistence living depends upon production. It's damn easy for you to say 'Yep, we've got enough now. We don't need any more. Progress stops here.' You're so eager to condemn the rest of the world to pastoral self-sufficiency, but you just try living totally off the land. It's a damn precarious living at best, and all it takes is one bad season and people starve. That's what makes trade and surplus and all those other dirty words so nice. They really *do* free people. A shitload better than 'wild nature.'"

Renfrew had been stuttering like a machine gun, trying to stem the outraged flow of words from Jasper, but the scientist ranted on, touching every element he found so offensive in the POW position. It wasn't organized—in fact, it was almost incomprehensible, but his passion couldn't be doubted.

Nor could Renfrew's. Where Jasper's face had turned a dark brick-red, the activist's pinched features had lost all color, and he seemed like a figure carved from ice, terrifying in his very stillness.

"I loathe and despise you! You're technocratic arrogance personified. Nature and the cosmos are mysteries forever beyond our grasp and comprehension, but you and your kind would rush ahead blindly into the unknown without any idea of the risks you may be posing to life itself. What's going to happen when you slam that asteroid into the pole—"

"It's going to release a shitload of heat and free up a shitload of water." Jasper's tone was amused and condescending.

"But you don't *know* that. It's never been done before. Something unexpected and potentially dangerous might happen—"

Jasper made a rude noise. "Boogey stories to terrify timid children. The odds are it won't, and anyway, we can't be caged by those kind of considerations. It requires daring to find the answers to scientific questions, and thank God there are still some adventuresome souls left in this antiseptic, cotton-wrapped society of ours that are willing to take the risk. It'll be our salvation."

"Or our destruction!"

"It hasn't been yet, and there have been doomsayers around for some eight thousand years. And back to your idiotic argument. An uncaring cosmos has been throwing rocks and ice balls onto planets for some four billion years, so it *has* been done before."

"And it destroyed the dinosaurs," Lucius said petulantly.

"Yep, but we're not dinosaurs, and besides, you won't be here, anyway. If you're worried about your skin, get back to Earth before we start. We're not afraid to take the risk."

"I'm not afraid!"

"Yes you are; you're fucking terrified. You distrust human effort, and you have an ignorant and superstitious awe of nature. You're pathetic."

He shrugged contemptuously and turned to leave, and Yeates slumped on the desk, relieved and unbelieving that Jasper had actually walked away from a fight. His relief was short-lived, however, for Renfrew leapt down the final three steps and, grabbing Jasper by the shoulder, hauled him around.

"Pathetic! I'll show you how pathetic I am. I'm going to stop you and break you. You'll never terraform this planet."

"Doesn't that rather depend upon me?" came a low, cool voice from the door. Everyone froze, and Cab folded his arms across his chest and calmly regarded the assembly.

Jasper gave a crack of laughter. "All right, Judge!"

"Don't crow, Dr. Mendel. That also doesn't mean that I'm going to rule in your favor. What you people have to understand—all of you—is that I won't be stampeded. I'll hear the evidence and rule accordingly. And I'm not going to try this case in the lobby of a hotel, so in the interests of peace I suggest that we end this little exchange now."

Mendel shrugged. "Sure, fine by me now that I've set these people straight." A glob of spit landed with a wet splat between his feet, and he looked up slowly, his jaw tightening until it had the malliability of a granite outcropping. "You know, I've always thought that leaders ought to have to take responsibility for the actions of their followers," he said in a conversational tone, and as he spoke, his arm was swinging in a wide haymaker. If Renfrew had been paying attention, it would never have connected, but the environmentalist had glanced back toward MacKinley, and the fist struck his nose, quite solidly.

The smack of flesh on flesh echoed loudly, blood gushed from Renfrew's nose, and then the room exploded in a welter of arms and legs and bodies as twenty-two people jumped on Mendel's tall, lanky body.

Cab cursed and went plowing into the dustup. He hoped that Jeanne had the good sense to get out of the way, and a quick look proved that she had. With his peripheral vision he caught a glimpse of her diving over the desk, being caught by Yeates, and the both of them vanishing below the plastic barrier. He was relieved to know the older woman was out of the way but incredibly aggravated with the sad-faced innkeeper for leaving him to face this avalanche of bodies alone. Apparently Jeanne shared his contempt, for he heard her shout, "Get out there and help the judge!"

"Call the police, call the police," Cab yelled back, then gagged as an elbow took him in the gut.

Setting his teeth, he seized the woman and, with a mumbled apology to abused womanhood, threw her over his shoulder. For a moment he was startled with what ease he accomplished the move and by how far she went, then he remembered the one-third gravity. He had grown accustomed to it over the past weeks but hadn't truly understood the full ramifications until now. Several bodies parted momentarily, and he had a glimpse of Mendel grinning out from beneath his tangled hair like a maddened sheepdog pummeling POW activists with the greatest abandon. Obviously he was having the time of his life, and Cab consigned him to perdition and promised revenge.

Ten minutes later it was over. The small Jared police force arrived, the combatants who were still on their feet were separated to opposite sides of the demolished room, and the colony's two doctors were busy treating the groaning casualties. Cab leaned against the desk and dabbed at a bleeding lip with his handkerchief.

Jenny came flying in the door and caromed into him, hugging him tight. He winced, and she released her embrace.

Grabbing away the handkerchief, she began dabbing ferociously at the cut. It hurt and he could have handled it better, but he allowed her to continue.

"Are you all right? What happened? Why do I always miss all the action?"

"Like the way you missed the action during that riot on EnerSun? Rabbit-punching unfortunate young soldiers," he teased, catching her by the wrist.

She smiled, an expression born half of exasperation and half of laughter. "Point taken. Still, I wish I hadn't decided to go home just now. How did you get embroiled in all this?"

"Jeanne came flying into the office and told me Jasper was in one of his moods." He shook his head. "God, that man is a lunatic. All of this could have been avoided if he had kept his temper. Hell, it could have been avoided if he had stayed away from these people like everyone else has had the good sense to do."

"Brilliant but erratic," said Jeanne, joining them. "That's how he's been frequently described. And possessed of an incredibly short fuse."

"Justice Huntington," called the chief of police, a small, square woman who looked capable of hefting several times her own weight even under Earth's gravity. "What do you want done with these people?"

"Lock them up."

"All of them, sir?" she asked with a glance from Jeanne Hudson to Jasper Mendel, who grinned challengingly back at her.

"*All* of them," Cab repeated firmly. "I'll sort it out tomorrow—in court."

"We have a very small jail," Jeanne said mildly.

"Good."

"There are only two cells, and Jasper can't have one all to himself."

"Then lock him in a broom closet." The scientist grunted in surprise and his long face took on the look of an abused horse.

Chief Riley was chuckling now. "We do have a good-sized storeroom. I guess I can put him there."

"Fine."

"Hey, Jasper," she called, moving to him. "Maybe you can sort out the shelves. It's a jumble of paint and turpentine and God knows what else."

"Thanks," he muttered glumly, but he didn't resist when she gave him a light tap on the shoulder, but moved out obediently. "Hell, it can't be any worse than that jail in Ecuador."

The room emptied. Jeanne said something about needing to apprise Darnell of events and left, and Peter Yeates fumbled about the room, moaning over the damage.

"Why do things always have to get confusing?" Cab asked plaintively.

"It's just Murphy's Law of jurisprudence in the System," replied Jenny, dusting at his coat.

Chapter Eight

"I am very sorry, Señorita Varllis." The bland-faced secretary put an emphasis on the diminutive, which made her sound like an unruly twelve-year-old who was interfering with her elders. "But La Presidenta Rodriguez is in a cabinet meeting and cannot be disturbed."

"I represent the American government," replied Lis, her voice low and cold.

"No, señorita, you represent the White House bureaucracy. It is President Long who represents the American government." Although his expression remained polite, his elongated black eyes were narrowing into slits of amusement. He was enjoying following Amparo's instructions—she had said he could be rude if he wanted—and this wasn't being *too* rude. It was more in the nature of a gentle slap to the brittle, Anglo beauty on the screen. "Now, if President Long should wish to speak to Presidenta Rodriguez, I'm certain she could be interrupted—"

Lis cut off the transmission with a vicious jab of her manicured forefinger. A dull silence fell over the office, broken only by the faint sigh of warm air flowing quietly in through the floor grates. For a long moment she considered the concept of power, analyzing it, caressing it, holding it, hugging it. And once it was perfectly constructed and sitting gracefully in the center of her desk (or so her mind's eye perceived it), she decided the time had come to exercise it.

She flipped on the intercom. "Susan, get me General Vogel at SPACECOM." She switched off without waiting for an acknowledgment.

A few moments later there was a gentle chime, and Susan's low voice presented the general.

"Hey, Lis. What can I do for you?"

"More Martian troubles. I want to know if you can actually stop a ship."

"In flight?"

"Yes. En route from the asteroids to Mars."

"Theoretically, yes, but it's damn tough. There's a lot of real estate out there, and it's tough to pinpoint something as small as a ship."

"Well, don't they have to file a flight plan or something?"

"Yes, but the regulation is largely ignored. There are so few ships flying that the chances of a collision are astronomically slim. Also, a number of the smaller space-capable nations don't require it. And if the ship . . ." He paused, then added, "This wouldn't happen to have anything to do with that ship you wanted us to ground on Mars because of safety and licensing violations?"

"Yes, it would." She stared down at her hands and picked nervously at her cuticles. "But we can't touch them on Mars now because that bastard Joe Reichart has convinced Nicaragua to grant registry to the ship and to sign an entrance-and-importation agreement with the Jared Colony."

Vogel's eyes flicked from side to side, then finally focused back on the screen. "This makes me terribly uncomfortable. If this ship can't be touched on Mars, why should we be able to mess with it when it's in free flight? That's treading awfully close to an act of war."

"There is precedent for it under admiralty law."

"This is a friendly nation." Lis made a rude noise. "Well, we all pretend that, anyway." He sucked on the inside of his cheeks, then worried at his busy eyebrows with his thumbs. "Do you really want this?"

"Yes. It's important. Terribly important."

His eyes dropped before her implacable blue gaze, and he

sighed. "Will you at least start a public-opinion blitz, so if I *can* find a loophole, strain at a gnat, and put a camel through an needle's eye, we'll at least have public opinion on our side? I really will look like an asshole if I randomly start ordering the Air Force to capture trading vessels of friendly nations. It'll play hell with trade in the System, and we need their trade."

"Oh, bullshit, Harold! This ship no more belongs to a friendly national than my old granny. The ship has been licensed and registered in this country for fourteen years, and I'm damned if I'm going to let a bunch of scumbags in the asteroids thumb their noses at the American government. And incidentally, that blade cuts two ways—they need us too."

"You haven't ever been off-world, have you?"

"No."

"Then forgive me for correcting you, but I think that's an erroneous, and possibly dangerous, conclusion. It would be a brutal existence, but they can survive without us."

She bridled, her thin nostrils becoming even thinner at the rebuke, but Vogel faced her calmly, his craggy face with its crown of white hair looking very grandfatherly, and again she had the sensation of being treated like a rebellious child. She forced a smile.

"Thanks, Harold. I guess I was getting a little hot and bothered. It's just so frustrating, when you're trying to make decisions and set directions for an entire nation and her territories, to have a small group decide that their private interests are more important than the nation's as a whole."

He nodded. "No offense taken, and I hope none given. You'll be informing the President about this?"

"Oh, of course." *Not,* she added to herself. She had made all of these decisions by extrapolating from Rick's instruction to her to "handle it," and she knew that he might be a little squeamish over some of her methods. But that's what she was there for. She was his hatchet man.

"Okay, Lis. I'll be in touch."

"Good." She snapped off the com and leaned back in her chair, lacing her hands behind her head. The feel of the silky strands of hair against her palms felt good, and much of her nervousness and anger drained away. She was young, beautiful, powerful, and she had just outmaneuvered a consummate political player. She wrinkled her nose at the ceiling, sending a delicate but very derisive little raspberry up through the roof of the White House and out toward the distant asteroids. She would take this ship, and by God, those people out there would know they had been in a fight. They would think twice before challenging the might of the Earth authorities again.

The only thing left to be done was to set the proper tone with the American public. Hit on the idea of unfair trade practices with Earth and leave a lingering fear about the security of people's jobs. That would handle the grunt workers, and for the more intellectual . . . ? Hint about irreplaceable natural treasures about to be lost through the dirty agency of human greed? Yes, that should do nicely. She leaned forward to call the press secretary, then decided that she didn't fully trust Susan out in the front office. The girl had the look of someone on the climb, and she sure as hell wasn't going to climb on Lis's back. Better to just go over to Fred Downs's office and arrange things there. Always keep the left hand guessing about what the right one was up to.

SYSTEM PRACTICES THREATENS JOBS.

Cab was so outraged and disturbed by the headline that he didn't bother to print out the paper, as was his usual practice. Instead he set the screen to scrolling and began reading through the article, his eyes flicking from line to line, and with each passing word his perturbation grew. He finished and leaned moodily back in his chair, his fingers worrying at his sideburns.

Might as well have used the word greed *in the headline instead of that wishy-washy* practices. *And I might have known Joe would be in the thick of it.* He glared at the sentence containing the entrepreneur's name.

"Jenny!"

She stuck her head in the door. "You bellowed?"

He frowned at her but didn't remonstrate. Rather he spun the screen around, offering her a clear view of the offending article.

She read, then lifted her eyes to his. "Why is it that we are always perceived in the press as being on the side of the devils?"

"Probably because a more ignorant bunch of sheep has yet to inhabit the planet," Cab replied testily. He pressed his lips together to silence any more outbursts. "Jenny, several weeks ago you speculated that all these woes that are besetting the Jared colonists might be related. We discounted the idea as being too farfetched, but now. . ." He gestured toward the quietly glowing screen. "There is a pattern. It has to be deliberate."

She settled onto the edge of his desk. "Now, for the million-dollar question: Why? What are the colonists doing that's so upsetting on Earth?"

The chair squeaked as he leaned back, closed his eyes, and began beating out a nervous tattoo on the arms with his fingers. "They're going to attempt to terraform the planet." He shook his head, a quick, dismissive gesture. "But that's centuries away, and I've never known a politician yet who thinks beyond the next election."

"They export nothing—"

Cab came forward in the chair and gripped her knee. "Wait, you hit on it weeks ago."

And they said in chorus, "The diamonds!"

Cab made a face. "But it still doesn't tell us who the shadow players are. Who's manipulating the agencies and the press? There hasn't been a peep out of Long over any of this." He rose and took a quick turn about the office. "Jenny, I can't do this—and you probably shouldn't—but if you're subtle, maybe we can get away with it. Talk to Darnell, urge him to file suit under the Administrative Procedures Act, requesting judicial review of the various agencies' actions."

"Grounds?"

"The only ones that apply; arbitrary and capricious behavior, and tell them to throw in § 706 (2) (D) (E) and (F)."

Reaching out, she caught his hand and pulled him to her. Resting her forehead against his, she said, "Cab, I love you."

The blood rose in his cheeks and he looked away. "Well, thank you, but I think there are going to be a number of people Earthside who won't."

"May I make an additional suggestion?"

"Certainly."

"I think we need a journalist of our own. Someone on our side to present the colonists' position and to show this maze of interference."

"Who . . . ?" he began.

"I'm going to send for Andy."

"This is a little beyond his beat. By about a million miles."

"More, actually, but I don't think Andy will mind."

"All right, call him." He reached for the com. "And meanwhile I have a call to make too."

"To whom?"

"Joe. I want to make sure he doesn't have any more little surprises waiting for me. Especially since his 'little' surprises usually make me feel like I've been blown off a mountain of dynamite that I didn't even know I was sitting on."

She hopped off the desk and shook down her pant legs. "I'll go call Andy, and he'll no doubt suggest that we open a brothel on Mars, or God only knows what else."

"Just so you don't agree to work in it," Cab replied absently, searching through his desk for Joe's private code.

"Only if I get to be the madam." But he was so preoccupied that he didn't even respond.

Joe had given him his code in the asteroids so he could be reached in case of an emergency, something Cab hadn't (naively, he realized now) thought would happen.

The wrinkles about Joe's brown eyes were crinkling with pleasure, but Cab didn't give him a chance to speak. "Joseph, would you care to tell me why you're beating on a hornet's nest with a stick while I'm seated on the ground beneath it trying to have a picnic?"

Reichart's smiled deepened. "Who ever told you life was going to be a picnic?"

"All right, admitted, but why do you have to keep things in such a constant uproar?" He waved his hands across each other in a negating gesture. "Forget I asked that. They made the mistake of poking you first, and you're responding in your own inimical style."

"I'm sorry, Cab. I realized that I should have talked to you and told you what was going on, but I was dealing with the colonists, and frankly—" He broke off.

"You just forgot about me, right?"

"Well, yes. But in my own defense let me say that it's because I didn't think you were going to be a major player this time around. I assumed you would hear your cases, deal fairly with us, and move on."

"It isn't exactly working out that way, and it's a damn uncomfortable position for me to be in."

"You could always deal yourself out. Get sick, retire, resign . . ."

Outrage and dismay coiled through him and came to rest like a bad taste on the back of his tongue as he considered what might happen and who might take over if he left. "Jesus Christ, Joe! Think what you're saying. They'd replace me with some rubber stamp, and then where would you all be? Thank you, no. I'll take care of my people and my district."

Shoulders shaking, Reichart turned away from the screen, recovered himself, then turned back. "Bless you, Cabot, you're becoming one of us. And don't look so horrified at the prospect."

"Not horrified—terrified. I don't know if I want this. My home . . ." He brushed at the air as if shooing away a cloud of biting insects. "I'm sorry, I'm babbling." He sucked in a deep breath and squared his shoulders. "You will keep me informed before you take any more of these Byzantine actions?"

"Yes. And there's something you can do for me."

"Oh?"

"There's a leak—a big one—on Mars. We need to plug it. So if you could kindly keep your ear to the ground . . ."

"Joe, I'm not comfortable with that. It comes perilously close to spying."

"Meaning that it's all right for the thugs on Earth to spy but not you? What, you're too pure?"

"I want to remain impartial."

"You don't have that luxury, not in the current situation. And I'm not even sure it's possible. When you don that black robe, you don't become a thinking machine. It wouldn't be right if you did. We've kept judges and juries rather than replacing them with computers because of the human qualities—mercy, judgment, understanding—they possess and bring to the administration of justice."

Cab leaned back in his chair and applauded. "Wonderful, stirring, correct as far as it goes, but an oversimplification. You'd be the first to scream if a judge betrayed that kind of bias in a case in which you were a party. What about the evidence, keeping an open mind, setting aside personal motives and biases, and ruling based on the evidence? Doesn't that count for something?"

"Yes, but when the other side's not playing fair, you'd better be prepared to set aside some of your cherished ideals."

"I am aware that there are strange shenanigans going on within the government agencies, but at this time I have no evidence that it extends to the POW case. I suspect it," he hastened to add. "But proof . . . ?" Cab shrugged.

"I wish you could see your way clear to back us."

"I *do*, but aside from the ethics I feel I owe to my position, there's the very real fact that if I start announcing to the world that I'm totally on the side of the colonists, I'll be yanked back to Earth, and you'll be saddled with some political hack that you'll have to retrain. And so help me God, if you say one word about how you've *already* retrained one political hack, I'll come to the asteroids and personally pull off all your arms and legs." The final words were punctuated with small spurts of laughter that wove a counterpoint to Reichart's deeper basso chuckles.

"Oh, no, Cab, I'd never say that, for although you were a hack, at least you weren't a stupid one."

"Thank you so much." He sighed. "All right, you've sufficiently reminded me that I am on your side. I'll do what I can to look for your leak, but I don't think I'm very good at this sort of thing. If it's right under my nose, I might stumble over it, but—"

"Stumbling with your nose—what an interesting metaphor. I must remember that. Isn't it rather painful?"

A tide of warmth flooded his cheeks, but he found enough grit beneath the embarrassment to reply. "Not as painful as a conversation with you. Good-bye, Joe. Please don't blow up the Solar System without telling me first."

"I'll try to see that you get some notice."

Reichart's grinning image faded from the screen, rather like a Cheshire cat returning to its own private pocket universe, and Cab tapped thoughtfully on the blank screen with a forefinger.

Jenny stuck her head into the office. "Mission accomplished. Our tame journalist is on his way. He bitched and moaned but he's coming."

"Did he proposition you?"

"Not this time. He's off brothels and call services and onto a new scheme. Selling Saturn-ring ice back on Earth. He's seems to think it would be the perfect gift for the person who has everything, and what a topic for cocktail conversation as you casually drop a chunk of extraterrestrial ice in someone's Scotch and soda."

"Did you spend all your time on this fascinating topic, or did you find a moment to tell him why we need him?"

"I found a moment, and that's when he stopped bitching and went off to pack."

"Pack? Andy packs? I thought he just shoved a fifth of bourbon and a change of underwear into a paper sack."

"A paper sack with a grease stain on the bottom," embellished Jenny, advancing into the room.

"And a dull razor so he can maintain his five-o'clock shadow."

She settled into his lap. "And an eggbeater to comb his hair."

He pressed his forehead against hers. "We're being very silly."

"Yes. Very poor form for a couple of professionals."

"We have a workmen's comp case to hear this afternoon. I think we ought to get back to work."

"Blah. Must we? Those damn federal regs are a bitch. Jenny, don't be vulgar," she quickly added in a tolerable imitation of his disapproving tone. "All right, Cabot. I'll be a good girl," she fluted, and folding her hands in her lap, she primly screwed up her mouth and looked heavenward.

He slipped his arms about her waist. "You're a dreadful woman and you ought to be spanked."

"Sounds great to me," she murmured. Her eyes were sultry green pools.

"Jenny, don't be lewd," they said in chorus.

Lis looked up, irritated at the interruption, but the look on Vogel's face, rather like that of a panicked cow, made her set aside her anger.

"What?"

"Rager's gotten wind of our plans to stop that ship, and he's going to call the President."

The woman's lips compressed into a thin line at the mention of the newly appointed chairman of the Joint Chiefs of Staff. Rager was one of the toughest and most brilliant men ever to be spit out of West Point, but he had also been a major pain in the ass to his superiors and to politicians alike. Although a career military man, he had a disconcerting habit of considering the rights of other sovereign nations, actively working for greater civilian control over the military, and scrutinizing every American overseas involvement under the powerful magnifying glass of his own sense of honor and ethics. Long had appointed him to the Joint Chiefs because he admired Rager's maverick ways. Lis had opposed the decision. It was one of the few times she had been unable to sway her boss, and she now sensed that her misgivings were going to prove to be correct.

"Jesus Christ. I don't want the President bothered with this."

"Then you'd better get to Rager first. He's on the warpath."

She didn't ask for an elaboration, but punched in the code for the Pentagon. As she sat waiting for her call to route through, she realized she was gnawing nervously on a cuticle, and she slapped her hand away from her mouth. It was a disgusting habit, and it made her look uncertain.

The screen flickered and stabilized on the chisled ebony features of General Isaiah Rager. Studying the implacable face, Lis abandoned the idea of a soft, cooing approach.

"Just what the hell do you think you're doing running to the President over a trivial matter like this Belter ship?" she spat.

"And just what the hell do you think you're doing? Trying to promote us into a ground war with an ally in Central America!" retorted the general.

"G-ground war?" she faltered.

"If the United States government is going to indulge in space piracy, that's exactly what we're going to get. President Rodriguez can't, and won't, sit still for that, and every other space-capable nation is going to wonder how long until we decide to attack them because they're carrying cargo that we don't like."

"This is a special circumstance. We're disciplining American territorial citizens."

"What, the Martians? Nobody's going to buy that bullshit! This is a registered Nicaraguan vessel."

"You know damn good and well that under international law capital ships can board sovereign ships of another nation if they suspect the ship is carrying contraband."

"Mining equipment? Mining equipment as contraband? Lady, that's a hell of a ploy."

"It's no worse than what they're doing. This is an American ship."

"I don't care what you call it. The fact remains that it's a hornet's nest. The Air Force is more than willing to go along with this crazy scheme because they've just been itching to do something with their fancy new space squadron. Then there's the little problem of interservice rivalry. You'd better add that into your equation. The Navy is still pissed over losing out to the Air Force in space, and if the fly-boys are going to get to tango, they're going to want to too. Mitchell is already pulling up maps of the Nicaraguan coast and dreaming of engagements with an enemy fleet. Fleet, hell! A few outdated gunboats and a cruiser or two. Well, maybe they can blow up some fishing vessels so Mitchell can feel like Lord Nelson."

"I am not about to start a full-scale engagement with Nicaragua. We're talking about one ship—"

"And how about the lure of congressional appropriations," Rager continued, as if Lis had never spoken. Pain was shooting up behind her ears from the tension of her clenched jaw as she fought to control her anger over the man's lecturing, scornful tone. "The old saying used to be: 'No guts, no glory.' Now it's 'No guts, no money.' The Navy's losing out to the Air Force, and they'll see a glorious little war in Central America as a way to recoup their position. My officers may be itching for a dustup, too, but as long as I command the Army, it ain't gonna happen. That's one voice for sanity, anyway."

"This is utterly preposterous! The scenario you're outlining is absurd, and Rodriquez is not such a fool as to make an issue over one ship that doesn't even belong to her. She's not about to challenge the United States."

"And if she swings the Pan American League behind her? Our efforts at economic imperialism and political interference haven't cowed all of them yet, and it sure as hell hasn't made us very popular in South and Central America. They'd just love a chance to pull our noses. And then there's world opinion. Remember world opinion? You know how sensitive the President is to world opinion."

She bit at her lip, her eyes shifting away from the screen.

"No, Madame Machiavelli, if you want to flex your political muscles at the expense of the Martian colonists, you'd better flex them to the fullest. Come up with some bullshit reason why Nicaragua"—his voice was thick with scorn—

"represents an awesome threat to the military and economic security of the United States and send in the troops. Of course, I'm going to be fighting you every inch of the way, and I'm going to start by calling the President. So though you may have delayed me by a few minutes—"

"All right, damn you! I'll drop it."

"Good girl."

"And if you ever take that tone with me or call me that again, you fucker, I'll break you!" She was on her feet, shouting.

"Like you're going to break the Nicaraguans and the Mars colonists? I'm not impressed. You've got three hours. At the end of that time I want to know that you've called off the space cadets and done some fence-mending with President Rodriguez. If not . . ." He gave an eloquent shrug.

She answered with a vicious stab that broke the connection and also broke her nail down to the quick. She sucked at the tiny well of blood, then folded her hands in her lap and stared at the far wall. For a long time she remained quiet and motionless . . . considering.

She had never seen any of the people on Mars, or the pilot who flew that ship, or the Belters who had supplied the equipment, but Joe Reichart she knew. Not personally but by reputation, and he became the focus of the bitter pantomime that played in her mind. His face loomed up before her like a grinning figure from a jack-in-the-box, and behind him danced and capered a chorus of faceless people, all laughing and pointing.

She was trembling, but she forced it down and reached deliberately for the hand-blown paperweight that glowed like a sapphire jewel on her desk. For a moment she caressed its smooth shape and considered the beauty of its swirling, luminescent heart, then launched it at the picture on the far wall. It struck with a violent crack, and a spiderweb of fine lines went radiating out from the frosted impact point. There was an instant of breathless silence, then the glass let go with a sound like a crystalline waterfall.

Rising, she crossed to the glittering pile and picked up the paperweight. It, too, was cracked and frosted. The door opened, and Susan, her eyes and mouth wide with concern, rushed in. Lis held out the ruined paperweight to her and said,

"Sometimes, Susan, you have to destroy a thing in order to save it."

"Yes, ma'am." She was edging back toward the door.

"Oh, and by the way. You're fired."

Lucius Renfrew snuffed out the cigarette with quick, nervous jabs and immediately lit another. The ashtray on the bedside table was littered with half-smoked cigarettes, and a blue haze filled the tiny hotel room. It was very late, and he knew he ought to be sleeping, but anger kept his mind churning in endless circles and refused to allow him to relax. He knuckled at his eyes, and an enormous yawn came billowing up. Before he could suppress it, his mouth gaped open and his injured jaw sent a stab of pain up through the top of his head. He yelped, cupped his face, and, swinging his legs off the bed, sat abruptly upright.

He cursed long and fluently, wondering why he continued to hurt this long after the fight. Maybe he had been more seriously injured than that quack of a Mormon doctor had said. Finally the last twinge had subsided, and he took a long drag on the cigarette. It was small comfort, but the knowledge that Mendel had come out of the fracas with a broken rib and a cracked wrist made him feel a bit better. Comforting, too, was the fact that Padget was preparing a civil suit for assault and battery, and by God, they were going to take that lunatic for every cent he had.

Folding his arms behind his head, he lay back among the pillows and considered the day's excursion to Olympus Mons. As he had stood on the summit of this mightiest of volcanoes, he had vowed again that it would not be lost to man's heedless pursuit of profit and development. Some things needed to be kept as a treasure house for future generations, and Mars was one of them.

If only Mars had proved to contain some native microbes, he thought sadly but with a tinge of irritation. They could have used the endangered species statutes, and that would have provided them with additional grounds upon which to challenge the terraforming project. And God knows they needed additional grounds. Padget had been pessimistic about their chances of prevailing over the Mormon colonists—particularly since Huntington would hear the case—but they had decided to go ahead. The issue was too important to stand back and wait. They had to take a stand here or see the rest of the Solar System raped and exploited.

His mother, a senior president of the First National Bank of California, had been a great outdoorswoman, and they had spent most of their weekends in the Sierra Nevadas. He could still remember how at a young age he had resented the presence of all those other people. He and his mother had backpacked through the wilderness, carrying their own food, using portable solar-cell camp stoves so they needn't cut wood, trying to blend with nature. And then there were the others. Getting back to nature with their palatial recreational vehicles. Ruining the silence and frozen purity of a winter's day with their snowmobiles. Interfering with their silent communion.

He had drifted through five years at Stanford, never quite managing to put together a coherent package of hours to produce a degree, but it hadn't mattered. After dropping out of school he had joined Friends of the Earth, and his flair for media manipulation and strident leadership had earned him a place among their officers. For seven years he had worked with the organization but broken with them over their accommodating stand on continued genetic experimentation. After a five-year study they had concluded that though some risks did exist, the benefits far outweighed the as yet undetermined dangers, and they dropped their opposition.

Lucius had been outraged and, leading a more militant minority, had broken off to form his own group. His mother's money, prestige, and backing had eased them over the first few years, and since then they had done nothing but grow. Now they were faced with their greatest challenge, and it was up to him to lead them to a successful conclusion.

"In the courts or on the streets," he muttered, and pleased with the phrase, he hurried to his lap-sized processor and entered it.

As he reflected on the words he thought wistfully of earlier times and wished he might have been one of those pioneers of the movement. Standing with Theodore Roosevelt in the early, giddy days when they first began to carve out a kingdom for nature. Or in the urgent 1960s or '70s when they had challenged governments and corporations and made them realize that *they,* the gentle people, were speaking for an entire planet. The movement had almost convinced the people of the industrial First World that there were limits to growth. Of course, the developing nations had hated it. They accused the West of attempting genocide, which was, of course, ridiculous. Of course, he abhorred hunger and need, but the way to solve it was by less, not more. The people of the Third World had been blinded by the false gods of production and consumption. A return to simpler, pastoral values would benefit all mankind. But then had come the explosion of space entrepreneurs, and the world had once more begun its headlong rush toward consumption, production, exploitation.

If only they would realize that only through denial and limitation do we learn wisdom.

He liked that one, too, and began tapping it into the machine when he was interrupted by the com. Frowning, murmuring the phrase over and over so as not to lose it, he crossed to the dresser and activated the screen.

"Dear God, you look like hell," said Lis, dispensing with any sort of formal greeting. "Who's been practicing tap dancing on your face?"

Surprise over her call and the rudeness of her opening remark drove his gem from his mind. Irritation made his reply equally sharp. "What do you want?"

"You know about the Belter ship?"

"I read."

"Oh, good," she purred. "I was afraid that might be one of those outdated skills that you've decided humanity could do without."

"Look, Ms. Varllis, I'm not interested in playing doormat to your bad mood. That crazy asshole, Mendel, came over to the hotel a few days ago and precipitated a fight. My people and I were going about our own business when he made rude and ugly remarks to us and, without any provocation, struck me!" His tenor voice was winding up into that shrill range he always got when he was angry. "But I'm not going to stand by for this. We have our rights, and I'm going to take him for every—"

"I'm not interested in your problems, Renfrew. Believe it or not, the fact that someone hit you in the nose is not major news. Life will go on, the cosmos will continue marching toward entropy—"

"Fuck you!" he forced from between stiff lips.

Lis stopped, raised a hand to cover her eyes, and when it dropped, she was back in control. "Excuse me. I've had a rather trying few days. Not to diminish your pain and suffering, but I've got some pretty major problems." And in a few quick words she outlined the situation of the Belter ship being careful not to overplay the diamonds, and their effect on the marketplace, but rather to stress the mining equipment and its effect on Mars.

"So you see, they're very busy trying to take advantage of this delay, before your case is heard, to strip a few more milions out of the ground to finance their terraforming project."

"I thought OSHA had closed them down."

"People who would resort to this kind of lawless action are not likely to be deterred by an OSHA ruling. They'll rip down that mountain to get at those diamonds."

"There's not going to be a terraforming project after the hearing."

"We hope. I assume that if the decision goes against you, you'll appeal?"

"Naturally."

She spread her hands expressively. "And there's more time for them to continue operations."

"We'll ask for an injunction."

She squeezed the bridge of her nose, looking weary. "Forgive me, but I don't think these people play fair. Look what they pulled over on the registration of this ship. They'll probably just ignore any injunction."

"So what are you suggesting?"

"I don't know." The tone was mournful, a wounded dove. "Maybe there's some way to keep that equipment from ever being unloaded. If the decision should go against us, of course."

"What are my assurances if my people and I take action?"

"Oh, no assurances. But you will know that you have a friend in the White House."

"That's good enough," he concluded grimly.

Chapter Nine

Cab flipped back to an earlier section of the agency report, and the whisper of the turning pages was loud in the silent apartment. He had always thought of himself as a loner, enjoying his times of solitude, but now the silence was oppressive and he realized that the months spent with Jenny had left their mark. He missed her and wished he had gone with her to Eagle Port.

Loneliness lapped at him like silent waters, and he shivered with a premonition of death. Born alone, live alone, and die alone . . .

And he was halfway there.

The thought was unnerving, and he bolted from the kitchen table, selected a tape, and soon the opening clarinet glissando of Gershwin's *Rhapsody in Blue* went coiling through the room. He returned to his work.

Nothing, he mused, and he flipped forward and backward through the reports. No sign of an employee complaint to precipitate OSHA's intervention in the mine. No explanation for SPACECOM's embargo of the diamonds. A feeble one for holding the equipment, but . . . His thoughts went ratcheting along, examining each action of the various agencies.

He shouldn't have been wasting time with this search. He had real work to do, but curiosity and a powerful sense of outraged territoriality had combined to push him into this investigation.

Since the 1960s there had been a growing tension between the judiciary and the regulators. Laws could be questioned and challenged by disgruntled citizens, but there was no relief from the faceless regulators. Armies of bureaucrats had carved out empires and passed regulations that carried the weight of law but were virtually unchallengable through the traditional court system. Further, these regulations had never been introduced, debated, reviewed, and passed by any elected representative body. It was ironic that America had fought a revolution over exactly that issue, yet now the public was tamely accepting laws that weren't laws, passed by men and women who had never been elected and could not be held accountable. And it permeated every aspect of American life.

We have such a negative view of people, thought Cab as he put on the teakettle to boil. *We think people won't be good unless we make them. So we set up institutions to govern them. And who runs the institutions? People—who are presumably just as weak and venal as the masses they're called upon to govern. Maybe Joe's right. Maybe it is enough to simply keep people from actively aggressing against each other and leave the rest to personal choice and a powerful court system to settle disputes between parties.*

He remembered one of his fights with Lydia when he had been on the EnerSun station. He had thrown up the example of the robber barons of the nineteenth century as an argument for why the colonial system of gentle anarchy couldn't possibly work. She had looked at him pityingly and told him to go back and read his history. *"First, that wasn't true capitalism, nor was it a free market economy. The federal government was busy helping the large companies stamp out competition and break the workers. Out here, if someone doesn't play nice, we don't deal with them, and we can't be coerced into dealing with them. They get run out of the marketplace real fast."*

Gershwin ended with a bang, and Cab replaced the tape with Rachmaninoff and forced himself back to work. He began drawing fanciful doodles in the margin of the printout while he tried to plan a way to put the agencies on notice that he was not going to stand by, waiting for their arbitrary actions. Fragments of ideas floated past, but he was distracted by images of Jenny. Had she reached Eagle Port yet? Had Andy arrived? When would they return?

There was a knock and he hurried to the door, grateful for the interruption. Amadea was in the hall and she was weeping. For an instant he was seized with the terror that afflicts all men when they're faced with a woman in tears, but chivalry won out over cowardice. Wrapping an arm about her shoulders, he coaxed her into the apartment and seated her on the bed. Offering his handkerchief, he knelt before her and began to chafe her slender fingers.

Her cheeks were blotchy, the tip of her nose red, and her eyes puffy and streaming. Even in the midst of his concern he noticed these signs of humanity and was grateful for them. Until now she had seemed too perfect to be real—Kuan Yin walking among mortals. The fact that she looked ugly when she cried was reassuring.

Well, not precisely ugly, he amended as his fingers stroked her hot, wet cheeks. More— his thoughts cut off, replaced by a head-ringing anger as he noticed the bruise beginning to form high on her left cheek.

"Who did this?" She shrank back as if frightened by his intensity, and he softened his tone. "Amadea, if somebody hurt you, you must tell me."

She shook her head, the black hair falling forward to shroud her face. "I ran into a door." The words were scarcely audible.

Cab caught her chin, gently forcing her head up to face him. "Don't give me that. You didn't come to my apartment in tears so I could beat the hell out of a *door*."

He had half risen, but her frenzied hands pulled him back down. "No, no, that will only make it worse than it already is. Let it go. Jeanne will handle him—"

"Him! Mendel, right? It's Mendel who hit you!"

"Yes, but he's very upset."

"That is no excuse to strike a woman!" He was on his feet now, raging about the tiny room.

"He thinks I'm a spy."

"Utter nonsense!"

"But someone is leaking information to Earth, and I'm the only outsider," she said mournfully. "If only I could think of some way to clear myself. I'd never harm these people. They're my friends."

"And if they have any brains, they know that. Jeanne hasn't gone along with this nonsense, has she?"

"Oh, no. She threw Jasper out of the apartment, but while she was yelling at him I ran." She gave him a tremulous smile. "Straight to you. Isn't that silly? I hope I haven't embarrassed you or put you on the spot." Her eyes slid nervously about the apartment.

"Jenny's gone to Eagle Port to collect our friend Andy Throckmorton," he explained awkwardly.

Amadea's head drooped forward as if its weight were almost too much for her slender neck. Cab quickly seated himself on the bed and pulled her head onto his shoulder.

She sighed. "I'm not a snitch. Honestly, Cabot. I wouldn't betray these people for the world. They're my friends. But Jasper was right when he pointed out that every time I come to visit, some bit of information gets back to Earth. It does look pretty damning."

"Only to an idiot," he growled.

"I don't even know anyone on Earth. Well, not in any positions of power. Just some old schoolmates, and I keep in touch only sporadically. Christmas-card sort of stuff. My life is out here. All my friends are here. The only people I talk to are my coworkers or other System dwellers. No grounder could ever understand the things that matter to us. Why, only the other day I was telling Jillian—"

The words died in her throat, and she pressed a hand to her mouth. She was so white that Cab feared she was about to faint, and he sprinted to the kitchen for some brandy. The liquor seemed to revive her, and a bit of color returned to her ashen cheeks.

"Cabot, maybe I *am* the leak." She pressed icy fingers to his lips to forestall any remark. "No, no, hear me out. Not intentionally, of course, but I tend to be a real chatterbox. Mother and Joe always used to tease me about it. When I'm comfortable with people, I just run on and on, and I've been talking back at the site."

"That project head of yours . . ." He snapped his fingers to recall the name. "Dave? You said something about—"

"How he's been making these sudden and unnecessary trips to Eagle Port."

"But you wouldn't talk in front of him, knowing how hostile he is to the project."

"Not in front of him, maybe, but you know how cramped our facilities are. You can hear anything from the galley, and that's where we tend to gather."

He chewed at his lower lip, considering. "So you think he's been eavesdropping and passing everything along to Earth." He rose, tugging urgently at her hand. "Come on, let's get right over to the Hudsons' and tell them that we've solved the mystery."

But she didn't move. Instead, she huddled closer to the bed like some small, frightened woodland animal. "I can't," she whispered. "How can I face them? They were right. I *am* the source of the trouble."

He sat back down, shaking his head. "But you're blameless. You didn't intentionally spy on them. They're reasonable people—or at least Jeanne is. They'll understand."

"I can't, I can't."

She was crying again, her hair flying about her face with each anguished shake of her head. A few silken strands caught on her wet cheeks, and he gently pulled them free. Her arms went about his waist, and she clung like an infant monkey. Her tiny form shook with the violence of her sobs, and Cab gathered her close. Later he could never quite recall how it had happened. He had been resting his cheek on the top of her head and stroking her hair when suddenly her mouth was raised to his and their lips met.

He had intended it to be a comforting brotherly kiss, a quick peck. But when her mouth opened beneath his and her tongue darted out to lick at his lips, he lost control. His tongue drove deep into her mouth, sucking in the taste of her. Her fingers moved quickly, pulling open his shirt, loosening his belt, and opening his fly. He was already at attention, his penis straining at the material of his jockey shorts. She pulled him free and rolled it between her hands. He groaned and reached for her, but she evaded his clutching hands.

He sat gasping while she languidly stripped off her pearl-gray and maroon jump suit and boots. Beneath it she wore only the briefest of lace panties. She arched her back, stretching her arms out to him, and the movement lifted her tiny bosoms, the dainty pink nipples already crinkled and erect with desire, and tightened the muscles in her flanks and belly.

He struggled out of his clothes and crossed to her, sliding his hands down her rib cage, over the swell of her hips. He snagged the panties and pulled them down while his lips traced a line from her breastbone to her navel. The wiry brush of her mons against his mouth brought a dryness to his throat and an ache to his pelvis. He knelt before her, bringing the briefs to her ankles. She stepped gracefully out of them, and he flung them aside.

He was shivering now, beginning to lose some of his rigidity as doubt and guilt began to intrude. She seemed to sense his distress and, taking him by the hand, led him to the bed. She pushed him down and, kneeling between his legs, began to pleasure him. Her lips played across his eyes and mouth and paused at his ears where her tongue darted in and out of the channel, sending an answering twinge to his belly. Down the chest, paying careful attention to nipples and navel. She rocked back and eyed his cock (where it lay limply across his thigh.) With a siren's smile she cupped it in her hands, rolling it back and forth like an artist working clay. He began to stiffen again. She lowered her head, her hair tickling across his belly and thighs, and ran her tongue up the length of his phallus, pausing to flick at the moist head.

He groaned—small, explosive sounds that were pulled from him with each breath—and all thoughts of Jenny were driven away in the white-hot flow of his passion. With a sound partway between a cough and a growl, he sat up, caught her by the shoulders, and forced her down on·the bed next to him. From a teasing tigress, she suddenly became a yielding doll, as soft and shy as any virgin.

He alternated between her thighs, dropping quick, nipping kisses onto the white skin, moving ever closer to her cunt. At last he was there, and he used his tongue to bring her to a fever pitch. Her small cries excited and gratified him. This beautiful girl had come to *him,* seduced *him*. Suddenly he could hold back no longer. He slid up the sweat-slick length of her and entered, gasping as her muscles tightened about him.

Once more she changed; transformed from deerlike innocence to a raging houri whose nails clawed at his back and whose hands gripped at his buttocks to aid him in his efforts. Her lips played across his throat, kissing, licking, and biting, all the while keeping up a running murmur of encouragement.

The blood pounded in his ears as his feet scrabbled for

purchase on the sheets, and he pumped frantically, trying to meet her frenzied demands. The pinnacle was approaching, and he felt stronger and more virile than he had ever felt in his life. He clutched at her shoulders and ejaculated in a burning flow that left him lying limp and exhausted across her breast.

For a long time he lay silent, listening to the gradually slowing rhythms of their hearts, and there seemed to be something profound in the way they matched one another; beating out a languid message of repletion.

"Cabot," she murmured softly, her hands running through his hair. "That was quite wonderful." He mumbled something, embarrassed by the light in her strange green eyes. "You're very exciting. There's an aura of power about you that I've never felt from any other man."

"Now that's flattery. You grew up around Joe Reichart."

"But Joe doesn't wear the mantle of his authority as gracefully as you do. You command without competing. You were born to it." She snuggled close, running her hand across his chest. "I suppose I'm jealous and I want to share *it*—whatever *it* is." Her eyes were sparkling mischievously when she looked up at him. "Do think it rubs off with prolonged bodily contact?"

Chuckling, he shook his head. "No, I don't think so."

"Can we continue to test out the theory?"

"Yes, but first I have to work out—"

"No." Her fingers pressed against his lips. "Don't do anything yet. Let's take it one day at a time, okay?" She smiled sadly. "You might get tired of me."

"Never." He gathered her close.

She gave a little spurt of laughter. "Well, this wasn't exactly what I had in mind when I came to you for comfort."

"Will it do?"

"Oh, yes."

He bounded off the bed. "Which reminds me. We really must let people know."

"I can't face Jasper."

"I'll be right beside you. Doesn't that make a difference?"

"Yes, but he'll think I'm so stupid."

"What do you care what that man thinks? He may be a brilliant scientist, but I think he needs a refresher course in how to be a human being." He rubbed the back of his hand gently against her cheek. "Any man who would strike a woman . . ." His lips compressed into a thin line.

"That's terribly old-fashioned and probably a bit chauvinistic of you."

"Whatever." He padded about, gathering up his scattered clothes.

Wrapping her arms about her knees, she watched him for a few seconds, then said, "You're really going to make me do this, aren't you?"

"Yes." He stood over her, studying the perfect oval of her face. "And if Mendel makes one remark, I'm going to knock him down."

"He's very big, and an accomplished barroom brawler."

"Nonetheless, I'll knock him down." Cupping her chin in his hand, he kissed her long and slow. "You've made me invincible."

She rose and started to dress. "You're talking like a man who was doubting himself."

"An hour ago I was reflecting on how half my life was gone. Now I'm thinking about how I have half my life to live."

She picked up the discarded jump suit, then paused at the table and flipped through the reams of printout. "What's all this?"

"I've been going over a record of the agency decisions relating to the Jared Colony. It indicates a clear pattern of harassment, and I'm going to do something about it."

"How? You can't pull things into your court, can you?"

"No, but Jenny's going to drop a word in Darnell's ear about bringing suit."

Dropping her clothes over the back of the chair, she lifted the sheaf of papers and fanned through it. "Cab, maybe there's a good reason for stopping the mining and the diamonds. The government may know things that we don't."

He laughed, removed the papers, and hugged her close. "That doesn't sound much like the daughter of that famous System firebrand, Lydia Kim Nu."

She jerked free, and he took a step back from the blazing anger in her green eyes. "That's because I'm *not* my mother!"

"Excuse me. I didn't mean to insult you."

A hand slipped down his cheek, and she peeped contritely

up at him from beneath the veil of her long lashes. "And I didn't mean to be such a witch. Forgive me?"

"Of course."

"You have to understand how hard it is to be the child of a legend. Everyone's always comparing me to her, and I want to carve out something for myself."

"I do understand. My family's rather like that. Senators, representatives, governors, ambassadors." He smiled. "And me, the only judge."

"Which makes you quite unique." They spent another few minutes embracing, then Amadea broke free and began pulling on her clothes. "When will I see you again? Privately, I mean."

"I'm not sure—"

"Soon. Please make it soon."

"Believe me, darling, I want that as much as you do, but there are difficulties. . . . I can't . . . I have a lot of trouble . . . lying. Maybe I should just tell Jenny the truth and move out. Good heavens, don't look so panicked."

"No, please don't do that. We don't know if this" —she gestured toward the bed— "is anything more than a passing madness. Please don't hurt Jenny and upset your life until we *do* know."

"That makes it harder."

"I know, but you're strong enough to handle it."

"It's not a question of strong. It's a question of feeling like a cad."

"Well, you're not one. You couldn't ever be."

"That's very nice, but—"

"No, listen to *me*, not to the guilt reflexes that have been built into you. You've helped me and comforted me, and I can never repay you for that. Surely Jenny wouldn't begrudge sharing you this little bit?"

"Well . . ." he said hesitantly.

"I'm a woman, too, and *I* wouldn't. Naturally we won't flaunt it. I just want you to have time to think and decide, and not be driven to something because you're such a chivalrous gentleman."

"You're turning my head with all these compliments, and before I become entirely too big for my britches, let's go to the Hudsons' and get this over with."

"You won't desert me?"

"Never."

• • •

Jenny keyed the door, it slid open, and she stepped aside, allowing Andy to negotiate his bulk through the door first.

A stained and battered case hit the floor, and Jenny tried to catch Cabot's eyes where he sat at the table. There was no response.

Andy peered about and released air in a long, gusty sigh. "Jesus, I hope I'm not supposed to share this place with you. There's not enough room to swing a cat."

"No, I made a reservation at the hotel."

"Right in the midst of those crazies. Gee thanks, Jenny."

Cab's silence was beginning to alarm her, and skirting the thrust of Andy's belly, she gripped him by the shoulder and gave him a little shake. "Hello, Cabot. Are you there? Here? Anywhere?"

"I'm sorry. My mind seems to have gone into neutral. Andy, it's good to see you."

The men shook hands, and Jenny took a quick glance about the apartment. The perfectly made bed caught her eye, and made her pause. Cab was almost finicky about his living quarters except for one area: the bedroom. The floor beside the bed was always littered with a profusion of books he was reading, the bedside table held a number of empty glasses whose contents could only be guessed at from the color of the ring in the bottom, and the bed was never made.

Curiosity tugged her closer, and her nose wrinkled as an unusual, but familiar, scent tickled her nostrils. Sweet but with an exotic bite just below the surface. More like incense than perfume . . . patchouli or frangipani.

Whirling, Jenny stared intently at Cab, noting the languid droop of his eyelids, the faint color in his pale cheeks, and the swollen lower lip, and she felt a shriek boiling up from somewhere deep within her. She clamped down on her back teeth, waiting for the anger and hurt to subside to manageable proportions. It did, at least to the extent that she no longer wanted to rage and beat on him, and she spent a few moments trying to excuse, justify, explain. That was quickly abandoned because she decided that she didn't want to be reasonable. This was *not* part of their agreement.

"When did Amadea come by, Cab?" she asked, deciding to give him the chance to be honest with her, though whether honesty was going to make her feel any better was problematical.

"She didn't" he said, the reply coming a shade too quickly.

"Oh, she said she might."

"Well, she didn't."

"Baby Amadea," rumbled Andy, stretching and scratching at his thinning hair. "There are unplumbed depths in that girl. She's as secretive as a mongoose."

"Interesting phrase," Cab said with a touch of boredom. "I didn't know they were."

"Hell, neither do I. I just like the image." His fat, round face creased into smiling folds. "That's 'cause I'm such a literary kind of guy." Jenny forced a smile. "Hey, Jenny, honey. You're not feeling good? You look kind of peaked."

"I'm a bit tired." She flicked a sideways glance to Cab, but he had returned to his abstraction.

"Then I'd better trundle."

"I'll take you."

"Nah, I can find my own way."

"Really, I don't mind. I want to take you."

"Okay."

"Cab, I'll be back in a bit."

"All right."

There was an instant of awkwardness while they stood, hands at sides, and stared at each other. It was Jenny who made the first move, and even as his arms closed about her she was cursing herself. The hurt was back, and she irrationally decided that she couldn't bear to be kissed by him. Not after . . . She shied away from the pictures her mind was forming. At the last moment she turned aside so his kiss fell on her cheek. His expression was that of a large dog who has found himself faced with evidence of his own wickedness—half embarrassed and half defiant.

"Come on, Andy." She didn't look back as they left.

For a long time she and the journalist didn't speak, then as they were approaching the hotel he coughed and said, "Jenny, honey, is there trouble between you and Cab?"

"No!"

He sucked at his cheeks. "May I have my head back now?"

"Excuse me, but don't be nosy."

"I get paid to be nosy." When she didn't say anything, he tried again. "Jenny, my sweet life, my wife, who is a clever person, says that a woman should talk to a woman about these matters."

"I don't know any women, and why don't you figure out who you're going to interview and leave me alone."

She left him at the door and walked hurriedly away. She considered going to Jeanne Hudson's, then decided that neither her pride nor her nerves could take it. What would be accomplished by raging over what was so far only a suspicion? And boring people with her problems had never been her style. No, she would tough it out and hope that Cab returned to his senses before she was driven to kill him . . . or Amadea . . . or both.

ALIEN ARTIFACT UNCOVERED ON MARS. WRITINGS ON THE CRYSTAL DODECAHEDRON TO BE STUDIED BY TEAM OF INTERNATIONAL EXPERTS.

Amadea switched off the reader, picked up her brush, and began pulling it through her long hair. She found it amusing that the press was desperately drumbeating in an effort to arouse interest, concern, *something*, in the breasts of the citizens of Earth over this "historic" find, and every effort kept falling absolutely flat. Oh, the scientists were interested, and a few of the crazier fundamentalist ministers had denounced it as a fraud perpetrated by the research team, or even a ploy by the devil to mislead mankind, for everyone *knew* that Man was God's only creation in the universe. But in the general populace the response had been underwelming.

And why not, thought Amadea, setting aside the brush. Whoever they were, they haven't been around for five, maybe six million years, odds are they've died out entirely, and who cares, anyway? The normal, everyday chores and dreams that make up life are what matter, not whether the universe will compress back to another big bang or die with a cold, gray whimper, or whether aliens passed through long before man had even started his climb out of the trees.

She sure as hell didn't care. Earth, herself, held too many wonders for Amadea to pine for the mysteries of the universe. She picked up the brush again thinking back on the six years she had spent on Earth. The longing was like a physical pain. The awesome sense of history one felt when standing before the Colosseum in Rome, skiing in Switzerland, watching the sun sink behind dark Scottish hills while the loch gleamed like molten gold.

Dave's high-pitched, nervous voice shouting through the halls of the encampment brought her out of her reverie, and dropping the brush, she reluctantly left the quiet of her small room. It was time to face their distinguished guests.

The galley had been converted for the press conference. All but one of the tables had been folded away in a quonset hut, and the one remaining piece of furniture was loaded with cheap refreshments: urns of coffee, hot water for tea, a bowl of sticky red punch, and plates of cookies. At one end of the long, narrow room a portable platform had been erected, and a podium and microphone perched precariously on the unstable risers.

The rest of the narrow room seethed and churned, as too many people tried to fit into too small a space. Little spurts of conversation kept popping up like bubbles in a boiling pot of oatmeal: "Excuse me"; "pardon"; "was that your foot?"; "I don't think it'll leave a stain." Amadea checked in the door and enjoyed the spectacle of eminent scientists, eminent journalists, even a few hoping-to-be-eminent politicians playing sardines. A shift of the crowd and she spotted Cabot, his pale face flushed with excitement, standing in a corner flanked by Andy Throckmorton and Jenny McBride. Amadea blew Cab a quick kiss but didn't really notice his response. Her attention had already moved on to Seth Mayburn Hudson, who was keeping the Jared youth group carefully out of the way and in line. She had invited them because she knew it would upset Dave.

And her project leader didn't let her down. A few moments later he fluttered up, asking in his breathless way, "Who the hell are all these people? Who are those children? There aren't going to be enough refreshments and the room's too crowded. I wish I knew who they were," he concluded querulously.

"The youth group from the Jared Colony. I invited them."

"I wish you hadn't. I really wish you hadn't." He wrung his hands, then ran a palm across his bald pate. "Religious nuts make me nervous. What if they may make a scene ranting about God and the universe and man's place in the universe—"

"I would say the chances of that are just about nil. They're properly brought up children, and many of them are planning on careers in science. Besides, Dave, it won't hurt for us to show a little friendship to our neighbors and to demonstrate that your feud with Jasper does not extend to the colony at large."

"I don't care about those people—what they do or what they're planning to do. But I don't want Jasper around here getting in the way."

"And stealing the glory? After all, *he's* the one who pushed for this excavation over your strong objections," she said with sweet malice. The top of Lucas's head turned red, and Amadea gave the knife one final turn. "In fact, I have a message for you from Jasper. He said to tell you that he wants to take a gander at the thing but that this is your big moment, Dave, so go for it."

Relief, shame, and resentment battled for command of Lucas's face. Finally he said in a low voice. "I don't begrudge Jasper his place in history, and he'll get it—being remembered as the man who began to terraform Mars—but he ran out on *this* project, and I saw it through to the end, and I think I'm entitled to some of the credit."

"Oh, by all means, Dave. In fact, take it all."

"You're in a funny mood today." He eyed her dubiously.

"Yes, and I need a drink."

"You and Jasper were feuding last I heard," he called as she moved away.

"That's all been settled. I'm on the side of the angels now." She smiled at his blank look, waved, and drifted away.

She noticed that Cab had been pulled away by one of the politicos, so she snagged a cup of the disgusting fruit punch and hurried to Jenny's side.

"Hi there."

"Yes?" The other woman's green eyes were veiled, and tension was etched in the tendons of her neck.

So she knows.

"Cabot's had an unfair advantage over you. He's already seen the sight. I wondered if you would like to go up early and take a look around. Feel free to go past the barricade and touch it if you want. I'll clear it with Conrad—"

"Thank you, but no."

"Hell, *I'll* go," Andy said. "And by the way, how are you, Amadea, sweetie?"

She nodded in answer to his query, then smiled apologetically. "I'm sorry, Andy, but I offered this as a courtesy to Ms. McBride, and I'm not supposed to let any journalists up. Of course, if you went with her . . ."

"Jenny," said the fat man, plucking at her sleeve. "You may not want to leave the party, but have pity. I'm still a journalist, and I'm doing you and Cab a big favor. Do one for me and let me get a scoop on this artifact. Please?"

"Oh, all right."

Amadea saw them safely on their way and returned to the galley, musing over the little tidbit that Andy had let drop. So Huntington had sent for Andy. Now why? Cab was wandering about looking puzzled and disconsolate. She slipped her arm through his, and he said, "I've lost Jenny."

"No, you haven't." She peeped up at him from beneath her lashes. "I was bad," she said in a little-girl voice.

"Oh?"

"Yes, I got Jenny out of the way so I could have a few minutes alone with you. Do you mind?"

He laughed, a forced, nervous sound. "No. No, I guess not."

"I tried to give her a fair exchange. I let her go up with just Andy and Conrad to look at the artifact. Now come here. I can't stand it any longer."

She bustled him out of the galley and to her room. The moment the flimsy door slid closed behind them, she had one hand behind his neck, the other plunged down his pants, and they were kissing frenziedly.

"Stop, please," he groaned.

His erection was hard and cool against her palm. "Let me give you some relief."

"No, we'll be missed."

"Are you crazy? The politicians still have to orate, and Dave has to congratulate himself, and then everyone has to get into pressure suits and troop up the pyramid. We won't miss a thing."

"But Jenny—"

"All right, love, we'll just cuddle." She pulled him down next to her on the narrow bunk and surrendered herself to his embrace. When he at last came up for air, she asked, "What is Andy doing here?"

"Getting out our side of the argument."

"*Our* side?"

"You're as bad as your mother about getting me to admit to where my sympathies really lie. Yes, *our* side."

"Then you do favor the colonists in the POW suit."

"I'm not saying that. What I am saying is that the Jared people have gotten a bum shake, and it won't hurt to have the people groundside get a different view of them. Not as rapacious capitalists trying to rape Mars but as ordinary, hard-working people trying to make a living. You keep bringing this up."

"Do I? I'm sorry, I don't mean to be a bore. I guess I'm just very anxious about how it's all going to come out. And don't say anything. I'm not angling for inside information—this time." She grinned mischievously.

He returned the smile. "I think I've given you enough so that you can make a pretty good guess."

"Yes, you have. Shall we rejoin the party?"

Jenny was back, and Amadea cursed her for having hurried Andy. She decided that saying nothing was probably better than fabricating a lame excuse for her and Cabot's absence, so she merely smiled, nodded, and moved on, leaving him with his clerk.

Dave was up at the podium, making a modest little speech. "I would also like to give credit to the man whose intuition is legendary and who first spotted the anamolay. Dr. Jasper Mendel." Lucas gestured to the tall, gangling figure, and Jasper came lurching through the crowd.

Mendel climbed onto the tiny stage, looking stunned but pleased, and held out his hand to Lucas. The smaller man hesitated, then they shook, and there was a yell of encouragement from Conrad and Jillian, who had served under both men. Jasper gave the crowd his toothy grin, waved his arms over his head, and retreated without saying a word.

"Well," murmured Amadea to herself. "A day of many surprises."

There was a stir from the door, and in came Lucius Renfrew. A number of reporters deserted the scientific cadre at the podium and ran to meet him. Renfrew was a lot more flamboyant and newsworthy than the cautious, pedantic scientists. Renfrew, who was not known for his manners, happily gave an interview while the final official speakers struggled to compete with that strident nasal voice. Finally Dave announced the end of the briefing and sent people in groups of five to suit storage and on up the pyramid.

It took over an hour to get everyone hauled up and reassembled before the dodecahedron. Amadea drifted back until she was standing with the kids from Jared. There were oohs and ahs from the crowd as Dave proudly pulled the cover from the great crystal artifact, and people strained forward, trying to see the fine, spidery writing that slanted in all directions across the surfaces. Seth jiggled on the balls of his feet and tried to peer over a sea of helmeted heads.

"Damn it, we can't see a thing from back here. I know Mom told me not to be pushy so I wasn't, and look what it got us."

"Tell you what, you kids come back in a couple of days and I'll give you a private tour."

"Honest? Oh, wow. Super" came the chorus of responses from the kids.

"Amadea, you're a darling," concluded Seth, putting a period to their feelings.

"Aren't I, though?" She tugged at his arm. "Could I talk to you privately for a moment? You're not really interested in listening to Dave tell in excrutiating detail every step we took to uncover the beast, are you?"

"No, what's up?"

They fell back to the lift and switched their helmet radios to the private mode. "I've thought about going to your parents with this, but I don't want to seem a talebearer, and they seem pretty enamored with Justice Huntington."

"You've got something on the guy?"

"I don't know if I would go that far. You know he's interested in me?"

"Yeah, it's all over the colony."

"Well, we talk a lot, and I don't like what I'm hearing. I don't think he's very sympathetic to us."

"You mean he's going to—"

She held up a hand. "I don't know and don't want to start false rumors, but a man who donates money to Green Peace and led a fight to keep his stretch of beach private and pristine, and who pulled what he did on EnerSun, doesn't seem the type to favor our goals. And he says . . . things."

"Maybe I should talk to the folks."

"That's a thought, or maybe we just ought to keep this

under our helmets until we have a little more information. I can keep you informed, and perhaps . . . but I shouldn't say that."

"What? Say what?"

"Your parents and the other elders are still tied very closely to Earth. Maybe . . ."

"Go on."

"Maybe you kids ought to be the ones making some of the decisions. A number of you were born up here, and the work of terraforming is going to fall to your generation. I'd hate to see you lose that because your parents are trained to obey the Earth authorities. No, don't say anything. But think about it."

From his expression he already was, and they returned to the ceremony. The official presentations had ended, and Lucius Renfrew was giving yet another loud and opinionated interview to the press.

"I'm certain that when the writings are deciphered, they will contain priceless wisdom for our species."

"They must have been real clairvoyant," grunted Andy. "Leaving messages for a species that didn't even exist when they rolled through."

Renfrew eyed him sourly. "That was probably their mission: to travel through the stars leaving messages for developing races."

"Or eating them," added Andy sotto voice.

"That's a narrow and provincial view. Any race that has achieved star drive would of necessity be far in advance of us morally and technologically. They undoubtedly learned how to live in grace and harmony with the cosmos, and by gently nurturing their world, it sent them forth on this mission of peace and teaching."

"Or, having raped and pillaged their own planet, they set out to find some others to supply their needs," countered Andy.

"You ignorant buffoon. You're exactly like all the rest of the ignorant masses. I'm surprised you haven't already started chipping pieces off this monument to sell as souvenirs."

"Say, now there's a thought. Hey, Jenny," Throckmorton bellowed. "I've got a new scheme. Forget the Saturn-ring ice, we're gonna sell pieces of the Rosetta stone here." Jasper and Jenny chuckled, Cab shook his head, and several other people expressed disapproval.

"Andy, you're a barbarian."

"No, I'm not, I'm a real sensitive kind of guy. I just hate pomposity. When I hear it, it reminds me of the time I had to wade through shit—"

"Andy, that will do." And seizing him by the arm, Cab hustled the journalist toward the lift.

"I don't know if I want to hear this story," remarked Jenny, following after them.

"You don't," Cab said firmly.

The last jump load of visitors had vanished over the pink horizon. Amadea stretched and sighed.

"God, what a day."

"Thank God it's over. Now we can get back to work," Conrad said, rubbing at his eyes.

"When does the next thundering herd arrive?"

Jillian looked up. "The experts will be here tomorrow. Along with the prefab equipment to build more living quarters."

"Sounds like tomorrow is going to be busy, and frankly, though I love you all"—Amadea dropped a quick kiss on the top of Conrad's head—"I'm sick to death of people. I'm going off for a flight."

"Don't be too long. It'll be dark soon," cautioned Jillian.

"Jilly, dearest, I'm not scared of the dark."

Once aloft, she sent her Light racing north toward Cebrenia. When she was well clear of the project, she flipped on the special radio that had been installed in her plane and punched in a code made familiar from frequent use.

"Bill, Amadea, here. I have tidings, and you're not going to like them."

"Then let's get them over with quickly."

"I don't think POW's going to get a favorable ruling out of Huntington, and he's urging the colonists to challenge the agency actions. The indication is he means to overturn them."

"That's not good news."

"I have the glimmerings of a solution, but it's rather drastic, and I wanted to know how hard you wanted to play."

"Very."

"What would happen if Huntington disappeared?"

"You can arrange that without implicating Gemetics?"

"Would I suggest it if I couldn't?"

There was a thoughtful silence from Earth. "Long would have to appoint a new justice for the Fifteenth Circuit; someone a good deal more favorable to our position if Lis has anything to say about it, and she will. And there would be a convulsion of outrage against the perpetrators, who I hope would be Mormons."

"They would be. I've got one problem."

"Yes?"

"I need something to prove Huntington's bias. To make it look like he favors POW."

"You'll need rulings against the EPA. I'll have Legal cook up some ideas and send them to you."

"Then I approach the POW lawyer?"

"Right, and for God's sake keep us out of this. Corporate action is as much of a red flag to Renfrew as government action."

"I'm not an idiot."

"I know you're not. That's why we do business together and why, if you're successful, we have a cushy job waiting for you groundside."

"If I'm successful? That was never part of our agreement. I was only supposed to keep you informed—"

"Your duties have just been expanded. Hard ball, Amadea, remember?"

"You son of a bitch."

"I wouldn't ask it if I didn't think you could do it. Look on it as a testament to your skill and my faith in you," he said in a caressing voice.

Her reply was to break connection. As she turned for home and stared down at the rugged landscape, darkening now as night came, she reflected that there was a lot of potential for harm on this unforgiving planet.

In the whole fucking system, she thought bitterly, and she tried to comfort herself with thoughts of home: blue-green and beautiful, as seductive as Babylon, a place for elegant and refined living. The place she wanted to be.

Chapter Ten

Padget MacKinley hadn't known quite what to expect. A mysterious call from a beautiful woman (he didn't know for certain that she was beautiful, but mysterious women who made mysterious calls ought to be) saying she had information that would be worth his while to hear was definitely an attention-getter. Eagle Port's nicest restaurant was doing a rousing business, and the lawyer, pursuant to his instructions, hurried through the main dining room to the private booths in the back. He counted three from the left and pushed through the hush-bead curtain.

The woman who rose from the table to greet him was no stranger. He was vaguely aware of having seen her about the Jared Colony, but she had looked nothing like this. Amadea's ebony hair was swept up into an intricate coiffure held in place with ropes of sparkling synthetic gems and several long pins, from which hung tiny crystal bells. A plain black dress sheathed her body, leaving one shoulder enticingly bare.

"Hello!" The bells chimed gently as she inclined her head in answer to his greeting. "This surpasses my wildest expectations."

"I'm so glad you're pleased, Mr. MacKinley." She held out

a hand, and he turned it, dropping a lingering kiss on her wrist.

"You are?"

"Amadea Kim Nu."

"Ah." He indicated the chairs. "Shall we sit down and"—he stroked the back of his hand down her bare arm—"get to know each other better?"

"Let's first take care of business. That way we won't sully the pleasure."

Her cool tone effectively doused his rising interest, and lawyer replaced Lothario.

They seated themselves. "You said you had information for me?"

She steepled her fingers before her face. "You're aware that Justice Huntington does not look with favor upon your suit?"

"We've guessed as much."

"And if you lose?"

"I don't talk or think about losing until it happens, and I win a lot."

"Congratulations, but you won't win this one. Believe me."

He frowned, piqued by her certainty. "You didn't call me all the way to Eagle Port to tell me this. I presume you have some solution?"

"Yes. I have sources on Earth, and they've indicated that if Huntington were removed, a successor would be selected who would support your position."

He half rose, saying as he did, "Thank you very much, ma'am, but no thanks. We've skirted the edges of the law and even slipped over onto its wrong side a time or two, but I'm not going to have any part in killing a federal judge."

"Interesting how your mind immediately leapt to the most violent solution. I could have been talking about any number of possibilities between here and murder."

"Are you?" He sank back toward the chair.

"As it happens, no. Oh, do stop bouncing up and down. I didn't say you would be involved." This time he returned to his chair and stayed there. "There's a group tailor-made to do it for you."

"Not the pious Mormons. Lady, you've got rocks in your head."

"Before you get so contemptuous, hear me out. I know the people of that colony very well. The adults would never take such a step, unless they thought it was necessary for the very survival of the colony, but the young people . . . now they're quite another matter. The MIA is led by a particularly hot-headed young man who's been in trouble before. I think Seth can be convinced that the colony is threatened by Huntington and will take action."

"Great, you've got it all planned out. So what do you need me for?"

"I need evidence to convince the colonists that Ca—that Huntington is against them, a spark to light the fuse, and that's where you come in. Rumor has it that you're a very cunning and unscrupulous fellow."

"Rumor has it right."

"Then it shouldn't be very hard for you to force Huntington into making rulings in POW's favor."

"Wait. If he's so against us, how in the hell am I supposed to maneuver him into doing this?"

"You're a federal litigator. I'm told that's how you make your living, filing . . . motions."

"A small aside, but to satisfy my curiosity, what were you about to say?"

Spurious motions, but I didn't want to be insulting."

"Thank you," he replied wryly. "But back to my lesson in legal tactics."

"The colonists, like most lay people, won't realize that these actions have nothing to do with the substance of the case. They'll just see Huntington ruling against the EPA and assume that he is going to overturn the Agency approval of the terraforming plan." She paused and took a sip of her cocktail. "Tell me, how good is the lawyer for the EPA?"

Padget gave a short bark of laughter and, leaning back in his chair, ran his hands over the top of his sleek black hair. "Terrible. I couldn't believe the feds did this, but they sent up a real rookie."

"My, how very improvident of them." She folded her hands in her lap.

"You look like a cat by an empty milk saucer. I take it that it was no accident that this youngster, fresh out of law school, got stuck with this job." She smiled, and her tongue peeped out briefly to wet her lips. "It's good to know we have friends in high places," concluded Padget, and laughed again.

"But where do you fit in, Miss Amadea? What are you going to get out of all this?" She remained silent. "It would make me feel a lot better if I knew you were as flawed, greedy, and self-interested as the rest of us."

She studied the tabletop before her and sketched out an intricate little pattern on the cloth with her forefinger before answering. "Speaking solely for my better nature, I favor your position. I think it's criminal the way we're tearing up the Solar System so people can have air-conditioning in the summer, and three video systems, and all the rest of the overconsumption that goes along with our society. But I know mere altruism isn't going to convince you." She stopped her nervous doodlings, laid her hands on the table, studied the perfectly manicured nails, then leaned in on him. "The fact of the matter is, I have a score to settle with Justice Cabot Huntington."

"Oh, my, are we talking sex and smut here?"

Her hand shot out, taking him firmly across the cheek and wiping the smirk from his face. She resumed as if he had never spoken.

"I met Cabot Huntington on the EnerSun station, and we became . . . close. He then went back to Earth and took up with his clerk, leaving me scraping away out here on Mars. He then turns up and immediately assumes that I'm going to hop right back in the sack with him."

"And did you?" inquired Padget, but he stayed prudently back in his chair, well out of her reach.

She laid her fingers across her lips and closed her eyes. "Yes, God damn me!" She released a held breath. "I thought I could separate him from Jenny, but he as good as told me that he liked having his cake and eating it, too, thank you very much, and I could take it on those terms or leave it."

"And you decided?"

"On neither. I decided to get even." She smiled, an intoxicating expression. "Is that enough self-interest for you?"

"Jesus Christ! Remind me not to jilt one of you System girls. Murderous little thing, aren't you?"

"It's easy to be murderous at a distance. I don't have to do the deed, see the body, take responsibility. I'm like a random particle, suggesting actions but never insisting on them. Perhaps I'll set in motion awesome events. That's a rather exciting thought. But what of you? Is this too unscrupulous for you, too much for your conscience and sensibility? Will you run away and report me? If you do, I'll deny it, and I'm well thought of here. No one will believe you."

"If your sources have kept you this well informed, they must have told you that the only thing that motivates me is my fee. As far as I'm concerned, we've discussed legal maneuverings to help promote POW's position. The rest—like you say—is up to random chance. How could I be held responsible?" He laughed, his black eyes dancing. "So is this it? Is business officially past?"

"Yes."

"Got any other plans for the evening?"

"If you're up to them."

"I think I can find it in me."

Later, as he lay snoring, she paced the six-foot length of the tiny one-room apartment she maintained at the port. What she had undertaken almost terrified her, but if she treated it as an equation, something divorced from reality, she would manage. Two days ago Devert had called back and outlined the plan. And now she was into it. Playing for high stakes, walking the tightrope; and as frightening as it was, there was also a sense of exhilaration. Disaster lay on every side, but she believed in her ability to negotiate it.

There was a danger in that she had had to tell one out-and-out lie to the attorney—that she had met Cab on EnerSun—but he probably wouldn't bother to check, so eager was he to accept her help.

She stifled a laugh, realizing it was the thin edge of hysteria and not humor that had evoked it.

They wouldn't be so eager if they knew who I really *worked for. Wicked, wicked industry. My ticket home.*

"Protectors of Worlds' motion for a more definite statement is accepted." Cab nodded to Padget MacKinley where he stood before the bench. The attorney for POW was looking smug and sleek, rather like a well-fed seal. Janet Jaschke from EPA's legal department was wilting under Cabot's steely gaze. "Ms. Jaschke, you will please clarify the indicated sections of your answer. Hearing is concluded."

He brought down his gavel and pushed back from the bench. MacKinley was already strolling back to receive the congratulations of his employer. A small knot of colonists was mumbling at the rear of the room, and Janet Jaschke still stood before the bench, literally wringing her hands.

Cab sighed and slid his chair forward. "Ms. Jaschke, off the record, have you been instructed to lose this case?"

"No, sir, and if you'll forgive me, sir, I think on the merits I've constructed a strong case. It's just these damn technicalities."

"They get easier with practice."

"That's not much comfort right now. I'm screwing up, and I know it. I should have become a plumber. I could have gone into septic tanks and filled a vital niche on the planet. As it is"—she made a hopeless gesture—"I guess I'm a bad lawyer."

"No, you're an inexperienced one, and you shouldn't have been assigned to a case of this magnitude."

"I know, sir," she replied softly.

Cab knew he was being unfair taking out his pique with the EPA on the attorney, but her inexperience was a problem and this was definitely *not* a learning case. It was too vital. Not only to the Jared colonists but to someone (or ones) Earthside. After the blowup on the EnerSun station he had become unnaturally sensitive to mood, and he knew that each time he was forced to rule in favor of POW, tension in the colony rose another notch. Last week it had been a motion to compel, today the motion for a more definite statement, next week . . . God alone knew what piece of creative lawyering MacKinley would come up with. Cab left the bench and returned to his chambers without another word to Jaschke.

Darnell Hudson was echoing aloud Cabot's thoughts in the back of the courtroom. Tugging at his bushy eyebrows, he rumbled, "This case is vital."

"And every time the judge ruling against us . . . against the EPA," amended Levi Coltrin.

"It's the same thing," ejected Seth. "He's down on us. Just like—" He bit off the words, and Jeanne wondered what he had been about to say.

Darnell gave a ponderous shake of his head, like a bull bedeviled by flies. "I didn't expect this from the judge. Joe Reichart said we could count on him."

"Count on him to screw us," muttered Seth.

"Show respect," snapped Coltrin, who had never liked the boy. "This is only preliminary stuff. Maybe he'll come through for us on the case proper. He did urge us to file that action against the agencies."

Seth bounced nervously on the balls of his feet. "Correction: It was *Jenny* who urged us to file that lawsuit, and she probably went behind his back to do that. You're all trying to make excuses for him. Face it, he's against us! At least Jenny's on our side. Wish she were the judge."

"I don't want to hear this talk about *sides*. We're American citizens, and we'll abide by the laws of our nation," said Darnell. "It may be *we're* not the ones destined to start this project, but it will be done. We may have to be patient."

"That's fine for you, but what about me? Your *acceptance* is costing me my future! Why should we be listening to the grounders at all? It's our money and our sweat and our blood that's put us out here. They've done jack shit to help us, and now they're trying to hinder us. Well, I'm not going to sit by and take it!"

The courtroom door slammed behind him, and Jeanne caught her husband's arm before he could plunge after Seth.

Coltrin pursed his lips. "You should do something about that boy. He's going to get into big trouble someday if you don't exert a little discipline."

"Levi, when I want a lecture on how to raise my son, I'll ask for it."

"The truth can sometimes be unpalatable," the elder concluded with dignity, and left.

Darnell's jaw worked and finally a temperate "Drat" emerged. "But maybe he's right. Maybe I am too soft on the boy. I should go after him."

"No, leave him to work it out himself. You know what his temper's like when he's pushed."

"I won't have him offending Justice Huntington."

"Seth is not likely to accost the judge. He'll rant and rave to his friends, then some new project will present itself and he'll forget all about being a fire-breathing revolutionary." He continued to frown at the door, and she gave his arm a little shake. "Darnell, don't make a bad situation worse. You know I'm right about this."

"Yeah, but I also know how much trouble he can get into if he's *not* deflected."

"Did you have to be so hard on Jaschke this afternoon?" The knife lifted for a moment, then resumed its measured chopping. "Cab, would you please pay attention. The damn onions can wait."

"Do you want to eat before midnight or not? If you do, then let me finish this. I can listen and work."

"Then answer my question."

There was a bang and a scrape as he swept the onion off the chopping board and into the skillett. After careful deliberation he selected a bell pepper and resumed his cutting. "It was a fair complaint, tricky but fair, and MacKinley's not about to let any advantage slip by."

"You didn't have to be so cutting and superior."

He faced her, gesturing with the knife. "I wasn't."

"It was in your tone and by walking off and leaving her standing there."

"That was not intended for her." He went back to the pepper.

"Oh, excuse me. What a shame she's not a mind reader."

"Has she been talking to you?"

"No, I could tell from her expression how she was feeling."

"Now who's the mind reader."

"This is off the point. The point is that you were young and inexperienced once too."

The knife slammed down onto the board, and tiny pieces of pepper went flying. "Meaning that I'm not now."

"Well, of course, you're not inexperienced, but I'm damn sure you made a few mistakes when you were first starting out." She stared at his rigid back. "Oh, you mean young." He remained silent. "Cab, what is your problem? You've been acting like—" She pressed her lips together.

"Like what?" The moment it was out, he wished he hadn't said it, but the guilt that had been sitting like a heavy stone in the pit of his stomach drove him to it. Emotions tumbled through him: anger, fear, culpability. To steady himself and to take his attention from Jenny's white, drawn face, he bent and began picking bits of pepper off the tile floor.

"Like a middle-aged Don Juan."

Panic joined the guilt, and they both began yammering at the top of their hysterical little voices. A confrontation with Jenny loomed before him like a yawning crevasse, and he knew he couldn't face it. He was confused and torn between his two women. Buffeted by contradictory emotions and, like a greedy child, wanting both.

Jenny; so warm and dear, his colleague, companion, friend, and lover. His love for her was a quiet glow, very comfortable and secure, and quite different from the madness that infected him whenever Amadea was near. The Eurasian was magical and volatile—cinnabar or quicksilver—and when he lay in her arms, he could shed the confining bounds of his upbringing, release his pent-up emotions. Fired by her passion, he was young, virile, powerful, a romantic in the finest and truest sense of the word.

But how could say this to Jenny? They had entered into their relationship agreeing to be monogamous. He couldn't ask to change the rules now. Besides, if he did, *she* would be free to roam, and the very thought almost choked him with jealous anger. The more rational part of his nature acknowledged that his double standard was outmoded and unfair, but he couldn't help himself. And his final, selfish conclusion? That for as long as he remained on Mars he wanted Amadea. And perhaps, after he left, the fire would burn itself out, leaving him free to continue in the comfortable, stable relationship he shared with Jenny. He gathered his scattered thoughts, looking for a way to soothe her. *Jenny, I absolutely guarantee that I'm not involved with Amadea.*

There it was, so easy to formulate and so impossible to say. And knowing he was being a coward and that he would probably pay for it down the line, he took the easy way out. He changed the subject.

"You may be right about Jaschke. The substance of her work is excellent, well researched and well presented; she's just inexperienced. Next time they come before me, I'll give her a stroke to reassure her. I don't want to drive her out of the profession."

He tossed the refuse, dusted his hands, and gave her a quick smile. Anger, outrage, relief, and frustration swept across her face like slides being rapidly fed through a viewer. For an instant he feared she was going to force the issue and continue the fight. She checked, as if she, too, had observed the chasm that threatened them, and a tremulous smile touched her lips, flickering in and out like a failing light bulb.

"You really ought to be dumping on MacKinley. He's taking far too much pleasure in humiliating Jaschke."

"I agree, but as long as he's finding genuine errors . . ." He shrugged and began dredging chicken pieces in seasoned flour.

Jenny joined him at the stove, lifted the skillet, and sent the pat of melting margarine sliding about the pan. Her shoulder was pressed against his, like a puppy nudging for affection, and he felt another stab of guilt. She shouldn't have to be a supplicant for his attention. Keeping his hands carefully away so as not to leave flour smudges on her hair and clothes, he leaned in and kissed her. The skillet banged onto the burner, and she molded herself against him, sucking feverishly at his mouth. There was a stirring in his groin, and he thrust his tongue past the barrier of her teeth, only to feel her withdrawing, shrinking back both physically and emotionally. He insisted, even taking a step forward to keep the contact, and her hands snaked up, dug into his shoulders, and forced him away.

"The margarine is burning," she panted. He accepted the excuse to save face, but inwardly he was seething.

Try to show her I care. That despite Amadea, she's still important to me. Get a come-on, then get pushed away . . . The thoughts jumbled together like flotsam in a whirlpool, and he aggrievedly decided that he was being badly used.

She muttered something about starting the rice, he grunted a reply, and while the chicken simmered, so did they. Hostility hung heavy in the room like a black tapestry shot here and there with threads of brilliant anger and unexpressed hurt. It was like being buried alive, and the cramped quarters did little to improve the situation. They sat almost knee-to-knee at the tiny table, pretending to concentrate on work while the printed words formed a meaningless stew.

The scrape of his chair across the bare tile was a horrible screeching sound in the leaden silence. Jenny winced but continued to stare resolutely at her reader.

"I left some material at the office." No response. "I need it." Still nothing. "I'm going to go get it."

"Fine."

"I'll be back for dinner."

"Fine."

"Well . . . fine!"

The slamming of the door supplied a momentary release, and in his depression he managed to imbue it with a significance far greater than it deserved, the final chord in a symphony of dissonance.

Cab was unaware of Amadea's scrutiny. She had found him in his office late the previous night, sullen and angry, and it hadn't taken much to convince him to join her in Eagle Port. Now the early-morning light was poking at the tightly closed curtains of her tiny apartment. The filtered sunlight through the amber-colored fabric sent a red-gold glow across the bed and splashed the bare white walls with color. It reminded Amadea of a bordello scene from a nineteenth-century French farce.

Cabot, his white, sinewy arms folded beneath his head, had his pipe clenched tightly between his teeth, and with each slow exhalation tendrils of blue-gray smoke wound themselves about his head. His eyes were focused well beyond the ceiling, looking at pictures that clearly didn't please him, for faint lines furrowed his forehead. Periodically he sighed, and each time it happened, his long lashes would drop to veil his eyes, brushing lightly on his high cheekbones.

As Amadea watched him lying there, sad and a little vulnerable, she felt a momentary flutter of doubt over her course. She had used this man, viewing him as an object, a tool to be wielded and then discarded, but it was difficult to keep emotional distance once she had slept with him. Women were more deeply affected by such joinings than their brethern who had been blessed with a penis.

She knew that such insidious emotions could only weaken her, so she used techniques taught to her by her mother. Carefully, dispassionately, she analyzed the emotions and set them aside. She had a job to do; a job that once accomplished would lead to the realization of her dreams. And if Cabot was in the way? Well, that was unfortunate and unavoidable. A certain amount of callousness was bred into each System child, for death was an old and familiar companion, and she was grateful for the toughness. It would keep her on course.

The silence was no longer to her taste, so reaching over,

she drew her nails down his chest, feeling the crisp curl of his hair against the soft pads of her fingers.

"You're sad."

Cabot pulled the pipe from his mouth and snagged a bit of tobacco off his tongue with thumb and forefinger. "I'm sorry. I have no reason to be but I am. Rather like one of those boring heroes in a 1920s surrealist novel indulging in post-coital depression."

"I thought the scene was rather more reminiscent of a French farce."

"That would be more fun. Champagne exploding over the walls, the gendarmes raiding the house of ill repute, and my wife pursuing me through the halls."

The frown deepened, and she tapped him on the tip of his narrow nose. "But you don't have a wife, remember?"

"Jenny and I almost had it out yesterday."

"Poor darling, there's nothing worse than a jealous woman."

"Except possibly a philandering man."

"You are determined to be hard on yourself. Do you want out? Is that what you're trying to tell me?"

"I don't know. One part of me thinks I ought to, but another part wants you desperately."

She showed her teeth in a wicked little smile, and her hand snaked beneath the covers to grip his cock. "I can guess which part." She sat up abruptly in her bed, her hair cascading over her hips. The silken tickle against her bare buttocks felt wonderful, and she threw back her head and laughed.

His deep, throaty chuckle wove a counterpoint to her bell-like laughter. "I can't stay depressed with you. You make me forget everything: work, duty, responsibility. I want to run away to the South Seas with you or seek out romance and adventure on the steppes of central Asia."

"You would look wonderful with a few days' growth of beard." The back of her hand stroked down his cheek. "A rifle slung across her back and a wiry little Arabian horse between your knees." Climbing on top of him, she gripped him between her knees and rubbed her thumbs across his hardened nipples. "And at night, in your tent, you would have your wiry little Eurasian between your knees."

"Stop. You make me sound silly."

"Not silly; you're my dear romantic." She lay along the

length of him and tangled her fingers in his thick black hair. "But tell me how I've interfered with your work?"

"I think about you . . . too much. And the thought of you keeps me in such good humor that I let that damn MacKinley get away with things."

"What things? According to the colonists, you're giving him everything he asks for."

He waved away the remark. "That's not true. He's comma-counting, but because the points he's raising are valid, I keep having to rule in his favor. I wish just once he would quit skating along the edge and actually fall right over into a real contempt situation. I'd slap him so hard and fast."

"He's contemptuous of you?"

"Yes, damn him. But I suppose I shouldn't feel abused. He's done this to every judge before whom he's appeared. There's something in his demeanor that's so ironic and scornful, it makes me want to hit him. I can tell you right now if he keeps harassing Jaschke and quibbling over form rather than substance, I'm going to take him to task. He's wasting the court's time and preventing us from coming to grips with the real issue."

"So you think the POW case will be heard soon?"

"Yes, and I'm going to enjoy the look on MacKinley's face when I tell him that I think the POW challenge is an unmitigated piece of garbage."

"Cabot . . ." she said faintly.

He grabbed her hands. "There, now are you happy? You now know where I stand. But please don't repeat what I said. As much as I'd like to be rude, I can't. A certain level of conduct is required from the bench."

Even though she had been expecting this revelation, she felt as if an icy fist had closed about her guts and given a hard squeeze. She wanted to grab Cabot by the shoulders, shake him, make him see sense.

God damn you, you arrogant, independent fool. Why couldn't you just play along?

Was he so dense that he couldn't read the signals from Earth? Could it be that he was truly devoted to a concept of justice and fair play? Or was his overweening pride so great that he thought he could yet again challenge the powers Earthside and emerge unscathed and a hero?

The third possibility infuriated her and managed to quiet

the guilt that kept springing up at the most inopportune moments to bedevil her. Her jaw tightened. So be it. If he chooses to be a person of moment, a man of destiny, he'll have to accept the consequences; men of moment are often broken or even die.

"Amadea? You're very quiet. You are pleased, aren't you?"

"Yes, of course. I was thinking how surprised Mr. MacKinley is going to be."

"Where are you off to?" Cab asked that evening and wished the words back the moment he'd uttered them. He had returned from Eagle Port about four, and Jenny had made no comment about his absence. She didn't now, even though he had given her the perfect opportunity, but continued to wiggle into leotard and tights.

Looking about distractedly, she spied her shoes and jammed them into a tote bag. "I've told you five times. I'm helping Jeanne with the talent review by choreographing a number for the girls."

"Oh, yes, that's right. Are you dancing?"

"Yes." She located her leg warmers and added them to the bag. "I suggested that you sing for it, but you're mind was—as usual—elsewhere, and all I got was a grunt for an answer."

"Hmmm . . . I'm sorry. I missed that."

"You've been missing a lot recently, Cab." She slung the bag over her shoulder and started for the door.

"Wait."

"Wait?" The tone was sullen and it both hurt and angered him.

"Is it too late?"

"Are we being metaphysical? Too late for what?"

There it was, another perfect opening, and again he dodged it. "Too late for me to sing."

"I suppose not, but we'll have to ask Jeanne."

He set aside his tumbler of wine, shrugged into his coat, and they were off. Knots and clumps of people were trickling across the open expanse of the dome, heading for the community center. Occasionally they merged, then broke apart, like spawning amoeba.

The main room of the center was a drafty, noisy barn, which judging from the basketball hoops and the raised stage at one end, doubled as both gymnasium and theater. The babble of conversation broke like waves on the walls and bleachers, then retreated mumbling, to rise anew. Women were setting out refreshments on several long tables, men stood in serious knots like military squares, and rug rats went diving through the legs of their elders. An occasional bumped head or scraped knee would elicit a bellow of outrage from a child, quickly soothed by a vigilant mother. The teenagers formed two phalanxes on either side of the room; boys on one side, girls on the other. There was much good-natured shoving and chaffing from the boys, and periodic squeals and giggles from the girls.

Cab, educated in a series of elite and expensive boarding schools, found the scene both strange, endearing, and faintly depressing. His all-male schools had usually had a female counterpart nearby, and though the students became adept at meeting and mingling, most of his contact with members of the opposite sex, at least until college, had been at carefully arranged social events. How interesting and exciting to have grown up in a mixed environment! The trauma of being almost grown, torn between childhood innocence, where girls were useless parasites, and adulthood, where they became so important. And in the middle, adolescent gaucheries and agonies.

Jenny had deserted him in the center of the room and was moving swiftly to find Jeanne Hudson. The sway and rhythm of her slim hips and the long hair bouncing lightly on her shoulders made his breath catch in his throat, and he suddenly felt a good deal less superior to the boys arranged against the wall.

It doesn't get any easier, fellas, he thought. But the stakes get higher, and the pain and the confusion definitely escalate.

A wave from Jenny brought him to where she and Jeanne stood by the stage. Jeanne embraced him in her warm smile. "I'm so glad you've decided to be in the review."

"You may not be after you hear me sing. I haven't done anything serious for years, and I'm badly out of practice."

"Oh, shoot, we won't know the difference."

Seth came up, paused momentarily, and blurted, "What are you doing here?"

"Seth!"

He grinned, abashed, at his mother. "I'm sorry, that really sounded rude, didn't it?"

"Yes," replied Cab, and was startled by the look of venomous hatred the boy shot at him.

"Barbara's playing the synthesizer for us, so you might go talk to her about your music." Cab nodded in assent.

"I'll try to get the girls organized," Jenny said, and headed off waving a leg warmer over her head like a semaphore.

By the time Cab and the pleasant little accompanist had decided on a couple of Schubert songs, Jenny had rounded up the girls and had them lined up on the stage.

"Where's Sarah?" she called, glancing from her list to the double line of giggling teenagers.

It was Seth who answered. "She's feeling a little under the weather and said I was to apologize for her."

"Okay, no problem. All right, ladies. Do you remember *anything* we did last week?"

There was a chorus of shouted nos and yeses, a few sarcastic remarks from the watching boys, and more giggles and wiggles from the girls. Cab, finding a vacant bench, settled down to watch while Jenny shouted and exorted and pranced the kids through their paces. Jenny was a delight, darting about like a particularly graceful and energetic butterfly, and Cab reveled in the smooth ripple of her muscles beneath the satiny material of her leotard; her flushed, sweat-damp face; and the eloquent play of her hands as she demonstrated and encouraged.

But after thirty minutes the sight of a bevy of gallumping teenage girls had begun to pall. It seemed to his jaundiced eye that they were all either too tall and skinny and gawky, or too short and fat and gawky. He sidled over to Jeanne and whispered. "I'm going to head back to the apartment. Tell Jenny where I've gone."

"Fleeing, are you? Well, I call that pretty poor-spirited of you, to sneak away after witnessing only one of our acts. No, don't apologize," she said, catching him by the sleeve, while her eyes brimmed with laughter and the lines about her eyes deepened and fanned. "It really is dreadful, but it helps promote that sense of community that's so vital to us." She had linked arms with him and was walking him out.

The door to the gym fell shut behind them, cutting off the

ragged clump of feet, the blare of the tape, and Jenny's shouted instructions.

"I find it intriguing, but also terrifying, this social unity that binds you all."

"It's our strength and why, despite what may happen in this court case, we'll someday terraform Mars."

"You're an amazing woman and"—he gestured, encompassing the entire colony—"an amazing people. I don't think any other group could do what you're attempting."

"Thank you, but that's not quite correct. Jasper has suggested that we support the founding of a Navajo colony once the project gets under way. They have the same philosophy of service to community that we have, and the same independent cussedness. I think it's a good idea and will certainly be a help to us."

He gave her shoulders a little squeeze. "You'll get your chance."

"My, is this the judge stepping down slightly from Mount Olympus and rendering an opinion?"

"It's a judge who's said too damn much. You make of it what you will."

They had reached the outer door. "I know what to make of it, and thank you."

He waved at her, thrusting away the thanks, and headed back to the apartment, hoping that Jenny wouldn't be late.

He had just settled down with his discarded book when there was a knock at the door. Grumbling over the interruption, he set aside reader and wine, pulled back on his high-heeled boots, and answered. Three bulky figures in pressure suits, the faceplates carefully darkened, were waiting. He gaped at the descending pipe fitter's wrench, moved too late to block it, felt an explosion of pain at the base of his skull, and knew no more.

Chapter Eleven

A bone-deep vibration penetrated the dark haze that had wrapped itself about his brain and sent a shivering along the length of his body. Slowly he became aware of a hot prickling in his arms. *Jenny. . . . Must have fallen asleep with her on my arm.* He tried to shift, to ease the annoying pins-and-needles feeling, and was startled when nothing happened. Or rather, the wrong thing happened. His arms didn't move, but his stomach started jumping, and a flare of agony lanced through his head.

He gagged, and a voice out of the darkness said, "You'd better not puke. You're suited and helmeted, and even if you avoid inhaling it and killing yourself, it's still awfully gross." The voice was frightening, a harsh, guttural sound, as if acid had been poured over the vocal cords.

Slowly memory returned: the knock at the door, the suited figures, the wrench. So he had been kidnapped. And by someone he knew. The distortion of the voice proved that. Huntington vaguely wondered how one altered a radio to create that effect. The continuing darkness was starting to concern him. Perhaps he had lost his sight. Then he realized that the darkness was due to his eyes being tightly shut, and he forced apart the gummed lids. Overhead, he could see a curving metal ceiling set with a number of glowing panels. The faint green light from the various panels scattered about provided the only illumination, and in the bilious light three suited figures seemed to go swimming about like deep-sea divers. He closed his eyes several times, and when he looked again, his captors had steadied.

"Who . . ." His voice creaked like an old, unoiled machine starting up after years of disuse. He coughed and tried again. "Who are you?"

There was a nervous explosion of laughter from one of the figures. "Oh, yeah, we're sure gonna answer that."

The pilot—by now Cab had concluded that he was in a rocket jump ship—growled at his partner to shut up.

"All right, how about this?" Cab was pleased to hear that his voice was now level and held even a hint of boredom. "What do you want with me?" Two helmeted heads swiveled to regard their leader, who said nothing. The silence lengthened. "For God's sake, what are you going to do to me?" he demanded, his calm suddenly and completely broken. He pressed his lips together to prevent any further outburst.

There was a subtle deepening in the thunder of the thrusters, then several abrupt braking firings that jerked the passengers. Whoever was flying the jump ship was clearly not very adept.

Could it be one of the off-worlders? But this is a little much even for Lucius Renfrew.

They landed with a jarring bump that took Cab off-guard, and his teeth snapped shut on his tongue. He moaned and indulged in a few moments of abject self-pity, then realized that his survival might depend upon coolness and control. He pushed back fear, the jabbing awareness of his physical agony, and the sense of being a limp, helpless victim, and prepared himself to *act*.

He was hauled to his feet, a move that made him feel as if a grenade had gone off in the top of his head, and pushed to the door. The ladder was down, shoved deep into the russet sand, and around the landing struts a few fitful drops of water glittered in the landing lights of the ship before evaporating.

"I can't climb this with my arms tied."

The pilot clumped back into the jump ship and returned

with a pump shotgun nestled in the crook of his arm. "Untie him."

The smaller of the three figures jumped to obey, but to Cab's irritation he or she was careful not to obstruct their leader's aim.

"Okay, down."

The judge and two of his captors climbed down while the pilot stood guard at the top. The shotgun was tossed to his companion, and the leader came quickly down the ladder. Cab peered about. Off to his right he could barely make out a looming wall disappearing into the darkness overhead. Nearby were a few tumbled boulders and the ever-present sand. The commander of this little gang of terrorists jerked his head, and the old oxygen pack was yanked out of the suit pouch and a fresh one dropped in.

"Okay, Judge. You've got eight hours of air, rations, and water—and the suit radio. I don't think you're going to make it to an outpost or manage to attract the attention of what few jumps might be passing by, but we're not out-and-out killers, so we're giving you a chance."

"How very generous of you. But your little sophistry won't save you. This is murder, plain and simple."

"We wouldn't have had to do it, if you hadn't driven us to it."

"Ah, so now it's my fault. See if that will salve your consciences years from now. There will still be blood on your hands." There was a funny little noise from the smallest killer. The leader growled at her, and she and her companion started for the ladder. "Would you at least satisfy my curiosity?"

"About what?"

"Could I know who's murdering me?"

"Who do you think?" came the reply, and Cab decided that his earlier impression was correct. His captors were very young.

"I had thought Renfrew, but he's not that stupid. He would never put together a snatch as poorly planned as this one. So I assume you're some of the colonists."

"Yeah, that's right."

"Why?"

"Because you're out to screw us, and the project is too important to be stopped by one man."

"You stupid boy! What do think will happen once I'm

gone?" The suited form hesitated, then shrugged. "No, you haven't thought about that, have you? Use your brains and take me back to Jared."

"No, I won't let you harm us."

"God damn you!" Cab bellowed. "I'm going to rule against POW."

"You'd say fucking anything to save your skin, wouldn't you? Well, Mr. Big Shot Judge from Earth, I know you're a liar, because . . . well, my source told me what you really mean to do."

"Source? What source?" he shouted, starting to run for the ladder as the boy went slithering up. There was the whine of hydraulics, and the ladder slid into its compartment. "Don't," he cried, but the door cycled shut and the engines began warming up.

Not wanting to be cooked in the backthrust of the rockets, he stumbled backward and watched the jump ship climb steadily upward. It soon dwindled into a blinking point of light and was gone. Cab found a chair-high boulder and sank, shaking, onto the rough surface. He was trying to concentrate, to formulate plans, but panic ran shrieking along his nerves and his brain was spinning like a gerbil on a wheel. The sky began to lighten, and tendrils of mist came sighing up out of the ground like the souls of the dead. He was soon completely surrounded by a billowing cloud of fog. The sun rose higher, and the mists blew away to be quickly evaporated by the thin, cold air, and he could at last get a look at his surroundings.

He was at the bottom of a vast cliff. The rock wall jutted up four or five kilometers like a rampart built by giants. To his left was a wide plain dotted here and there with mesas. On Earth they would have been enormous, but measured against the wall behind him, they were like small pimples on the face of the planet. He tried to recall everything he knew about Mars and finally concluded that he was at the bottom of the Valles Marineris, the greatest canyon in the Solar System. After some struggle he brought to mind a fuzzy map of the planet showing the canyon thrusting through the Syria region, pointing obliquely toward Tharsis.

Tharsis—that was where the colony had its mining outpost. It was closed now because of the OSHA ruling, but Darnell had left a skeleton crew to guard the site. If he could move in that direction, he might have a chance. But first things first. He had to get out of the canyon. He studied the cliff face and discovered that it was shifted and offset, forming a series of ledges and handholds. It was going to be an absolutely terrifying climb, and by God, he'd better not look down, but he thought he could make it. Sucking in a deep breath through his nose, he took a sip of water, cycled an asprin out of the tiny first-aid kit in the helmet, swallowed it, and began to climb.

Some time later, as he blinked the sweat from his eyes, he wondered what picture he would present to any watchers. A tiny white-suited figure spread-eagled against a red escarpment like a modern-day Christ. He giggled and quickly bit down on his lower lip, realizing it was exhaustion and terror, not humor, that had elicited the laugh. He also didn't have air to waste.

Breathe, rotate your head to relieve the tension in your neck, stretch, climb.

He wondered how much time had passed, then decided he didn't want to know. *Only eight hours of air.* Measuring his life, not in falls of sand through an hourglass but by the drop of oxygen in a canister. Not as romantic or evocative an image, that, he mused as he reached a new handhold. What he had taken to be a knob of rock was in fact crumbling clay, and he yelled in terror as it pulverized in his hand, and he went scrabbling back down the cliff. Sliding in an avalanche of tiny pebbles, he felt the suit catch and rip; and the sharp hiss, like the exhalation of an angry cobra, as it resealed itself. He groaned as he came abruptly to rest on a ledge some three hundred feet below. A fist-sized rock was gouging him in the side, but for a long moment he didn't move, terrified that he would begin to fall again. The ledge held and he didn't. Instead, he gave way to terrified sobs. He was snorting like a frightened horse as he tried to draw a breath and control his tears. It took a few minutes, but he succeeded, then discovered that if puking in a suit was unpleasant, crying wasn't much better. His nose was streaming, and already the salt from his drying tears was beginning to prickle and itch on his cheeks.

He pushed cautiously to his feet and faced out across the canyon.

"God damn you!" he screamed. "I'm not going to die here!" It was uncertain whether the challenge was directed to the canyon or his kidnappers, but it made him feel better, and he soon resumed his climb.

"Jenny," he whispered during a rest. "Please notice I'm gone. Please come find me. Oh, and by the way . . . I'm sorry."

Jenny prowled the small apartment like a caged tigress. Occasionally she would stop and eye the com, wondering if she ought to call the Elysium station. But Amadea would only deny that he was there.

Maybe I should go instead. Just fly right over and walk in on them.

"And do what?" she asked aloud.

Shoot them both like a heroine in a bad Western? Throw a temper tantrum? Cry? Scream? Crawl in bed and join them? Maybe three would be better than one? Not as satisfying as two, but something.

"How could he do this to me?" she inquired of the silent room.

She had returned at midnight to find the apartment empty. A half-finished glass of wine sat on the table next to the gently humming reader. Cab had obviously left in a hurry. Couldn't wait to get his ashes hauled by that green-eyed slut! Very deliberately she picked up the glass and flung it across the room. It shattered, leaving a wash of red down the white wall sending sparkling shards of glass in all directions.

With quick, jerky movements she cycled the bed down out of the wall, stripped off her clothes, and crawled beneath the covers. "I don't know where he is or what he's up to, and I don't care. Screw him!"

She must have slept a little, but mostly all she remembered from that night was the sticky clinging of sweat-damp sheets as she tossed and turned, scrabbling about for lost pillows and sitting up, wide awake, at the least sound. Finally, at four A.M., she got up and decided that something was seriously wrong. Even if he'd been off humping Amadea, he should have been back by now. She suddenly realized that he couldn't have gone to Elysium. He didn't fly worth a damn and would not have set off at night. So they had to be somewhere nearby. Like at the hotel. She threw on clothes and went.

There was no night clerk, and she had to rouse Peter out of his apartment on the ground floor.

"Huh . . . wha . . . ?"

"Cab. Has he been here? *Is* he here?"

Peter stretched and yawned cavernously. "No, he hasn't been here since—" He broke off and rolled his eyes, trying to avoid her gaze.

"Oh, so he has been here."

"A time or two."

"With Amadea, I presume? Come on, Peter, yes or no?"

"Yes," he muttered.

"But he's not here now?"

"No."

"Thank you."

She was steaming as she headed across the dome toward the tunnel entrance leading to the Hudsons'. How many people in this colony knew about Cab's philandering and had been sniggering behind her back? *I'm really going to kill him,* she thought, *humiliating me this way.*

Jenny pulled up in front of the Hudsons' door, lifted her hand to ring, then hesitated when she heard Darnell's angry bellows.

"Where were you and Sarah last night? We know you were together because Sarah admitted it to her mama." There was an inaudible muttering then the sound of flesh hitting flesh. "God damn you, boy, you were raised better! If you ruined this girl, I'll have your balls."

More inarticulate murmuring, Jeanne's voice this time.

"Marry her? Of course he's going to marry her. I won't permit this in my colony."

Jenny didn't want to walk into the fight that was raging in the apartment, but fear for Cab won out over embarrassment, and she rang. The door was yanked open, and Jenny took a step back at the sight of a vein beating darkly in Hudsons' temple and the unhealthy brick-red color of his face. The Prophet apparently realized what a terrifying aspect he was presenting, ran his hand across his hair, and forced a smile to his lips.

"Oh, hi, Jenny."

"Darnell, is Jeanne in?"

"Well, yes, but we're sort of in the middle of a family crises." The door was starting to close. "So if you could come back later . . ."

Jenny wedged her shoulder against the door. "Darnell,

please. I'm sorry to be rude and pushy, but I'm worried about Cab."

"Cab?" Jeanne's voice came floating from the front room. "What about him?"

Darnell gave up, stepped back, and Jenny tumbled into the apartment. Jeanne was looking haggard, in a faded blue bathrobe with her gray hair stringing down her back. Seth, who was fully dressed, stared sullenly into a corner of the room. He glanced briefly at Jenny, then his eyes slid away.

"When I came back from rehearsal last night, he wasn't there, and he still hasn't come back. I'm afraid . . ." Her fingers knotted as she considered how foolish and almost melodramatic her next remark was going to sound. "I'm afraid something's happened to him."

Jeanne and Darnell's eyes met for an awkward moment, and Jenny writhed inwardly with chagrin, and even a little hurt. Everyone did know, came the sad, sighing little thought. She sucked in a deep breath and squared her shoulders.

"And no, I don't think he's with Amadea. Cab doesn't fly well enough to have gone to her, and she doesn't seem to be here." She hung her head as she admitted, "I checked."

"Why do you think something's happened," asked Seth, ignoring his father's boarlike glare. "Couldn't he just have gone off for a walk or something?"

"For the entire night? No." She shook her head. "I can't pinpoint why, but I'm certain something's wrong. He went off and left his reader running. Cab would never do that. Books are too important to him, and he wouldn't risk damaging a disk that way."

By now the Prophet was beginning to frown. He tugged at his bushy eyebrows and gave a grunt. "Could be there is something wrong. I wouldn't put it past those POW people to try something underhanded." Jenny wondered about Seth's look of surprise and confusion at the suggestion that POW might be behind Cab's disappearance, but she was too worried to spend much time analyzing it. "I'll call the elders and see if anyone noticed anything last night. Will you be here?"

Jeanne crossed swiftly to Jenny's side and slipped an arm about her shoulders. "Of course she'll be here. I'm not going to let her sit home alone to brood and worry."

"Can I help, Dad?"

Hudson glared and his jaw worked. "No! You stay here.

We're still not finished with that little matter we were discussing before Jenny arrived, and I mean to pick it up when I get home."

The door slammed behind his burly frame, and Seth sidled toward his bedroom. "I'll leave you two. Got some stuff to do."

"Fine," Jeanne said, and waved him away.

"You looked exhausted."

"I haven't had much sleep."

Jeanne guided her to the couch. "Something to drink? Some juice or herb tea? How about breakfast?" Jenny jerked a shoulder. "No, of course you wouldn't feel like eating at a time like this."

"I swear to God, Jeanne, if he comes waltzing in three hours from now saying he's been out watching the sun rise, or some other damn thing, and asks why I was being such a hysteric, I'll kill him. I . . . no, I won't. I'll be too damn relieved at seeing him."

Twenty minutes later a call came from Darnell reporting that a suit and an extra oxygen canister was missing and that one of the jump craft had a number of unlogged miles on it.

"You're sure Cab couldn't have taken the ship out?"

"Not a chance, Darnell. He can't even fly a Light, or at least not very well. He wouldn't be stupid enough to mess with a rocket-powered ship."

"Then it looks like he's been dumped somewhere, but whoever did it is giving him a fighting chance—leaving that extra canister." Jenny clung to the back of a chair, doubled over from the gripping pain in her stomach. "The chief's hauling in those POW people, and I'm sending out search parties. Now don't worry, Jenny, we'll find him." But there was an undercurrent of doubt running beneath the encouraging words, and Jenny acknowledged how hopeless it was. In the old hackneyed phrase: It was a big planet.

Andy Throckmorton came slouching in, his fat face pulled down into sympathetic folds, but his eyes were bright and probing, and as soon as he had lowered his bulk onto the sofa, the questions began.

Jenny answered the first couple without thinking, then leapt to her feet and glared down at the journalist. "Andy, are you writing a fucking story?"

"Sorry, babe, but yeah. That's the name of the game. This

is news, and I'm going to report on it. So sit down and let's go over it. Who knows, aside from helping me earn a living—"

"Don't you care about Cab at all?" Her hands were shaking and she gripped them tightly.

His head dropped, and he pushed out his lower lip, which made him look like a miserable baby. "You know I do," he said quietly. "But it's hard for me to say things like that. Cynicism is my stock-in-trade. I'm sorry. And like I was going to say: If we talk it over, we might pick up something."

Jenny dropped limply onto the sofa next to him. "There's nothing to pick up. He's just gone."

He patted clumsily at her shoulder. "Have faith."

"I thought cynicism was your stock-in-trade," Jeanne said in an undertone, and went to stir up a pan of brownies. Like many older women, she was convinced of the efficacy of food in a crisis.

Andy and Jenny were still talking when another grumbling call came in from Darnell, announcing that the POW activists seemed as clean as a baby's bottom and had been released. Hearing that, Andy heaved himself off the couch and headed for the door.

"Gotta go and pulse this home before those pet journalists of POW beat me to it. God, it's a dog-eat-dog world," he remarked as he left, but Jenny and Jeanne were paying no attention. They were too busy listening to Darnell telling them how he was about to go out with a search party, and how every available Light and jump ship was in the air, and how he had alerted the various scientific stations within their search radius.

"Nothing to do but wait now." Jeanne sighed as she snapped off the com.

Jenny hugged herself, as if the enfloding arms could somehow keep her from flying to pieces. A scream was beating its way free, making her throat ache and her chest feel like a slowly exploding bomb. She was torn between crazed behaviors; to curl up in a ball on the floor, beat at the walls with her fists and scream her throat raw, or run crying through the colony and out into the Martian desert to search for him.

"Jeanne . . ." She barely opened her lips, fearful that the maelstrom of emotion would come boiling out. "He's going to die, I know it."

The older woman took her in her arms, in a way Jenny's

own mother never had, and rocked her gently back and forth. But her words were comfortless.

"If God wills."

President Richard Long spun to face his White House Chief of Staff, his expression both concerned and confused.

"Lis—"

"I just heard and came right away. I'm shocked, Rick."

"What in hell is going on up there?" The President ran his hands over his hair. Huntington kidnapped . . . maybe dead, embargoes on diamonds, ships getting reregistered, OSHA and SPACECOM investigations."

"I discussed this with you."

"The hell you did. All you said—"

"Was that Gemetics was counting on us to give them a little help, which you thought was a good idea. You also didn't like the way the money from the sale of those diamonds was going to be used."

"Refresh my memory."

"That big terraforming project." Her hands sliced the air. "But this is pointless. What matters is that a government official has been kidnapped and possibly killed by the colonists."

"You have proof of this?"

"I have a very reliable source that indicates that the colonists are behind this. Naturally I'll want more proof, but in the meantime we should do something."

"Such as?"

"Send a message to the System that this kind of lawless behavior is not going to be permitted."

"Uh . . ."

"Stop gobbling. We're not going to end up in a deBaca situation. *We* didn't start this, but we're going to look like pricks if we don't finish it."

"That's sounds pretty damn grim and threatening."

"I'm not talking about napalming babies," she snapped, exasperated by his recoil from the thought of force. Sometimes she damned the fates that had put her behind the throne rather than on it. This was one of those moments. "All I'm suggesting is that we put the deep-space squadron on standby alert with the clear indication that we'll send it in if the colonists don't straighten up and fly right."

He dithered, his hands opening and closing into halfhearted

fists. "I don't feel like I have a very clear picture of all this. Could you—"

"I'll get a report to you. Now will you put the squadron on alert?"

"Well, I suppose—"

"Good. Oh, yes, I've drafted a statement. If you approve, I'll have Fred release it."

He stared at the four lines of spidery scrawl and nodded slowly. "Okay, that's fine." He was looking like a puzzled child faced by a new object that might or might not contain a threat.

She smiled reassuringly and bumped his chin lightly with a fist. "It'll be okay, really. Somebody's got to take a stand on the System sooner or later, and you're the best person to do it because they know you're not their enemy."

"Are they going to know that after today?"

"Rick, even the most loving parent occasionally gives the kids a whack." She whirled and headed for the door.

"They're awfully tough kids," she heard him mutter, but she didn't dignify the remark with a reply. She had things to do, and a quick and quiet celebration she wasn't going to miss.

The brutal winter had ended abruptly, leaving weathermen worldwide scratching their heads and predicting something freakish from the—so far—perfect spring. In Washington the cherry trees were in full bloom. Lis, having finished her arrangements, strolled a walkway flanked on both sides by the colorful trees. She felt like a figure out of a Salamith Wulfing painting, the pale pink petals dancing about her, carried by a bracing wind. In one hand she carried a small wicker picnic basket while the other held on to her wide-brimmed straw hat, its multicolored ribbons streaming behind her.

William Devert was waiting on a bench in the park. He grinned.

"What's with the virgin milkmaid look? You're supposed to be the Mona Lisa of politics, not an escapee from a fairy tale."

She pirouetted before him, the ankle-length pink skirt with its lacy white petticoat swirling about her. "Don't you like it? I thought I would soften up my image. Richard Long's baby doll instead of his lady Machiavelli."

"Lis, my darling, even if you were attired in nothing but feathers and lace and had a sucker in your mouth, you'd still look exactly like what you are—the Iron Maiden." She frowned, and the irritation she felt was half feigned and half real. "It's the eyes that give you away. Far too calculating." He reached out and flicked a petal from the bodice of her dress. "You're also looking inordinately pleased with yourself."

"So should you, and why didn't you tell me? Why did you wait for me to get it off a bulletin on the comnet?"

He shrugged. "I didn't want to gloat." He smiled again, but the pleasure faded fast. "Seriously, unlike your beautiful self, I take no pleasure in the removal of Huntington. But it was something that had to be done."

"And this regret, of course, makes you pure."

"No, but you seem positively delighted by the news."

"I had nothing against Huntington personally and I'm sorry for him, but you have to take the long view in all of this."

"Yeah, like the next election."

She stiffened, then shook her head. "Bill, I'm not going to fight with you. We're both in this up to our necks, you for business reasons and me for . . ."

"Yes, why?"

"I really do think the System has got to be cemented back to Earth," she said.

He blew a loud and long raspberry.

"Fuck you too."

"Lis, cut the crap. This has nothing to do with philosophy. It has to do with pride and power, and you know it."

She smiled at him from the corners of her strange, elongated eyes. "If I say yes, will you be nice and drink champagne with me?"

"Oh, I suppose so."

She twisted off the wires, pushed out the cork, and poured two glasses. "Up Joe Reichart."

He drank, then said, "So that's it."

"Um-hm. He's been bedeviling administrations for thirty years, but I'm going to be the one who beats him."

"Here's to winning." But his mouth twisted as he said the words, and he knocked back the remaining champagne like it was water.

"Amen."

• • •

Jeanne shifted the casserole pan and wished she could have just this once pushed this particular duty off on someone else. She hadn't wanted to leave Jenny, but at least the girl had agreed to lie down, and perhaps she was even sleeping. Then Jeanne remembered that it was her day to provide meals to the Schmidts, and she had flown about the kitchen, throwing together a casserole. Ernie had been the chief designer of the colony and had worked like a white-haired Prometheus to deepen the crater, build the dome, and drill out the living quarters. But in recent years he had begun to fail, and when Susan, his wife of forty-seven years, had been reduced to a breathing husk by a sudden stroke, he had lost all ability to cope. The Relief Society had stepped in to care for them. Jeanne had recently begun to pray that Susan could be taken, for Ernie became feebler every day, and what would happen when they were both invalids did not bear thinking about. Obviously homes would have to be found for them with other families, but what a blow to a proud old man who had been one of the founders of the colony.

And Darnell and I are getting up there too. How long until something comes on one of us? At least we have Seth . . .

"Yoo hoo, Jeanne." Jerked from her melancholy reverie, Jeanne looked up to see Evie Standish hailing her from the door of her apartment. "On your way to the Schmidts'?"

"Yes."

"Well, I won't keep you. I have a little question." Evie's fingers made nervous pleats out of the edge of her pullover shirt. "Now, I'm not accusing Seth of anything, but last night Ben didn't come home until almost five o'clock. He wouldn't say anything, but then his daddy put the fear of God in him and he finally admitted he'd been out with Seth. I'm sure it's some foolish prank or other, but I don't like them behaving so—"

Relief swept over her, followed by a sick certainty. "Evie, please take this to Ernie." She shoved the casserole into the woman's hands. "And send Ben over to the apartment right away. Do you know where he is? This is critical."

"He's right here. Dan grounded him."

"Good, then he can walk back with me." She turned the younger woman and pushed her into the apartment. "Hurry."

With Ben trailing behind, Jeanne paused only to collect

Sarah before hurrying home. Ben had been sulky and bored, but with the inclusion of Sarah in the little party his expression shifted to one of nervous fear. Jeanne burst into the apartment, calling for Seth and Jenny, then checked and moderated her tone, for they were already present in the front room, and they had a guest. Amadea was seated on the sofa next to Jenny, looking solicitous and occasionally reaching out to give the attorney's hand a sympathetic squeeze. Each time it happened, Jenny would stiffen and try to withdraw. Amadea seemed oblivious to the body language, however, and Jeanne wondered if she was really that insensitive or simply didn't care. She needed to get the Eurasian out of the apartment, and there didn't seem any polite way to do it, so she bluntly said, "Amadea, could you please leave. We have something to discuss."

"Is it something I could help with?"

"No." She opened the door, making it impossible for the girl to refuse.

Seth stood in the background, agitatedly shifting weight from one foot to the other. There were a number of pregnant glances being exchanged by the three teenagers.

"Jenny, I think I'm about to solve the mystery of Cab's whereabouts, but—"

"Where? What?" She came off the couch like she'd been launched.

She held her off. "Before I do this, I want a promise from you."

"What? Yes, of course, anything."

"I want you to convince Cabot to show a little leniency toward my foolish children once he's back." There was a babble of outraged denials from the kids, quickly quelled by a look from Jeanne. "I should have realized it a lot earlier. The clues were right under my nose, but it took Evie to put it together for me. You walked in on a fight this morning. Sarah's father called, snorting fire and ready to emasculate my son because he had been out with Sarah all night. Having dirty minds, we all assumed there had been some youthful rutting going on." Sarah turned pink and shook her hair forward to hide her face.

"Then a few minutes ago Evie Standish asked what Seth and *Ben* had been up to last night. Now, I know darned good and well that Seth may be randy, but he's not kinky, and taking a buddy along on an amorous outing makes about as much sense as wings on turtles."

"So you think the kids . . ." Jenny's eyes slid from guilty face to guilty face, reading the answer. "Oh, God," she whispered, and sank back down on the couch.

"This whole affair has been so badly planned and carried out—from the missing suit to failing to log the jump ship miles so it became apparent there had been an unauthorized use—I should have seen immaturity written all over it."

Jenny had regained the use of her legs. Running to Seth, she gathered the material of his jacket in both hands and gave him a shake. "Where's Cab? Where did you leave him?"

Seth glanced at Ben, who shrugged. "Better tell her. I guess the games up."

"This is not a game! Cab is out there dying! Now where is he?" The words were being forced past clenched teeth.

"Out near Melas Lacus. I can show you on a map."

"Get it!"

Sarah was crying. "We thought it was for the best, Mrs. Hudson. We knew he was against us and we were just trying—"

"Where did you get that idea? Cab never said anything, and I'll tell you now that he intended to rule in favor of the project!" cried Jenny.

Seth erupted back out of his room, a map fluttering limply in his fingers. "I don't believe it. I was told—" He bit down on the words and turned a bright red.

"Told what? By whom?"

"I heard it here and there," he said lamely.

"I don't have time to pursue it now, but I will want an answer. Someone's been sowing suspicion and misinformation ever since we arrived, and I'm going to find out who. Now show me where Cab is."

"Are you going to tell Pater?" Seth asked Jeanne in an undertone as she moved to the com.

"Not now. I'm going to give the searchers the location. But he will have to be told." Tears pricked at her eyes, and she suddenly felt every one of her sixty-seven years. "I only hope it doesn't kill him."

"I really fucked up. Can *you* ever forgive me?"

"Yes, but it will be a lot easier if we get this man back alive."

Jeanne punched through to her husband, but what came back was not encouraging. "Okay, we roger, but it looks like it's trying to come up a blow, and we may get grounded."

Jenny was raging about the room, weaving an intricate pattern about the furniture. "I want to go too." She snatched back the map. "That's about five hundred and fifty, sixty miles?"

"Yeah, about that."

"In a Light I can be there in about three hours. I'll carry a couple of extra canisters and—"

"If it comes up a blow, you can't get back in a Light."

"Then we'll wait it out until a jump ship can reach us."

"Every available ship is already flying," Ben offered hesitantly.

That stopped her but only for a moment. "Then I'll take Amadea's. She flew over from the site. She won't mind."

Seth's lips twitched, then folded tightly together. Jeanne, knowing Amadea's curiosity, pulled open the door and, as she had expected, found the girl waiting in the hall outside.

"Amadea, Jenny needs your Light. She's a good pilot, so I'm sure you won't mind lending it. She's going after Cab."

"Then you know where he is."

"We have a pretty good idea."

"I could go."

"No," Jenny said flatly.

"I think this is something Jenny should do, and has to do. I would feel the same if it were Darnell." Amadea flushed under the cool appraisal in Jeanne's eyes.

"Please, take the Light," the Eurasian said, as if it had been her idea all along. "We'll all be waiting anxiously to hear from you."

"Can we . . ." Seth gestured to himself and the other teenagers. "Can we . . . help you get ready."

There was a momentary struggle, clearly presented on the redhead's delicate face. Then she nodded abruptly, and Jeanne released a pent-up breath. Maybe things were going to work out, after all.

Chapter Twelve

The extra canisters were a soothing hardness beneath the palm of Jenny's gloved hand, as for the hundredth time she reached back to reassure herself of their presence. The flight was going well, and the horrible, numbing pain that had been her constant companion for the past eight hours was gone. In its place was an almost manic feeling of confidence. She was going to find Cab, he was going to be all right, they were going to get him safely home, and then she was going to kill him.

No, that was wrong. If nothing else, this ordeal had served to show her exactly how much she did love him—warts and all.

"And right now he's a positive toad," she said aloud. "But, God, I'll be glad to see him."

She checked the time on the suit chronometer and decided that in thirty minutes she would start calling for him. He should be in radio range by then. Thank God Darnell's prediction of a big blow seemed to be exaggerated. The landscape was quiet, quieter than she had ever seen it on Mars. No tiny dust devils played coyly about the foot of the range of eroded hills that thrust up out of the red sand like old, worn teeth from a beggar's gums. The only motion was from the thin wavelike clouds skittering across the salmon sky like frightened white hares. Darnell, or any other longtime resident of Mars, could have told her the significance of those racing clouds, but she was alone, and the little plane droned on, taking her farther and farther from any safe haven.

Abruptly the plain ended, and she was staring down into the vast depths of the Valles Marineris. Rags of mist were whipping around the sides of a tall mesa in the center of the canyon like the ghost pennants of some long-defeated army. The Light bucked under the buffeting down drafts generated by the rift, and Jenny sensed the great wings thrumming with strain. For the first time since setting out she felt fear, and she wished she hadn't flown so casually across the canyon. Still, it seemed necessary, for she was relying on Cab having discerned where he was, then heading north toward the Tharsis mines. She reached the opposite wall of the canyon and the turbulence stopped. It was time for the radio. She only hoped Cab was listening.

"—bot Huntington. I believe I'm somewhere to the south of the Tharsis region, moving away from the Valle Marineris. I'm extremely low on oxygen, so—" Here the control broke momentarily, and he muttered, "So could somebody please hurry?"

His voice sounded like sandpaper being pulled across slate, but he was alive and calm and in fair condition.

"Cabot, you scumbag, you're wonderful," Jenny muttered as her throat squeezed shut and tears pricked her eyelids. She coughed hard to clear her throat and called, "Cab, Cab."

"Jenny?" Disbelief filled the word.

"Yes. Where are you? Give me a landmark, something to sight on."

"No landmarks. I just finished dragging over a range of hills, and now I'm in the middle of a dune field."

"Hills, right, I see them. Now let's see if they're the right hills and if you're on the other side." Jenny kept her voice as level as his, but a pulse was jumping in her throat, and she was torn between wanting to shout, scream, cry, or laugh.

He was easy to spot; a little white-suited figure standing on the crest of a dune. Jenny found a reasonably level stretch in the midst of the wind-carved sands and set down. Only now did she allow herself to lose control. Scrabbling for the extra canister, she hugged it to her chest, pushed back the canopy, jumped, and ran. The deep sand grabbed at her booted feet, making her lurch and sway. Cab advanced more slowly, and as she drew closer she could see that he was limping and that his right arm was cradled in his left.

They met, and she didn't waste time with questions or embraces, but yanked out the old canister and slammed in the new. Her knees almost gave way when she saw how little oxygen remained in the old tanks. and she pulled him into her arms. He winced as she touched his arm, then began to shake as reaction set in.

"I knew you'd come," he finally said.

"I knew I'd find you."

"So there, see? Nothing to worry about." A hysterical little titter shook him.

"Are you badly hurt?"

He drew in several breaths and shook his head. "No, I slipped climbing out of the canyon and hurt my leg, and the arm I did in the hills."

"Broken?"

"I don't think so, but I wouldn't be averse to a hot bath, a stiff drink, and some painkillers."

"Then let's get you some." She was helping him back to the Light when he suddenly looked up and frowned.

"This is Amadea's Light."

"Yes," she snapped, angry at even a reference to the Eurasian. "I commandeered it."

He seemed to sense that any further reference to the geologist might cause an explosion. "How did you find me?"

"Later." She had suddenly become aware of a faint whistling about her helmet and how the wind plucked at the exposed surfaces on the suit. She scanned the horizon but saw no sign of a storm. It didn't reassure her. There was a prickling at the base of her neck, and fear lay like a cold knot in the pit of her stomach. It was a long way back to Jared. Heedlessly she gripped Cab by the elbow and bundled him into the Light, ignoring his protests and cries of pain.

As the Light soared into the sky she wondered why she had been so rough. If there were indeed a blow coming, a few extra seconds spent easing Cab into the cramped backseat wouldn't have made that much difference. For a few minutes she sat probing at the hard knot of emotions that sat like a frozen lump in the center of her breast. What surfaced was a perverse, bitter pleasure at the pain she had inflicted. What she really wanted was emotional pain—to hurt him the way he had hurt her—but that seemed beyond her right now. So she had settled for physical hurt. It wasn't pretty, and she was ashamed of the response. It was also very human, and she tried to excuse herself on those grounds. The excuse didn't work, and as they skimmed across the bleak Martian landscape her sense of euphoria died to be replaced by an angry sense of ill usage.

Cab said nothing. In fact, he had rested his head against the clear canopy and seemed to be asleep; his response infuriated her. He should have said something, showered her with compliments, with gratitude. But even as the thought flickered past she realized that if he had opened his mouth, she would have gone down his throat.

"So you're a goddamn irrational bitch!" she muttered aloud, and that made her feel worse than ever.

"Dr. Singh is of the opinion that the writings are unconnected, while Beals thinks they are a complete message. I personally hope that Beals is right, because otherwise there's no real coherent message, and that would be—"

"Amadea, shut up," Jeanne Hudson said wearily.

"Well!"

"Was that rude?" the older woman mused almost more to herself than her unwanted companion. "Yes, that was rude." She gave herself a little shake and faced the younger women. "But I'm not going to apologize. Amadea, I'm really not in the mood for chitchat, so if you're going to stay, could you please be quiet?"

"What else can I do, since you let that woman take off with my Light?"

There was a load of venom in the words, and Jeanne stared. She had never before heard such a tone out of the lovely Eurasian.

"I'm sorry—" they both began, then eyed each other warily.

Amadea raised a hand to her eyes. "I was babbling, and I'm sorry. I guess I thought—stupidly—that conversation would comfort us. I'm very worried about Cabot."

"I'm very worried about *both* of them."

"Jeanne, have I done something to offend you? I wouldn't for the world, you know that, and if you'd just tell me—"

"Oh, Amadea! Really!" Jeanne rose and took an agitated turn about the room. "We're not blind. The way you've been carrying on with Justice Huntington . . . well, I'm ashamed of you."

"Not all of us share your views on morality."

"I'm not talking about morality. I'm talking about simple decency. To jerk that girl around." She pressed her lips firmly together. "In a less close-knit or polite colony she would have been made a laughingstock, and I admire the way she handled the situation. She never whined or made a scene. She displayed breeding and dignity."

"Meaning that I haven't?" They stared hard at one another. "I told you weeks ago I was attracted to the man."

"So that makes it all right? Ethically you should have talked with both Cab and Jenny, to get everybody's feelings out on the table, and if they didn't have an open relationship, you should have backed off. Actually I'm ashamed of Cab for not discussing the matter." She paused and considered. "No, that's foolish of me. Men are always a little crazy where sex is concerned."

She looked up and was startled by the hard, almost predatory, green light in Amadea's exotic eyes. "I get what I want, Jeanne, and I apologize to no one for wanting. Now if you'll excuse me, I think I'll go talk to Seth."

She had scarcely left before the door flew open and Darnell came stumping into the apartment. Jeanne started toward him, then checked herself with momentary indecision when she realized that she still had not made a decision whether to tell him about Seth, Ben, and Sarah. As a devout Mormon woman, she should instantly appraise him of his only child's sin, not only because he was father and husband but because he was Prophet. But what might such a revelation do to him? And worse, do to the relationship between father and son? In that instant she decided—she would say nothing and pray that Jenny could convince Cab to do likewise. The decision made, she moved swiftly to his side and helped him out of the pressure suit.

"What are you doing here?"

"We had to turn back and get to ground. There's a hell of a

blow coming up." He scrubbed at his face with his hands, then, becoming aware of her silence, looked up. "What's wrong?" He glanced about the apartment. "Where's Jenny?"

"Gone."

"Using what?"

"Amadea's Light."

"Are you out of your mind? Why did you let her go?"

"I would like you to have seen me try to stop her."

"I told you there was a blow coming up."

"You said there *might* be." They glared at each other, then she took a quick turn about the room.

"Oh, this is pointless, the recriminations."

"She shouldn't have gone. *You* should have had more sense even if she didn't."

"I understood how she felt. If it had been you out there in the desert, I would have gone and probably killed anyone who tried to keep me from it. I would have crawled on hands and knees to reach you." She gripped him by the front of his shirt, gazing intently up into his face. "And Jenny loves Cab. I couldn't—wouldn't—have stopped her."

"And if they both die?"

Her hand went to her throat. "You can't mean that."

He grunted. "It looks like it could be a bad blow."

She pulled in several quick breaths to steady herself, then met him squarely, eye to eye. "Then at least they'll die together. And with God's mercy it won't happen."

"Amen." He lowered himself wearily onto the couch and stretched out.

"I'll fix you some soup, and then you'd better sleep. You'll be heading out as soon as the wind dies."

He caught her by the hand as she started to pass. "Always the practical one."

"It's woman's gift. Somebody has to keep her feet on the ground while you men go rushing about saving or losing the universe."

His eyes were soft as he looked up into her lined face, and the stern set of her jaw relaxed. "Jeannie, when was the last time I told you that I loved you?"

"Too long. So tell me."

"And the soup?"

"It can wait."

• • •

Cab was asleep, his snores rattling and wheezing over her helmet radio. Jenny glanced back over her shoulder, noting how exhaustion and strain had deepened the hollows beneath his cheekbones, heightening the foxy cast of his narrow face. Reaching back, she stroked a hand down the curve of the helmet, thinking again how close she had come to losing him, and with an emotional, mental sigh she released her anger. Better that she remember that gut-wrenching sense of completeness, joy, relief, and anguish that had gripped her as she went stumbling across the sand, and she finally closed her arms around him. People took things too much for granted, forgetting in the mundane day-to-day grind what made a relationship special. She had had a forceful and terrifying lesson, and she didn't intend to forget it.

There was a faint peppering on the tedlar wing covering, and the fiberglass pod of the Light, and Jenny jerked her attention back to the front window. What she saw choked off the breath in her throat and set her heart to hammering. A mountainous wall of sand was marching toward the Light like an avalanche of ochre snow. Giant dust devils preceded it like the outriders of some terrifying, elemental army. The small, thin clouds were seized by the wind and ripped to shreds, helpless prey in the teeth of a hunter.

Jenny started to turn the Light, then realized that she could never outrun such a monster. Her only hope was to land. A low outcropping of hills beckoned, and she headed for them, hoping that within those stubby mounds they could find some shelter. She had time only to scream out Cab's name before the wind slammed into them, sending the fragile craft tumbling end over end. The judge awoke with a yell of terror and clutched with his good arm at the back of her seat.

The plane was vibrating like a plucked string. Jenny fought with controls that seemed frozen and at last righted the Light. But they weren't flying. They were at the mercy of the wind, and it was not compassionate. The Martian ultra-lights were designed with snap-off wings for easy storage. Under normal circumstances it represented no danger, but in the grip of such a monster storm it was a disaster. There was a sharp crack, and Jenny jerked her head to the left just in time to see a wing fold like an origami bird. It was carelessly plucked free and went spinning off into the billowing clouds of dust.

She had no idea how close to the ground they were, and as she felt the other wing go, she wanted to say something—some cry of love and loss, a farewell to Cab—but nothing emerged but a sliding scream. A dark shadow loomed up, and the Light slammed nose-first into the obstruction. For a long moment Jenny hunched over the controls thinking that it wasn't fair for every bone and muscle to hurt after she was dead. A hand closed like a vise on her shoulder, and she let out a squeak.

"Jenny?"

She rotated slowly in the shattered seat, as if fearful that parts of herself would fall away if she moved too quickly, and focused on Cab. A trickle of blood was running from a cut over his eye and down his nose where a large drop hung trembling on the tip. She choked down a desire to laugh and said instead, "We're alive."

"Would you mind terribly if I said I wished I weren't?"

"I understand. I feel like a road pizza myself."

She became aware that they were shouting. It wasn't strictly necessary, the suit radios were working well, but the shriek of the wind as it blasted past the ruined Light made it seem necessary. Sand was peppering in through the broken canopy, and suddenly a pile of the stuff let go with a sigh and slid down into her lap. She yelled and shoved ineffectually at the encroaching softness.

"What do we do now?"

"I don't know."

Cab tried to peer out through the dull ochre pall. "If we can turn the Light so it's facing the hill, and the bottom of the pod to the wind, we'll have some shelter."

"Some shelter."

"Better than nothing."

"But we'll have to get out in the storm."

"We're not exactly *out* of it now," he shouted back as one of the exposed LegerSteel ribs shivered in the wind, producing a strange, almost musical moaning sound.

"Okay, we'll try it."

The hole in the canopy wasn't big enough to crawl through, so she had to kick at the cockpit canopy to get it open. It popped back with a screech, and she wriggled free of the wreckage. Cab followed more slowly because of his injuries. Though the Light weighed only four hundred and fifty pounds (less now that the wings were gone,) the howling wind made turning it an interesting proposition. Once, when they were on the verge of making the flip, the wind seized the ruined aircraft and sent it cartwheeling across the rocky foot of the hill with Jenny clinging to it like a circus stunt-rider. Cab yelled and plunged, limping, after her, gripped an exposed rib, and dug his heels into the coarse sand. They finally wrestled the plane to a stop and found that its move had been fortuitous. They were now between two outcroppings of rock.

Again they fought with the ungainly Light. Sweat was pouring down Cab's sides and stinging the cut on his forehead, but still the beast refused to move. Jenny, driven almost to distraction by the dentist's-drill quality of the shrieking wind, suddenly dropped her end, clapped her hands to her helmet, and let out a scream of vexation.

"That . . . won't . . . help," panted Cab, hugging the Light to remain upright.

"I can't stand it!"

"Well, I'm not exactly enjoying this, either!"

They stared, snorting at each other, then Jenny set her jaw and plunged like a blocking tackle at the beached plane. It creaked and moved, and Cab snatched quickly at the edge of the canopy to help it on its way.

"You fucker!" wheezed Jenny, and this time Cab didn't remonstrate with her for crudity. Under the circumstances it seemed entirely justified. With a groan the Light settled onto its side. Blowing like spent horses, they leaned against the shaking frame and slowly linked hands.

"Are we having an adventure?" rasped Jenny through a dry throat.

"Yes. Can't say I think much of it, and people who would actually go looking for one are nuts."

Lying on her belly, Jenny rolled into the fuselage. "At least we'll have the satisfaction of being able to bore the snot out of our grandchildren by constant repetitions of this story."

She reached back to help Cab, and he gratefully accepted the proffered hand. His leg and arm seemed to be on fire, and his head reverberated to the poundings of a migrain headache.

"Assuming we live to sire and produce children." They were faceplate-to-faceplate, and her white, strained face with its shadowed eyes stared out at him. "We're in a hole, aren't we, Jenny?"

"If this thing lasts too long, yes. We'll run out of air. If it doesn't, we should be fine. Jeanne knows where I was headed. All they have to do is backtrack me."

"And if we've been blown far afield by the wind?"

"Don't be such a goddamn pessimist! I don't think we tumbled that far."

"Does the radio work?"

She reached up and flipped the dials several times. "Nope. But the ones in our suits work, and the automatic distress beacon on the Light is working."

"Both of those have a really limited range."

"You're driving me crazy."

"Sorry," he snapped, irritated by her tone. "But you haven't been out here as long as I have. I've used up my quota of optimism."

She rolled onto her side, presenting him with her back. He nearly gave into a weak desire to cry but bit it back. Still, the momentary emotional storm had served one purpose. It brought home just how foolish it was to fight. This might be their final hours together—better to spend them lovingly supporting each other. He inched closer and slipped an arm around her. After a moment the rigidity drained slowly from her body and she snuggled close.

"Let's sleep awhile."

"Okay, but not too long. I don't want to just drift on in to . . ."

"We're not going to die out here. I'm utterly determined to get back and get even."

That brought her up. Staring down at him, her faceplate a dark, reflective surface, she shook her head. "No."

"No? What no? In case you haven't noticed, someone tried to kill me and may succeed in fortuitously killing us both."

"It was a terrible misunderstanding," she faltered, and as if realizing how lame that sounded, tried again. "I promised Jeanne—"

"Jeanne?" he exploded, and forgetting, he pushed up on his injured arm. He dropped back with a groan.

"No, no, she wasn't involved."

"Well, the colonists sure as hell were."

"Not exactly. It was a handful of silly children, thinking they were being big heroes." He muttered something so rude and vulgar for him that it shocked her into a momentary silence. She shrugged as if dislodging something unpleasant from her shoulders. "Okay, it was shitty, but I know Jeanne isn't going to let this pass, and I think it would be a lot better to keep it an intercolony thing rather than involving the entire System by hauling them into court. They believed you were against them, and when they found out differently, they were devastated. I don't think anything you could do would equal the guilt they've already endured thinking they had killed an innocent man."

"So that makes it all right."

"Do not take that tone with me! I'm not saying that and you know it. I'm pointing out that these are not hardened criminals, and this experience has scared the shit out of them."

"So what in hell am I supposed to say once I get back? Assuming I get back?"

"That you don't know who did it. Besides, those kids are the wrong item. We really need to go after the person who convinced them that you were going to rule in POW's favor."

That brought Cab up short, and he recalled his kidnappers' reference to a "source." "That's going to be damn near impossible if these 'kids' don't tell us."

"I don't think they will. They're shielding someone."

"Which implies that a colonist was behind this whole thing and intensifies my desire not to be forgiving."

"Oh, Cab, just hear this damn case and get it over with. The sooner POW—and we—are off Mars, the better."

"You're biased, Jenny, terribly biased. You'll protect the colonists who tried to kill me but remain adamant against POW."

"That is a really shitty thing to say. You try to crucify me for getting involved, for having opinions. But I say you're a damn liar if you deny that you have them too."

"Fine! Then my *opinion* is that I ought to prosecute my kidnappers to the limit of the law. I want my emotional satisfaction by seeing them punished."

"Oh, for God's sake! They're children!"

"I hardly consider them to be below the age of rational thought."

"It must be nice to be as morally ascendant and unforgiving as you are. But there's a danger, Cab. Someday you might need a little understanding and forgiveness, and you're not going to find it."

She skittered away from him, drawing her knees up close to her chest as she maneuvered in the tiny cockpit of the wrecked Light. He hugged himself close, ignoring the stabs of pain from his injured arm. It was both a sheltering gesture and a control, as if the pressure of his arms could hold back the flood of guilt, anger, and justification that was threatening to erupt. It was pointless to pretend he didn't understand. They had slid away from the issue of the colonists and on to Amadea. *Amadea,* whose presence filled the sand-choked darkness. He even fancied he could discern the rich odor of her perfume with every breath he drew.

"We're not talking about the colonists any longer, are we?"

"No. At least not those colonists."

"I don't suppose it would help if I said I was sorry."

"It might."

"Then I'm—"

"But only if you mean it."

In another setting he might have chuckled. She sounded so young and vulnerable. But it was not another setting, and her hurt beat at him, ripping away at the facade of justifications he had erected about himself, just as the Martian sand ate at the surrounding hills. It had seemed so easy a day—a lifetime—ago. So very romantic and macho. Jenny would understand or, better yet, would never find out. So he had run the internal tape, but it was a lie. And in the hostile world, far from friends and comfort and in danger of dying, he realized just how much he had risked. Perhaps lost. Certainly lost if he couldn't bring himself to speak and soon.

His hand shot up, reaching for his falling forelock, ready to sweep it back. But his fingers met the metal and plastic of the helmet, and the hand dropped back into his lap. In one of those strange, encapsulated moments he had an insight that, although it was illuminating, was also embarrassing and diminishing. Young, bright man, truly a young turk, brash and charming, tossing back his unruly forelock . . . And how ludicrous in a man his age.

He set his jaw, feeling the muscles tighten and jump at the sudden pressure. Separate the teeth—a real act of will, that—and speak.

"I am sorry."

"Can I ask you one thing?"

"I wish you wouldn't, but go ahead."

"Could you at least tell me why? What did I fail to give you?"

"It wasn't you." He smiled and knew it wasn't a very successful attempt. "Amadea's like an Act of God. She falls within the category of typhoons, hurricanes, and tornadoes. Beautiful, wild, and completely irresistible. She wanted me. She says she loves me, and she's the most beau—"

"Go ahead. I'm not blind. I know she's prettier than I am."

They sat in uncomfortable silence for a few seconds, then he resumed. "It's flattering to have a woman that young and that gorgeous pursuing me. She makes me feel young."

"Meaning that I fail to?"

"Don't make me analyze that. There's nothing logical about this. It's a complete arousal, a blood fever."

"And you want to wear it out."

"I'm not sure I follow you."

She shifted, and the opacity of the faceplate lifted. Her teeth kept closing and gnawing on her lower lip, then the tip of her tongue would appear, lick quickly at the chapped skin, and withdraw.

"Are you going to stop seeing her?"

"Are you asking me to?"

Tears brimmed over in her eyes and went streaking down her cheeks. "Oh, Cab, you're hurting me so much."

"I don't mean to. I don't want to." He swallowed past the swollen knot in his own throat. "I love you, Jenny, but I love her, too, and I don't know if I can make a choice. At least not yet."

"So you're not going to stop." Her gloved fingers writhed through each other like frenzied snakes, then knotted tightly together.

"I will if you ask me to."

"And I don't want to have to ask."

"Stalemate."

"This is a little hard to take . . . on top of everything else," she whispered.

"Jenny, this entire conversation may be rendered pointless if we don't get lifted off this desert."

"What do you think I've been referring to? God, what a comfort you are."

He gripped her hands. "Jen, I'd rather be out here with you than anyone else in the world."

"That's nice. I'd always sort of hoped to . . . be with the man I loved."

"Meaning that you aren't? I mean, you don't?"

"I don't know if I can answer that, Cab. At least not yet," she mimicked cruelly.

"By God, you can be a bitch." He jerked away and rested his head against the fiberglass wall of the pod, then straightened and stared back over his shoulder at her. "The wind, it's dropping."

"Then I guess it's not going to be rendered pointless. They'll be coming. Best to conserve air while we wait." She curled herself onto her side, pillowing her helmeted head on an arm.

"Jenny."

"No, Cab, there's nothing more to say. You've been nice and candid and honest; so now I'll try to be mature and understanding and supportive, and we'll just have to see how well this works out."

Fifteen minutes later he said softly, "I'll let Jeanne handle things . . . about the kids."

"Thank you. Any and all bribes are gratefully accepted."

"Oh, shit!"

"Sounds about right."

Chapter Thirteen

Cab shifted uncomfortably on the chair, trying to dislodge the sand grains that had lodged in the folds of his scrotum, and tried to concentrate on Lis Varllis's running monologue of apology and comment. He wondered how in hell the sand had gotten through a pressure suit, then decided that it must have happened during his slide down the cliff when the suit ripped. That reminded him of his cut and bruised leg, and the pain instantly crescendoed. It was a question that jerked him back to the conversation.

"Who was it who kidnapped you?"

"I don't know. They kept their faceplates darkened and set the radios to distort their voices."

"You must have some idea."

Irritated by her insistence, he glanced up from an inspection of his hurt arm and was arrested by the expression in her violet eyes. There was an intensity about her that put him on edge, on-guard.

"No, I have no idea."

"The President is naturally very upset over this event and concerned, lest it represent . . ."

Not upset enough to call me himself, Cab thought. *Instead,*

I get stuck with this jumped-up bureaucrat. I thought when that jump ship arrived, I'd be bathed, shaved, and in bed in no time. Instead, I'm being grilled. Damn Jenny, anyway. Jeanne too.

Jeanne Hudson had been in the crowd that had gathered at the dome lock. Both he and Jenny gave her reassuring nods, but he was very glad the three juvenile delinquents weren't present. He might have forgotten his promise to Jenny with that kind of provocation. Darnell and the other two men in the rescue mission formed a flying wedge and forced a path through the throng. Murmured questions, comments, and queries from the waiting people amalgamated into a droning rumble pierced by an occasionally recognizable word. The end result was a sound closely resembling the gurglings of the gastrointestinal tract of some large, dyspeptic animal. It succeeded in heightening Cab's sense of claustrophobia, and he limped doggedly toward the tunnel mouth, eager to escape the mob.

Andy came charging through the crowd with all the grace and elegance of a cow going down to water, and people scattered before the great, thrusting prow of his belly. He dropped a hand on the back of Jenny's neck and squeezed, like a mother cat assuring herself of her kitten's presence, and wrung Cab's good hand.

"Shit, it's good to see you! Any idea who snatched you?"

"No."

"That's succinct." He turned to Jenny. "Any idea who snatched him?"

"No."

"My finely honed journalistic instincts scent a story—"

"Drop it, Andy," Jenny warned.

"Oh."

"Glad to see your journalistic instincts also tell you when to shut up," Cab growled as his leg sent a twinge of agony shooting up into his groin.

"You should see a doctor."

"Later. All I want now is a wash, a shave, and bed."

"It could be something serious."

"It's not."

"Man of steel," Throckmorton grunted. "Okay, if you're in

that great a shape, you may as well call Joe as soon as you reach the apartment."

"Why?"

"He was worried."

"Touching. Jenny can call."

"Better you should call."

"Why?"

"A little problem with the deep-space squadron. They're on full alert."

"They should be. I'm a federal court judge. I've been kidnapped." His tone was acid.

"Yeah, but you're back now, and Joe's afraid they won't cancel the alert."

"Andy, forgive me, but I frankly don't give a fuck about the geopolitical or spacial political problems between the Earth and the System right now. I am going to sleep for fourteen hours, and *then* I will worry above saving the universe. Not that I think it's necessary. Joe is overreacting."

"Like he overreacted back on the Reichart station."

Cab winced and Jenny stepped in. "Andy, stuff it." She took Cab's arm protectively.

"Everybody's in a rotten mood."

"Yes," she replied, and they pushed on.

Lucius Renfrew was the next interruption. He stopped in front of Cab, opened his mouth, then, instead of speaking, pulled off his glasses and gave them a brisk polish on the tail of his coat. The gesture seemed to give him inspiration, for he suddenly blurted, "For the record, I want you to know that my people had nothing to do with your kidnapping."

"I know." Cab shouldered past him.

"Then—"

"Then nothing. Drop it, Mr. Renfrew, and concentrate on your case. I intend to hear it tomorrow."

"Tomorrow? But we're not scheduled for another two weeks."

"I just rescheduled. We're going to settle this matter *now*. Before someone decides to dump me on Demios next."

"We had nothing to do—" he began shrilly.

Cab cut him off with a slashing gesture. "I know!" He and Jenny pushed on.

"Are you sure that was wise?" asked Jenny in an undertone. "He might put something together and accuse the colonists."

"I agreed not to indict those children, but I'm not going to shield them totally. If their guilt is established by another source, I'm not going to interfere."

Her jaw worked, but she kept her teeth clamped firmly together to prevent any outburst, and she dropped his arm as if he had burned her. The action left Cab feeling bereft, and then embarrassment was added to the melange of conflicting emotions that already churned within him, for Amadea came running out of the throng and flung herself on his chest.

Despite his best effort, he yelped in pain, and she jerked back, her hands flying to her mouth. "I'm sorry. Oh, I'm sorry. I didn't mean to hurt you. Have you seen a doctor? No, of course you haven't. You must have that looked at. Oh, your leg too? Oh, Cabot, I was so worried." She burst into tears.

Cab, feeling panicky, patted her awkwardly on the shoulder, his gray eyes periodically shooting to where Jenny stood in rigid outrage. "There, there. It's all right. I'm all right. I only need some rest."

"Yes." Jenny pushed between them and tucked Cab's arm possessively beneath hers. "And it shouldn't be delayed. We'll see you later, Amadea."

He tried to balk, but Jenny propelled him ruthlessly forward.

"What about my Light?"

"It's wrecked," Jenny brutally replied.

"That was really nasty," muttered Cab as she again hustled him toward the tunnel entrance.

"Yes. I'm not feeling very charitable right now. Guess Andy is right. Everybody's in a rotten mood. No, don't say anything. It will just make me mad and we'll have another fight. I don't want to fight."

"Neither do I. I don't have the strength to fight. I just want to sleep."

But that escape and solace continued to elude him. The com had been chiming as they entered the apartment, and Jenny had made the mistake of answering. Now he was stuck with Lis Varllis and not enjoying the conversation.

"Are you listening? Did you hear anything I said?"

"No."

Her chiseled lips compressed into a thin line, deepening the grooves about her mouth. She didn't look as young or attractive now. "Then I'll repeat it."

"Must you? I'm terribly tired—"

The smack of her hand striking the desktop resonated over the net. Because of the transmission delay, it seemed to hang, echoing, in the room. "I'm representing the President on this, and you will *listen!*"

"I'm not very impressed. If the President's that overwrought, let him call me himself."

"He's too busy to deal with you!"

"A minute ago this affair was uppermost in his mind. Get your story straight, Ms. Varllis."

"I want to know who kidnapped you!" She was shouting, so he shouted back.

"I don't know!"

"I don't believe you."

"And I think you're abnormally fixated on this. What are you so concerned about?"

Her eyes narrowed, and she pursed her lips, considering. "I am concerned because you are a federal employee. Naturally the President is worried, lest this represent the first violent break between Earth and the System, and he wants to handle the situation."

"Then let him handle it by pulling the squadron off alert. That would be a profound reassurance to the colonists."

"Not until we have the whole picture. There's no formal law-enforcement agency on Mars. We may need the military to get to the bottom of your kidnapping."

"No. Keep the Air Force off Mars. The Jared police can handle the investigation."

"These people have consistently challenged and evaded our rulings. I have no faith—"

"If you're referring to the government's punitive and unreasonable actions toward this colony, I personally must side with the colonists. President Long told me he wanted to build bridges between the System and Earth. Beating the colonists over the head with federal regulations and agency harassment is not the way to do that. I don't know who's behind the actions that have been taken, but whoever they are, they're idiots!"

And he knew the minute the words were out of his mouth

that the woman in the screen before him was the "idiot" and that he had made an enemy for life. Her expression was positively reptilian, and he wondered how anyone could ever have thought her beautiful. He briefly considered apologizing, then rejected the idea. The woman *was* an idiot.

"I think you're shielding someone, Judge, and my recommendation to the President will be that he send in the squadron."

"I hope the President has better sense than you do. Oh, and you might tell him that I'm hearing the POW/EPA case tomorrow. He should be pleased with the outcome."

"What do you—" she began, but he cut the connection.

Jenny stared admiringly down at him and gave him a round of applause. "Thank you, but I think I just pissed in my own pool."

"Cabot! How crude."

"Life in the System is slowly destroying all my cherished belief and morals," he retorted as he headed for the bathroom.

"Poor baby. Uuup."

"Don't answer it!" But he was too late, she had already accepted the call.

"Joe."

"No."

"Take it," she coaxed.

"You and your damn beloved colonists. Hello, Joe, what is it?"

"Glad to hear you're okay."

"I'm not okay. I'm mad, tired, in pain, and I have sand up my . . . never mind. What do you want?"

"For you to exert your charm and social standing on the great and the powerful and get that squadron pulled off alert. It's causing tremors from the Moon to the Belt."

"Sorry to disappoint you, but I just fell from grace. I completely alienated Lis Varllis, and she's planning to push the President to land troops on Mars."

"Don't they ever learn?" Joe sighed, and rubbed at his eyes.

"So you're not blaming me?"

"No, I personally have always thought you had the patience of a saint to be willing to deal with these assholes. After all you've been through I'm not surprised you lost control."

"Maybe the President will have more sense."

"I doubt it."

"He's a good man."

"He's a politician."

"All politicians are evil, Richard Long is a politician, therefore he is evil. Is that the reasoning?"

"Something like that."

"I think you're being simplistic."

"I think you're being overly optimistic."

"Five hundred says I'm right."

"Done."

"I'll call you in ten or twelve hours, after I've had some sleep, and we'll see who's right."

"This time, Cab, I'm actually hoping you win."

Jenny rested her elbows on the bench and cupped her chin in her hands. Behind her, the courtroom was filling with spectators drawn to the final salvo in *Protectors of Worlds* v. *Bartlett*.

"How did your bet with Joe come out?"

Grumbling under his breath, Cab pulled a fold of his robe from beneath a sore buttock muscle and leaned back with a sigh. "In a draw. Joe wanted to concede the victory to me since the squadron hasn't moved in on Mars, but I felt only half vindicated since they're still on alert."

"Any luck getting through to the President?"

"Are you joking?" He drummed fingers on the case folder. "Lis Varllis is turning into a worthy opponent."

"Wish for once they'd be an ally." Cab lifted a single sheet from the folder and frowned at the words written across it in his own elegant, flowing script. "Are the cases what you needed?"

"Yes, you did a good job. And so did Jaschke. After a somewhat bumbling start her presentation was articulate, scholarly, and erudite."

"And MacKinley?"

"Strident."

"Sorry I missed most of the presentation, but it's tough to find case law that basically says that a person's position is stupid."

"If Jaschke had moved for summary judgment, we wouldn't have this problem. *That's* the time to be saying something's stupid. Now I'll have to make it look like a reasoned and learned decision with judicious arm waving, bootstrapping, and energetic tap dancing."

"Should be entertaining for the multitudes." Her green eyes danced as she considered the image of Cab doing a buck and wing atop his bench.

"Whatever you're thinking, Wickedness, I can tell it's very detrimental to my dignity."

"Very." She turned, rested her shoulders against the bench, and surveyed the room. "All the players are present. Shall we get under way?"

"Yes, have Chief Riley call the court to order."

The whisperings and mutterings subsided, and Cab scanned the room. The twenty POW supporters held down two benches immediately behind Padget MacKinley at his table. MacKinley had lost none of his insouciance, but Lucius Renfrew twitched and bounced on the hard plastic bench; a tug at an earlobe, a cough into a fist, a polish to the glasses, a twist at the hair of his long sideburns. It agitated Cab to look at him, so he shifted his eyes to the Hudsons, who sat with quiet dignity in the front row.

Mormon attendance at the hearing seemed based upon position and standing in the church: elders, high priests, patriarchs, a couple of bishops, and the Prophet all sat in gray-haired eminence. And Jeanne—the only woman. It was a testament to her power and position in the community that she held a place of honor next to her husband. Cab was struck by the incongruity of a woman so capable and powerful who served loyally in a church that (to his mind) diminished and denigrated their female members. Perhaps there was something to Mormonism if a woman such as Jeanne could embrace the faith. His own rather tepid Episcopalianism had faded over the years, until now, when he was left with a vague, amorphous sense that *something* existed beyond the seen and observed, the here and now, but exactly what it was, he couldn't say.

He shook his head to clear it of the pointless metaphysics. Was it yet another symptom of his advancing age? Or what he perceived as his advancing age? Why, then, hadn't he thought about death and God and eternity when he had been footslogging across that god-forsaken desert? Perhaps because he hadn't gotten close enough to the edge; close enough to smell the sweet, nauseating odor of death.

I'm only forty-three. Stop it for Christ's sake.

His eyes found Amadea, standing against the back wall. Her eyes were locked on him, but she didn't really seem to see him. There was no acknowledgment of his nod. *Children.* They were the one sure path to immortality. So maybe it was time. His attention flicked between Jenny and Amadea. No, the decision was too hard. Not yet. First the hearing. People were waiting for his pronouncement. Talk about godlike.

He picked up the folder and tapped its edge on the bench. All eyes focused attentively on him.

"I wasn't going to be rude," he began, and as soon as the words left his mouth he knew he had made his decision. He *was* going to be rude, very rude, and he had the license to do so. It came with the robe. "I was going to hand down a decision based solely on law and precedent," he went on. "I'm still going to do that, but first I'm going to have the satisfaction of stating that in almost twenty years of legal practice I never have before seen a more spurious and pointless lawsuit. All right, that's said."

There was a gasp and murmur from the colonists, and a deeper rumble of discontent from the environmentalists. Padget MacKinley's hand had tightened on his pen, almost warping the soft metal, and Lucius Renfrew was on his feet. Before he could erupt into one of his famous diatribes, Cab fixed him with a frigid eye and Renfrew subsided. The tiny exercise of transcendental dominance felt good, and with a small smile playing about his lips he returned to his decision.

"First a short recap of the case, and then an even shorter ruling. Three months ago the residents of the Jared Colony submitted an environmental impact statement to the Environmental Protection Agency, pursuant to its regulations and in preparation to beginning a long-term terraforming project on Mars. The statement was accepted, and permission granted to begin the work. The organization, Protectors of Worlds, hearing of the action of the EPA, exercised their right to judicial review as established in Overton Park, 401 U.S. 402, and filed suit in this court.

"POW's challenge to the action of the EPA rests upon a pair of precedent-setting cases and a United Nations treaty. If any one fails, the POW case falls, and in fact I believe I can dispense with all three.

"POW first raises *Sierra Club* v. *Rucklushaus*, which mandated that the EPA not only has the obligation to protect the environment, they are required to enhance it. Counsel for the plaintiff has stressed the element of protection, combining it with the U.N. Outer Space Treaty, 18 U.S.T. 2410 January 27, 1967, which states, in a nutshell, that the Solar System be preserved for the benefit of all mankind. POW's argument runs as follows: The environment of Mars represents the perfect natural state of this celestial body and must therefore be preserved as is. That to do otherwise is to cheat the peoples of the world of their birthright and heritage.

"This argument can be dismissed on several grounds. First, the Sierra Club case mandated an *enhancement* of the environment. I find it incredible that anyone would argue that terraforming a planet is in fact not an enhancement but rather a denigration of the environment. Obviously such would be the case if the world were currently inhabited by intelligent creatures, or perhaps even by native flora and fauna, but such is not the situation on Mars, and I leave that decision for the time when humans encounter such a world.

"Furthermore, the creation of a new Earth-type world would, to my mind, seem to be in the best interest of mankind. The Jared Colony's articles of incorporation contain the guarantee that the Martian land made available by the project will be sold—for a reasonable sum—to any interested parties, whatever their national origin."

Cab thought he was being uncommonly virtuous in even addressing the United Nations treaty, for in intervening years most of the space treaties had been ignored, and the old cliché "Possession is nine-tenths of the law" had come to be the rule.

He took a sip of water and resumed. "Then there is Protectors of Worlds v. Salazar 923 U.S. 501. This case held that a national park in New Mexico should be forever closed to any activities save those of hikers and campers. The court adopted the words of numerous tracts on wilderness literature stating that such havens of solitude were basic to the rights of the people, that civilized men had to have a place where they could get back in touch with the infinite and timeless forces of nature and the universe. In short, they were saying that it is a good thing for city dwellers to have vacation spots. And this court does not dispute that finding. I do, however, dispute the conclusion that this current case falls within the parameters of *Protectors of Worlds* v. *Salazar* and that Mars must be left a pristine showcase for the sole enjoyment of a handful of scientists and those wealthy enough to afford a Martian wilderness vacation. Such an action would represent the tyranny of a privileged minority over the vast bulk of humankind.

"A final matter: Should the EPA, for whatever reason, choose to rescind their approval of the terraforming project, or should any other federal agency step in to block the action of the Jared Colony, this court is prepared to rule that this situation is totally on point with Florida Rock Industries v. U.S. 22 ERC 1943, which held that a federal agency's removal of land from the private sector represented a taking for which just compensation was due." Cab split a thin smile between MacKinley and Jaschke.

"I shudder to think what the value of a terraformed Mars would be. And I rather doubt that the United States possesses sufficient wealth to adequately compensate the colonists of the Jared settlement for that taking."

This last remark was clearly beyond the scope of the case, but as he had sat musing in his office after the conversation with Joe, he decided it might be a good idea to send a clear and very pointed message to Ms. Lis Varllis. Ever since his conversation with the autocratic White House Chief of Staff, he had known that she was behind the agency harassment of the Jared Colony. He, of course, had no proof to back this assertion, but Lis reminded him strongly of his mother during her less lovable moments, and he had seen just such cunning maneuverings out of Cecilia.

The silence of the courtroom was shattered by the fall of his gavel. "Plaintiff's challenge to the action of the EPA is therefore denied."

Bill Devert lolled deeper into the cushions of the couch and stared up through the bottom of his wineglass at the rising champagne bubbles. Raising it still higher, he announced, "Here's to the proud colonists of Jared and to Justice Cabot Huntington, jurist extraordinaire!"

"Oh, Bill, go fuck yourself!" He flinched as a gout of icy champagne struck him in the face. Blinking to clear his eyes, he focused on Lis, who stood quivering with anger.

"You're problem, my love, is that you don't know how to admit defeat gracefully. Huntington survived, the diamonds will flow, and someday the rivers of Mars will flow too. Something very Zen about all that."

"And how *Zen* is it going to be when you're tagged as a co-conspirator in a murder attempt?"

"Ah, but I won't be. Either Huntington really doesn't know who snatched him or he's choosing not to act—which, incidentally, would show how very devoted he is to the System and its goals—and finally there's no way to trace it back to us. If Amadea's fingered, she can always look innocent and declare how she 'never thought the children would react in that way.' *Voilá!* Perfect!"

"There's nothing *perfect* about it. This administration has lost face."

"How? You undertook this little affair as a favor to Geme-tics. If *I*, as a senior vice-president, am not upset, why should you be? As far as the world is concerned, you won. Huntington upheld the EPA action."

"They're arrogant and wayward, and I will not be defeated by a gang of raggedy-assed misfits who can't make it in normal society."

Devert swung his legs to the floor. "You're being stupid. No one knows that your pride has taken a drubbing except thee and me, and if you treat me nice, I'll never tell." He grinned, but she ignored the sally.

"DeBaca was right. The System has got to be brought back under control."

The muscles in her upper arm were rigid beneath his fingers, and he gave her a firm shake, trying to bring her back to reality. "Now just hold on. Whoa, now. Those people out there are prickly as hell. They probably suspect, because of the agency action you took, that the administration is dicking them, but they don't have any *proof*. For Christ's sake, don't give them any by stomping on them with an iron boot heel."

She jerked free. "I'm not an idiot, for God's sake. I do have some subtlety. I'm going to set an example on Mars, but I've got to arrange things so that we'll be coming in as the white knights."

"Arrange what, and how?"

"I think I can count on Renfrew to come up with something creative."

"That antitechnological thug."

"You were more than willing to use him when it suited your purpose."

"*Touché*. But back to your grandoise plan."

"We need a trigger, something to justify use of the deep-space squadron. Once we've got one and have moved in and restored order, the administration will look decisive, just, and powerful. It should give Rick's popularity a real boost."

"On Earth maybe! No one in the System will buy that. We've got people working out there. I know what they're like and they'll—"

"I don't *care* what they're like, and I don't care what they think!"

"Then you're an arrogant fool!"

Her nails raked four lines of exquisite pain down his cheek, followed by the warm flow of blood filling the gashes. Fumbling a bit, he lifted a napkin and blotted at his face while Lis coolly prepared to leave. The act seemed to have steadied her, wrung the anger from her soul, leaving only calculation. And seeing the expression on her perfect face, Devert wondered how he ever could have thought he loved her.

"You're going to land us all in hell."

"I'm going to win."

"That's what I mean."

The pretty blonde tossed Renfrew's pajamas into his case and stared mulishly down at the inexpert packing job. "Lucius."

"Shut up."

Jana chewed at her bee-stung lower lip, shook her hair over her face, and pouted. Then, raking back her mane with both hands, she determinedly tried again.

"I really think it's awful that we're just packing up and going home."

"We're not, honey. Don't you think Padget and I have already talked this out?" Condescension edged his words, though Renfrew would have vehemently denied a charge of sexism. Nonetheless, it was there. Little had changed in the hundred and some years since the New Left revival in America, and the inexplicable—but very real, alliance of fundamentalist Christianity and the extremist environmental groups had heightened the unspoken but firmly held notion that a woman's place in the movement was on her back. "Just get on with the packing. I've got some thinking to do."

He didn't get much done before there was a knock, and MacKinley entered the room without waiting for an acknowledgment. "I've got our event."

"Yeah, what?"

"The Belter ship. The one that pulled all those shenanigans to get reregistered."

Renfrew's face fell. "I still want to take the artifact."

"I don't think that's a good idea. In her conversation with you Lis Varllis indicated that she'll cover and pardon almost anything we do up here, but let's not push it too far. Her power only extends so far. Any action we take has to be directed against the colonists. Let's leave the scientists out of this, especially since they're on our side. They don't want Mars fucked with any more than we do. Also, we've got to consider the media angle on all this. If we attack innocents, we're in deep shit, but these Mormons are not the most popular—"

"Fascist racists! All they're concerned about is making money. Selling off Mars to other white, rich Mormon pigs. It should belong to the people."

"Yeah, right, Lucius, but let's save the slogans for the press."

"Fuck you too!"

"Temper, temper. Don't alienate your lawyer, who still has to file an appeal for you."

"Sorry. I'm still stunned by this outrage. Okay, the Belter ship."

"It's carrying heavy mining equipment that it will deliver, and then take on a cargo of diamonds."

"We could stop the delivery."

"No, I think we should take the diamonds."

"The angle?"

"That this is wealth that should belong to the people of Earth and is instead being used by a few selfish individuals for their personal aggrandizement."

Renfrew nodded enthusiastically. "I love it." An uneasy thought intruded and his face clouded. "But how long are we going to have to squat on that ship?"

"That will rather depend upon your friends in high places. Varllis must have some ideas on how to turn this to her advantage. It's up to us to give her the opportunity. The ship is due to land in three days."

"Then let's clear out for Eagle Port." Padget nodded. "Maybe you ought to head back to Earth."

"Not this time. Just once I want to be macho and militant."

Renfrew gave a short bray of laughter. "Yeah, you have missed out on some of our earlier festivities."

"That's because I had to be on hand to bail you out."

Whipping off his glasses, the leader of POW gave them a quick, delighted polish, replaced them on the bridge of his thin nose, and clapped MacKinley firmly on the back. "Okay, you're in."

There was an excited little noise from the corner, and Renfrew remembered Jana. She was staring adoringly at him, a pair of his Jockey shorts clutched to her chest. The adultation was pleasant, but he was slipping into his he-man mode in preparation for one of their terrorist actions. His thin, pale brows snapped together over his nose.

"Aren't you done yet? We fucking well haven't got all day."

Chapter Fourteen

"I propose a toast to Captain Sakti Gupta. May her presence here presage a new era of friendship between Mars and the asteroids."

Darnell's face was flushed and shiny, and he was gripped by an intoxicated cheerfulness. This despite the fact that his glass contained only sparkling cider. He had reason. The day had been a good one. A locked warehouse on the outskirts of Eagle Port held the recently unloaded extracting and processing equipment only waiting to be transferred to Tharsis so mining could resume. And Gupta's ship, the *Gray Goose*, now held a fortune in diamonds; the first trickle of what would someday be a flood of wealth to Earth. Wealth that would finance their dream.

Sakti Gupta listened impassively to the fulsome toast, but that wasn't unusual; she was an impassive person. Her short-cropped black hair was liberally streaked with gray, which seemed to reflect in the pale winter's-gray of her eyes. They glowed eerily in her dark face. She was not a pretty woman. The planes and angles of her face seemed to have been sculpted with a hatchet, and the faded blue coveralls bulged at the waist and hips as though she were hiding inner tubes within the folds of her clothing. Still, she was a powerhouse; working as hard as any of the men from the Jared Colony or the three men who made up her crew. A strange woman to Darnell's mind, but this evening he was in love with the world, and he thought her the most beautiful woman he had ever seen. Some of his pleasure faded, however, when, heaving up from the chair, she offered a toast of her own.

"And here's to the Earthers, fuck them all." The shocked silence was broken by Jasper's braying laugh. Sakti glanced at the rigid faces about the table. "You don't agree?" The pale eyes settled on Seth. "The young ones do. They know. And you'll learn. I started out on one of the stations, but it wasn't far enough. They were always there, prying and poking, interfering. I went to the Belt, but even there . . ." She shrugged. "Wish there were someplace else to go. Maybe ten or twelve light-years would be far enough to escape their niggling.

"But I've upset you being a cynical old bitch." She seized her glass, which did not contain fruit juice. "To peace, prosperity, and happiness. And a long life in which to enjoy them. Better?" There were relieved nods and smiles all around the table. "Better."

Eddy Calder shifted the wad of bubble gum from his right cheek to his left and decided that maybe this was just as disgusting a habit as tobacco. The one difference being that Sakti had okayed gum and absolutely nixed any further tobacco chewing aboard her ship.

He wondered what Tom and Pedro were up to, and if Eagle Port was unfolding its fleshy delights to the wandering Casanovas. Assuming, of course, that Eagle Port had any fleshy delights. They had never done a run to Mars before. He was trying to picture his crew mates dry and lonely in order to relieve his own sense of boredom and ill use. Of course, the only person he could blame for his ill use was himself. He had fucking *volunteered* to stay on the ship and guard the cargo. From what, he couldn't imagine.

But Sakti had thought it important to watch the diamonds, and seeing the hungry expressions on the faces of his younger crew mates, he had nobly offered to stay behind with the ship. He had wanted to read his newly arrived Yeats collection and perhaps work on his own poetry a bit, but now he was sorry. Even aging poets with a useless degree in English literature needed love. For seven years after receiving his doctorate he had bounced about the country from university to university, pursuing the ever-elusive dream of tenure. Finally he had decided to chuck it all and go off-world looking for adventure, inspiration, a steady paycheck. Why? He wasn't sure anymore. Oh, there had been adventure and inspiration aplenty, but it hadn't translated itself into poetry—at least not very good poetry—and now here he sat, alone and lonely when he could have been out drinking and whoring.

But only if one of the other fellows had stayed behind, he reminded himself, and with a shake of the head he settled the lap reader in a better position and called up the book.

He lifted his head as a new thought intruded. Maybe he shouldn't be trying to delve the soul of man in a few perfect sentences. Maybe he ought to be writing novels, Hemingwayesque treatments of life and love and loss and pain. After all, he was on the modern-day equivalent of a tramp steamer. What better source for real mean and gusty prose?

A banging on the lock shattered his concentration, and the perfect plot went spinning off into chaotic oblivion among the synapses of his brain. Grumbling, he set aside the reader, unfolded his long, skinny legs, and stilted over to the lock. He didn't inquire as to the identity of his caller. He assumed it was Tom or Pedro, back for some item they had forgotten. He punched in the code, releasing the lock on the outer door. A suited figure stepped into the lock and an elusive sense of something not quite right shot through him. But before he could pin it down, there was a scraping sound, and his attention was distracted by the ship's cat, Archimedes, who was busily dipping his front paw into Eddy's tea and licking off the milk-flavored beverage. For an instant his hand wavered over the locking mechanism, then a final dip by the cat pushed the mug to the edge of the table. With a yell Eddy flipped the lever and leapt to capture the teetering crockery. Archimedes eeked, bounding off in another direction.

Order restored, Eddy turned back to the lock as the inner door swung open. "What did you forget . . . hey, who the hell are—"

A gloved hand came up, palm flat, and the heel took him hard in the nose. It felt as if splinters of bone were flying into the top of his head, and he had the sensation of falling. His vision disintegrated into flashes of black and red as the metal floor came up to meet him. The last thing he heard was Achimedes yowling and spitting, and the scrabble of claws as the cat headed for a bolt hole.

Candelight played softly over Amadea's face, giving her skin a delicate gold-and-rose glow and heightening the shadows beneath her eyes. Concerned, Cab reached out and placed his hand over hers.

"You look tired and unhappy. What's wrong? Can I do anything to help?"

"Forgive me, Cabot, but you're part of the problem." His hand jerked back. "I feel very awkward being out with you this way."

"I moved out so you wouldn't feel awkward, but you've been avoiding me."

"I've been busy."

"Amadea, I'm trying to figure out where we're going. That's why I moved out." He brushed back his forelock, then grimaced. He had promised himself he would drop the habit. "I thought you'd be pleased and we'd spend more time together. Instead, you've become increasingly quiet and withdrawn. Ever since the hearing. And you haven't said anything about the outcome."

She shrugged. "What's to say?"

"I thought you would be pleased."

"I am."

"You don't sound it."

"What do you want, Cabot? For me to hire a brass band and fireworks? Is your ego that fragile? And I thought you did what you did out of principle, not to gain points with me."

This time more than his hand retreated. He pulled far back into his chair and stared uncomprehendingly into her beautiful, closed face.

"Amadea."

She gave herself a shake and clutched at her head with her hands. "I'm sorry." Her voice was muffled. "I don't know why I'm such a bitch recently. Tired, I guess, and I'm taking a lot of shit off Dave."

"So our secret player is not happy with the outcome of the case."

"Oh, no." She looked away, then back again. A soft, tremulous smile now curved her lips. "The linguists are making real progress on the artifact," she said brightly.

Cab smiled. "Are we starting the evening over again?"

"Yes. And this time I'll be nice."

"But what about the artifact?"

"Many of the words seem to be proper names."

"Crew list of the brave explorers who came through here?"

"Who can say? At least not until they figure out the interlinking words." She twirled her wineglass, carefully studying the circular imprint the base left in the white tablecloth. "Cabot, if I married you, would you take me to Earth?"

"M-married?"

"You don't want to marry me?"

"I . . . I don't know. There's Jenny . . ." He scrubbed nervously at his face. "And my circuit. I still have three months here, and then on to the asteroids."

"And you'd want your wife to accompany you?"

"It wouldn't be much of a marriage if she didn't," he said firmly, certainty having replaced his earlier stammering response.

"Oh." The tone was hollow. "But I shouldn't even have brought it up. You were right to remind me about Jenny, and you have to have time to make up your mind."

"Do *you* want to marry me?"

She gave a tinkling little laugh. "Oh, I was just talking."

"Oh." He sounded hurt.

"Oh, Cabot, you men take love so seriously."

"And women don't?"

"No. You men play mind trips. Women know there's no romance. It's a matter of basic survival. Of self, of the species."

"You depress me."

"Don't let me. Pour me some more wine, and after I've drunk enough I'll stop being meaningful and devote myself solely to your entertainment."

Jeanne paused with the fork halfway to her mouth and regarded the sweating, red-faced man who had just run into the restaurant. His outthrust belly gave him the look of a particularly agitated pouter pigeon, and he kept mopping at his face with a large purple handkerchief. She nudged her husband.

"Isn't that Mike Despopolous, the port master? You dealt

with him when we were importing the organ." Darnell looked up, chewed, swallowed, and nodded. He returned to his meal. Jeanne continued watching while the maître d' indicated their table. "Darnell, stop stuffing your face. I think something's wrong."

"What could be—"

"Captain Gupta," panted Despopolous. "Ah . . . er . . . the Port Authority just got a call from your ship." He gulped, his Adam's apple bouncing up and down in his fat throat, the jowls wobbling. "It's . . . ah . . . well, hmmm, been seized by the Protectors of Worlds, and they're calling a press conference." Sakti came out of the chair, and Despopolous backpedaled. "They're holding your crewman as . . . um . . . er . . . guarantee for your good behavior. I've got port security out there but—"

"My ship," rasped the woman.

"My diamonds!" echoed Darnell, looking sick.

"The crewman," Jeanne reminded them both pointedly. She threw her napkin onto the table.

"Are they armed?" snapped Gupta.

"Yes."

"They couldn't have boarded an antimatter drive ship carrying arms. They must have obtained them here," Darnell accused.

Despopolous spread his fingers across his chest. "Not from us."

Jasper was now on his feet. "You're so fucking naive. Do you know how easy it is to bribe a luggage handler or attendant? Or they might have shipped the guns to—"

"None of this matters! The fact is, they have guns, they're holding the ship, and most importantly, they have a hostage."

Darnell clasped Jeanne's hand between his. "Thank you, my dear, for putting things back in perspective." He turned to the port master. "What do you suggest we do?" Despopolous goggled. "*You* have the security force," Darnell added patiently.

"Oh . . . oh, right, but don't ask too much of us. I've only got three men." He wheezed and mumbled for a few moments. "I . . . ah . . . ummm. I guess the first thing to do is hear their demands and try negotiating."

"Negotiating! Fuck that!" Seth panted, his fists clenching

and unclenching at his sides. "We should *negotiate* with the talking end of the gun!"

Jeanne turned on the young man with a look on her face that Darnell had never seen before. His son gulped, choked, and slunk back into a chair where he sat with his back half turned to the other Mormons. And in that moment a suspicion became a certainty. His son had had a hand in the kidnapping of Huntington. His son had attempted murder. He took two steps toward the huddled boy, then Jeanne caught him by the arm.

"No. We have other matters to concern us now."

The throng of Mormons, led by Sakti, with Despopolous trailing behind, were pounding for the door. Darnell's eyes slid restlessly between wife and son.

"Huntington . . . ?"

"He knows."

"And you. You knew and didn't tell me," he said in a harsh whisper.

"No, I didn't. This was something better handled by women."

"Women!"

"Yes. Jenny, Carol, Julie, and me."

"This should have come before the elders. . . . Where are you going?"

"To the ship. I have more pressing matters than digging up dead cats." Darnell pivoted back toward Seth. "And you leave him be!" They were the focus for a number of interested eyes as the other patrons of the restaurant watched the little drama being played out without understanding precisely what it entailed. Jeanne ignored them, and the world retreated, leaving only the two of them—eyes locked—battling for control. His eyes dropped first and he stepped to her side, and side by side they went to retrieve their suits.

There was quite a crowd gathered about the base of the ramp. The ship itself was wedge-shaped, with a tangle of communication towers near the front end of the craft, which gave it the look of a scaly gray beetle. Three great columnlike legs set at each end of the triangular-shaped ship sank deep into the red sand. In fact, it reminded Jeanne of a Ouija board pointer as it sat with its blunt nose pointed toward a line of distant hills. She found herself framing questions in her mind:

Will the crewman be all right? Can this be stopped without a confrontation? Bloodshed? And suddenly there came a memory from her childhood. A silly, old-fashioned toy called an Eight Ball. Ask it questions, shake it, and it would float an answer into a tiny window set in the base of the ball. But the only answer that came to mind was the one that had arisen with distressing regularity during her childhood: "Answer cloudy, ask again." She felt like crying.

Renfrew, with his usual talent to milk any situation for its maximum benefit, had planned his takeover before most of the journalists who had been present for the unveiling of the artifact, and the POW hearing, had left Mars. They made up most of the interested spectators, the residents of Eagle Port having wisely decided that putting themselves within range of armed lunatics was not a good idea. The door of the lock stood open, and four or five suited figures were observed moving back and forth, automatic weapons at the ready. On top of the ship sat a mounted laser rifle, protected by a pile of crates.

Jasper gave a low whistle when he saw the state-of-the-art weapon. "These guys are planning on playing rough."

"Hope they let Eddy suit up before they blew the air," Sakti said in a voice so flat and level that it revealed her strain better than any amount of shouting and screaming. "Archimedes is already dead. He hasn't got a suit."

"Archimedes?" asked Jeanne.

"Ship's cat." The muscles at the hinge of her jaw worked. "Stupid to be upset about a cat."

"So much for the great nature lovers; defenders of the innocent," snorted Jasper. "And as crass as it sounds, we should use that." He waved an arm toward the milling journalists. "This is going to be a media war."

"As long as it stays a war of words," warned Jeanne.

"That rather depends on them," grunted Young.

"And on Earth," added Sakti.

"Earth?" came a chorus.

"They're not going to let an opportunity like this pass."

Darnell drew himself up. "I don't like these broad and suspicious generalizations. Who's *they,* and what will *they* do?"

Irritated by his reprimand, the woman just shrugged and stared back at her ship. Actually it wasn't hers. Only a small fraction of it belonged to her. The rest of the drive ship belonged to a syndicate. She shivered, thinking what would happen to her if the ship somehow got tied up in a maze of legal red tape. But maybe the fact of its Nicaraguan registry would save them. Maybe.

The cameras were up and running. One of the journalists skittered up the ramp, keeping a wary eye on the guns, and handed Renfrew a microphone.

"Peoples of Earth . . ."

. . . "I stand before you not as a criminal or a terrorist but as an Earthman attempting to rectify a terrible wrong. The criminals aren't on this ship. They're out there." His arm shot out with that stiff, mechanical gesture that had become his trademark. "Criminals who would cheat you of your birthright. The wealth and beauty of a world."

He dug into an open crate. When he straightened, his gloved hands were filled with dull, gray rocks of varying sizes. "Do you know what these are? Of course you don't, because the greedy have kept this information from you, fearful that you would demand a share of this wealth. They're diamonds. And there are crates of these stacked in the hold of this ship. They're going to be used to finance a terraforming project, a plan to turn Mars into a garden. But will you have any share in this? No, because a corrupt official has given this planet into the hands of the few."

"Cabot Huntington ruled that POW could not oppose this travesty. He gave away your birthright. But we will not stand by and merely accept this judgment. The Protectors of Worlds will hold this ship, her cargo, and her crew until the American government—and other world governments—move to correct this terrible miscarriage of justice."

Lis touched the controls set into the side of the President's desk and exchanged glances with her boss.

"Well . . ."

His palm hit the desk with a sharp *thwapping* sound. "That's not much of a response. What have you unleashed up there?"

She folded her hands and placed them against her cheek. "So now it's my fault?"

"Well, is it or isn't it?"

"No. It's the fault of a group of people who think they don't have to play by the same rules as the rest of us."

"Are we talking about Lucius Renfrew and POW, or the colonists?" Long asked sarcastically.

She shot him an irritated glance. "From the beginning the colonists have tried make their own rules. Using Mars as a private preserve, ignoring the embargoes and dealing with the asteroids, the reregistration of the Belter ship. It's all a symptom of an underlying infection. They don't need us, Rick, or at least they don't think they do. I say it's time to disabuse them of that notion."

"And Huntington . . ." She rushed on before he could speak. "He's part and parcel of this. He's completely biased and has obviously thrown in his lot with the System. I think something has to be done about him."

"What do you suggest? Shall we impeach him after I dropped the impeachment proceedings against him not three months ago? I'd look like a perfect idiot. Besides, I'm not sure I accept your characterization of the man. I think he still believes in us."

Lis studied her perfectly manicured nails. "Then how do you explain the fact that he's shielding the people who kidnapped him?"

"What!" Long was half out of his chair. "But that's just crazy. . ." His hand went to his hair, flinging back the famous forelock.

"A faction within the colony kidnapped him, but he's choosing to keep quiet. How would the country react if it knew the colonists were resorting to violence? The people would be outraged, and Huntington knew that. So he kept quiet and ruled in their favor. Now is that bias or is that bias?"

"Where did you come by this information?"

"From an absolutely reliable source. Also, guess who he's had several long conversations with?"

"I'm not in the mood for guessing games." He was looking like a sulky five-year-old.

"Joe Reichart. Not the sort of person with whom a loyal federal employee should be consulting."

Long took a turn about the office, his stockinged feet *shooshing* softly on the eagle-embossed rug. Reseating himself, he slipped on one shoe, frowned, and looked up at her.

"Can we keep this from becoming a media event?"

She gestured toward the blank television screen. "I thought it already had."

"No, I mean Huntington."

"Depends upon what you have in mind. A public slap on the wrist? A private White House reprimand?"

"What were your thoughts on the matter?"

The gut-wrenching anger that accompanied any thought of the judge seized her, and she struggled to control her face. If Rick suspected how deep her anger ran, or how personal her battle with Huntington had become, he would never turn the handling of this crisis over to her.

"I think we should send in the Air Force. You've never taken the squadron off alert, and they could be there in a couple of days. That would relieve the very small security force at Eagle Port of the responsibility of dealing with Lucius. It would also send a very clear message to the System."

"And Huntington," he promoted.

"I think we should have him arrested and returned to Earth."

"Jesus! On what grounds?"

"Numerous; shielding known felons, misuse of office." She made a circular gesture in the air over her head. "And by the time it grinds through the courts you will have replaced him with an appointee of your own. Someone who will serve the interests of both Earth and the System."

"And the press?"

"They'll be told that the squadron is being sent in to restore order. They'll find out about Huntington once he's bound for Earth, and meanwhile Fred Downs and I will be doing some groundwork to prime them. By the time Huntington gets here, there won't be a person in America who won't believe he's a rebel and a traitor."

His thumbs were rasping up and down, up and down through the curly cinnamon-colored hair of his sideburns. It was an annoying habit that he did only when he was nervous and uncertain. He gripped his hands beneath his chin as a new thought intruded. "This thing isn't likely to get out of hand, is it? Renfrew and his people are armed. I don't want any American blood spilled. Especially not by other Americans."

She made a derisive noise. "Don't be silly. POW has done this sort of thing a number of times before, and there's never been any violence. People are basically sheep. Lucuis knows this and plays on it. They'll hold the ship, whip up outrage on

Earth over the greedy Mormons, the Air Force will arrive, and that will be that. Everybody will be happy."

"Except the colonists," he commented dryly.

"Richard! The greatest good for the greatest number, remember?"

The thumbs were back in action, and she reached out and grabbed him by the wrists. "It will be all right. Really. That's what I'm here for, remember? To make it all okay and to be your heavy." She smiled into his troubled eyes. "So you can go on being the beloved young leader of the free world."

That drew a laugh, and he nodded. "Okay." He lifted one of her hands to his mouth and dropped a kiss onto the soft palm. "I'll leave it in your capable hands. And I think Jennifer and I will retreat gracefully and strategically to New York. She's planning to attend that American Ballet gala. I'll accompany her and give them all a thrill."

"And your faithful troops will get down and get dirty."

He caught her before she could reach the door, his hand warm and heavy on the curve of her hip. "Does it bother you, the way you have to take the heat for me?"

"No," she said truthfully. "Your armor must remain untarnished, and"—she gave him her best little-girl smile, an expression totally at variance with her next words—"I love the exercise of naked power."

"Right," he replied, unfortunately not realizing that she was in deadly earnest.

On Mars the leaders of Jared had listened to Renfrew's statement with varying degrees of response; outright fury from Seth, weariness from Darnell, disbelief from Young and Coltrin, dramatic posturing from Jasper. After the pointless trek out to the ship they had trooped back to Despopolous's office where they now waited and argued. Five hours' worth of argument and they were still miles from a consensus, much less a decision. Gupta wanted to rush the ship; Jeanne was still opposed to that, though weakening. Coltrin favored negotiation, a very unpopular position.

A call came through, and Despopolous picked up the wire-thin headphone, trying to hear over the din in the small office. As he listened, an odd, strained expression slipped across his plump face. He logged off and crooked a finger at the Prophet.

"Darnell, could I speak with you a moment? Privately."

Hudson heaved to his feet and followed Despopolous into the hall.

"I shouldn't be doing this, but you're neighbors and friends, so I'm going to tell you." He sucked at his cheeks and gave his head a ponderous shake. His sad, drooping eyes and wobbling jowls gave him the look of a melancholy basset hound. "I just got a call from the commander of the deep-space squadron. They're on their way here with orders to . . ."

Padget MacKinley was not part of the occupying force. He needed to be free to file papers, arrange for bail, issue press releases, whatever. But he had come to the ship in response to a call from Lucius. The leader of POW darted back and forth across the ramp like a manic metronome. Padget almost grabbed him to stop the irritating perambulations. Through the faceplate he could see that Lucius's pale face was flushed with excitement, and the tip of his tongue protruded from between his lips.

"Two things." Two gloved fingers shot up, in case Padget had failed to understand the words, and quivered between them. "Lis called to tell me that the military is on its way. Normally I wouldn't depend on those jackbooted pigs, but this is a special case. Anyway, all we have to do is hold tough for a few days and it'll be all resolved. And even better"—his fist drove into his other hand—"she wants Huntington. The commander has orders to arrest him and return him to Earth for trial."

MacKinley started. "Good Christ, on what grounds?"

Renfrew gave a dismissive gesture. "Who cares? Apparently they've made up something. The point is he's out, and his rulings are suspect, so even if we don't get a rehearing, we'll win this one on appeal." He shot to the other side of the landing ramp and came skittering back. "But I wanted to do something for Lis and win a few points for us. Let's see to it that Huntington is here, all tied up with a red ribbon for the Air Force. Take Luke and Stan and send them back to Jared to grab Huntington. I don't want to give him a chance to run or those assholes at the colony to hide him or something."

"Are you sure that's wise? He is a federal—"

Renfrew waved him down. "Don't be stupid. We've got Varllis behind us."

• • •

He had been very understanding about her "not being in the mood and really just needing a cuddle" and had held her in his arms, talking, until he had finally drifted off to sleep. The part about her "mood" had been true. Amadea had tried for several days after the hearing to get in touch with Devert, but he was always "unavailable." Then a blank-faced assistant had called and informed her in the kindest tones imaginable that her Earthside job had been delayed, and they couldn't say when another position might open up.

She had wanted to scream in fury at the man who had cost her her dream, but there was still the illusion to be maintained; for her coworkers, for the colonists, yes . . . even for Cabot. After the first convulsion of rage passed and rational thought had again been possible, she realized that the judge might still be useful. So she had begun her ruthless campaign to maneuver him into marriage. Her first tentative overtures in that direction had almost sent him fleeing into the Martian desert, but there was time yet. He wasn't due to leave for another three months. Still, she didn't much feel like putting out with no reward in view. So she walked a tightrope between a complete break and the wholehearted fucking she had done earlier.

The com chimed, and she ran to answer before it could wake Cabot. If he awoke, he would start to talk, and she couldn't stand having to listen to him talk. He really wasn't her type, anyway; too intense, too conservative, too proper. Thank God for divorces and good lawyers. If she could bring him to the sticking point, she wouldn't have to live with him long, and a good settlement . . . Her palm hit the accept button, and the screen settled on the brushed and polished features of Padget MacKinley. She stared and facetiously thought that the shysters were so good today that they responded to psychic communications. Remembering Cabot's recumbent form in the bed behind her, she swiftly blocked both sound and picture and lifted the delicate, private headphone.

"See, I caught you being indecent. Wish I were there." The leer came slopping over the comnet, making her wish she could take a bath. "You're tough to track down. Finally found someone at the site who knew where you were—"

"Just get to point, MacKinley," she whispered.

"My, we're touchy today. Wish I were there to do a little touching. Heh-heh." This sally having failed to elicit any response, he cleared his throat and dropped the sexy act. When he resumed, he was all business.

"I did a favor for you, now I need one in return."

"Oh, what favor?"

"Do you agree?"

"Depends upon what it is."

"Is Huntington there with you?"

She glanced over her shoulder. "Yes."

"Then keep him there."

"Why?"

He quickly apprised her of the situation, and in the silence that followed she did some fast calculating. Marriage to Cabot? An iffy proposition at best, and she would have to stay with him for at least six months to a year. A chance to regain lost ground with Gemetics? That was even less likely. At least with Cabot she had sex on her side. Or . . .

"If I do this, I want something in return."

Now it was his turn to be cautious. "Yeah, what?"

"A job with POW, on Earth, and a professional salary."

"What can you offer the organization?"

She snorted quietly. "You know what I can offer."

"Sweetheart, we've got more tail than we know what to do with," he said brutally. "Give me something worth bargaining over."

"A masters in geology."

"That's worth something. Okay, it's a deal, but remember who you owe this to."

"Don't worry, you'll get your piece," she replied ironically, and broke the connection.

For a long moment she sat staring off into space, then rose and moved to the bed. All that was visible of the judge was a shock of tumbled black hair and the top of one ear. Periodically a sonorous snore would shatter the quiet of the room and set the edge of the sheet to fluttering. Carefully she pulled back the covers until his face was revealed. Dispassionately she studied the deep hollows of the cheeks; the high, prominent cheekbones; long black lashes; thin, aristocratic, disdainful nose; sharp, pointed chin.

She had sweetly and artfully tried to influence this man. When that had failed, she had moved on to new puppets whom she manipulated, and the result had almost been death. Now she was going to hand him to his enemies.

How dramatic, she thought, her mouth twisting with disgust. But despite her scorn, guilt fluttered at the edges of her mind. She firmly suppressed it. She was not, at this late date, going to behave like the villain in a cheap movie thriller and be saved. She looked back over the past weeks and decided that despite a few setbacks, she had done very well indeed. Only her tools had failed her. In her own way she had been as capable and admirable as her *perfect* mother. At twenty-two Lydia hadn't been playing games with a world. And how it would hurt her if she knew that her youngest, most taken-for-granted child, had fucked over Cabot Huntington and, through him, Lydia and Joe and their precious System's rights movement.

Her troublesome conscience having been dealt with, she dug a long forefinger into Cab's side, knowing how ticklish he was. He erupted from the nest of sheets and blankets with a bellow and stared blearily and belligerently about the room. His confused and pugnacious expression softened as he focused on her beautiful face.

His arms snaked about her waist. "You look much happier this morning. Bad mood passed?"

"It's much improved, thank you. Room service again, or do we dress and go downstairs?"

"Downstairs. If I keep eating and lying in this bed, they're going to have to roll me out." He frowned down at his belly.

She didn't reassure him because she knew it would bother him. It was his middle age angst that had allowed her to attract and enthrall him in the first place, and now that the charade was almost at an end, she had no interest in pacifying him.

She was in the bathroom brushing the heavy, black cloak of her hair when she thought she heard voices from the other room. Opening the door a crack, she peeked through. Jenny's back was to her, the other woman's long red hair like a waterfall of fire over her slender shoulders.

". . . leader of the rebellion out here, and you're to be arrested and returned to Earth."

Chapter Fifteen

"I had no idea this was going on," Cab said, the bed creaking under his weight, and Amadea searched the bathroom for something to wear.

"If you had emerged from your sex-drugged womb, you might have noticed," Jenny retorted.

"This is utterly insane. Oh, not Renfrew seizing the diamonds, that's right in his line. But me? On what grounds could I possibly be arrested? It's just insane."

"Yes, you said that before, but it doesn't alter the facts. They're coming after us—presumably with some kind of trumped-up charge—and we've got to make a decision. Jasper is on his way back here for weaponry and reinforcements, and I think we should go back to Eagle Port with him."

"Weaponry!" Cab exclaimed. "What are they thinking of? If they attack the enivronmentalists, they will have played right into the hands of the White House. They should wait for the Air Force and get things straightened out then."

"Cab! How can you keep defending this administration? They're not going to deal honorably and justly with us or the colonists. If they're willing to—without proof—accuse you of bribery and collusion, shielding known felons, and God only knows what else, they're not going to *straighten things out!*"

Amadea entered with a rustle of lace and chiffon. Seating herself on the bed next to Cab, she wrapped her arms around his neck and gave Jenny a challenging look. "Cabot is right. We must have faith in the system and in our leaders."

"I don't recall inviting you to join in this conversation."

"Nonetheless, she has a right."

A quickly indrawn breath hissed between Jenny's teeth, and she gave her head a sharp shake. "No," she said, more to herself than to the other people. "I'm not going to get side-tracked onto our boring little soap opera."

Amadea spoke up. "Instead, you want to turn it into an espionage drama. But tell me, exactly what do you think you'll do once you get to Eagle Port? Join in the free-for-all that it sounds like Jasper is planning to brew? That would really give the authorities something to complain about."

"The colonists have decided that they have a right to recover their property, and the captain to recover her ship. I happen to agree with them."

"Vigilantism. What about the rule of law, Jenny?" asked Cab.

"It's failed. Can't you see that? If the people at the top aren't willing to play by the rules, what the hell's left for us? To endure anything they choose to dish out? Captain Gupta has offered to take us with her when she goes, and Jasper said that Jeanne only agreed to the retaking of the ship in the interest of helping *us*. They care, Cab. Don't denigrate their sacrifice by going meekly back to Earth. Do you really want to go home as a felon and face disgrace?"

"The courts would not permit that to happen."

"Courts can be bought! *You* were."

Cab went white. "Damn you, Jenny, how could you?"

Her nails dug into her scalp. Then she threw back her hair, and faced him. "I'm sorry. But, Cab, I'm afraid for you. Afraid of what will happen if you go back. I couldn't bear it if anything happened to you." She was crying, and her anguish reached him.

He rose and tried to move to her, but Amadea's clinging arms held him back. "Cabot, no. Think what you'd be doing. You would be abandoning your principles. If you flee, it would prove what she's saying; that the rule of law in the System is dead."

Jenny dashed tears from her cheeks. "Not in the System, on Earth. May I point out that there's no order for Renfrew's arrest, just for Cab's," interrupted Jenny. That angle hadn't occurred to the judge before, and his eyes narrowed.

"You're a major figure, Cabot, trusted and respected by both sides."

"Oh, yes, so respected that they're going to arrest him and return him to Earth in disgrace," Jenny muttered ironically. Amadea shot her a look of burning hatred, but the face she turned to Cab was beautiful in its gentle distress.

"Cabot, use your power, position, charisma, and *be* that voice for sanity and justice. If you acquiesce to this momentary injustice, you'll be setting an example for everyone. Showing that *you* at least believe in the . . . the rule of law. That you will trust the legal system to vindicate you rather than taking matters into your own hands. I'm certain that you'll come through just fine, and law and civilization in the System will be strengthened by your actions."

Amadea's body was molded to his, and Jenny wondered bitterly if sex was how it would be settled. Maybe she should enter into the battle of bodies and become a piece of velcro on his left side. She rejected the thought almost as soon as it formed. She was not going to lower herself to Amadea's level. She would win this with reason, or not at all.

"Cab, you've always said that you had no patience with martyrs. *Then don't be one*. Action has always struck me as a better choice than noble posturing. If you elude them now, you'll have a chance to make all the statements you want . . . but on your terms."

"I'm afraid of what will happen if I return to Earth," he admitted slowly.

"You should be. You've outraged the power brokers, and it could go beyond mere disgrace. You might go to jail." She drew her sleeve across her eyes, angry at her tears, for just as she didn't want to use sex to influence him, nor did she want to use emotionalism. "I can bear losing you to *her*, Cab, but I can't bear losing you needlessly in an ugly power play. . . ." She choked, turning away so that all he could see were her shaking shoulders.

The moment seemed crystallized. Perfectly etched in mind

and spirit. Amadea clinging to him like a perfumed limpet. Jenny lonely and isolated, but dignified as she fought for control, struggled not to emotionally blackmail him.

And the arguments; trust and nobility versus flight. But had he any reason to trust them? Sure, it was a different group of players—Long instead of deBaca—but the rules seemed to be the same. Cindered bodies on the Moon—certainly one way to exert control—and here on Mars, a more subtle game. Agencies designed to help and protect people being used to destroy them. It was like a juggernaut running out of control. Chewing up the landscape, crushing people like saplings, intent only on its own advancement. *Once instituted, the sole purpose of a government is to survive*. The words rang in his ears, but he couldn't remember who had uttered them.

For himself it was less of a question of nobility as it was of pride. When he learned from Jenny of his impending arrest, his first response had been one of panic—yes, by all means run—but then other considerations had kicked in. What would his mother think if he cut and ran? Wouldn't it be braver to stay and face them down? Could he make a difference, as Amadea was suggesting?

He looked down at the Eurasian, and rising to tiptoes, she pressed a passionate kiss onto the corner of his mouth. "I know you won't leave me, and I know you'll do what's right for all of us."

His eyes slid to Jenny, who had turned at the other woman's words. Her eyes were filled with contempt. For him or for Amadea? He dithered, once more filled with that horrible sensation of being a bug on a pin.

"What do you want me to do?"

"I want you to run, but if you don't"—she shrugged—"I'll understand and I'll go with you . . . be with you whatever happens."

And finally, after all the weeks of agony, guilt, and confusion, he chose. Gently he disengaged Amadea's hands from his neck, folded them together, gave them a little squeeze, and stepped to Jenny. Her face seemed to glow as if lit from behind, and she reached desperately out to him. The first time in all of this madness—or soap opera, as she had called it—that she had. If only she had done it sooner, he thought. But she had been too proud and too sensitive of his feelings to place any pressure on him.

His fingers closed over her icy ones, and they started to the door. Behind him he heard Amadea scrabbling in her luggage, so at the threshold he paused and turned back, ready to make some attempt at an apology. But the words died in his throat, for he found himself staring down the barrel of a pistol. Jenny let out a gasp, and tumbled through the door and behind the sheltering hall wall. Her abrupt abandonment of him, after just professing a Ruth-like devotion to follow him anywhere, left him bewildered. Almost as bewildered as the gun in the hands of his mistress.

He forced his attention from the weapon to her face, and what he saw left him dry-mouthed. No longer was she the embodiment of delight, a modern-day houri. Her face was as cold and implacable as a death mask, and it conjured up other ancient memories, of Kali or Cerridwen the Hag.

"Come here and shut and lock the door." He hesitated, and she smoothly leveled the gun on his crotch. "And don't think I won't use this. I have too much riding on your safe delivery." He made a minute gesture toward the gun. "I said safe, not undamaged. And my mother saw to it that I hit where I aim. I won't kill you by accident."

It never occurred to him to doubt her claim. He knew Lydia Kim Nu, and now, at last, he knew the daughter. Quickly he locked he door, horribly aware of her target, and then stood, trying to keep his hands from straying protectively to his groin.

"Why, Amadea?"

"A ticket to Earth. And when one passing train crapped out, I grabbed another."

"I don't understand." She just shrugged. "You owe me at least an explanation."

For a long moment their eyes held, gray to green, then she hunched one shoulder as if dislodging an irritating insect. "Well, why not." Her teeth closed momentarily on her lower lip, but it didn't signify indecision, only calculated consideration of where to start.

"I originally worked for Gemetics." He raised his eyebrows in puzzlement. "Largest manufacturer of synthetic diamonds in the world. About a three-billion-dollar-a-year industry. They were pushing for a POW victory. Without a terraforming project the Jared colony wouldn't need to become a major new supplier of diamonds, and Gemetics would avoid a new competitor who could substantially undercut them in the marketplace. I had been hired as an information broker. When you arrived, you became part of my duties, and I got close to you. I soon realized that you were predisposed toward the colonial position and that I couldn't sway you, so we decided to kill you . . . or rather, get you killed." Her matter-of-fact presentation sent a trickle of ice down Cab's spine.

"I needed Padget MacKinley to push you into ruling against the colonists so I could manipulate Seth and the other kids. Which happened, but the kids weren't murderous enough, and your little honey was too determined to rescue you. You came back and fucked up everything, and Gemetics cut me loose. When Padget called, I had another chance, and I'm taking it."

"And Lis Varllis?"

"I'm not sure about her part in all this. I was just Gemetics little girl Friday."

"Then none of it was real . . ." He motioned between them.

"No." She indicated a chair. "Sit. And if you don't mind, I really don't want to talk about it anymore. We're going to have a wait until the POW people arrive, and it'll be boring enough without having to listen to any whinings and snivelings from you."

Amadea had settled onto the foot of the bed and was watching him with an expression of cool disinterest. For a few minutes he indulged in the careful concoction of several escape plans, each more fantastic than the last. Unfortunately none of the useful items always scattered about in the movies lay at hand, and as he stared at the pistol he realized the truth in the old adage that one should never fuck with a gun. Thinking back to his experiences on the EnerSun station, he wondered now how he had ever had the nerve to attack the assassins sent after Evgeni Renko. Probably because another person's life had also been at stake.

A flicker of movement attracted his attention. He frowned and realized that the door to the adjoining room had opened a fraction and closed again. *Jenny.* He hurriedly forced his attention back to Amadea. *She'll need a diversion.*

"Amadea, can't we talk about this?"

"No, I'm sick to death of listening to you talk. Droning on and on about case law and jurisprudence—"

Jenny erupted into the room wielding a room-service tray

still piled high with dirty dishes, and a large, white teapot. Amadea slewed around on the bed, and Cab leapt out of the chair, hoping to draw her fire if she should decide to shoot. She never had a chance. Distracted by Cab, her eyes flicked back to the chair, and Jenny clouted her across the side of the head with the tray. Dishes and cutlery went everywhere while Amadea screeched like an angry hawk and clutched at her head, the gun falling unheeded to the floor.

Realizing her mistake, she scrabbled for the weapon only to have it kicked out of reach by Jenny.

"Nice . . ." began Cab, only to have the rest of the sentence swept from his mind as his sweet, gentle, ladylike law clerk seized Amadea by the hair and yanked her up off the bed.

Yowling with pain and fury, the younger woman clawed at Jenny's hand while kicking desperately at her legs. Jenny yelped as a kick connected, then set her jaw and delivered a hard right to Amadea's nose. A smack like the sound of a large piece of raw meat hitting a chopping board cut through the room, and blood spattered over the two combantants. Cab took two steps forward, hands patting at the air, trying to stop the free-for-all, was narrowly missed by one of Amadea's flailing hands and prudently retreated. Judging from the look on Jenny's face, she would neither welcome nor heed any interference. The morbid interest that people always have at the sight of a fight or an accident, combined with the complete fascination that grips men in the presence of battling women kept him watching while Jenny methodically beat the snot out of Amadea, and he realized with a start of guilty pleasure that she was exacting this vengeance on the girl because of *him;* paying her rival back for all the weeks of hurt and jealousy.

In a few minutes it was over. Jenny dropped the inert bundle of tears and blood back onto the bed and stepped back sucking at her knuckles. She was relatively unscathed; blood trickled from a pair of gouges in her cheek where Amadea's flying hand had caught her a glancing blow, and she was limping from the kick, but that was all. As for the other side? It had been a complete massacre. Amadea's eyes were blackened, several handfuls of black hair lay scattered across the floor, her nose was bleeding, and her lower lip was swollen and trickling blood over her chin from where the tender skin had been driven against her teeth. The only sounds in the room were Jenny's sharp pants and faint mewling sobs from Amadea.

Jenny shot a glance to Cab, her expression half guilty, half defiant—fully expecting a reprimand. Instead, he held out his arms. She came into his embrace with a soft little sound that was part tears and part laughter.

"Thank you. That was quite a rescue."

"Then you don't mind? I was—"

He buried his face in her hair. "Jenny, I've been such a fool. Can you ever forgive me?"

She pushed him away and held him at arm's length, staring intently into his face. "I forgave you days ago. When I thought I'd lost you." Her eyes slid away, and she stepped beyond his reach, as if embarrassed by her own emotionalism. "Jasper should be here soon. If we want to take anything other than the clothes on our backs, we'd better get packed. Oh"—she grinned and pulled a silver key card from her back pocket—"and I guess I'd better return this to Peter."

"So that's how you got in. But why didn't you bring some help?"

She stared at Amadea, who had stopped crying and was blotting at her nose with the edge of the sheet. "This was something *I* needed to handle . . . and then there's Lydia to consider. Coming?"

"I'll meet you at the apartment."

Her gaze flickered between Cab and Amadea, then she nodded. "Okay, but don't be long."

"This won't take long."

The door closed behind her, and Cab swung the chair around in front of the drooping figure of his former mistress, rested his arms on the back, and stared mutely into her ravaged face. He felt like a too taut violin string, vibrating dissonantly as each new and conflicting emotion swept through him. He tried to cling to the warm sense of his love for Jenny, nourish his shame, fan his anger against Amadea. But not . . . not to examine the love he had felt for *her*. The fact that it had been based on sex and very little else added to his sense of stupidity, but a small part of it, divorced from passion, had existed—still existed—and he feared that if he looked too closely at the emotion, it might break him.

Memories of their frenzied lovemaking lanced through him, but where in the past it had brought an answering physical reaction, this time it felt as if his balls were trying to retreat up into his body. He rested his forehead on his arm, wanting to cry but feeling too stupid to deserve the luxury of that release. He had brought this pain on himself, for Jenny's assessment had been correct. In a desperate attempt to recover what he perceived as his lost youth he had flung himself into an affair with a girl young enough to be his daughter, and all semblance of rational thought had vanished in the hot surge of his passion. He had indeed been thinking with his gonads.

He raised his head and saw something in Amadea's face that reminded him of her mother. His own self-pity was lost in a rush of sympathy for Lydia. Lydia Kim Nu, one of the foremost leaders of the System, architect of the independence movement; what would the knowledge of her daughter's betrayal do to her? Could they keep it from her? And how . . . how could the girl have done this?

"Amadea, why?" His voice grated out, husky with unshed tears. She stared sullenly at him, and a flash of anger drove back the hurt and confusion that lay like an aching weight in the center of his chest. "How the hell could you do this to your mother?"

She jerked off the bed. "Oh, yes, my *wonderful,* sainted mother!" she mumbled around her swollen lip. "How could I *possibly* forget about my mother! Christ, I'd give anything to be free of her, of the memory of her. Everyone always throwing up to me what a fucking paragon she is. How I must share her goals and desires. Well, I don't!" she screamed down at him. "I hate it out here! I'm sick to death of dirt and canned air and provincial shit-kickers who think they're something special because they're taming the new frontier. I want wealth and ease and comfort and elegance and the company of witty, intellectual people. I want to swim in Tahiti, ski in Switzerland, do the theater in London, not dry up and blow away before I'm fifty because of the radiation and the work, and all the rest of it. I don't want to work hard and be virtuous. I want what Earth and only Earth can offer. And as far as I'm concerned, the System can go straight to hell!"

She gagged and choked; wiped furiously at the tears which the violence of her emotions had elicited. This moment of weakness passed quickly, however, and she turned her blazing green eyes back on him. "And you . . . I loathe you. I *endured* you because of what I was to receive in return. And then you ruined me. Ruined it all. Fuck you, Cabot. I hope they catch you before you can get off-world. I want you to know the kind of loss and ruin I'm experiencing."

"I am . . . right now."

She jerked her head up and stared at him incredulously. Then a slow, pleased smile crossed her face. Because of her split and bleeding lip, it looked more like a grimace than an expression of pleasure. Sickened by her malevolence, her enjoyment of his anguish, and by his own stupidity, he rose and left, carefully closing the door on her lest anyone see what lay behind it.

"Shit! Those look like bodies down there!" yapped Jasper peering through the front windows of the jump ship.

Cab placed a hand in the center of Jenny's firm rump and shoved her to her feet, then tried to extricate himself from the jumble of ammunition boxes, long, heavy-barreled target rifles, and the legs of their fellow travelers. Being by far the smallest people on the jump, they had been relegated to the floor. Cab now wished he had protested more vigorously as Chief Riley's booted foot came down on the fingers of his left hand as the fourteen volunteers from Jared all rushed forward to see. He yelped and, sucking at his fingers, limped forward to join the others, all huddled about the view ports.

He was not in the mood for politeness or finesse, so he merely elbowed his way to the front. The ship swept in over the two large reactor cooling towers, flashed over the body of the port proper, and circled back for another look. It wasn't hard to locate the Belter ship; it was the only one currently on the field, squatting like a heavy, gray-armored insect on the russet sand. And between it and the port warehouses lay several tiny, huddled forms. It looked like a heedless giant's child had strolled across the plain, scattering action figures from its toy box.

"Jesus Christ! Get off me! I can't fly with all of you on my back," bellowed Jasper.

Then the ship bucked as a beam of blue-green light split the pink sky directly in front of the nose of the craft. Even inside they could hear the muted crack as the neon-argon laser ionized the thin air of Mars.

"Shit, shit, shit, shit, shit!" screamed Jasper, slewing the ship over and diving in for a landing behind the security of the warehouses. The abrupt maneuver sent people and weapons flying about the tiny cabin. The radio came to life, and the placid, almost moronic voice of the port computer intoned, "You are landing in a nonapproved zone. Please acknowledge and return to the field."

"Fat chance," muttered Jasper.

"You are lan—"

"This is Despopolous . . . ah . . . Dr. Mendel . . . er . . . is that you?"

"Yes! Who the fuck else would it be?"

"Please land behind the—"

"I am! I am."

And with a bump and a lurch the ship touched down. Peeved by the loss of their target, the laser crew set about randomly firing up the sand crawlers that were parked about the warehouse area. A ray of blue-green incadenscence would pulse out, followed by a terrifying crack as the air rushed back to fill the vacuum formed by the passage of the superheated beam. Though quieter than it would have been on Earth, it still sent the exiting relief force from Jared scurrying for cover.

Following almost instantly on the heels of the first sound would come the actual explosion as another crawler took the full force of the laser and went bouncing and tumbling end over end across the sand, rather like a piece of popcorn on a hot griddle. By the time the little band of colonists, all clutching weapons and looking like raggedy-assed extras in a remake of *The Kuwait Emergency,* reached the safety of the administrative building, twelve sand crawlers lay in twisted ruin. Cab looked for flames and smoke, then realized there wasn't enough oxygen to keep the fuel ignited.

It was an excellent demonstration of the firepower controlled by POW, and it had the proper effect on the people come to challenge that power. By the time the breathless, nervous, and chattering people gathered in Despopolous's office, they were all busily telling each other how hopeless it was to go after the ship. Darnell looked like a grim-faced stone effigy. Despopolous's conversation was punctuated with more ums and ahs than normal, and Captain Gupta raged from one side of the room to the other.

"What in the hell happened out there?" demanded Cab over the excited conversation that filled the room. He dropped into a chair, propping his injured leg on the edge of the port master's desk.

"Certain people decided that Renfrew and his bunch would be a pushover, and didn't want to wait for reinforcements from Jared."

Sakti rounded on Darnell. "I've acknowledged eight or ten times that you were right and I was wrong. What more do you want?"

"If you had—"

"Shut up!" roared Cab, and he was surprised when they and everyone else in the room obeyed. All eyes were riveted on him, and he shrank back in the chair as he realized that without any desire on his part, command had shifted to him. "Somebody give me a coherent explanation of what happened."

Sakti hitched up her pants and glowered at the far wall. "I didn't know how long it would take for Jasper to get back from Jared with the target rifles, and with the military on the way I decided to move. I didn't figure those people had much experience with populaces who would shoot back, and I thought we might be able to rush them. A number of locals broke out their private weapons for us, and we went."

"But that damn laser just tore us up," broke in Seth. "Sakti was right . . . at least partially. The people holding the main bay just about wet their pants when they saw us coming and that we were actually shooting, but then the laser kicked in, and the troopies in the door got their morale back and figured out how to shoot again. They're not very accurate, but they can pour out a lot of lead with their automatic weapons, and eventually they got lucky."

"Because you got stupid. And look at the end result," growled Darnell.

"I lost one of my crew out there. You don't have to remind me what a fuck-up it was."

"So what do we do now?" asked Jenny.

"We've got three choices." Huntington held up three fingers. "Negotiation." There were head shakes all around, and he folded down his forefinger. "Wait for the authorities to arrive and let them settle this—"

"And us too," murmured Jenny.

"Or try again," Cab ended on a sigh.

"Goddamn right we try again. I'm not having my ship impounded."

Cab shifted his gaze to the Prophet. "The decision has to be yours, Darnell. Jenny and I have a compelling reason for wanting off Mars." *And I have a compelling reason for wanting to get even with at least one of the parties that tried to kill me,* his thoughts added. "And Captain Gupta wants her ship. But we'll be leaving, and you'll have to stay behind to face the music from Earth."

"And it ain't gonna be pretty," added Jasper, and sucked loudly at his teeth for emphasis. "Almost as bad as that time down in Ecuador—"

"Judge, we want to see you get away. The charges against you are ludicrous, and I don't think you're going to get fair treatment back home. But more than that, there's our pride. Nobody has a right to do us damage and not take the consequences. They've seized our property and shot our people, and we have a right to settle it."

"They'll say it's vigilantism."

"Vigilantism, my left tit," ejected Chief Riley. "I'm the duly elected sheriff for the city of Jared, and Despopolous here commands security for Eagle Port. We don't need Earth to stick its nose in here. What right do they have, anyway?" She stared belligerently around the room.

"Um . . . little problem," said Despopolous. He stroked sadly at his fat cheeks. "My people and I . . . um, are Earth appointees, and I've . . . ah, been ordered to take no action."

"You goddamn toady! Is your cushy job more important—"

"Seth, shut up," ordered Darnell. "I understand, Mike."

"But . . . ah, you're neighbors, and . . . um, we want to help. So . . . er, here's the key to the arms locker. Might, um . . . ah, be something there to . . . hm, help you."

"They'll have your ass for helping us," warned Cab.

"That's okay. We're System. They're not."

Darnell accepted the key card. "Stephen, Seth, check out the arms locker."

"So what do we do?" Cab asked after the door closed behind them. "I haven't had much—hell, *any*—experience at this sort of thing."

"But I have." Jasper tugged at his upper lip; his eyes narrowed into thoughtful slits. "Now that we've got range, I think we ought to use it. Even up the odds a little before we try crossing that field again. Who's had experience with long-range target weapons?"

"That I have," Cab offered.

"You're not going. You're hurt, and we want your skin in one piece when we put you aboard that ship." Cab subsided, but he was already considering how to get around the ban. He was neither an old man nor an invalid, and he had a score to settle.

Jasper seized a piece of paper and began a rough sketch of the landing field and its environs. "Okay, here's what we do."

The arms locker contained gas grenades, and while they would do fuck-all against suited opponents, they would at least lay down cover when they did start the actual assault. But before that happened, Jasper wanted to even the odds, and finding that the locker contained several military assault rifles complete with computer-corrected laser-dot scopes made that goal a good deal more attainable. According to Gupta, POW had taken no casualties during that first ill-organized rush, and Jasper aimed to change that. Four of the colony's best marksmen were making their way to various elevated positions spotted about the ship. Using their jet-powered backpacks, Wraight and Crenshaw were perched like vultures on top of the two cooling towers, Darnell was making his way into the hills above the Belter ship, while Jasper was holding down a position on the top of one of the warehouses.

He had a good view of the evironmentalists milling about in the mouth of the loading bay, but the piled crates, which formed a nest about the laser, effectively blocked from view the crew that manned it. He hoped Wraight and Crenshaw would have an actual shot at it. Cursing a little, he chinned on his radio, hoping that POW wasn't listening on the frequency they had chosen. It was an odd one, so maybe they would get lucky. God knows they were due for a little luck. They'd had precious little of it thus far.

"Everybody ready?"

"We're in place," said Wraight. "But, God, it's exposed up here."

Jasper ignored the small snivel. There were no safe places for anyone involved in this little party. "Darnell?"

"I'm fine. Get on with it."

"Are you in place?"

"I'm getting where I need to be."

"Now, dammit, don't be a hero. Darnell, Darnell?"

Disgusted with the pigheaded old coot, Mendel raised his rifle and held down on one of the suited figures in the bay. "Wraight, Crenshaw, let's do it."

He drew in a slow breath, released it halfway, then held it and squeezed back on the trigger. An instant later one of the figures threw up its hands and jerked backward into the shadowy depths of the cargo bay. Switching targets quickly, he blew away another of the guards before the rest went scuttling and tumbling back into the ship, out of sight and out of range. He couldn't see what success Wraight and Crenshaw were having with the laser crew up top, but suddenly the laser fired, the hellish, death-dealing light exploding the top of the nearest cooling tower.

"Wraight," he croaked, knowing it was too late but needing to try.

A tiny figure lifted off the second tower and went scooting toward the hills as the beam blew pieces of the tower in all directions. A flying bit of debris struck Crenshaw, but he kept moving, and Jasper, watching through his scope, started to breathe again. His relief was premature, however, for the laser pulsed once more, the beam taking Crenshaw in the center of his back. Steam erupted from the body as the cells released their supply of water under the hellish assault of the laser.

Jasper realized that the laser obviously had sighting equipment equally as sophisticated as his own, and a hell of a lot more range. Clutching the rifle to his chest, he rolled desperately to the edge of the roof and plunged off, waiting until he was below the level of the building before cutting in his suit jets. Wouldn't do to pinpoint his position any more than he already had. He waited for the laser to come into play again, raking across the top of the warehouses, but it didn't happen.

"Amateurs," he muttered. "Fucking amateurs."

"They were good enough to take out two of ours," Gupta grunted in rebuttal.

"What are they doing now?"

"Buttoning up."

"Like I said . . . amateurs."

• • •

"Carl's dead, he's dead!" Jana screeched, her hands clutching frantically at his shoulders. Lucius threw her aside and surveyed the carnage in the hold. Two people were down: one with his helmet shattered, and bits of hair and brain clinging to the ragged edges of the faceplate; the other with a small, neat hole in the center of his chest. Inside, he wouldn't be so neat. Those tiny slugs did grotesque tissue damage when they penetrated. Up top, one of the marksmen had taken out Dick.

"Only fourteen of us left," he muttered to himself, and wished he hadn't sent Stan and Luke back to Jared. "You got the doors closed?"

"Yeah," a young man forced past chattering teeth. "But, Jesus, maybe we ought to give up. We haven't got a chance against them—"

"Shut up! We did just fine before they set up those marksmen, but the laser's handled them and it will continue to handle them. All we have to do is stay put until the squadron gets here."

"What if they've got more marksmen, what if they take out—"

"If they had them, they'd have used them!"

"Nobody's ever done this before," bawled Jana, hugging herself. "Nobody's ever shot at us before."

"Yeah, well, these people are fucking terrorists. What did you expect? And the goddamn feds should have kept this kind of heavy armament out of the hands of colonists! Maybe *now* they'll see the dangers inherent in their policy and *do* something about it. These people are a fucking menace!"

He flung himself up the ladder and out of the lower cargo hold, trying to maintain his sense of outrage. It was the only way he could hold the terror at bay. He had taken part in a number of these seizures on Earth, but they had been fun. He got to tote around an automatic weapon, hold forth for the press, overawe the civilian populace, and best of all, they usually won. Or at least delayed whatever action it was they were protesting, costing the developers or the government additional millions.

But *this!* It felt like he had a hole in his stomach that extended all the way to his backbone, and he doubled over. Tears pricked at his eyelids as he considered the dead and the fact that he might be joining them. He knew he couldn't reveal his fear to his people, so he decided to stay on the bridge rather than take part in the fighting. He would be of more use monitoring the situation as it developed.

And maybe they wouldn't come again. He clung to the thought for a moment, then realized with a sense of hate and fear that people who were willing to kill for objects *would* come again.

Cab had been stashed in the emergency room of the port's hospital with the wounded from the first ill-advised assault. Jeanne moved quietly from bed to bed, talking gently with her people, and Cab waved her over.

"What do you need?"

He rubbed his thumb along his jaw, considering. "Out of here."

"Jasper and Darnell want you out of harm's way."

"But Jenny's with them, and I need to be with her."

"So the two of you are back together."

He flushed and looked away. "I didn't know you knew."

"It was a little hard to miss. I'm surprised Amadea isn't here. She's always been closely involved with our little dramas."

He stared at her, choosing his words with care. "She's back at Jared. Being no fool, she's not about to come to a place where people are shooting at each other."

She stared at him curiously for a moment, then let it drop. "No."

"You have a husband and a son in the middle of this. You must understand how I feel."

"But I wouldn't be much use out there, and the shape you're in, you won't, either."

"Jeanne, please," he begged, gripping her hand.

She studied him for a long moment, closed her eyes, and released a long sigh. "God forgive me. All right, go. I suppose you gotta do what you gotta do."

He sat up and hugged her. "Very profound and very wise."

"The meaning of life according to Jasper Mendel. You will come back so I won't live to regret this?"

"I promise."

Returning to suit storage, he retrieved his and was soon hobbling from building to building, taking advantage of the cover. At last he reached the assembly point, a large warehouse set well back from the Belter ship and shielded by several other buildings. There were a lot more people there than could be explained by the Mormon reinforcements Jasper had brought, and he realized that some of the Eagle Port population must have joined in. This further example of colonial solidarity struck on a raw nerve, almost bringing into focus something that had been bothering him for days. A figure loomed up and he lost it.

It was Seth, and Cab automatically stiffened. It helped some to know that the boy had been duped by Amadea, but he still found it difficult to face him. "Is Jenny here?"

"She's over on the other side with Jasper. We're going to try hitting them from both sides."

"Goddamm it!" He drove his fist into the side of a carton. "I want to be with her. I've got to get over there."

"You'll never reach them in time. We're set to start in"—his eyes flicked up, checking the suit chronometer—"four minutes. Aren't you supposed to be in the hospital?"

"No."

Seth grinned. "I get it. Jasper's gonna hate it, but he's not here. Welcome aboard." He held out his hand, then remembered, and it dropped limply to his side.

They stared at each other for what seemed like a long time, then Cab offered his hand. They shook.

"Shotgun or handgun, Judge?"

"Pistol, please."

Seth tossed him one. "Sir," he said, switching to a private frequency.

"Yes."

"I just wanted to tell you that you're . . . okay. If I hadn't been so stupid and listened to—"

"Don't worry, you're not giving anything away. I know about Amadea."

Seth goggled. "But when? I mean, why didn't you say something?"

"First of all, I only learned of it today. Then there's my pride and, more importantly, her mother. Lydia is a good friend of Jenny's and mine. I don't want her to learn of her daughter's actions."

"I take it back. You're more than okay, Judge. And if it's not too late, I'd like to say I'm sorry."

"Apology accepted."

"And if I eat a round out there, it'll be no more than I deserve."

"Don't you even think about it." Cab's finger pointed threateningly at the teenager. "You've got to grow up and amount to something so that years from now, when I'm old and irascible, I can remind you about what a little prick you were in your foolish youth."

Seth laughed and held up his hands, gloved palms out. "Okay, okay."

Darnell inched forward on his belly, expecting at any moment to feel the burn of the laser across his back. But it didn't come. Maybe the defenders were too busy watching for the attack to notice a lone man on a promontory high above their heads. He wanted to ascertain their positions but resisted the impulse. He wasn't going to move until the assault started. Then he'd come up and pick them off. He was his people's insurance. He couldn't screw up now.

"You're enjoying this," Jenny accused as she squatted in the sand, watching Jasper prep the grenade launcher.

"Yep."

"And I don't think this is standard training for most scientists."

"Nope."

"Oh, stop that."

"You don't like my John Wayne imitation?"

"Who's John Wayne?"

"Poor benighted child. You're not an old-movie junkie?"

"You and Andy. He's an old TV junkie. It's all pretty lousy now. I can't believe it was any better years ago." She put a hand up to her faceplate. "And I'm babbling. Sorry. Nerves."

"I'd be worried if you weren't. And to where I learned this . . . I've knocked around the globe a lot before coming out here, and I love to be in trouble. Learn a lot of interesting skills when you're constantly in trouble." He checked his chronometer. "Ooops, almost time to go." At her expression he laid a hand on her shoulder. "Okay? You don't have to do this. Probably shouldn't. It you get hurt, Huntington will cut off my nuts and feed them to me." He settled the launcher onto his shoulder and darted forward, using the cylindrical control room module of the power plant for cover. "By the way, why are you coming?"

Because I think one of us should share in the risk. This entire party has been planned because of us. And then there's my need to be melodramatic. I keep fantasizing about Cab weeping over my fallen body and being sorry because he treated me so badly. Still, this is a hell of a way to get even, if that's what I'm doing. I'm scared, I don't want to get hurt.

She eyed her armed companions and the ship, squat and threatening on the plain. She was still trying to think of an acceptable answer for Jasper when one of the young Eagle Port colonists who had been listening to a commercial radio station broke in.

"Jesus, shit! Guess what? They've translated the message on the alien crystal."

"No shit?" said Jasper. "And what do our brothers from the stars have to say? Some great words of wisdom that will make all of this"—he gestured toward the ship—"unnecessary?"

The man had an odd, pinched expression on his face. "Nooo, the linguists say this thing is basically an inscription rock, you know, like the one in New Mexico that the conquistadores marked up. Things like 'Ribblesnitch was here,' complaints about commanders, and what seem to be comments on sexual prowess."

Jasper looked sour. "Well . . . shit!" Then he laughed, settled the launcher, and fired off a grenade. It erupted from the mouth of the launcher with a dull *phut,* and thick white smoke came billowing up from its impact point. "So fuck all the metaphysics and let's drive on!"

Chapter Sixteen

Ghostly figures lumbering through thick white smoke, the vanguard of some strange, alien army.

But most soldiers fight in suits now, Cab thought inanely, and clutched at his injured arm. He pushed harder, struggling to keep up, his leg sending flashes of agony to his brain with each desperate step. Another attacker lumbered/glided past. *Wait, don't leave me behind.* He tried harder to emulate their long, ground-eating, flying strides. Jenny was somewhere ahead, beyond the now invisible ship.

If this was the first skirmish in a planet-spanning war between Earth and the System, there would soon be men fighting in suits across a radius of many millions of miles. Women too. The colonists apparently did not share their Earthbound brethern protectiveness toward women. Jenny and Lydia going after the assassins with only Peter to back them. Ah, Jenny.

But it couldn't come to that—musn't come to that. He should have forestalled this attack, awaited the arrival of the Earth forces, and accepted whatever punishment was meted out to him. A little late now to think about that. And as he analyzed his turbulent emotions he realized he wasn't feeling that noble. Between them, POW and Amadea and Gemetics had caused him a lot of grief and damn near cost him his life. No, he was going to be neither noble nor forgiving.

There came the muted crack of the laser, and the smoke glowed a bilious blue-green. Cab went facedown and tried to become one with the red sands. His suit radio reverberated with the sounds of agonized screaming as the beam found a target. Suddenly it became real. That had been the death cry of a human being. His stomach tried to climb up into his throat.

"Shit!" screamed Seth. "That damn thing's just tearin' us up!"

"Go on! Go on!" roared Jasper's voice, rising above the hysterical chatter that filled the radios.

Crack!

Several people raced past him with elbows pumping, heading back to the safety of the buildings, unable to face that withering fire. He struggled to his feet and ran on, driven by one thought: to find Jenny. Something that seemed a good deal more likely now than it had only moments before. A light breeze had risen, dissipating the thick smoke, carrying it away toward the nearby hills in long, tattered streams. Very soon the laser crew wasn't going to have to guess about the location of their attackers.

High on his promontory, Darnell cursed the smoke but for different reasons. As soon as the grenades had gone, he had popped up, looking for targets. He had managed to squeeze off one shot before the smoke completely obscured his view, and his last, satisfying sight had been of one of the defenders being blown back into the protective nest of crates surrounding the laser. But now he was stymied. Firing randomly would only bring the laser down on him before he had accomplished his purpose, but while he waited for the smoke to clear, his people were being chewed up by that beam of coherent light, and once the protective cover was gone, their situation would be even more desperate.

He had counted four people manning the laser. One was down. The question was how fast he could take out the other three without sacrificing accuracy. The smoke was clearing. Sucking in a breath, he propped the rifle and waited. Shadowy form, release partway, squeeze. Another body collapsed.

More screams from colonists as the laser blasted holes in the plain. One of the environmentalists panicked and ran for the top hatch. Darnell fired, missed; cursed and fired again. The bullet slammed into the man, and that, together with his momentum, pitched him right off the side of the ship.

The smoke was almost gone now. It made it very easy to see the laser swinging around to bear on him. *One more, one more. Must take him.* They fired simultaneously.

Cab saw the top of the promontory blow away and didn't make the connection until he heard Seth sobbing and cursing somewhere nearby. His ears seemed deadened, and then he realized why. The laser had fallen silent.

"Go, go! Before they get somebody back up there!" screamed Gupta.

The survivors raced the final few yards and reached the ship. The rungs on the side were high, and with his injured leg, Cab couldn't jump for them. He reached, reached, and suddenly someone grabbed him around the waist and boosted him up to the first rung. The judge looked back, nodded his thanks to the burly giant who had helped him. Six-foot-six if he's an inch, he thought resentfully as the man reached up, and coolly pulled himself up behind Cab.

His arm was shivering with strain by the time he reached the top. A final effort and he belly-flopped ungracefully onto the top of the ship and lay panting. His large companion went charging forward and bulled into the piles of crates surrounding the laser. They toppled like children's blocks, and the hatch lay revealed. A ragged cheer went up, and the colonists swarmed forward. Cab spotted a tiny figure in among the men and croaked out, "Jenny!"

"Cab!" Dropping her rifle so it hung by its sling, she pulled him to his feet. "What are you doing here?"

"Being with you."

"Oh, Cabot."

Her arms went around his neck, and he held her close. Physically it was less than satisfying, separated as they were by their suits and helmets, but Cab had never felt closer to her.

Jasper's shout pulled them apart. "No time for kissy-face. Save it for later. Let's get 'em!"

But as a fight it was disappointing. The remaining POW members had been utterly demoralized by the loss of their invincible laser and quickly surrendered. Sakti Gupta had located Eddy being held in one of the crew quarters and released him. She then spent a few moments holding the frozen body of Archimedes before returning briskly to the task of preparing the ship for lift-off. As air cycled back into the ship the triumphant raiders held a quick nose-count and discovered that Lucius Renfrew was missing. People scattered in search of him.

Cab was poking through the mid-level cargo bay when he heard voices. As he drew closer he recognized Seth's voice, raised in anguish.

"You killed my father. And now I'm going to kill you."

A breathless, inaudible reply whispered through the bay, and Cab limped hurriedly to intervene. And found himself standing in a moment that was etched with glasslike sharpness on his consciousness. Seth, taut with guilt and the dimly growing realization of the totality of his loss. Renfrew, slack and blubbering on the floor of his hiding place; for the first time actually confronting the ramifications of his actions. And what of Darnell? Had he for belief or bravery sought death on that mountain? Or had he, discovering his son's attempt at murder, taken the guilt upon himself and carried it down into oblivion with him?

And had Cab himself not also played a part in bringing them to this? Arrogance disguised as impartiality. Playing at judgeship, enjoying the propitiation of both sides like some oracular figure dispensing wisdom and justice. Trying to remain aloof from all sides, and in the end, ironically, being manipulated by all.

The gun lifted slightly, the muscles in the boy's forearms tightening as he prepared to fire, and Cab said softly, "Seth, no."

The boy whirled, tears staining his face. "My father was on that hill."

"I know."

"He wouldn't have been there except for this bastard."

"You could make the same argument about me. He authorized and took part in the attack partly so I could leave Mars. Are you going to shoot me too?" Hand outstretched, he took a step forward. "Give me the gun."

"No! He's got to pay, and if he gets back to Earth, he never will."

"That may well be the case, but if you do this thing, you'll never have another peaceful moment. You came close to making a tragic mistake once. Don't risk it again." His hand closed over the boy's wrist, and he pulled the gun from Seth's nerveless fingers. "There's been enough killing for one day."

The boy slumped, and Cab closed his arms about Seth's bony shoulders, holding him while he sobbed. "It should have been me. It should have been me. I should have paid the price for being bad, not him."

Cab held him while he wept.

"It . . . ah, takes time to fill fuel tanks. Er . . . can't be done in . . . um, five minutes."

Sakti lifted her hands as if contemplating throttling the port master, then turned the action into an expressive gesture in the air over her head. "The squadron is almost here. It will be a hell of a note if after all this trouble we are caught, as the Americans say, with our pants down." She took a quick turn about the bridge of the *Goose*. "I have enough anti-hydrogen to go six times around the entire Solar System, but I can't get off the planet because I have no maneuvering jets."

"We're . . . ah, working very . . . um, hard."

Jasper came striding in. "We've got Renfrew and his little band of loonies locked up in the brig, and I had that shyster thrown in with them."

"And the two who were being sent after me?" asked Cab as he lay in one of the acceleration couches.

"They found a warmer-than-expected reception at Jared, and they're locked up."

"We're *all* going to be locked up!" Sakti again threw her hands into the air and stalked from the bridge. Despopolous rolled his eyes expressively.

"Do you know where Jenny is?" Cab asked.

"With Jeanne."

"I should probably go over there. Looks like we won't be leaving for a little while yet."

"Yeah, me, too, but I'm a coward. I dread facing her."

Not as much as I do, Jasper, my man, thought Cab as he eased himself out of the acceleration couch.

Down in the main hold he wearily climbed back into his suit and limped off to the hospital. Seth, Jenny, and Jeanne were seated about a table in the cafeteria. Jenny with a cup of steaming coffee, the other two with fruit juice. This dedication to belief, even in the face of terrible loss, summed up Jeanne's character. Cab was sorry that he wasn't going to have a chance to get to know this remarkable woman better.

Lydia, Lis, Amadea, Jeanne, Jenny. He looked back over the women who, over the past year, had played such profound roles, both good and bad, in his life.

It was uncharacteristic of him, but he came around the table, dropped his arm over Jeanne's shoulder, and pressed a kiss onto her wrinkled cheek. She smiled, though tears glittered in her eyes, and gave his hand a squeeze.

"It's hard to know what to say," Cab said. "Words are so inadequate at times like these. But I am very sorry. I owe you and your husband a great debt."

"Knowing that you and Jenny are safe will help settle the debt." She took a sip of juice. "And I know Darnell would feel the same. It's very hard for Seth and me to accept God's wisdom in this matter, but we'll try not to mourn too long or too hard. Darnell never wanted to slide down into helpless old age."

They sat in silence for several minutes, then Jeanne pushed away her glass. "You'd better go. Sakti Gupta is a good woman, but her ship is the most important thing in her life, and if the refueling finishes and you're not aboard, she might just go without you."

Jenny and Cab rose reluctantly. "I hate to leave you all to face the wrath that's going to be generated by events here."

"Don't worry. We Mormons are used to wrath, and we always endure." She stood and hugged Jenny. "Come back soon?"

"We promise, as soon as matters on Earth are settled, Cab's going to hire a good lawyer to fight the charges. . . ."

"Take care of your mother," Cab said, gripping Seth's hand.

"I will, and you take care of Jenny. And about Amadea—"

He shook his head. "No, leave it. I really would prefer it if you would."

"But how can I face her, knowing what I do, and not say anything?"

"I don't think she's going to be on Mars much longer. And for our friend Lydia's sake, please keep silent."

"Yes, sir."

But the two seemed reluctant to let them go and insisted on escorting them back across the field to the ship. Jenny and Cab waved once from the small lock set in the nose of the craft, and the pair were lost to view as the door cycled closed.

"Glad you're back," grunted Gupta. "We're close to leaving." Martinez was running the final checks, the complex control board glowing as numbers, graphs, and charts flowed across its screens.

A sudden pounding cut through the rising hum of the engines.

"Shit! Now what!"

It was Jasper, demanding entrance. As soon as he stepped through the inner door of the lock, Sakti was on him. "What? You want to come along?"

"No, wanted to let you know that you've got about twenty minutes, maybe less. Despopolous says the squadron's preparing to deploy landing shuttles, so you might be cutting right under the noses of the big ships."

"I can handle that. But why didn't Despopolous tell me this? Com broke down?"

"Nah, I wanted to bring you the message because I had something else for you."

Unsealing his suit, he reached in under his arm and emerged with an outraged kitten. White with an irregular blotch of black over her left eye, she looked like a pugnacious and punch-drunk fighter as she hung, spitting and yowling, in the scientist's hand.

"Jasper Mendel, you're a sweet man," Jenny said, and gave him a quick hug.

Gupta's long fingers caressed the cat. "You're also going to be a Belter if you don't get off this ship." The scientist slammed his helmet back on and headed into the lock. "And thank you." The smile that curved her lips softened the harsh planes of her face. "And tell those Mormons we'll get their damn diamonds to Earth somehow."

"Hey, that's a thought. How do I know you're not just decamping with the riches—"

"Out!"

"Good-bye, Jasper," chorused the judge and his clerk.

"Go strap in."

• • •

From their small crew cubicle they couldn't witness the *Gray Goose*'s screaming escape from Eagle Port under the very noses of the incoming shuttles or the fast maneuverings that Gupta pulled to avoid the main body of the fleet, but they felt them. Acceleration drove them into the restraining straps, and Cab moaned, wondering why every time he came to the System people used him for a punching bag.

Once Sakti signaled the all-clear, he discovered another fact about the *Goose;* unlike the luxury liner they had taken to Mars, the cargo vessel had no artificial gravity. He fought the growing nausea, but two hours into the voyage he was puking up his guts, and Jenny had put him back in the bunk. She stayed with him for a long time, but at last her growing desire to see something of the voyage and visit with the crew and talk about life in the aseteroids won out over her concern, and she left him to rest.

He didn't want to whine, but her abandonment and her obvious enjoyment of the entire situation served to increase his own doubts and depression. During the EnerSun crisis he had clung to his belief in the American democratic system and the men and women who administered it. When Tomas's perfidy finally had been brought home to him, he had been shaken but had not lost faith in the institutions. Evil people might occasionally reach the helm, but the ship always righted itself. Now even that comfort had been removed, for it had been the very agencies of government that had been used to oppress the Jared colonists, and when that failed, Lis Varllis had authorized an illegal act to achieve her goals.

Still, didn't that support his original premise, that it was the people, not the institutions? No, that was sophistry. Opponents of the decentralized System always pointed to the necessity of government as watchdog to contain the evil tendencies of the people. But if human beings were so evil, who would watch the watchers? And were they not made more dangerous by the placement of such power in their hands? Over the past hundred and fifty years government had continued to grow unchecked, invading every aspect of life. This growth had been excused as an effort to protect the citizenry, but was it, or was it instead a convenient way for the government to centralize ever more power in itself?

"The purpose of governments is to perpetrate themselves," and at last he remembered who had said that. He had, to Kenneth Omi Furakawa during some of his darkest days aboard the EnerSun station.

He felt very empty as his last defense fell, and the final foundation that supported his belief in the political system he had served his entire life collapsed. He turned his face to the wall, tasting bile as he remembered how eagerly at the inaguration he had embraced the President's position.

Once more the perfect dupe.

"Cab?" Her warm hand touched his cheek. "How are you feeling?"

It disturbed him to have her floating upside down next to him as he lay in the top bunk. He closed his eyes, still struggling to find up and down in this alien world.

"Terrible."

"Sakti's going to take us to Ceres to join Joe. Then we can start the legal machinery in motion."

"I don't want to be doing this, Jenny. I keep thinking about home. Will I ever see my house again?"

"I'm sure." She wriggled inside the sleep sack and pulled him close. "It's okay to be homesick. It's not a sign of unmanliness."

"You're not."

"A man?"

"Homesick."

"But I've always been a renegade."

"So you welcome this?"

"Not the circumstances that led to it, no. But being a part of the System? Yes."

"You'll fit in well, and they'll make good use of you. You're a natural leader, Jenny."

"And what about you? Don't tell me you can't inspire loyalty."

"I've been lying here thinking about just that, and I find I distrust my motives. My playing the great white leader led to disaster on Mars."

"That's not true."

"Maybe it's better if in the future I stay out of any decision making. These bunch of hardy individualists are going to view me with suspicion, anyway. I'm tainted by privilege."

"I think you're tainted by silly notions because you don't feel well. Things will look better when you have some gravity to settle your stomach and your leg and arm heal."

"We'll see."

"Cab, if there is trouble between Earth and the System, you're going to be very important. You're the only person who can mediate between the two sides. You have wealth, position, and respect on Earth, and you have respect and position out here. Don't deny them that help. And don't assume that everything you do is motivated by a desire to accumulate power. There's also the little matter of responsibility, and that is something you take very seriously indeed. You'll disappoint me if you fail to take it this time."

"I don't want to disappoint you."

"Good."

"I just don't want to make any major decisions."

She frowned down at him. "That's your job. What, are you going to resign from the bench? That really will make Lis Varllis's day."

"I may not have a choice."

"And if people in the Belt want you to adjudicate for them?"

"They have the hearing boards."

"No, they don't, you disbanded them. So are you going to leave them hanging?"

"No."

"Are you going to let me down?"

"No."

"And are you going to leave Joe to handle everything himself and take all the heat?"

"No." He could feel the skin around his eyes tightening and crinkling as he began to smile.

"Then it sounds like you've made a decision, haven't you?"

"Is it hard to make love in free fall?" he asked, ignoring her final comment.

"It is if you're going to puke all over me. So maybe we ought to settle for making love in what amounts to a sleeping bag and graduate to free fall later."

"Yes, ma'am."

Her fingers were busy with his shirt, releasing the strip

fastener and pushing it off his shoulders. Her lips played over his chest, teeth teasing at his nipple. “And, Mr. Huntington, Judge, sir. If you call me Amadea anytime during this act, or even talk in your sleep, I’m going to kill you.”

“No chance of doing that, Jennifer. I’ve made my decision, remember?”